SOLVING US

Susan Renee

SOLVING US

Original Copyright 2015 by Susan Renee

All Rights Reserved. In accordance with the U.S. Copyright Act of 1976, the scanning, uploading, and electronic sharing of this book without the permission of the publisher or author constitutes unlawful piracy and theft. For use of any part of this book please contact the publisher at authorsusanrenee@gmail.com for written consent.

This book is a work of fiction. Names, characters, places, and incidents are the product of the author's imagination or are used fictitiously. Any resemblance to actual events, locales, or persons living or dead is coincidental.

Except for the original material written by the author, all songs, song titles and lyrics mentioned throughout the novel SOLVING US are the property of the respective songwriters and copyright holders.

Cover art created by <u>Indie Solutions by Murphy Rae</u>
Editors: Devon Anderson, Lauren Brocchi, Joyce Camlin
Formatting: Douglas M. Huston

To Peg Flynn
God places people in our lives for a reason.
Thank you for changing mine with one unexpected gift.
I would absolutely not be the person I am now
had I never opened it, taken the leap, and started to read.

PROLOGUE

"She looks like some sort of zombie freak now."

"I don't think this is working anymore."

"She used to be so pretty. Pity, really."

"It's not you, Liv, it's me."

"I wonder what happened to her."

"I'll always care about you. I just feel like we're moving in different directions."

"Who would want to put a hickey on top of those scars? I mean, is that even possible?"

"It's not like we were getting married or anything."

"Yeah, she'll never see any action. No guy wants that when he can have someone who looks...normal."

"We're both headed to college soon, Liv. It's bound to happen anyway."

"Maybe instead of modeling, she should think about being a makeup artist. She's going to need some help covering that up."

People can be so mean.

Chapter 1

"Liv? Are you coming out of there anytime soon? I have to get ready for work." The knock on the bathroom door brings me back to my senses. I've been staring at myself in the mirror for too long.

"Yeah sorry," I tell her as I run my hand down my neck, my right side, and over my hips. The scars are pretty faded now at my neck and shoulder but still not invisible. The largest ones on my stomach, hip, and right thigh, though, are dark enough to see that I look like a woman with tiger stripes on half of my body. It has been years, but sometimes I just can't help but stare at myself. It is a constant reminder of the pain and torture and loss that completely changed my life. Autumn and winter are now my favorite seasons for the sheer fact that I can be covered up for months, but summer will be here before I know it. I am finally comfortable with some tank tops, but shorts or short skirts are still out of the question. Nobody needs to see these legs.

"You're not staring at yourself in the mirror again are you?" Abby groans from the other side of the door.

What the?

Is she psychic or something?

I dart my eyes all over the bathroom walls and behind the mirror to see if there is a camera in here that maybe I don't know about. I really try hard to not look at myself so much when she is around. Although we are best friends, Abby and I, there are just parts of my life that I don't want to worry her about, and this is one of them. Who cares if I have some scars, right? It's been years. No big deal….to everyone but me.

"Olivia?" Abby asks gently as she softly knocks on the door prompting me to answer her. "Can I come in?"

I wrap my body with my towel quickly and open the door while trying to wipe the lone tear that falls from my eye, careful not to reveal the evidence of my personal pity party. Abby steps in the bathroom

Solving Us

hesitantly, and when she looks into my eyes, I can't hide my thoughts. Her head tilts as she looks at me knowingly. "Spill it girl. You used to do this all the time in college when you were feeling down. We've been friends far too long for you to feel the need to keep secrets."

"I know, and I'm sorry I monopolized the bathroom - and the hot water," I cringe. "Rough morning, I guess. You would think after seven years I would be over this shit, and most of the time I don't even think about it but today…well, you know…seven years ago I left that hospital a different person, and I just…" I take a deep breath and blow it out glancing back in the mirror at my pained and sad reflection. "I was just thinking about life and throwing myself a pity party."

Abby nods and smiles at me, but I know she's ready to debate the validity of my emotions. "I looked at the calendar, Liv; I know what day it is, but you know what?"

"What?"

"April twenty-fifth comes every year, Liv. Yeah, it's been seven years, but at some point you do have to let it go and move on. You're a survivor, Liv. On all accounts you should've died that day, but you didn't. You lived, Olivia, and you have so much to be happy about! You graduated from the Rhode Island School of Design at the *top* of your class! You moved out here with me. Everyone loves your work. You're such a talented photographer. You really *see* people! You capture your environment with ease. You're bound to find the perfect job! You have great friends, a family who loves you so what's the problem? Any guy would be lucky to find you, and he will, soon! I have a good feeling about you being here in Boston with me. We'll paint the town red together, or purple, if you would rather!"

Catching a glimpse of my neck and shoulders that are not covered by my towel in the mirror, I whisper, "Any guy would be lucky to find me, as long as he never has to lay eyes on my baggage."

I roll my eyes partly at Abby for thinking I'm some sort of catch and partly at myself. I know I am just being emotional and feeling insecure. I just can't get myself to snap out of it today. Abby hugs me as she says, "Olivia Grace McGuire, the *only* person who looks at those scars and sees you as anything *other* than beautiful is you. I mean, I understand you were picked on in high school, but kids are stupid douchebags sometimes, and," she says nodding towards my neck. "Your top scars are all but invisible now. You were young; they were young. Girls, especially at that age, can be bitches, but you got through four years of college without much problem. You've grown up. Seriously, do I need to pull out my cheesy lines about how beautiful you are inside and out because you've heard them a hundred times?"

"I know. You're not telling me anything I haven't heard before from Mom and Dad, but I'm a single twenty-four year old. Guys seem to like what they see until they try to get to second base. My body makes guys uncomfortable the closer they get. I strike out every time. Remember Chris in college our sophomore year, the guy from my Studio Photography class? That was a nice couple of dates. He told me he liked me, that I was beautiful - until he got my shirt off," I shake my head as I continue. "He tried to act like it didn't bother him, but you'll never convince me that I wasn't the reason we broke up. I was just another notch on his bedpost."

I frown at my reflection in the mirror. "It's not you it's me," I recite. "I think I've heard that one about four times since high school. Speaking of which, do I need to bring up Archer?"

Abby's head snaps in my direction. "Archer? The guy you dated in high school? The one who cheated on you? Honey that was...."

"Seven years ago," I said. "Yeah, I remember. He used to think I was beautiful, too, but even my steady high school sweetheart couldn't handle my physical changes after the accident. That's not love," I dismiss, shaking my head in disappointment. "Me and guys and love...maybe it's just not for me, ya know?" I shrug like it's no big deal, even though my heart feels heavy.

"That's bullshit, and you know it Liv," Abby argues shaking her head. "Not that I'm defending Archer because I know he hurt you; and as your present-day BFF, if I ever meet this guy, his balls are going to meet my foot with my favorite pointy shoes on." It makes me laugh because I know just how much Abby loves her very pointy, very high heeled pumps. She has a bit of a shoe fetish. She can't live without the newest pair of Jimmy Choos.

Abby continues, "But...he was just as young as you, Liv. People change in time. They grow up a lot. I would like to think Archer isn't that insensitive now, though maybe you'll never know, and that's okay. Good riddance to bad rubbish, as they say."

I sigh and close my eyes for a moment before shaking my head to snap out of my funk. "I'm sorry, Abby. I didn't mean to turn this morning into a 'pity me' morning. You're right. I know, I just...."

"Haven't found your knight in shining armor yet." Abby shrugs. "He'll come. You'll find yourself a great job and meet someone who will love you for you and make you feel like the Cinderella that you are; I can just feel it! Your focus just needs to be on losing your insecurities and embracing who you are! I love you for *you*. All your friends love you for *you*, or they wouldn't be your friends. Shit happens to us, and it sucks when it does, but that doesn't mean we have to let it define us. Until that happens, don't be so afraid to live a little! Go have fun in the city, date several guys, have lots of sex! Find a great job that you love."

I turn and give Abby a huge hug. "And let's hope that job comes sooner than later 'cause our rent isn't going to pay itself."

"Damn right, it's not girl. Don't worry, though, I'll just be your sugar mama for a while."

I smirk at her and run a brush through my hair before heading into my bedroom to get dressed for the day. Before she starts the shower and can't hear me, I shout down the hall "Thanks for the confidence boost breakfast, Abs! I love you."

"Right back at ya girlfriend. That's what friends are for!"

Abby and I graduated from the Rhode Island School of Design a year ago and wanted to move together from Providence to Boston in hopes of landing great jobs and living the dream together. Abby landed an internship with an interior design firm out of Boston before we graduated, so she already had a plan. I hadn't really found what I was looking for, so I spent two years at home making a little money with the local newspaper as a freelance photographer so that I could afford to live away from home on my own. Newspaper photography jobs are starting to dissipate now that the digital sharing world thrives, so I knew it was time to take a leap and put my skills to the test. It was nice to 'flee the nest' as the say and begin to live a life of my own, and my BFF Abby was just the person I wanted to share it with, at least for now. After four years of rooming together in college, we know each other's strengths and weaknesses. We complement each other well and can help pull each other through our depressing life moments. I know her favorite ice cream flavor is Rocky Road and always have it available when Abby goes through her latest break-up or bad day at the office. And she knows ,when I feel down, I either want to blast my music, sing really loud, and dance away the stress, or I want a snuggly blanket, a bowl of Hershey Kisses, a tall glass of milk, and a good chick flick. I think we both have the lines to the Princess Bride completely memorized by now.

From our apartment, we can see the Charles River, which leads into the beautiful Boston Harbor. Really, for the price, we can't ask for a much better view every day. The owner of this particular apartment community is a friend of Abby's parents, so she got a nice deal on a two-bedroom apartment with the understanding that she would use her interior design skills to help outfit some of the business luxury apartments at the top of our building. She was all too thrilled to accept, and so far, it's worked out for her.

Our apartment is a great fit for Abby and me in that we are close to the social life and have many amenities we both take advantage of, like the gym, the pool, the outdoor grilling area, etc. We both enjoy being outside and both are social people, she more so than I. We're acquainted with many people throughout our building and many in the surrounding apartment community. My only wish is that the building weren't pet-friendly. Yes, I used to be a dog person and spent my entire life around animals, but now? Now I feel like every dog that sees me smells my fear.

Chapter 2

I decide to get dressed and go for a walk through the park, maybe down to the river to take some pictures. I'm aching to try out one of my new lenses that I received as a going away present from my parents. I throw on my Capris and favorite blue and white striped t-shirt, slip on my grey jersey flats, grab my camera and wallet, and walk out the door. Taking the elevator down to the lobby, I quickly exit through the front doors of the building, greeting a few of my neighbors who are just getting back from their morning runs. I slept in too late for my run, so I vow to myself that I will do it tonight before dinner.

I lift my chin for a moment and take in the sights and sounds around me, something I'm getting good at in order to find the right photo opportunity. It's a beautiful late spring day. The sun is already past sunrise stage and is beginning to heat things up for the day. It's supposed to be an unseasonably warm day, though the breeze off the harbor always knocks the temperature down a few degrees. I can smell freshly cut grass from the neighboring quad next to the building, and along the walkways are tons and tons of fresh daffodils. Those suckers pop up everywhere in the springtime. Just like dandelions that scatter yards like weeds throughout the summertime. Birds are chirping animatedly amongst themselves and are flurrying about, most likely creating their nests for the season.

There are a few boats preparing to leave their port for a day on the water and a few more I can see already heading for the harbor.

Today would be a great day to spend in the water

Taking a nice deep breath and closing my eyes momentarily, I put behind me all of my morning depression and begin my walk in hopes of finding that picture perfect opportunity.

People watching is one of my favorite things to do behind a camera lens. I try to tell a story with the pictures I capture, and from the reviews I have received of my work in the past, it seems like I have a good eye for really seeing people for who they are. Good judge of character? I don't know; I suppose the guys who waltzed into, but ran out of, my life would be evidence to the contrary, but at least I know how to take a good picture. I stand in the middle of a grassy quad in the park a few yards away from my apartment building and begin to shoot picture after picture. First, there is the old couple sharing a coffee on the nearby park bench. They look so much in love. I hope one day I'll find that guy who shares his everything with me, or at least a good cup of coffee. I turn around and spot a woman sitting on the grass with her little boy who can't be more than a year old, maybe two. She and the boy are singing pat-a-cake, pat-a-cake, and he is all giggles. The little boy's mom lifts him up high above her head and brings him back down blowing little kisses on his tummy as he giggles and writhes in her arms. It puts a smile on my face, and I snap the picture quickly hoping she won't think I'm some sort of voyeur.

Soon I am immersed in taking picture after picture: snapping, checking my camera, editing out the bad pictures, and continuing. I sit down on the ground when I spot a small chipmunk sitting just across the path from me. I don't want to scare him, but he just sits there as if he is posing for me. I crouch as low as I can to the ground without startling him and begin to snap pictures of the little animal. He moves a few times, and it looks as if he is holding some sort of morsel of food to his mouth. Second breakfast, I guess.

I watch the chipmunk run away and bring my camera down from my face just in time to witness the most heart stopping moment I have had in…well…I can't remember ever experiencing this feeling before. I don't usually make it a habit of gawking at people, but in this case, I don't know what comes over me. He is gorgeous! He is hot! I don't know who he is, but he is shirtless and running towards me on the path next to where I'm crouching. I couldn't *not* notice him if I tried. His body is long and lean, his chest toned and showing off his clear six-pack? Eight pack? Wow, I feel bad trying to count, but his chest just draws my eyes to him like a moth to a porch light. The sheen of sweat on his chest and abs gives him a sexy glow that I can't help but admire. His biceps are like two huge boulders that I would never be able to get my hands around, but I wouldn't mind holding onto them as long as I could. They flex effortlessly as he swings his arms in his natural forward movement.

Mmmm...those arms.

What is it about a guy's arms?

In a moment of morbid curiosity, I allow my eyes to roam up to his face as he approaches right where I'm sitting. I lean back and meet his eye instantly. His eyes are a piercing shade of blue that hypnotize me immediately.

Close your mouth, Olivia!

Close your mouth!

My brain is trying to speak to me, but my body just isn't listening. I continue to stare at him, his beautiful blue eyes, messy brown hair just long enough for me to run my fingers through. He is the epitome of attractive.

My breath leaves my body as his eyes meet mine and hold my gaze for what feels like an inappropriate amount of time for two complete strangers to look at each other. I narrow my eyes just a bit as I look at him in that moment because I feel like, for the first time in a long time, I am the one in front of the camera, and he is studying me. Just me. Maybe I'm just imagining things, or I just want to feel pretty for a moment, but he holds my gaze and slows down his running pace as he approaches me.

"*Beautiful* morning isn't it?" he says to me clearly surveying me head to toe.

"Uh, what?"

He's talking to me?

Holy shit! Hot runner guy is talking to me!

"I mean, um, yes it is a beautiful morning," I stammer.

Ugh! The one time I can make a good impression, and I stumble my words and feel so flustered. I'm not convinced he was talking about the morning weather though. I blush, and when I look back at him, he is smiling at me. He has a panty-dropping, megawatt, million-dollar smile that is obviously infectious because I can't help but smile back. It's like my lips are attached to strings, and I am being manipulated by some master puppeteer. He is stunning.

"You live around here? I run this route all the time, but I've never seen you."

"Yeah um, I'm new. Well new-ish. Just moved here a couple weeks ago."

Hot runner guy smiles at me. "Ah. Well, welcome to Boston!"

I return his smile as I sweep a wisp of hair that has fallen out of my ponytail away from my face.

"Thanks."

"See ya around...I hope." He whispers that last part, *I hope,* and maybe he thinks I didn't hear him, but I so totally did! Whoa!

As he picks up his pace again, he glances down at my camera and then back up at me. With his eyebrows raised and smirk on his face he continues on his run. My mouth still open in wonder, I watch him run past me further down the path. He turns around one more time to glance at me, and damn if I'm not still gawking at the fine specimen that has just run by. How embarrassing! I throw my head down and look at my toes while pretending to fix my camera lens. I still can't help but smile to myself, though.

He smiled at me.

He talked to me.

He hopes to see me around.

Around his waist maybe...

I take a deep breath to try to compose myself. I raise my hand to my cheek and feel the heat of my flushed face. I wonder who he was and why I hadn't seen him on my morning runs before. I make a mental note to ask Abby about it when I see her again. She runs earlier in the morning than I do, since I don't have a job yet; but if she tells me he's an early morning runner, I may just find myself changing my routine.

I spend the next hour down at the docks taking several shots of the incoming boats and goings on in and around the marina before I feel the urge to take a break. My energy level was jolted this morning thanks to

Solving Us

the adrenaline rush I had experienced with the hot runner guy, but that doesn't stop me from walking in to Starbucks for my favorite double chocolate chip Frappuccino.

While I am sitting outside on the Starbucks patio, I toy around with the settings on my camera, taking a few shots of my Frappuccino and my blueberry yogurt muffin, for lack of any other photographic subjects. I don't even look up when the patio door opens, nor do I pay any attention to the sound of a chair scraping along the pavement of the patio.

"Do you always take pictures of your food?" a male voice asks me amusingly.

I freeze and can feel my eyes widen at the voice that has just spoken obviously to me. I don't remember anyone else sitting on the patio when I came out here, and certainly nobody else with a camera. I lift my head and make eye contact with the man speaking to me. It's him! Hot Runner Guy, except he isn't running, of course. In fact, he isn't all sweaty and panting either. He is fully dressed in business attire, which somehow makes him even hotter than when I saw him this morning. His black suit pants and stark blue dress shirt combination give him a bold air of confidence. The blue of his shirt brings out his deep blue eyes. In the heat of the morning, he had rolled the cuffs of his shirt sleeves about half way up showing off those beautiful forearms I admired so much earlier. He has his newly purchased cup of coffee with him and is standing right next to me, but I can't bring myself to think of coherent words!

Think Liv, think! I swallow hard and stare at him.

"Mind if I sit with you?" he asks me.

I finally remember to close my mouth this time, so I'm not gawking at him and his very hot body, that I'm sure many girls take advantage of. I did, however, notice that there was no ring on his finger…so at least I'm pretty sure that there isn't just one girl who is winning his affection. I fantasize for a second that I am the girl he dreams about, being held in his arms, tasting his lips.

His lips.

"Sure, yeah I guess," I reply back to him, praying that he didn't just notice my wandering fantasy. "Sorry, no, I don't usually take pictures of my food." I chuckle softly as he slides the chair across from me out a little further so he can sit down. "I'm more of a people-person when it comes to pictures, maybe animals from time to time or landscapes. I was just playing with a few settings on my camera while passing the time."

"Ah, I see. So you're a photographer by trade? I noticed you snapping pictures this morning while I was running." He sits back in the chair across from me holding his coffee and makes direct eye contact with me while he speaks. His gaze is intense with his head cocked to the side, almost like he is trying to figure me all out in one conversation. "I'm sorry I didn't stop to say more to you this morning, but I had a quick conference call and didn't want to be too late. I swear, I'm not a stalker, but if I'm being honest, I saw you come in here as I was leaving for work so I followed you."

I raise one eyebrow and half smile at him. "You followed me? Sounds pretty stalker-ish to me," I tease.

"Ooh touché," he says nodding at me and wincing slightly. "I'm sorry you just… piqued my curiosity this morning…I guess. So, when I saw you again I figured it was fate or something telling me I should talk to you. My name is Finn." He smiles at me shyly, which catches me off guard. For someone who appeared so confident a moment ago, he seems almost nervous now. I can see the pink rising in his cheeks; he is blushing. How cute!

He followed me? He noticed me? Am I on some episode of Candid Camera or something? I look around quickly for a camera just in case.

"Nice to meet you; I'm Liv. Olivia," I stammer. "I mean most people call me Liv." I smile at Finn and hold his gaze until I just can't do it anymore. His stare is intimidating yet makes me feel those little flutters in my tummy that I haven't felt in a long time. What are those? Nerves? I take a deep breath and relax enough to continue our conversation. "To answer your question, yes, I'm a photographer by trade. I graduated from college with a focus in photography."

"Where did you go to school?" he asks me.

"Rhode Island School of Design."

Finn nods. "Impressive. Did you just graduate?"

"No. 2012, actually. I spent two years working for the newspaper in my hometown before moving here to Boston to live with a friend of mine."

"A boyfriend?" he interrupts quietly.

Frowning at that thought I reply, "Uh, no, my college roommate actually. Abby is her name. She's an interior designer with the Stark Firm in the city."

Finn's eyebrows shoot up "Stark Firm. Also impressive, and what do you do? Do you work for the Boston Herald now?"

"No. I actually just moved here a couple weeks ago. Now that I'm all unpacked and settled, I'm actually looking for work in my field. I am not exactly sure what that means yet, but I'm starting to research a few job opportunities. I like being behind my camera. It's a passion I've had since high school and one that really brings me joy. It's almost like…therapy for me."

I don't know why I feel the need to explain everything to him. I'm nervous sitting here talking to him, but he seems to have this knack for making me feel comfortable, so I try not to think about it too much.

Finn's eyes are warm and hopeful as he looks back at me with a slow sweet smile rounding his face. His teeth are perfect, and the way he looks into my eyes makes me blush every time. "Rhode Island School of Design, eh? That's something to be proud of. Have you heard of The Kellan Agency? It's a marketing and design firm that provides services for many of the largest companies in Boston." He talks about the Kellan Agency with swelled pride, and I most certainly have heard of it. It is one of, if not the, best marketing firm in Boston. He must work there.

There are those flutters in my tummy again.

Don't get your hopes up Olivia; he's just being a nice guy.

"Yeah I've definitely heard of The Kellan Agency. It was one of the more popular firms among my peers looking for internships before graduation. I would kill for a job there, but I'll have to work my way up to that company. Mr. Kellan would never take someone with so little experience."

Finn studies my face for a minute, and I can't figure out what it is he's thinking, but I swear I see his lip twitch up just for a second.

"Why didn't you apply for an internship?" He raises an eyebrow.

How did he know I didn't apply?

"Oh, um, well, I wasn't quite sure at the time that moving from my hometown was what I wanted, so I stayed with my parents for a couple years and worked there instead. I knew that I had made the wrong choice, though," I inhale steadily before continuing. "Once you go away to college and enjoy the freedom of the real world, going back home is a bit pathetic. Not that I don't love my parents and love the peacefulness of being at home, but…" I rub my hand nonchalantly on my neck and look past Finn for a second before continuing my thoughts. I don't know why I do it, but as I speak I instinctively rub my fading scars on the right side of my neck. "Sometimes being at home just digs up a past that you don't want to live in anymore." I raise my head to look at him again. "I'm ready to move on and be on my own."

Finn takes a sip of his coffee and lowers his cup as he watches me talk. I don't miss the fact that he is watching my hand as I rub my neck. I forget that I clipped my hair up earlier at the docks. He must notice my scars when I'm talking because his eyes widen momentarily, and his lips separate like he is going to ask me something. I slowly lower my hand back to my lap trying to be as inconspicuous as possible. I tilt my head to the right in an effort to cover up my scars with my shoulder. I hear him take a deep breath before he speaks again, appearing more relaxed than he is probably letting on.

Please don't ask me what happened to me.

Please, please, please…just not today.

My body tenses as I wait for him to speak.

"I admire your tenacity, Olivia" The way Finn says my name makes my insides melt like softened butter. Nodding his head at me, he confidently says, "It takes a pretty strong person to want to fly the nest and do the grown-up thing on your own without a definite plan. I like it."

Thank you, God!

I feel my shoulders relax, and I sit back in my chair. "So what about you, Finn? What is it you do besides run?" I ask smiling at him. We both chuckle nervously. I wipe my mouth with my napkin just in case I had drooled thinking about him without his shirt on.

When would I get to see that again?

Could I please see that again?

Finn blushes but gives me that megawatt smile again that reaches all the way to his eyes. "I've taken over the family business, which means I can get pretty swamped with clients, business meetings, conference calls, important decisions...a lot of wining and dining executives and new clients. You know..."

"A business man, huh? Sounds exciting," I say.

"It has its moments, and I really enjoy the people I work with, so I don't experience really bad days very often. Today, for example." His eyes roam over the parts of me that he can see. "So far, today has been...pretty great."

"And what kind of family business do you run, Finn?" I ask tearing off a piece of my muffin and popping it into my mouth.

In an act I can only describe as surprisingly tender, Finn reaches across the table with a napkin and wipes the corner of my mouth.

Oh my God, did he just do that?

Did I drool?

Oh my GOD how embarrassing...and...hot!

I can feel the warmth shoot through my entire body at his touch.

"A...crumb," he says quietly discarding the napkin.

I smile shyly. I can feel the heat rising in my face and gaze down at my hands for a second, twisting my ring around on my finger. It's my favorite silver ring that has the word LOVE engraved on the top and a tiny paw print engraved on the inside. I wear it always on my right pinky finger. It is sort of my pinky promise to myself to never forget what happened to me and the hero who saved my life. I never take it off. Not for seven years. When I look back at Finn, he is admiring me from across the table while taking another sip of his coffee.

What is he thinking?

I know he's thinking something.

"I'm in the photography business," he finally says. "That's why I noticed you this morning…you taking pictures."

"Ah." I nod my head in understanding, but he's holding my gaze. Our eyes haven't left one another, and my body is starting to feel like it's in a trance, like Finn is sitting across from me playing his music, and I'm the snake being charmed out of the basket as he beckons me.

"I'm sorry, Olivia, I haven't done this sort of thing in a while, but I'm…intrigued by you. You seem like a great girl with a very down to earth personality. I think getting to know you more could be great." Finn glances down at his watch quickly. "I would love to keep you company here this morning, but I have a meeting I need to get to."

"Oh, yeah, sure, that's okay. I totally understand. You're probably super busy with calls and meetings and…businessy stuff." I smirk at him. I don't expect him to stick around, though I would have no objections if that were what he chose to do.

"No," Finn corrects me. "What I mean is I would really like to take you out…if you would be interested. You're new to the area, right? And what I've learned about you today is that you're not living with a boyfriend, you have a passion for photography, and you sometimes take pictures of your food." He smirks and then chuckles when I look at him embarrassed.

Sheepishly chuckling and nodding in agreement I reply, "Correct on all counts, I guess."

"Kidding," he says. "I remember you said you were more of a people or animal person, and I think I know just the place to take you. Do you like being out on the water?"

Whoa! Hot runner guy just asked me out?

Hell yeah I'm interested!

But water...does that mean swimsuit?

I gulp down the knot of panic in my throat at the thought of having to wear a swimsuit. "Yeah, I love the water. I haven't gotten to get out much since I've moved here, so that would be great, except umm, I'm not the best swimmer." I lie. I'm actually a great swimmer. I had to be growing up on the river and doing a lot of white water rafting, but he doesn't need to know that, yet. I'll say anything to not have to wear a bathing suit.

"It's okay." He shakes his head. "We won't be getting in...well unless we fall in or something, but don't worry, I'll save you if that happens." He winks at me and chuckles shaking his head at the cheesy line he just delivered. I snicker back at him but try to help his ego a little.

"I think that sounds amazing," I say, smiling excitedly, but not too excitedly. I don't want to seem desperate after all.

"Great! It's supposed to be warmer than this tomorrow, so dress casually, and be sure to pack your camera." Finn reaches across the table and grabs my iPhone that is lying on the table next to me. He swipes his finger across and starts pressing his fingers around my screen. I have no idea what he is doing, but I don't speak up and ask either. "Here you go. Now you have my number. Text me later with your address, and I'll pick you up tomorrow around noon if that's okay?"

I look down at my phone when he hands it back and see that he added himself as a contact into my phone. A laugh escapes me when I see that his contact reads

FINN from STARBUCKS

"Thank you, umm, Finn from Starbucks. I can't wait! And...thank you...for asking me, I mean. It was really nice meeting you."

Finn puts his hand out in an effort to shake mine. "It was a pleasure to finally meet you, girl who takes pictures of food," he says with a warm smile.

Ahh, that panty-melting smile.

When I grab his hand in a return handshake, I gasp softly and try to hide it in my deep breath. The flutters are back in my stomach as I focus on the softness of his skin and the heat of his hands. I am blushing; I can feel it.

"I'll wait to hear from you later with your address." He looks down at our hands wound together and then tugs forward on my arm as he lowers himself enticingly close to my ear and whispers, "You're beautiful when you blush, Olivia." He straightens up and smiles at me again. "Until tomorrow," he whispers and walks away, leaving me almost panting for breaths as I watch the hot runner guy, Finn, walk away.

Standing up from my table, I gather my muffin wrapper and Frappuccino cup and throw them away before starting my walk home.

You're beautiful when you blush Olivia.

His words play over and over again in my head. Had I just imagined that entire conversation? Was it just me, or did he seem more than interested in me? I frown momentarily remembering my early morning flashback. My past always makes me insecure around guys, and this was no exception, really; but for the moment I can't help but smile at the thought that, though the morning may have had a rocky start, it is quite possible that my day is going to turn around. I text Abby immediately about what just happened, but I know she is too busy at work to reply and then is traveling out of town for the weekend. Hopefully, I will catch her at some point before she leaves to tell her all the details!

I wait an hour before I send a text to Finn with my address for tomorrow's date. I don't want to come across as too eager. In reality, it was all I could do to not text him while he was sitting there at the table with me. I thought at least an hour was a safe bet and am startled by his immediate response. He must've been waiting for my text.

Will pick you up at noon. Excited to spend the day with you!

I send a quick reply:

Solving Us

Me: Ditto! C U tomorrow. Have a good evening :)

Finn: I hope it's a fast evening so I can see you sooner!

His text makes me blush and smile…. and smile even bigger. I feel like a giddy little school girl who was just approached by her school girl crush. My phone beeps one more time, alerting me to another text message.

Finn: I'm imagining you blushing because you're beautiful when you blush!

I'm not sure which reaction I am most aware of first, the growing smile on my face, or the warmth that spikes through my body, but either way I am a very happy girl for the rest of the afternoon thanks to "Hot Runner Guy" and what seems to be a mutual attraction. I have to find something to productively occupy my time before tomorrow comes! I am still hoping to get to talk to Abby, but in the meantime, I leave my camera at home and decide to take advantage of the gorgeous day by walking through town to do a little shopping. I want to look perfect for my date, and a new outfit will help.

Chapter 3

The intercom bell goes off near my front door at precisely noon. The apartment manager at the front desk calls up to let me know that Finn is in the building and is heading up, since I had already added his name to our security list. It dawned on me that I didn't have a last name for Finn when I added him to my list, so I made a mental note to ask him what his last name is. Nothing hugely important, I suppose; but I guess if I'm going to date the guy, I should know his full name, right?

Whoa, slow down, Liv.

It's one date!

Don't get your hopes up!

I am alone in the apartment since Abby left for the remainder of the weekend to spend a few nights in New York City with her latest boyfriend, Trent. I never did get ahold of her, except for a quick text to tell her I had a date. I don't mind, though, as it gives me more freedom to be with Finn, should the first date go well, and not feel like I'm ignoring Abby. I allow Finn to knock on the door and wait the appropriate amount of time before opening it. I never want to come across as desperate, but I am very eager to see him in a more personal environment. I have no idea what he has planned, other than we will be spending the day on the water.

I open the door and look up to see Finn standing casually in the hallway outside of my apartment. My breath hitches as I take in the sight of him. He is dressed in faded worn jeans that look like they were made specifically for his body. The way they hang off of his hips and hug his legs perfectly is nothing short of ridiculously sexy. There is a rip near the knee on the left leg that gives him that sexy bad-boy look that I am drawn to immediately. Although a loose fitted black V-neck t-shirt covers his chest, I can still very much make out the shape of his pecs underneath. His aviator sunglasses are the perfect accessory hanging from the V of

Solving Us

his shirt. There isn't much left to my imagination, but my imagination is certainly running wild. I can't believe I'm about to spend the day with this guy; moreover, I can't believe this guy wants to spend the day with *me*.

"Hey, Finn," I say smiling at him. I don't want to make too much eye contact because I fear the heat in my cheeks will never leave.

"Olivia," he gasps in a deep breath. He takes a moment to gaze at me with this appreciative and excited look in his eye. He looks like he is happy to be seeing me after months of not seeing each other, but it has really only been a little over twenty-four hours. On my shopping trip yesterday, I purchased a new pair of capris jeans that were slightly ripped on each thigh and paired them with a navy blue cotton t-shirt with cap sleeves. I chose my old UGG brown wrap sandals since they were comfortable for walking. I didn't accessorize much, since I knew I would have a camera around my neck, so I went with a small pair of silver dangle earrings and my ring, the ring I never take off. I pulled half of my long brown hair back into a ponytail but left the back down in an effort to hide the scars on my neck. I know they aren't that visible, but I would much rather relax and enjoy the day with Finn than be forced to talk about things I don't want to talk about. Not yet anyway, but maybe someday.

"You look beautiful, Olivia. It's great to see you again."

"Thank you," I say. "Come on in for a second; I need to grab my keys. I left them on my desk."

Finn walks into my apartment and looks around. "This is a great place and with a pretty nice view too." He seems impressed. The apartment I share with my roommate, Abby, is a two bedroom, one bath apartment. Guests walk through our door into our living room that is spacious enough for us to have a couch, loveseat, bookshelves, coffee table, and television armoire. It is more for storing our DVDs since the flat screen TV is mounted to the wall. Because Abby scored a corner apartment, there are two side-by-side large windows that present a view of the neighboring quad where I frequently roam to people watch. Our kitchen leads into our dining area, which includes a French door entrance onto our patio with a view! It's a beautiful view of the Charles River, and because we're up high enough in the building, on a good day, we can see right out into the sound.

"Yeah we really like it, and we couldn't beat the price. Abby agreed to help the manager decorate their penthouse apartments for business clients pro bono, so in exchange, we get this apartment for a steal!"

"That's good business." Finn's eyebrows raise up for a moment, and he chuckles. I think he is impressed. I wonder where he lives.

"Yeah, I guess, that and the manager knows Abby's parents," I smirk.

"Ah, yeah that always helps."

"Let me just grab my keys, and I'm ready to go." I run back to the desk in my bedroom and grab my keys that I had thrown there after my run this morning. It was nice to get some exercise to use up some of this pent up energy. I also pick up my camera bag. I meet Finn back at the bar to our kitchen. Abby and I eat many of our meals here together, instead of the dining room table, to catch up on each other's day.

"Ready!"

"Great!" Finn smiles. He reaches out his hand to take my camera bag so I won't have to carry it, *ever the gentleman,* and then takes my right hand with his left. He holds my hand all the way down to the ground floor and outside the building, letting go only to open the door. It's good that we make small talk on the way to his car. I welcome the much-needed distraction to keep my legs from shaking. Finn's car is parked along the street outside and around the corner.

"Your chariot awaits, my lady," Finn announces swiftly opening my door for me.

"Thank you, kind sir," I try to hide my huge smile as I sit down in his car and look around quickly. Holy smokes! I am sitting in a sleek black Corvette Stingray with dark tan and black interior. This car is made for a man. As Finn rounds the front of the car to get in on his side, I can't help but watch him. Holy hell, he is sex on legs. I shouldn't even be thinking of sex with Finn, as there is no reason for me to think we will ever make it that far, but a girl can dream.

"A 'Vette huh? It's a beautiful car. It fits you," I tell him as I watch him get in and start the car.

"Yeah, she's my baby, and I only get to drive her when the weather is great. Can't drive her all year long because our winters are so brutal, so on a day like today," he says looking over at me while sucking in a deep breath. "I like to take full advantage." Finn's eyes begin to wander up and down my body, and for the moment, I let him because he shows no evidence that he doesn't like the view. He makes me feel pretty. Hell, he's even told me a few times that I'm beautiful, not that that means anything.

"I have something for you before we leave." Finn reaches behind me and pulls a gift bag from the floor of the back seat.

Oh my gosh, he bought me a gift?

He hands it to me and quietly explains, "I thought you might be able to put this to good use today, and I'm assuming you don't have one yet since, um, they only just hit the shelves a week ago, and you were probably busy moving."

I frown in confusion, not understanding what Finn would buy for me, or why he feels the need in the twenty-four hours that we've known each other, to get me anything at all. I mean coffee, maybe, or a bouquet of flowers. Nevertheless, I am not going to be rude, so I excitedly open the gift bag. I pull out the tissue paper sitting on top and gasp in shock at what is sitting on my lap. I whip my face towards Finn who is anxiously awaiting my reaction. My eyes widen in surprise.

"Seriously?" I exclaim. "A Canon Zoom EF-S lens?" I am all smiles, but I'm not sure of the appropriate reaction.

This sucker had to have cost him a fortune!

"Well, I noticed the camera you were using the other day and thought you might be able to put this new lens to good use today while we're out on the water. From what I've researched, it's fantastic for landscapes, people, nature, and wildlife. You said those are the things you like to photograph, so I figured you'll make great use of it."

"I....I'm not sure what to say, Finn. It's too much. I know you spent too much; I mean, this is our first date. You....you barely know me." I feel guilty for the amount of money I know he spent. Whether he can afford it or not, I guess, doesn't matter; but still, I feel guilty. I am happy and excited yes, but I feel guilty, nonetheless.

"I want you to have it, Olivia. It will allow you to do so much more with your camera, and I know that your work brings you joy - and I like seeing you happy." Finn looks down and inhales a breath of what appears to be courage before he looks at me and says, "I don't make a habit of showering women with extravagant gifts. Please don't think I'm trying to impress you with money or something, but there's something about you. You're a beautiful girl with a beautiful smile, and knowing that I put that smile on your face today makes *me* very happy in return. Well, that and you said our *first* date, which implies that there will be at least a second and third." He smiles nervously. His nervous smile is so damn cute.

"I don't know what to say. I mean, I'm not a girl who needs extravagant things." I say shaking my head as if I gave him a bad first impression. "I mean, are you sure about this?" I know what I want to do. I want to kiss him. I want to reach up with both of my hands and pull his face to my lips. I want to taste him and forget about our date. I could just sit here with him all day, our lips connected, my hands on his chest. Holding his hand earlier was so comforting. I haven't felt that way in over seven years. I wanted to revel in it.

Facing me from his seat, Finn reaches his hand out and pushes the stray hair that has fallen out of my ponytail away from my face. It's a nice excuse for him to touch me, and I wish he wouldn't stop. I try very hard not to tip my head in the direction of his hand. I'm sure as his fingers glide past my face he can feel the heat in my cheeks.

"I'm sure." He smiles. "Just say 'Thank You', Olivia. That's all you have to say," he says peering into my eyes. I want to shrink back just a little bit because I feel like he is peering into my soul, like he can see me and all my insecurities. However he does it, I feel completely at ease with

Finn. I reach my hand over to his leg and rest my hand on his thigh. He stiffens slightly at my touch, but then I feel him relax.

"Thank you, Finn. Thank you very much for this. I...I can't wait to use it!" I frown slightly. "Umm...just where are we going today anyway?"

"It's a surprise," he says, smirking. He lowers his hand to hold mine on his thigh. He slides on his aviator sunglasses and pulls out onto the street. Holding his hand is giving me major butterflies. The energy between us is almost palpable. I look out my window, expelling a few deep breaths to control the flutters in my stomach.

This really nice guy asked me out.

He bought me a gift.

He was thinking of me. ME.

He's so hot.

How is this happening to me?

Please Olivia don't fuck this up.

Not knowing how long we'll be in the car, I decide to use the time to playfully learn as much as I can about this hot runner guy named Finn.

"Well, since this is our first date, and we don't really know each other that well, I need to get to know you. I mean, I don't date just anyone who asks, so I need to make sure you meet my standards and all." I'm smirking at him.

Finn turns his head to see my expression and releases a quiet chuckle. "Ask away, Olivia."

"Hmmm, chocolate or vanilla?" I ask.

"Twist if I have a choice. Chocolate if I don't."

"Coke or Pepsi?"

"Diet Coke or beer." He shrugs smirking. I laugh.

"Beyoncé or Carly Rae Jepson?" I ask narrowing my eyes.

His eyebrows furrow, and he purses his lips, I think a little embarrassed. "Who's Carly Rae Jepson?"

I laugh heartily at that one given the irony of how we met, how he gave me his number, and told me to call him. "Guess that answers my question. How about this one: who's singing the song on the radio right now." I recognize it as one of my favorites.

"Not a Bad Thing by Mr. Justin Timberlake." Finn looks over at me with raised eyebrows. I'm immediately impressed, though I don't know why. I smile in response and chuckle.

"Ah, very good, very good. I'm impressed. How about favorite food?"

He thinks about it for a moment before he says, "Cheeseburgers."

"Oh good pick! I love a good cheeseburger"

"Yeah? I've made a mean burger in my day. Perhaps you'll get to experience my culinary prowess sometime."

I don't think I could ever turn that offer down.

"Perhaps." I can feel my face flushing.

"My turn," he says.

"Okay, shoot."

He thinks for a minute before asking, "Star Wars or Star Trek?"

"The force is always with me. Next question." That gets me a chuckle and a positive nod.

"Favorite Book?"

"Right now or like of all time?" I ask. I have to be able to answer correctly.

Finn shrugs. "Both, I guess, if they're different."

"They are. My favorite book right now is called Happenstance by Jamie McGuire, but my favorite of all time is Harry Potter and the Order of the Phoenix."

His head snaps towards me as if he's shocked by that answer. "Really?"

"Yeah. Really. I'm a Potterhead just like everyone else in my generation. Aren't you?"

He nods his head slowly but deflects my question by asking another. "Favorite color?"

"Blue," I say quickly.

"Favorite vacation spot?"

Solving Us

"Umm, well I haven't been to that many places, but I would love to see Ireland one day. I hear it's beautiful there."

"It is. Stunning," Finn mutters. He looks over at me once more. I can't see his expression through his sunglasses, but he gives me a sheepish grin and turns his focus once more to the road.

I take a minute to look outside my window while enjoying the drive. I don't realize I'm humming along to "Play It Again" by Luke Bryan on the radio, until Finn looks over at me and smiles.

"You have a beautiful voice. You like Luke Bryan? Why doesn't that surprise me?"

I roll my eyes from behind my sunglasses and smile, thankful that Finn can't see them. "Umm, yeah I guess, but I don't swoon over him or anything like lots of girls do. He was just sort of popular among my circle of friends in college."

"Well, sing away. I like listening to you." He looks amused which embarrasses me slightly.

Ten minutes later, we are parking at the New England Aquarium and walking to the wharf near the Boston Harbor. I can see a huge blue and white catamaran that is emblazoned with **Boston Harbor Cruises** on the side. I look over at Finn who is smiling like a little boy on Christmas morning. He is so excited that I am obviously sincerely surprised to be here.

"We're going on a cruise?" I ask him.

"Not just a cruise, a whale watching cruise!" He exclaims squeezing my hand as we walk to the dock to board the vessel. "Boston Harbor Cruises are the best cruises in the country to be guaranteed a wonderful whale watching experience! I thought maybe you could use that new lens on those big beauties in the water!"

"WHALE WATCHING??! Are you serious Finn? Oh my God! I've never been in my entire life!" I cannot stop smiling. I also can't contain myself anymore. A small kiss wouldn't hurt anything, right? I tug on his arm to get him to stop walking or at least slow down. When Finn turns to look at me, I quickly reach up on my tiptoes, grab his left bicep, and plant a quick peck on his left cheek.

"Thank you for this, Finn! I'm so excited! Oh my GOSH I can't wait! Come on!" My eyes are beaming with elation. I tug on Finn's arm, this time to get him to continue on with me to the catamaran. I definitely shocked him with that little kiss, but I'm pretty sure he is completely fine with it. He puts his hand on the small of my back and leads me up the dock. My confidence is boosting, and I cannot wait to show Finn what I can do with a camera.

We spend the first hour of the trip just walking around the boat discussing our hobbies and our friends. I tell him a little more about Abby, and though he doesn't have a roommate, Finn mentions that he has a very good friend named Toby who he gets to see on the weekends when he's free. About ninety minutes into the ride, the catamaran slows down, and we venture up to the top viewing deck. There are several people up here with us, but we have a great spot right next to the railing to see out into the ocean.

I take a minute to get my camera out and put my new lens on so that I can take a few test shots. I just get my lens snapped on when I hear a loud gasp behind me. I don't even have time to lift my head to see what is going on when Finn suddenly grabs me by the shoulders and turns me around in front of him to look out to the water. A gigantic humpback whale shoots up from the surface of the water about one hundred yards in front of me! It shoots up and leans over to the left splashing back down into the water. It is magnificent to see! I can't believe how close we are!

I turn my head back at Finn, who is standing behind me somewhat, caging me in between him and the railing. "OH MY GOD did you SEE that?" I shout. I laugh out loud in astonishment. This is completely surreal.

"I sure did," Finn says from behind me. "Sorry if I startled you. I just didn't want you to miss it!" He's laughing, too.

We watch the water for the next hour as more whales, one after another, shoot out of the water, lean to the side, and smack back down under the surface. Many times we can hear the whales come to the surface to breathe and turn just in time to see a fluke dipping back down in the water. Dolphins swim parallel to the boat every once in a while, jumping out of the water with each other like they are playing leapfrog. I must snap a thousand pictures while we are standing there. I am amazed at some of the shots I am getting, and in all honesty, as guilty as I had felt at first, I am extremely grateful for my new lens. A few times I feel Finn watching me and look up just in time to see him look away, not wanting to get caught staring at me. It makes me smile every time I catch him. I really can't help feeling like I'm at SeaWorld, and this whole date is a prepared show! How is it possible that I am simply watching nature happen around me? Incredible.

I lower my camera from my face, still gazing out at the water, as the catamaran heads back to the wharf. I feel Finn's arms come up on each side of me, literally caging me in next to the side of the boat. I let out a comfortable sigh of contentment. I feel safe with Finn, and I know he is testing his limits, so I let him know I am okay with the closeness by leaning back into his chest. For a minute he doesn't move, but then he slowly wraps his arms around my chest at my collarbone. He is definitely trying to be careful not to cop a feel accidentally on purpose. I lay my head back on his chest and smile. He smells so good, woodsy like mahogany, but with splashes of apple and citrus. I wonder what cologne he is wearing. I could become addicted to that smell. I haven't felt this happy in a long time. What a freaking amazing day this has been! Finn places a light kiss in my hair while he is holding me.

"Well? What did you think?" he whispers in my ear.

"Finn, this was without a doubt the most amazing thing I've laid eyes on in a very long time! Thank you so much for bringing me here! If I had a trophy to give you, I would definitely proclaim you the winner of the Best First Date Award." I raise my eyebrows and shake my head in astonishment. "Seriously, this was an amazing afternoon." I can't stop smiling.

I don't want our time together to end.

Get a grip Olivia; it's the first date.

"Good. I'm really glad you enjoyed it. I had a feeling you would." He kisses my hair again. "And it was incredible to see you in your element with your camera. I couldn't stop watching you. You really have an eye for what's around you."

I turn around so I can see his face, but he doesn't let go of me. Instead, he moves his arms to hold me in a light embrace while I lean back against the railing enough to speak to him. "Well I hope you stopped watching me enough to see some of those whales because that was an amazing view!" I tease him

The look in Finn's eyes says everything he doesn't have to say but does anyway. "Yeah...I did have an amazing view." He is staring at me. His eyes move between my eyes and my lips; he wants to kiss me. I can feel it. I can feel his body lean slightly into mine. My breath hitches, and my lips separate as I feel that spike of warmth shoot through me all the way down my legs.

Kiss me, Finn.

From behind me, Finn's right hand comes up to my hair, and he gently runs his hand down the left side of my face to my chin. I see his Adam's apple move as he swallows. He seems almost nervous. With his fingers, he slightly raises my chin and then tilts his head slightly to press his lips against mine.

I close my eyes and allow myself to give in to the taste of him. He brushes his tongue lightly against my lips asking for permission to enter, and I grant him access immediately. Finn is an exceptional kisser.

I wonder how much practice he's had?

He is smooth and gentle, never overstepping any boundaries, and always making sure I'm comfortable. I feel protected by him. As my tongue meets his, I hear the slightest groan from the back of his throat. He moves my camera out of the way so he can pull me closer to him. Since his left hand is holding me to him at my back, I grab on to his bicep, moving my thumb back and forth slowly feeling the firm muscle beneath my hand. My left hand lies gently on his chest.

Bystanders be damned, this kiss is turning me on. I don't want to stop kissing him. As we stand here brushing our lips against one another in a mutually passionate moment, I begin focusing on my body and how it feels to be in a man's arms this way again. My body temperature is rising with each stroke of his tongue against mine, and soon all I can think about is how wet I'm getting...

Wet.

I'm wet.

No, I'm really wet.

Why am I wet?

What the hell?

I'm wet....and people are laughing.

I open my eyes and look up at Finn, who also has no idea what is going on, but he is wet, too, and looks startled. We take a second to survey our surroundings just in time to see a huge whale fluke sink back into the water. That whale shot up out of the water close enough to our boat that it splashed all of us standing on the upper deck when it re-entered the water! Everyone is laughing and shouting! I look up at Finn, feeling the drips of water from my now wet hair, and he looks at me trying to hide his smile like he doesn't want to ruin our semi-private moment, but in this situation it can't be helped. We both break down into a fit of giggles over the fact that we missed the whole thing.

I guess now I don't have to worry about that awkward moment after a first kiss when nobody knows what to say.

We are all laughs for the rest of the ride to the wharf. By the time we dock, we are mostly dried out from our surprise whale attack, but Finn notices the goose bumps on my arms and pulls me into the cruise gift shop. He quickly finds and purchases a long-sleeved t-shirt for me to put on before we leave.

He's so compassionate.

With the breeze coming off the water it is slightly cool, and the warm shirt is indeed comfortable. I love how thoughtful Finn is.

Finn takes me to one of the local pubs on the way home so we can get a bite to eat and talk some more. I have a feeling he could skip dinner and come right to my place, and I could be okay with that decision as well; but this is the first date, and I know he is trying to be a gentleman.

I respect that very much. Quite frankly, I'm not ready to end my day in tears if Finn were to get my shirt off and see how unattractive I really am. I'm content to just share my day with Finn, getting to know him as much as I can. We are seated in a booth towards the back of the pub. It's quiet enough that we can talk and still take in the social atmosphere around us. The televisions around the pub are playing the Red Sox game, and patrons are cheering the team on after a few home runs.

"So, Olivia," Finn says before taking a sip of his Yuengling. "You obviously love what you do behind a camera. There's no way anyone can deny that after watching you today, so what's stopping you from finding your dream job? Not sure where to start? Don't know what you're looking for?"

I munch on a French fry while I consider Finn's question. "Well, yes to both in a way, I guess. I spent almost two years working for a newspaper already, and that had its moments, but I want to be able to get paid to experience moments like I did today, or work on a team where I feel like I have a hand in the end result, ya know? I don't want to be out snapping pictures of the local town parade or local sports team all the time...not that I'm belittling that or anything. I loved it while I did it back home."

"I get that. You're a passionate artist who isn't afraid to think outside the box, but you don't always have to hold the reins, right?"

"Yeah...yeah that's pretty much me exactly," I smile approvingly. As I'm sipping my drink, I watch Finn's eyes. He's looking at me again like he really gets me. He seems to understand my personality, even just from the short time he's known me, and I like that about him. I like that I don't have to pretend around him. Well...not entirely anyway. I move the hair hanging down my back around to the right side of my neck instinctively, trying to hide my scars from Finn. I don't mind that he sees me; I'm just not ready for him to see *all* of me. Finn is watching my every move though and is perceptive enough to pick up on my sudden insecurity. He clears his throat quietly and nods his chin in the direction of my neck.

"So, what happened?" he asks. I look up at him panicking because I know what he's referring to and he knows I know.

Solving Us

"Sorry. I noticed them the other day," Finns explains quietly referring to the scars on my neck. "I wasn't going to bring it up, but I can see it bothers you at least a little, and I don't like that you feel uncomfortable. I don't like that whatever went through your mind just a moment ago took your smile away."

My head bows, and I focus on the ring on my finger. My thumb and pointer finger instinctively start rotating the ring around and around my finger. It's my nervous tick.

"You don't have to tell me; I know it's none of my business. I just…like seeing you happy."

"Oh, um, it's no big deal really, just an accident from high school," I lie. It is a big deal to me. It was a life-altering accident and one that I'm scared I'll never fully come back from, but there is no way Finn needs to know that now. Not today. He either doesn't want to push the issue, or gets the message that I'm not ready to talk about it, because he purses his lips and shakes his head like he understands.

"I'm sorry. I'm sure it was a frightening experience for you," he replies. I can tell he's trying to decide what to say next. "Look I know this is our first date but…I just - I mean, I want you to know, as I've told you already, that I think you're beautiful, Olivia, stunning even! You're such a breath of fresh air, and a few scars aren't going to change that for me."

Be still my melting heart, I might have to love him soon!

I wonder if his view of me will change when he learns my scars are more than a few.

I am flattered, though, so I smile at Finn and then take another sip of my beer, wishing for a moment that it were straight vodka.

"So, about your epic job search," Finn changes the subject, for which I am grateful. "Why don't you consider a job with The Kellan Agency? The photographers at the agency have opportunities for world travel to work with international clients, and they're always an imperative asset to our marketing teams."

"Hmm, spoken like a true advocate for the company, Sir,' I tease him. "So if I had to guess, I would say you've either worked for the Kellan

Agency before, or you know Mr. Kellan? You never did tell me what your family business is."

Finn looks down immediately searching for words. He frowns for a moment, and I don't quite understand why that question catches him off guard. What's the big deal if he works there or not, other than the fact that I would see him every day if I worked there, too. "I don't just work there, Olivia," he says with quiet breath. Finn looks up at me with a slightly pained expression.

"I own it."

"Oh."

Wait…what?

The crowd around the restaurant starts whistling and cheering as the Red Sox score another double.

The smile on my face dissipates and immediately turns into a confused frown.

"You?" I ask loudly enough for Finn to hear me. "You're the Mr. Kellan of The Kellan Agency?"

"Yes. Well, no. Mr. Kellan was my father." Finn begins to explain. "When I graduated college, my dad was diagnosed with Hodgkin's Lymphoma and passed away two years later. I inherited the company from him; regardless, I would've ended up here anyway. I love the people in this company and have great respect for how my father ran his business. It's my pleasure to do it now."

"Oh. Wow." I take a deep breath and swallow the drink I just took. God this was awkward. "Um, I'm sorry to hear about your father, really I am," I say anxiously. "But Finn, I…" I could feel my heart beating a little harder, a sign of my nerves and anxiety. I'm now anything but blissfully calm as I was an hour ago. Is he offering me some sort of opportunity without knowing anything about me?

"You haven't even seen my portfolio…or my resume…"

"I don't need your portfolio, Liv," he interrupts while taking another drink. "I've seen your work."

Solving Us

I frown at him. "How?" I shake my head in confusion. "I never even told you where I was published...or that I *was* published for that matter."

What the hell?

Why does this feel all sorts of weird?

Finn looks as if he doesn't want to reveal his secrets, so, hopefully, whatever he is about to say will be the truth. "Dr. Tursly at the Rhode Island School of Design was a friend of my father's. He used to send my dad info on all of his top students so that we knew who we might want to extend internships to each summer. Obviously, being at the top of your class, I heard about you over a year ago...but you didn't apply for an internship."

My eyes are wide with surprise. Obviously, I get that things like this happen; schools share info on top students all the time to help them get ahead, but never in a million years did I think about people talking about me. I'm just a normal person who lives behind a camera, nothing special. It dawns on me right then that perhaps his running by me yesterday morning, and our conversation at Starbucks, may not have been just chance encounters.

Was this a set up?

He knew who I was?

"Did you seek me out yesterday morning because you already knew who I was?" I ask.

"No!" He looks confused as to why I would even ask that question. "I had no idea who you were when I saw you yesterday other than..." Finn looks at the bottle in his hands, not wanting to look at me. I can see the blush on his face again. "Other than I thought you were beautiful lying on the ground taking pictures of something I couldn't see. You were in your element, and I could tell you were doing something you loved doing. It just so happens that something you're passionate about, and very good at, is photography; and I have a job opening in my company for a marketing photographer that I think you might be perfect for. Why wouldn't I want someone with that much passion working for me?"

I don't know what to think. I'm blown away. Why didn't he tell me this afternoon...or yesterday morning? About a hundred thoughts race through my mind as I look at him, and then it hits me.

Oh God! Was this all some sort of hoax?

Was he wooing me like he probably wines and dines a client so that I would work for him?

He's the freaking CEO?

He kissed me!

"*Why* did you take me out today?" I ask suspiciously. "I mean I feel like I must have crossed some sort of imaginary line because I really thought you were interested in me....in *me* and not just my photography skills. I don't have any marketing experience, and I've never really done anything in advertising. I'm just a girl who takes pictures."

Finn looks up at me with sheer confusion on his face. "Olivia, you're much more than just a girl who takes pictures. Please, stop selling yourself short."

I tilt my head as I look at him sadly. "Was this all one of those wine and dine experiences you told me about this morning?" I ask him. "You know, just take the girl out and show her a good time so she'll come work for you? Extra points if you can get her into your bed as well?" The heaviness in my chest is confining. It's taking my breath away, and it's all I can do to keep the tears at bay.

Don't go crazy, Olivia.

This could all be a huge misunderstanding.

Breathe!

"What?" Finn gasps. "Olivia, no, please that's not what I meant at all. I just know you're looking for a job, and I think you would be *great* at The Kellan Agency. I could give you great career opportunities, and I *really* enjoyed this day with you so much. I thought I made that very clear. I *like* you! You're a beautiful girl and..."

"I'm NOT a beautiful girl, Finn. Please stop saying that," I interrupt emphatically. I'm looking down at my lap now, fidgeting with the ring on my finger. The ring I never take off. I slump in my seat in utter disappointment.

"Olivia..."

"You saw the scars, Finn. They're not beautiful, and what you've seen isn't even the worst of them. I look like a shark has attacked me for Christ's sake. I'm flawed. I'm sure you've been with many girls who far surpass my plain girl looks. If you're anything like the other guys I've dated, I know what you're thinking, and it's okay. Every other guy has had the same reaction, and I get it."

Finn is frowning at me from across the table. "Olivia....please, I don't know how many other guys you've dated, but I can probably bet everything I own that I'm not like most guys."

I'm disappointed and upset, and I can feel the water works coming on strong. A lone tear streaks down my cheek as I look up at Finn for the last time.

"I guess I was just hoping you would prove me wrong, that maybe you were that guy I've been waiting for who sees me for *me*, and who can be honest with me about *who* he is." Trying as hard as I possibly can to keep the tears under control, I stand up and look down at Finn who looks crestfallen and shocked. I almost feel bad for what I've said to him. Almost.

"Olivia," he breathes. "Please, hear me out. I swear it's not what you..."

The crowd around the room is screaming at the television sets now, clearly not agreeing with the call of the referee. The noise gives me the chance to get my wits about me and stand up without causing much of a scene.

"I'm sorry, Finn. I guess this isn't going to work out. I'm so sorry to have wasted your time." I quickly take the new camera lens Finn purchased for me out of my camera bag to give back to him.

"No, Olivia, please don't give this back. I bought this for *you*! It made me happy to give it you," he pleads.

"No Finn. Please, give it to the person you hire for the job. I'm sure he or she will make great use of it. Thank you, though, for the thought and again for today. I really had a nice time. I'll see myself out."

And with that, I leave as quickly as my legs can carry me without running. Once I'm out of the pub, there is a line of cabs waiting at the curb to be designated drivers, so I choose one and hop in before Finn can chase me from the building and make a scene.

Every relationship I have ever had with a guy in the past starts out the same. I allow myself to be comforted and complemented by smooth words and gentle touches. With some, I even start to believe I really am beautiful again, but in the end every single relationship I have goes south faster than I expect. I'm beautiful until the guy I'm with sees more of my body than I show to the everyday world. A bikini body I no longer have, and there is nothing I can do about that. I allow myself to shed the tears I had bravely held back before on the way home. This had been one of the best days that I could remember, and I'm heartbroken that it has ended less than happily for me, but should I have been surprised? Probably not.

Did I just totally mess up and run away from the one possibly nice guy I've met in seven years because I'm scared?

Perhaps.

I think I really liked him.

Chapter 4

I can feel the fight leaving my body as I'm dragged one more time down the road. My right leg is a bloody mess, I'm pretty sure my right arm is broken, and who knows what my neck looks like. I can feel the warmth of blood on my body, but until the fight stops, I know I won't truly know how bad the damage is, to either of us. I hear more growling now. It sounds louder to me, but maybe it's because the bigger dog is closer to us now, or maybe it's because there is more than one dog attacking Max…or maybe…

Oh my God!

IS IT A BEAR?

"MAX!!!" I try to scream, but I know my voice isn't traveling through the growls and barking.

I can't breathe. My chest isn't letting me get the air I need. Before I black out, I hear Max yelp again and cry as he slumps down next to me. I stop hearing anything going on around me. I fall deeper and deeper into the black hole of oblivion and am content to stay there, forever.

*****

I'm alive. How am I alive? When I open my eyes and look around, I'm lying on the living room couch in my Boston apartment, drenched in sweat. I can feel the bile rising and know what's coming. It happens every time I have a flashback nightmare. I roll myself off the couch and stumble down the hall to the bathroom, making it just in time to be sick. When I finish, I wet a washcloth and wipe my face, take a sip of water from the Dixie cup sitting on the sink, and then lay my head down on the bathroom floor and sob. I sob for Max, who I miss terribly. I sob for me, for all the mean comments I endured during the years following my accident; and as I remember this morning and afternoon, I sob for that as well. Fuck this day, and fuck my life.

I hear the door to our apartment open and the jingling sound of keys hitting the kitchen counter.

"Olivia?"

It's Abby. What is she doing home? I don't answer her. I just want to lay here and be left alone to my misery.

"Olivia, I'm home; where are you?" She comes around the corner and, obviously, sees me lying on the bathroom floor. "OH MY GOD, WHAT HAPPENED? Are you okay?"

"Yeah I'm okay," I sniffle as I start to sit up. "I fell asleep on the couch when I got home from my date, and I guess I had a nightmare." I think for a minute about what day it is before I look back at Abby. "What are you doing here, Abs? Shouldn't you be in New York still?

"Yes, but Trent got called back home to cover for someone at the hospital, so we came home early. I was just walking in when I heard you."

Abby studies my face and narrows her eyes at me, and then as she finally registers what I said, her eyebrows shoot up.

"Date...*what* date...OHHH yeah, your date! I totally forgot it was today!"

"I know. You were out of town, so I didn't remind you; and I knew I would see you on Sunday anyway, but it's a long story."

She sees that I'm comfortable, or at least not ready to move yet, because Abby throws her shoes off, grabs me another drink of water, and sits on the floor next to me. "So, spill it girl; tell me about your date! That is...unless you would rather talk about your nightmare?"

"Just another flashback. They're happening more often right now, and it's really pissing me off." I look at her with sad pained eyes, and she can tell the story of my date isn't going to be a happy one.

"Oh, Liv. I'm so sorry you're still living with this pain. The last thing you should have to experience is living that nightmare over and over again."

"I know," I say in a whisper. "But I can't really control what I dream about, you know that."

"Your day was that bad?" Abby asks worryingly.

"Yes...no...I don't know. It all just happened so fast, Abby; I haven't even given myself time to think about it. Maybe I was overreacting, and if that's the case, I can't ever show my face in front of Finn Kellan again; and if I wasn't overreacting, then Finn Kellan might possibly be a fucking douche bag who wines and dines women to get them to work for him." I crush the Dixie cup I drank out of and throw it towards the garbage can, but miss. I watch it crash to the floor.

"Wait, Finn Kellan?" Abby asks quickly. You would think I just told her I met Justin Timberlake. "THE Finn Kellan, as in Owner and CEO of The Kellan Agency? That Finn Kellan?"

"Yeah. That's the one," I sadly confirm. "I met him yesterday morning in the park while I was taking pictures and then again at Starbucks. We got to talk, and he asked me out. Oh, but I forgot to tell you that he never told me who he was or that he owned the Kellan Agency. He never told me his last name. I had no idea who he was. I thought he was just some hot guy named Finn who was kindly offering me a great day, except after our so-called great day, he offered me a job."

"That's amazing, Liv! If Finn Kellan offers you a job you say YES." She pauses and looks at me expectantly.

"You said yes, right?"

My face falls and I bow my head. Her face falls, too. "Oh God, you didn't say yes. What the hell happened?"

I continue to tell Abby about my encounters with Finn, starting from the very beginning and ending with my stepping out of the pub earlier this evening. I grab a Kleenex and pat at my eyes as I start to cry again, while I explain what disappointed me the most.

"He told me I was beautiful, twice! He also told me that I was a breath of fresh air and that he liked me. He even kissed me!"

"Damn right he did! Haha, that's awesome...how was it? Is he a good kisser?"

"Well, okay, I may have kissed him first, but then he really kissed me later; and to answer your question, he's a fantastic kisser. But what the hell, Abby? Who does that and then turns around and offers someone a job? He was sooo hot when I saw him running yesterday, and then by some chance, he said he saw me later walking towards Starbucks and followed me so that he could talk to me. We had a great date; he even bought me an awesome, albeit ridiculously expensive, lens for my camera."

"No shit!" Abby's eyes narrow. She obviously feels just as I do that getting a gift like that on the first date is a bit odd.

"Yeah, but I feel like now it was all a planned interview. He watched *me* all day - watched me work - then he offered me a job over dinner."

"Okay," Abby says shrugging her shoulders. "It sounds to me like he digs you, Liv. What's wrong with that? If Finn Kellan offered me ANYTHING, I would take it! He's a catch, Liv! Like, he's Boston's hottest young bachelor, and he showed interest in you! He could give you a hell of a career, yes; but it sounds like he would like to know you more than just as an employee"

"That's just the problem, Abs. Does he want me to work for him because he likes me and wants to have some sort of relationship, albeit inappropriate if he's going to be my boss, or was he just smooth talking and flirting with me so I would accept the job? We didn't even talk about what the job would be! I was so turned around by what he was saying that I felt confused and hurt….and cheap….and a little used, so I left. He kissed me, Abby! I mean, seriously, does he come onto and sleep with all the women in his company just to get them to say yes to working for him? I can't imagine that works out well in the long term."

Tilting her head to the side with a sorry expression, Abby says, "Oh, Liv, I can understand what you must've been thinking, but you know what? I think there's a possibility you could be wrong. Finn Kellan is a pretty popular name around here, and from talk at the firm, I've never heard gossip about Finn being anything but a nice guy. If he was showing interest in you, Honey, he was probably actually interested in you!"

"So, you think I was overreacting?"

"Well, I think it's a possibility that your reaction was a bit unwarranted; but I'm not going to downplay your feelings, either. You have a past that has created certain strong insecurities for you, so it's understandable that you would react that way a little. Perhaps Mr. Hot Runner Guy CEO should've gone about courting you differently at least or made himself a little more clear, so don't sweat it. Men are like...blenders, Liv."

"Umm, what?"

"Blenders. You want one, you think you need one...but you're not really sure why."

I laugh through my tears at Abby's ridiculous humor.

"Look, you can either call him and explain your thoughts or just chalk it up to a bad date and move on."

I blow my nose one last time and nod my head. "You're right; maybe I should call him tomorrow," I agree softly. "Ugh, I have no idea what I'll say. I'm really attracted to him, Abs. And his smell...oh, Abby, he smells so good." I take a deep breath remembering Finn's scent of wood and apples and...what was giving off the sweet smell, violet maybe? I don't know. I let out my breath and smile shyly at Abby before frowning as I remember my earlier confusion. "I was just afraid that he was leading me on to get me to work for him. Maybe I was being a stupid emotional girl, because if I'm being honest with myself, I *want* him to like me. I was *hoping* he really liked me."

"Nah, I wouldn't say you're a stupid girl, and maybe he really does like you," Abby stands up and helps pull me up off the bathroom floor. "We all have our really bad days, and perhaps if this job conversation would've happened tomorrow instead of today, the outcome would have been different. Call him tomorrow, though. You'll know he's a nice guy and worthy of your attention if he agrees to see you after everything that happened today. Just be patient; the best guys out there are like...coffee...the best ones are rich, warm, and can keep you up all night long." As Abby smirks at me, her stomach growls loudly, and we both chuckle.

"I know it's a little late, but I think this night call for some girl time. How about some milk, a big bowl of Hershey Kisses, and a chick flick? Want to watch the Princess Bride? 'No more rhymes now; I mean it!'"

I chuckled at Abby's quote from the movie. The Princess Bride is our go-to comfort chick flick. "Ha! As you wish, Abs." I say smirking. "I'll get the snacks; you get the movie."

On my way to the kitchen, there is a knock on our apartment door.

"I'll get it, Abs!" I call to her since I am already heading that direction.

We don't have tons of friends in the building and aren't really expecting any visitors. I walk over to the door and peer through the peephole. I freeze right where I'm standing and grab on to the doorknob to keep from falling to the floor when I see who is standing outside my door. Familiar warmth shoots through me, and I can immediately feel my face flush.

What the...?

How did he....?

I swallow hard and take a very deep breath to stop myself from shaking and open the door. My eyes lock with the man standing in front of me. "Hello, Finn."

Chapter 5

Finn's shoulders fall, and his expression full of sadness and guilt. "Oh God Olivia! Please tell me that the sadness on your face isn't my fault," he pleads, shaking his head. I take a quick stock in my appearance, noting that I must look ridiculous with my hair pulled into a messy bun that was previously sweat-ridden, blue capris sweatpants, and an old, worn pink tank top. My eyes are puffy and swollen from crying, and my makeup is nonexistent at this point. Could I look any worse? I'm a hot mess.

Well Finn, what you see is what you get, I guess.

"I...please," Finn pleads. "I never meant to hurt you. Allow me to fix it; I *need* to fix it because I can't have you being sad and upset because of my own stupidity."

The look of sincerity on Finn's face makes me want to hug and console him. He looks lost, like a man who is desperate to get out of the doghouse, or like a little boy who just dropped his ice cream cone.

Damnit, Olivia, get a grip!

I take a deep breath before asking, "What are you doing here?" This time I'm going to learn from my mistakes and shut my mouth and listen rather than react irrationally.

"I didn't want to follow you and make an uncomfortable scene this evening; but I texted you...um...well...probably more often than a normal person to make sure you made it home safely, and you never answered, so I feared something had happened to you and...I'm sorry; I just had to check to make sure you were ok and ..." Finn stops and takes a deep breath. He slides his hand through his hair, clearly frustrated that he can't think of how to say what he wants to say. "I'm sorry, Olivia. I'm so sorry; please let me explain." He bows his head and closes his eyes for a second before peeking up at me. "Can we go for a walk?"

I look myself over quickly and raise my hands to my hair to make sure it isn't ridiculously disheveled, though I had it all pulled up in a messy bun on the top of my head after my nap. I swipe my hand across my forehead. I feel like a hot mess and most likely look the same. Finn knows exactly what I'm thinking, though, and quickly puts my mind at ease.

"Olivia you couldn't look cuter than you do at this very moment," Finn says looking me over. "Well, maybe you could if there was a smile on your face that I had a part in; but right now, in your comfy clothes and hair all pulled up and off your neck, you're perfect." He holds his hand out for me. "Walk with me?"

I wait a second before smiling shyly back at him.

Time to walk the walk, Liv. You said you wanted him, right?

"Ok." I say quietly. "Just let me tell Abby where I'm going." I turn around to walk down the hall to Abby's room but stop short when I see her standing in the living room. She steps over to the door to see who I'm talking to.

"You must be Abby," Finn says looking up from the doorway. "I've heard a lot about you. I'm Finn. Finn Kellan." He holds out his hand to Abby as he introduces himself to her.

Reaching out to shake Finn's hand, Abby replies, "It's nice to meet you, Mr. Kellan, I've heard a lot about you, too. Can we help you with something?"

"Finn," he corrects immediately. It isn't lost on me that his eyes quickly dart to me. "Please, call me Finn, and um, yeah you can help me." Finn nods his head in my direction and says to Abby. "You can help me convince this beautiful girl here that I'm worth her time if she'll just give me a chance to apologize for being a huge douche earlier today."

Abby and I both laugh at Finn's self-proclaimed douchiness, and already I can see that Abby is impressed. "Well, it does take a real man to admit when he's a douche, so I might be willing to help you out this one time, Finn Kellan," she says with a wink to me. "Liv", Abby says turning to look at me. "You and Finn go ahead. I'll jump in the shower while you guys are out, okay?" Abby looks at me and raises her eyebrows to let me know she's asking if I'm ok being with Finn.

"Yeah, sure. I'll be back soon."

Solving Us

"Go. Take your time. I'll see you soon," Abby says waving us out the door. I can see her meet Finn's eye with her stern "don't mess with my friend" look. I smile at her protective mommy behavior as Finn takes my hand and heads down the hall to the elevator. Abby grabs my other hand swiftly and gives me a reassuring squeeze. This is why I love her.

Standing in the elevator with Finn, I can feel the tension between us. I don't know if I can call it sexual tension, but the desire to turn towards him and hug him comes over me so strongly I have to fist my hands at my sides to keep from relenting to my urges. My breathing is getting heavy, and I can feel my cheeks warming. I'm not sure where this conversation with Finn is going to go, but I remind myself that tonight needs to be about hearing him out and not reacting so irrationally. Something feels so right standing with Finn, though, and I know in my heart that I want something to work out between us. He really is a nice guy. If he didn't care, even a little bit, about me he wouldn't have shown up tonight.

"Finn," I turn slightly to look at him. I can tell he is anxious because he's fidgeting as we stand together in the elevator. The fingers on his right hand are drumming softly on his thigh, and his eyes are apologetic but hopeful. His cheeks are also slightly pink, telling me that he can feel the connection between us just as I can. "I think I owe you an apology."

Finn turns and cups my face with one hand since I'm holding the other one. "No Olivia, listen, you really don't. I'm sorry, I…I just went about this all wrong, and I want to be able to explain myself because…I like you, and I fucked up on our first date. I was so stupid, and I'm sorry."

The elevator bell dings, and we walk out the back door of the apartment building to stroll through the quad outside. The street lights give the quad a romantic glow but not so bright that you can't do a little stargazing when the weather is just right, and tonight, it's perfect. It's a cloudless night with a warm breeze, which is lucky for me considering I walked out without a jacket in just my tank top. The local restaurants create a smell in the air of fried food, and the sounds around us are of people docking their boats for the night after a day on the water. Finn and I find a bench along the quad that is deserted and in a quiet spot where we can talk.

We both sit down on the bench, and Finn lets go of my hand rubbing both of his hands nervously on his legs, cupping his knees and back up. I sit next to him and watch him for a couple minutes as he gathers his thoughts. I'm not about to start talking first. I put myself out there with my apology, so at least now he knows the ball is in his court. I'm ready to see where he goes with this.

"When I'm at work," Finn starts. "Running a company really isn't necessarily as hard as some people might think it is. I inherited this job a lot younger than I expected to. No, scratch that, I never expected to inherit this job. I expected my Dad to be around forever, but life doesn't always work out the way we plan. Lucky for me, I have a staff that works very hard, and we all share a mutual respect for one another. I do a great job of making them feel appreciated and needed because I *do* appreciate them, and I *do* need them. Mrs. Hoover, my secretary, keeps me very organized and on task up until the minute I leave the building and sometimes even longer than that. I'm a confident guy, and I rarely question my decisions in the office, but Olivia," he says turning to look at me.

"That's where it stops. Outside of work I..." Finn's shoulders slump, and he shakes his head. The next words out of his mouth are spoken so quickly and softly that if I wouldn't have been looking at him, I would've missed what he said.

"I haven't been on a date in three years."

Whoa! Did I just hear that right?

Three years?

That's pretty much all of his adult life.

He can't be over twenty-five.

The sides of my mouth twitch up slightly when I think about the fact that after a three year dry spell, Finn picked *me*. Somehow he found *me*.

Or did I find him?

Stop grinning you goof. He's opening up to you!

"You find that amusing?" he asks me trying to hide his embarrassment with a smile.

I lean over and softly nudge his shoulder with my own and grin at him. "Yes. No. Keep talking. I'm listening."

Finn let's out the deep breath he was obviously holding in. "The thing is Olivia, I had such an awesome carefree day with you. Watching you light up when you saw where we were going, watching you work in your element, doing what you love doing...sharing in your smiles, your laughs, your kiss." Finn's eyes fall to my mouth. I bite my bottom lip to keep from smiling too much.

That kiss!

"That means a lot to me, Olivia. Probably more than you realize. It means something to me that you were willing to share all of those parts of the day with me."

Finn bows his head in defeat. "I guess when we started talking about work I got excited and carried away and didn't even think about what my proposal must've sounded like to you. I'm so sorry."

I watch Finn as his eyes retreat back to mine. He brings his hand up to my face and brushes a stray hair behind my ear. "When you left, I replayed our conversation in my head over and over, and I get it Liv. You were right. I can see how you felt like I was wining and dining you; but Olivia, I promise you that was not my intention. I never would've wanted to make you feel that way, and I am so sorry that I hurt you with that perception."

I stare at him a moment before I ask what I feel is the obvious question. "Why didn't you just tell me yesterday when we met, or earlier today? About who you are, I mean?"

"Would you have gone out with me if I had? Would you have even been interested knowing who I was? I don't always want to be Finn Kellan the CEO with the weight of the world on his shoulders. Sometimes I just want to be Finn, the guy who gets to date the gorgeous girl."

I consider Finn's questions for a moment. I knew of The Kellan Agency before our meeting yesterday but obviously didn't know anything about Finn. I suppose if I had Googled him, I may have learned a few things; but not everything you read in print or online is real, so I usually don't waste my time.

"I don't know," I contemplate. "I know I would've still found you unbelievably sexy, but I probably would've felt way out of your league. So had I known who you were from the start I guess I probably would've tried to impress you professionally instead. And I'm sure no matter what Finn you choose to be, there's always a gorgeous girl waiting to date you."

Finn chuckles at my response and shakes his head.

Oh God! I said unbelievably sexy out loud didn't I?

"You wouldn't have had to try hard to impress me professionally, Liv. I was already impressed by what I saw in the park, but don't you see? You admit you wouldn't have even given me much consideration personally because of who I am professionally."

I frown at him and am almost ready to argue his point when he continues. "I know I said I haven't gone on a date in three years, and I'm being honest about that, but that doesn't mean women don't try to throw themselves at me whenever they can…and please, I'm not saying that to brag or look even douchier than I already have. I hate when it happens more than anything. Those women don't know me. They don't know my past; they don't know who I really am inside. They see a young, rich guy who might throw his money around on lavish gifts, but all for what, pretend love? I don't want to live that way."

His words literally take my breath away. Listening to him is very nearly like listening to my own inner monologue.

Pretend love.

I don't want to live that way.

They don't know me. They don't know my past.

They don't know who I am on the inside.

My eyes are wide with wonder, and I can feel my head tilting as I study Finn in amazement.

Solving Us

My lips separate and I draw a quiet breath before I say anything. "I get it," I say shaking my head slowly. "I understand *exactly* how you feel."

"You do?"

"Yeah," I slowly nod my head. "People judge you based on what they think they know, but it's what they don't know that really defines who you are. But they'll never see that side of you because they don't want to. They see what's in front of their eyes and not what's really underneath, in your heart."

Finn's eyebrows shoot up in surprise, and his wide eyes of wonderment match my own as we look at each other. I look down realizing I just let the proverbial cat out of the bag. If he's perceptive, and I'm sure he is, he now knows I have another layer to myself that I've not yet revealed.

"Sometimes I bet you really feel…"

"Alone." Finn finishes my sentence for me and that is exactly what I was going to say.

Whoa!

Connection!

Finn has baggage…

I blink.

Finn blinks.

His feelings really are sincere, and I feel guilty now that I obviously overreacted earlier; nonetheless, I'm relieved that he gets it and seems to get me. I'm comforted by the fact that he understands my feelings and doesn't belittle me in any way and actually seems pleasantly surprised that it looks like we have something in common: a defining past that neither of us is ready to share. I don't wish the feelings of insecurity on anyone; it can be debilitating at times. And the fact that Finn isn't perfect and doesn't want to be perceived that way bewitches me. I tilt my head to the side and study him a moment more.

I can't believe what I'm about to do but it just feels right.

I take his face in my hands as I feel my heart race. I close my eyes and kiss his lips slowly and gently, allowing the warmth to overtake my body. Kissing him makes me feel like I'm snuggling into the warmest and softest blanket. Finn puts an arm on my back to fold me into him and keep me steady, as we share in a lengthy, soft kiss. He is forever a gentleman. When we stop kissing. we're both flushed and breathing erratically. I rest my forehead on Finn's.

"Forgiven," I say to him grinning bashfully after a minute. I lay my hands on his chest, feeling the rigid muscles of his physique underneath his t-shirt. "And I'm sorry again for…"

"No," Finn stops my lips with his index finger. "You don't ever need to apologize to me for how you reacted. You were justified. I'm the one who sounded like a complete asshole…and, Olivia, I don't know that I can promise you that I won't fuck up again, but I want this with you, a relationship, I mean. Like I said, it's been a long time since I've really paid attention to a girl. I haven't wanted something like this in a long time, well ever actually, but I can promise you that I will do everything in my power to think before I speak so that I don't hurt you again. I really like you, Liv. You beguile me. Something about you grabbed me the first time I laid eyes on you. When you're not around, I can't get you out of my mind, and when you are around I just want to be near you. I want to protect you. I want to make you feel the way you deserve to feel."

Flattered doesn't even begin to describe how I feel that Finn is choosing me. He makes me feel pretty and makes me feel protected, but why has he never wanted a relationship like this before? Has he ever had a long-term relationship?

Who am I to judge? I haven't had a long-term relationship since high school.

Is his past not a happy one? He seems to have beaten himself up more than I expected over hurting my feelings, but he melted my heart with every word he said. I know if I choose Finn, as he is choosing me in this moment, I will find the answers to my questions. I take a deep breath and follow my heart.

Maybe someday he'll be the prince that saves me from my own wicked spell.

Solving Us

The Beauty to my internal Beast.

"I like you too Finn, and," I swallow gazing at him. "I'm pretty sure you beguiled me first."

I can hear the deep breath that Finn takes before he whispers my name.

"Olivia."

Our foreheads still touching; he grabs my legs, dangling from the bench, and brings them both up to rest on his lap. I shiver when a cool wind gust blows through the quad. I'm not dressed for any less than summer temperatures, and as we've been sitting here, the breeze through the quad has definitely come with a dip in temperature. Finn immediately wraps himself around me to help shield me from the cool air. I relax into his embrace. Both of Finn's hands are behind me. His left at the small of my back, he moves his right hand to the nape of my neck and guides my lips to his, kissing me a second time. The world around us falls away, and we're together in a bubble of warm heavenly bliss. I feel Finn pulling me closer to him as if he can't get me close enough, and something in me explodes. Knowing that this man I'm sitting with cares for me and is showing me his heart and showering me with affection is more than my head and heart can take at one time. I can get used to kissing him. Kissing Finn is nice. Better than nice, actually.

For what feels like long minutes, I lose myself in the feeling of Finn. I think about nothing but the warmth of his body enrapturing mine paired with the sweetness of his breath, the obvious mint he must've had on the way over here tonight mixed with the beers I had with him earlier. I feel the electricity on his fingers as he touches me, holds me, but that feeling comes crashing down as soon as I feel his hand move up my body. His fingertips are only centimeters away from the scars on my neck. The proximity scares me because I can't remember how it feels to have someone else physically touching them. I recoil, bringing my right shoulder to my ear out of habit, squeezing my eyes closed when I realize what I just did.

Shit!

He was just kissing you Olivia!

"I'm sorry; did I hurt you? I'm sorry!" Finn exclaims holding his hands up in front of him like I'm the kissing police. The concern in his eyes is agonizing.

"No. No, you didn't hurt me at all." I shake my head. Crushing my eyes closed again, I release the breath I didn't know I was holding. "Damnit! I'm so sorry, I just…"

"Fuck." I whisper.

Two hands are on my head softly smoothing my hair back on each side. "Olivia, it's okay. I'm sorry. I didn't mean to scare you." Finn's hands are strong and comforting. He makes me want to relinquish to his soft touch. Kissing him was definitely great, until I screwed it all up.

"No, Finn you didn't. It's me. I just…" I take a deep breath and look down too timid to look at him; and quite frankly, I'm just not ready to have this conversation. "It's just been a while….I guess."

Maybe I'm really not ready for this.

Maybe I really don't want it.

"I understand." Finn tilts my head back to capture my attention. He studies me while stroking my cheek with his thumb. "Olivia, I get that something horrible must've happened to you in your past that you're not ready to talk about, and that's okay. Hell, it's okay if you never want to talk about it, but if and when you do, I'm here. I'll be here."

How can he read me so well in just a short time?

He kisses my forehead, an affectionate show of compassion. "We all have parts of our past that we wish never happened Liv, and even though sometimes I don't want to believe it, I have a respect for the saying 'What doesn't kill us makes us stronger'."

I look at Finn questioningly. I wonder what he's referring to. The death of his dad I suppose.

"Yeah." I take a deep breath. "Stronger, right." I nod.

He leans forward and places a feather light kiss on my lips and again on my cheek.

"Come on; let me walk you home."

Solving Us

As we walk back to my apartment, he keeps his arm around my shoulder, stroking my arm now and again to keep it warm.

"So…I know we never really talked about it further," I start. "And, well…I can totally understand if you would rather I didn't after tonight, I mean, it's not very apropos to date your boss and all…"

"Wait." Finn stops walking and turns my body so I'm standing right in front of him.

"You would consider it? Working at The Kellan Agency, I mean? Is that what you're asking?"

"Well, I don't know. I guess…maybe…I mean…you didn't actually offer me a real position; you just sort of mentioned the possibility. I should probably hear more about the job first, but…"

"But what?"

"I just told you tonight that I liked you. I don't want to be that girl." I wince at the thought.

"What girl?"

"The girl everyone in the office thinks is sleeping her way to the top, so to speak," I say apprehensively.

Finn takes a deep breath and dons a shit faced grin. It makes me chuckle to even consider what he may be thinking about right now. "Well, first, who cares what they think is going on? And second," he laughs out loud. "You could give sleeping with your boss a try, but then I would be very disappointed to have missed it because I wouldn't be your boss. We wouldn't even be working in the same part of the building. Yes it's my name on your paycheck, but I actually wouldn't really be your supervising administrator, well not unless you do something really bad, and I have to get involved. Think of it this way. You're a teacher who reports to a Principal, and I'm the Superintendent."

I frown at him, confused. "Oh." I laugh and smack Finn on his chest playfully. "Okay I guess I deserve that. But Finn, you do understand that sleeping with the CEO of the company you're working for is sort of frowned upon in most places right? I mean surely you know that."

"Nonsense. I mean, I do understand that but…wait…did you say sleeping with?" Finn's eyebrows raise practically off of his face.

Oh Shit!

You and your damn big mouth, Olivia!

"Did I? I didn't. I mean, I didn't mean it. Sleeping with you, I mean. I just meant in general. Not that I mean I don't want...or that I wouldn't..." I stop talking and cover my face with my hands. "Oh God, this isn't happening. Shut up, Olivia. Shut up, shut up, shut up!"

Finn laughs heartily at my obvious embarrassment.

"It's okay, Olivia. I didn't mean to embarrass you. I just meant that you haven't experienced The Kellan Agency yet. The members of my staff are mostly like family. They watched me grow up in my Dad's office, which is now my office. They all know my mother, and they all knew my....um." He frowns. "Well they all want to see me happy, and really, you wouldn't be dating me to get to the top in this business if photography is what you really want to focus on. I don't do anything cool like that. I just sign my name to a bunch of boring contracts and sit in a bunch of sometimes boring sales pitch meetings." Finn leans forward and whispers in my ear, "I don't always get to wine and dine the heavy clients. Sometimes my people have to do that for me."

His breath tickles my ear, and my shoulder immediately comes up in defense. "Is that so, huh? Well I guess that means you'll have plenty of time to um...wine and dine me then?"

Finn cups my face in his hands. "It would be my pleasure, Olivia." He leans down to kiss me, and I return his kiss, short and sweet, and then he takes my hand.

"Come on. Let's get you home; it's not getting any warmer out here."

I'm not so sure about that. I smirk as we walk hand in hand back to my apartment.

"Thank you," Finn says prayerfully standing in front of my apartment door. He bends down to kiss my forehead and runs his hands up and down my arms to warm me up. He doesn't know that I'm already plenty warm just from his touch. His contact always sends sparks of heat right through me, and I'm not about to tell him to stop.

"For what?" I ask him.

"For hearing me out, for believing me, for seeing me, for choosing me anyway."

"That goes both ways, Finn. You could've gone home thinking I was a total ungrateful bitch, so thanks for making me hear you out and for believing in *me*…and for choosing *me* anyway."

"Can I see you tomorrow?" he asks.

"I'm counting on it. You still have lots to tell me about this job if it's something you really think I'll be perfect for."

"Okay then. How about brunch?"

"How about lunch? I should catch up with Abby a little since we haven't talked in a couple days. She'll want to hear all about my first date with this guy I met yesterday." I grin.

"HA! First date, huh? I hope he didn't take advantage of you." Finn's expression is playfully stern.

"Never," I shake my head trying to hide my smile, but I fail. "He was a perfect gentleman and, regardless, I kissed him first, so if anyone took advantage, it was me."

"Is that so? Well, I'm pretty sure he probably enjoyed every moment, so I imagine he'll ask you out again soon."

"I hope he does, and I'll look forward to it."

Finn smiles and embraces me in strong warm hug. "As do I," he says kissing my hair.

"How about I take you both out for lunch tomorrow and then for a tour of the Agency? That way Abby can learn all about your new job first hand."

"That sounds fun! Let's do it." I squeeze my arms tighter around him.

"Great. I'll contact you tomorrow then. Until then…" Finn kisses my temple while he slips his fingers into my hair, holding me to him. I feel him take a deep breath. God, he still smells so good. "Sleep well, Olivia."

"Thanks," I whisper. My eyes do feel heavy, and I stand there imagining what it would feel like to fall asleep in Finn's strong arms. I'm excited for the possibility of that day to come.

I look up at Finn just in time for his lips to meet mine. His fingers still in my hair, he tugs slightly so that my head is at a better angle for him. He has no idea how much his hands in my hair turns me on. My lips part for him, and smoothly our tongues meet, tasting one another. It is the sweetest goodbye kiss that really feels like a promise for more. I let out a small whimper, which, to my surprise, must have a strong effect on Finn, according to the movement I feel near my waist. Finn is aroused. He opens his eyes and connects with mine just long enough to breathe in deeply, wrap his arms around my waist, and pick me up.

Whoa!

He quickly puts me down and holds me at arm's length, his hands holding my shoulders.

What?

"Whoa." Finn says taking a few deep breaths and blowing them out slowly.

"Yeah." I agree feeling a bit flushed.

Finn steps toward me and trails his fingers across my forehead, moving the stray hairs away from my eyes. "Good night, Olivia," he whispers.

Wow...he has more control than I do!

"Good night, Finn." I smile, turn the doorknob to the door that was right next to me, and slowly walk inside my apartment, never turning my back on Finn. He waits until I'm inside and have closed the door to walk away, but not before I peek through the peephole in my door to see him back up against the adjacent wall, put his hand on his chest above his heart, and sigh. He has the happiest, most satisfied smile on his face. So this is what guys do when girls aren't looking. He is so cute standing there. I have to cover my mouth to stifle my giggles when I see him adjust himself before he goes. I guess I'll just keep that little visual morsel to myself. My own little Finn secret.

"Well I take it from the shit-eating grin and look of infatuation all over your face that you two must've worked things out just fine, eh?"

Abby asks amused as she walks into the living room to see me standing at the door.

"Uh, yeah…" I sigh. "Abby, I don't know what wrongs I righted to deserve him, but if the Finn I was with today is the same Finn I'm with, in a few weeks, months, or years…" I shake my head in disbelief. "Abs, I could fall for him. Hard. Oh, and before I forget, he's taking us to lunch tomorrow and to the Kellan Agency to tell us more about this job."

"Perfect! I can't wait, now get your ass over here and tell me every damn detail of the last two days!"

"Ha! Gladly!"

Chapter 6

Olivia I'm so sorry. I never meant to hurt you.
Please allow me to explain.

Did you get home safely?

Olivia...please at least tell me you're ok.

Liv, I know u don't want to talk now but
I NEED to know you're ok.

If I don't hear from you in 30 minutes
I'm coming over to check on you.

Finn was right. He did send a lot of texts last night. Scrolling through them all this morning for the first time, I have to swallow my guilt at keeping him hanging and worrying about my safety. I can tell after our conversation last night that he really does care about me, and truth be told, I think I'm beginning to care about him, too. I really don't want to jump in too soon, but it's just been so damn long since a guy has showed sincere interest in me. I know things may change, but I'm excited to spend the day with Finn and Abby. If they're both going to be in my life, I'm happy to get to see them interact with each other. I send Finn a quick text so he knows I'm thinking about him.

Me: Just looked at my phone. Sorry to scare you last night.
See you soon!

Finn obviously keeps his phone with him at all times for work because he replies immediately.

Solving Us

Finn: Don't mention it. Gave me a good excuse to see you again. Can't wait for today. See you soon Beautiful.

Lunch was a lot of fun. Finn took us to an old fashioned diner in town that served just about whatever we could imagine. I had fish and chips, Abby ordered a cheeseburger, but Finn chose a spectacular pancake and bacon brunch. We were like little kids giggling over just about everything we talked about. Finn told us about some of his travels with his father, and at times, he and Abby were able to share travel experiences. Abby used to travel a lot during the summers with her parents, but my family really didn't travel much and certainly never out of the mainland USA. Part of that was my fault I think. After my accident, I never really wanted to venture out far from home. College was the biggest step I had taken, and getting to know Abby over those four years was the best thing that could've happened to me.

After lunch, Finn takes us on a tour of The Kellan Agency. Taking up the fiftieth through the fifty-fifth floor, the Agency is housed in one of Boston's most popular skyscrapers: the sixty-story Hancock Place. Luckily for Abby and I, the Stark Firm, where Abby works, is only a block away which means we can meet each other frequently for lunches during the week.

We enter the lobby of The Kellan Agency on the fifty-fifth floor and immediately meet the receptionist and personal assistant to Finn's office. She greets Finn with a huge knowing smile and professional, "Good afternoon, Mr. Kellan." Obviously she's working on a Sunday because Finn asked her to come in for me. She seems to be the only one in the building besides us.

"Hello dear, you must be Olivia." She addresses me.

Probably in her late fifties, early sixties, she looks like she could be my mom. She is very pleasant in appearance wearing a grey sleeveless dress shirt with ruffles down the front. Her smile is very welcoming, and I immediately feel like I could confess my biggest secrets to her. The sign on her desk reads **Mrs. Grace Hoover.**

Ah! We share a name. Shouldn't have any problems remembering hers.

"Yes," I shake her hand and return her smile. "Olivia McGuire. It's a pleasure to meet you. This is my roommate, Abby Sheridan." I clear my throat, not knowing what to say next. This is a little awkward given that it's Sunday, not a typical work day.

"Finn." I shake my head correcting myself. "I mean - Mr. Kellan - is giving me a tour of the building and telling me more about the commercial photographer position. I suppose if I may be working here I would hate to be lost on my first day," I joke. When I say Finn's name, I feel his hand on the small of my back.

"It's okay, Olivia," Finn says kissing the back of my head and smiling at Mrs. Hoover. "Grace here practically helped raise me because I was around this building so much. She knows all about you and our date yesterday; and if she doesn't hear it from me, she hears it from my mother so there are no secrets between us. I asked Grace to come in today in case you wanted to, you know, sign paperwork and all that stuff. And she keeps my important messages for me. I couldn't run this place without her." Finn speaks as if the relationship between CEO and Executive Assistant is always so relaxed. I can't help but smile in awe a bit at the atmosphere in this office. I can tell immediately that Finn loves and appreciates Mrs. Hoover very much. I blush anyway knowing that someone in the office knows I went out on a date with Finn.

How is this going to work exactly?

"Have fun looking around, Olivia, and please feel free to call my desk or ask me any questions you may have as you get situated. Finn, I have a few messages here for you."

"Thank you very much, Mrs. Hoover. I appreciate the warm welcome!" I say, smiling as confidently as possible at Grace. While Finn goes through his messages with Mrs. Hoover, Abby and I take a quick moment to look around the lobby of the reception area. The walls are a warm cream color and filled with several large posters of advertisements for several different companies. I see an advertisement for a local college, one for the Boston Aquarium, one for a local brewery, and on the far wall closest to the window with a view, there is one of a cover print for

Solving Us

National Geographic Magazine that I practically drool over! It's a beautiful landscape photo of the Cliffs of Moher in Ireland. It's a crystal clear picture with the brightest green cliffs I have ever seen. The picture is breathtaking, and I stand and study it for minutes.

"My pride and joy and one of the best trips I've ever taken," Finn says quietly from behind me. His voice is warm and gentle and sexy and mmmm yummy. I turn with a knowing smile to look right into his brilliant blue eyes.

"You took this picture?" I don't know why I'm flabbergasted.

"Yep. That was a couple years ago on a trip with my father," he says with pride. "Why don't you guys follow me, I'll take you to my office, and we can talk more about the job there. It's much more comfortable."

Abby and I follow Finn through the double doors and down the hallway to his palatial corner office. From fifty-five floors up, both corner walls of Finn's office are floor to ceiling windows providing a breathtaking view of the Charles River leading into the Boston Harbor. It looks like you can see for miles. The rest of the office has a modern feel to it. With clean lines and straight edges, the room is painted completely white, taking in all of the natural color from outdoors. The beams from the building structure that show through the windows are a light grey that actually compliment the color palate of the room quite well.

I wonder if he planned that.

There is a conference table to the left of Finn's desk that sits atop a natural tan colored rug. Around the room are a few green plants, and along the walls are pictures of more landscapes. Waterfalls, mountains, sunsets, ocean; I'm guessing each picture is a souvenir taken on one of Finn's expeditions. The room as a whole looks like it lives outdoors. It's peaceful and open and makes me smile.

"Holy Hell!" Abby exclaims. "This place is like a peaceful nature walk and a trip to Ikea all wrapped up in one room!"

I turn my head and look at Abby, my eyes growing wider to remind her why we're here and that I don't want her to mess this up for me. She just laughs at my expression, and I shake my head.

"Yeah I guess it does," Finn answers. "There was a time that I lived in my office, or so it seemed, and I'm an outdoors kind of guy, so this space is one that I can work in all day and still feel like I'm not shut up in the corner of a skyscraper for hours at a time."

I notice the block of colors sitting on Finn's desk that looks almost like it doesn't belong. It certainly isn't something I would expect to see in the office of a CEO; but then again, I have a strong feeling I understand why it's there. I ask anyway to make conversation.

"What's with the Rubik's Cube?" I say nodding my head in its direction and smirking at Finn. "Do you play with it during recess?"

"Ya like it?" he laughs. "Puzzles are sort of a thing for my family, or at least they used to be. It's a stress reliever sometimes to just sit back and figure out someone else's puzzle instead of solving my own day to day issues. And what's cool about those things," he says pointing to the Rubik's Cube, "is that you can mess them up however you want, but if you can find the patience, there's always an answer...the right solution. At some point it all just clicks."

I nod my head in agreement with Finn and continue to look around. "It really is breathtaking in here."

"Thanks. I'm really glad you like it." Finn looks at me adoringly. I could stare back at him all day, but off to the side of the room I hear Abby clear her throat to break us out of our trance.

"So," I say, "tell me about this job I'm perfect for."

"Well, the job entails work in both advertising and commercial photography, which means you would shoot on location whenever warranted, edit your digital images, and then you would lead a team when needed to use those images in the development of promotional material to meet the needs of our clients. You would also work with our marketing teams to help rebrand existing products for our clients."

I shake my head. "Sounds interesting. So ,for example, the whale photos I took the other day could be used in creating a new marketing campaign for the Boston Harbor Cruises?" I remember looking through one of their brochures on the catamaran and thinking it looked a little outdated.

Finn smiles at me. "Spoken like you've been working here for years. Yes, absolutely; and it just so happens that the Boston Harbor Cruise line is already a client of ours. I'm sure with your passion and obvious creativity you may be the perfect person to spark a renewed interest for an old client."

Okay, I like what I'm hearing. This could be an outstanding opportunity for me.

"Olivia, this business that you would be stepping into can be an extremely lucrative business, and I'm not just talking about money, though yes, the money is great. I won't lie about that. Some of our clients are major businesses that willingly drop millions of dollars on their marketing campaigns if it means their business stays on top. Take Mass. General Hospital for example. They're the leading hospital in Boston, so they take great strides to stay ahead of the others, even in their promotional materials. They've been huge clients of ours since my Dad got sick and was in their care. He had a ton of respect for how that hospital is run."

"It's not about the money, Finn. I'm content in the way I live, but I would be lying if I said the ideas now running through my head and the opportunity to unleash my creativity didn't excite me a great deal."

"Good. I like that your wheels are already turning. Our commercial photographers are constantly helping our marketing teams come up with the best way to present our client's products in the best light. It's stressful at times because there's always a deadline, and for creative people sometimes deadlines are frustrating and a bit imprisoning; but Olivia, when you're driving down the road and you see the billboard you designed, or you open a magazine and see the promotional spread that you developed…"

"Or you see a picture of the Cliffs of Moher on the cover of National Geographic…" I finish Finn's sentence for him.

Finn sighs and smiles so large his smile touches his eyes. I return his smile in total understanding of the euphoria he must've felt seeing his work published.

"It's every photographer's dream," I say in awe, "to be published in National Geographic."

"Yeah." Finn raises his eyebrows and nods his head at me, his eyes never leaving mine.

"You could have that, Olivia. All of it," he whispers.

Abby nudges me in my side and whispers in my ear. "Liv, don't you fucking think about walking out of this room without your name on a contract. This job is your dream job."

I whisper back at her still never taking my eyes off of Finn's. "Yeah, I think you're right."

"So, um," I clear my throat "My boss. You said you wouldn't be my boss?"

"Correct. Well, yes, technically I suppose I would be your boss; but Karen Elena, my Advertising Account Coordinator, sort of oversees all of the marketing photographers since your projects go through her in the end anyway. You have to remember, though, that we're not a huge advertising agency. My father believed in keeping us small and united, and it's worked for us very well for many years. As long as everyone is completing their projects and keeping the workplace drama free, I don't have to get involved. I'll introduce you to Karen tomorrow; you'll like her. She's intuitive and creative and always open to ideas outside the box, but she doesn't have your talent or education. Like I said before, she's more the principal of your department and you're the "special art" teacher. She's always had an interest in photography and can do Photoshop edits like you wouldn't believe, but her job isn't as exciting as yours. It doesn't come with travel perks or the reward of seeing your work in someone's advertising. Like me now, she gets paid the big bucks to be the office administrator, to make sure your department and your collaboration with the marketing staff runs smoothly, and helps with questions or problems with clients as they arise. She's a good friend of my mom's, as well; I told you the staff around here are like family. We've all been together for a long time."

"Sounds great."

"Yeah? So that means you're in? You'll take the job?"

I take a deep breath.

How do I talk about my fear?

How do I bring up the beginning of our relationship?

Am I overthinking this?

I glance over at Abby, and she sees the trepidation in my eyes immediately and knows what I'm thinking without a doubt. She has my back.

"Hey, Finn," Abby asks. "Can you point me to a restroom? You guys can talk job particulars while I step out for a minute."

Finn directs Abby down the hall towards the bathrooms. Once she has left his office he turns and steps towards me.

"You're scared. I can see it on your face, Olivia. Talk to me."

Damnit, why do I wear my emotions on my sleeve? "I'm not scared, Finn, really. I just…um…" I take a deep breath and close my eyes to steady myself. "Tell me how this is going to work. With us, I mean."

Finn mirrors my deep breath. His head tilts as he studies my hesitation. "Well, I don't have any rules here about my staff not being able to date each other as long as it doesn't interfere with their jobs. It's easier to let it go than forbid it and have it happen behind closed doors. That just stirs up a lot of unnecessary drama, and so far it's worked for all of us."

"Oh, so will I see you every day?"

"Not always. We'll be working on different floors, and I'll try my best to stay out of your way. I would never compromise your integrity or reputation by taking advantage of our relationship at work; but I would be available if you, you know, if you needed me or whatever," Finn says shyly. It's cute to watch him try to piece together his professional and personal life at the same time.

"I like that."

I shake my head and frown at myself. I'm such a fruit loop. "I mean, I like that you would be around not that I mean you would just be around for me. Obviously you wouldn't just be around for me, that's not what I mean. What I mean is…"

"Olivia?" Finn is smirking at me.

"Yeah?"

"Take the job."

I grin back at him. There is no way he's going to let me walk out of here without the job, and truth be told, I don't want him to. I want this as much as I can tell he does. I swallow any fear I have left and take the leap.

"Ok." I nod. "Thank you for the offer, Mr. Kellan. I think the job sounds perfect."

Finn's shoulders release from the tension I hadn't noticed before, and he lets out a breath before lifting me off the ground and swinging me around in his arms. I can't help but giggle at the ridiculously cute show of affection.

"Olivia, you amaze me. Thank you…for this whole weekend…for saying yes, to this job…and to me."

Finn kisses me quickly. His kiss deepens, and his hands cup my hair. He wraps one of his hands around my head to hold me close to him, but the other slides softly through my hair, and oh my God his touch ignites something in me I haven't felt, well, ever actually.

Seriously, how the hell does he do that? Turn me on just by touching my hair?

Abby is going to be back any minute from the bathroom. A girl can only pee for so long, and I don't want her walking in on us making out in Finn's office. I have to stop.

Stop kissing him, Olivia.

Mmm he tastes like pancakes.

Olivia, seriously, stop now. You have to stop kissing him!

But he's so damn kisstastic!

I'm still giggling in his arms when our lips separate. "I'm really excited, Finn. This job sounds like a dream come true. Hell, this whole weekend has felt like a dream I don't deserve. I feel like someone is going to pinch me, and I'm going to wake up and none of this will have happened."

"Believe it, Liv. Whatever your dreams are, I want to give them to you."

"How about dinner to celebrate?"

Finn flinches quickly. "Do you mind if I take you out after work tomorrow? Then we can celebrate your first day. I'm supposed to spend time with my buddy Toby tonight or else I would…" He furrows his brow like he was deliberating with himself.

"Well…why don't you just come with me to meet him. I'm pretty sure…"

I interrupt Finn quickly. "No, it's okay! You go. Do your thing tonight. I'm pretty sure Abby is going to want to celebrate tonight anyway."

"I am?" Abby walks back into Finn's office. "Celebrate what?" Her eyes widen, and she smirks at me. "You took the job?"

"I took the job."

"HA! It's about damn time girl! Let's go celebrate! Oooh maybe we can try that new dance club over on Thirteenth! I hear they have a wicked DJ."

I look back at Finn grinning from ear to ear. "See? I told ya."

He chuckles at both of us.

"Yeah I see what you mean. Dance club huh?" He raises an eyebrow at me. "I hope to get to see that someday." Finn tries to hide the look of desire on his face but fails miserably. His eyes roams from my face to my chest to my legs and back up.

"Whoa there, Tiger." Abby laughs. "You can have her any other time, but tonight, she's mine. Girls night it is!"

"Come on ladies," Finn says shaking his head at both of us. "Since she came in just for us let's get the paperwork done with Mrs. Hoover, and then I'll drive you home."

There's always tons of paperwork when starting a new job, but Finn and Mrs. Hoover did such a great job of making time fly. Within fifteen minutes, Finn takes my hand and leads us out of the building and back into the warm spring sun. It's shaping up to be another absolutely beautiful day. I peek over at Abby on the sidewalk who winks at me as she looks down at my hand entwined with Finn's.

"Sooo cute!" she mouths to me silently. I chuckle back at her and squeeze Finn's hand before stopping to allow him to open his car door for me. I'm deliriously happy at this very moment and praying to myself that I'm not making a huge mistake mixing business and pleasure.

Chapter 7

My first day at the Kellan Agency arrives quicker than I expect, but I'm feeling positive and confident as my morning progresses. I choose a black, sleeveless pleated A-line dress, which I accessorize with a blue belt, the same color as Finn's eyes. I find a coordinating pair of earrings and a silver bangle bracelet in my jewelry box. I'm already wearing my favorite silver ring, so after looking myself over in the mirror before leaving, I feel comfortable and just sexy enough for Finn to take notice. I don't consider myself a drop dead gorgeous girl, but I have my moments.

Thankfully, though, for my first day, Finn notices that I'm nervous and keeps his distance enough that nobody knows we're dating, or at least to those who don't know, it's not obvious. I know a few people already know about us, but I still don't want to flaunt it on my first day, or ever for that matter. Finn takes me around the building and introduces me to a few key people, including my new boss, Karen Elena. She seems outgoing, outspoken, and excited to meet me. With her auburn, shoulder-length hair and dark green eyes, I can't help but think of Susan Sarandon when I look at her. We talk a little about my daily job responsibilities and she shows me to my office, which is a room I share with four other photographers. It's spacious and filled with computers, editing equipment, cameras, backpacks, and four desks that are laid out in a cubicle design on the side of the room. The layout provides enough privacy that I feel like I wouldn't have someone looking over my shoulder watching me work all day but is open enough for conversation to flow freely among the photography team.

Karen has to take an incoming call, so she leaves me to get situated in the office and to meet the rest of the team.

"I'm pretty sure this must be your desk over here, and you must be Olivia!" I turn my head in the direction of the female voice that is speaking to me.

"Yeah, that's me. Olivia McGuire."

"I'm Mandy. It's nice to meet you! Welcome to the team. This is Austin Rivers, everyone calls him Riv," she says pointing to a rough-looking man in the cubicle next to her. "And that over there is Luke Prescott."

I smile and say hello to my new team. I hate being in the spotlight, so I want to make introductions as quickly as possible. I always consider myself a social person and want to make a good first impression, instead of being misjudged as the freak girl covered in scars. So far, so good; everyone seems pretty nice, and nobody has stared at me yet.

"It looks like you must have an admirer or a really great friend. There are a few things waiting for you over here at your desk," Mandy says, walking over to my cubicle.

Sure enough, sitting at my desk is a vase of white roses. They're beautiful. They have to be from Abby or maybe my parents. They're the only ones who know I'm starting a new job today. I quickly open and read the card that's sitting amongst the crisp white blooms.

Congratulations on your first day!
Can't wait to see your dreams come true.
F

I'm blushing like a love-struck idiot, so I look down to try to hide it from anyone who's watching me. There's another gift for me sitting on my desk as well. Wrapped in a cute blue gift bag that has a picture of a whale on the front, I recognize the bag right away as one from the Boston Harbor Cruise gift shop. This has to be from Finn. I open the gift bag and sigh happily shaking my head. I pull out the camera lens that Finn had given to me the day he took me out whale watching. The card attached to the gift bag makes me blush again.

You told me to give this to whomever I hired to fill the position.
I'm happy to return it to you with fond memories
of a spectacular day spent with a beautiful girl. See you tonight!

Seriously, how did I get so lucky?

"Boyfriend?" Mandy asks me, smirking at the smile I'm trying very hard to hide.

"Umm, sort of...well...I don't know...it's complicated."

"Wow. Lucky girl," she says. "Can't wait to hear all about him."

"Yeah well, um it's still early. I don't even know yet if it'll last or if it's really a thing." I really don't want to bring attention to my relationship with the CEO on my first day. I know they would all judge me, and they certainly won't want to be my friends if they think I'm spying on them for any reason. I'm going to have to be very careful with this, and it makes me anxious.

"I understand. Well given the attention he just paid you, he seems like a keeper! Hey, you want to grab lunch in a bit? I could help answer any other questions you have about work and could give you the rundown on office gossip."

"Yeah." I smile at her. "That sounds great. Thanks."

I settle down at my desk and open my new office email. I shake my head amused at the first email I see.

No, we really won't see each other much.

We work in different parts of the building.

Geesh...

FROM: FINN KELLAN
SUBJECT: WELCOME
DATE: MAY 19 2014 10:30
TO: OLIVIA MCGUIRE

WELCOME TO THE KELLAN AGENCY, OLIVIA. I TRUST YOU'VE FOUND YOUR WAY AROUND AND HAVE BEEN INTRODUCED TO YOUR TEAM BY NOW. I HOPE KAREN WAS HELPFUL TO YOU THIS MORNING. IF YOU NEED ANYTHING, FEEL FREE TO CONTACT ME, OR MRS. HOOVER IF I'M UNREACHABLE. I ALWAYS CARRY MY CELL.

FINN KELLAN
CEO, THE KELLAN AGENCY

Was that his way of telling me he would always be available to me? I could text him anytime? I quickly type out my response to him.

From: Olivia McGuire
Subject: Thank you
Date: May 19 2014 10:34
To: Finn Kellan

Thank you for the very warm welcome, Mr. Kellan. I've been given the tour around my floor and have met and spoken to my team. I'm excited to get to work. It's not lost on me that the Boston Harbor Cruise file is sitting at the top of the files on my desk. Thank you for that, and thank you again for this opportunity.

Sincerely,

Olivia McGuire
Commercial Marketing, The Kellan Agency

Once I settle into my desk and get to work, the rest of the morning flies by. I'm enjoying my research into the client files I had waiting for me on my desk when I arrived this morning. One of my new projects, besides the Boston Harbor Cruise Line, is for a winery.

A winery in Napa Valley.

Someone pinch me.

I get to travel to Napa Valley…and get paid?

I must be dreaming.

"I love this job already!" I mutter to myself.

"Hey Girl, you ready for lunch?"

I hear Mandy call for me from the cubicle next to me. I look at the clock on my computer which reads twelve-thirty. Wow, time flies!

"Yeah, just organizing my work for this afternoon. Ready in a sec."

I take a quick second to check my cell phone for texts or voice messages in case I need to return any during my lunch hour. There are two texts, from Abby and my parents, wishing me a great first day. I have one voicemail from Finn letting me know he's thinking about me and wishes he could be more around for my first day but is respecting my wishes to figure things out on my own like any other employee.

He is so attentive and excites my heart with those nervous flutters every time I hear his voice. I feel a little like Christine bewitched by her Phantom of the Opera…except I can't sing nearly as well…and I'm the one with the scars.

Mandy and I walk out of the building and across the street conveniently to a sandwich bar for lunch. We grab our meals and choose a small table on their outdoor patio to escape the busy atmosphere inside. It's much easier to hear conversation out here even with the bustle of traffic on the street. It's not quite "New York City busy", but there are cabs honking their horns and trying to weave through traffic and many people walking up and down the sidewalks to their respective lunch breaks, meetings, etc.

"So, Mandy, how long have you been with The Kellan Agency?" I ask, biting into my turkey sandwich.

"Since I graduated college actually, which was only two years ago. The Kellans are sort of like family, and the agency is very much a family business. You'll learn that."

"Yeah Finn, uh, Mr. Kellan told me that when we spoke about the job."

"Yeah, Finn and I grew up together. Karen Elena is my mom and a good friend to Finn's mom, so we've all known each other for a long time."

I look up at Mandy and study her face. She is a stunning girl in her late twenties with shoulder-length auburn hair that's layered around her face. I can't tell the exact style, since she has half of it pinned back off her neck on this very hot spring day. Her eyes are a beautiful green color, and her face is speckled with little freckles over the bridge of her nose. Really, if she had any type of accent other than a Boston accent, I could believe she stepped right off the boat from Ireland. I can definitely see the resemblance to her mother with the dark red hair and piercing green eyes.

I'm suddenly finding it hard to swallow. It makes me a bit anxious knowing that I'm working on a team with people who are so close to Finn and his family. If they don't like me, or we don't get along, how will that work for Finn and me in the future?

"Oh, so what about your Dad? Does he work for the Kellens as well?"

"No, my parents are divorced, actually. When I was about eight years old, he left and never came back. Truth be told, I don't remember much about him except for the few pictures I have. Good riddance, I say. If he can't be bothered to be a dad, I don't want to waste my time knowing him. So yeah, I really just hung out with Finn's family and my friends a lot."

"You grew up with Finn? What was that like?" I take another bite of my sandwich. I'm trying to dodge a bullet and praying it works for the next hour.

"Well, really, I grew up more with his younger sister, Sydney."

I choke on the bite in my mouth. "Wait, what? Finn has a sister? He never...I mean, I didn't know that." Fuck! Did I just give it away that I have anything other than a professional relationship with Finn? Damn me and my big mouth!

"Had...Finn had a sister." Mandy explains. "She committed suicide our senior year of high school."

I gasp out loud. "Oh my God! That's so...wow. I had no idea." I shake my head. "How long ago was that?"

"Our class graduated in two thousand and eight, but she left us before that. So about seven years now, almost eight." She clears her throat and takes a drink to hide the emotion I see in her eyes. I look away momentarily to give her a minute and because I need a minute to process what I've heard so far. I am speechless. Like, literally speechless. All the air leaves my lungs, and I can feel the pain and loss of air from my chest, like someone has just punched me in the gut.

How could Finn not have told me this?

Don't be stupid Olivia. You've been on one date.

Solving Us

And I can't believe I'm learning all of this from Mandy.

Is this okay? Should I stop this conversation? Keep it going?

How much do I want to find out without hearing it from Finn's mouth first?

And how do I tell him that I know all of this?

"I'm so sorry for the loss of your friend, Mandy." That's all I can think to say.

"Thanks. Sydney and Finn were really close, so obviously, it really affected him when she died. She was a beautiful girl and loved by so many. She had so many friends, but then she had this accident our junior year."

My body stiffened, and my stomach turned. "Accident? What...what kind of accident?" I didn't want to know. God, I didn't want to know, but I couldn't stop myself from asking.

"Finn was home for the weekend visiting and had taken Sydney out to the movies. They were both huge Harry Potter fans and went every year together to the newest movie premier. It was just sort of their bonding thing." Mandy smiles as she recalls her memories of Sydney and Finn, but then tears started to well up in her eyes.

"Anyway, after the movie, they were driving home, and out of nowhere, this pick-up truck slammed into Sydney's side of their car. A drunk driver it turned out. Sydney was so torn up and broken but she was alive. She lived."

Mandy chuckles softly through her tears. "She used to call herself 'The Girl Who Lived'," she says, shaking her head at her friend's humor. I have to chuckle a little, too, understanding the Harry Potter reference.

"But she had so many scars from the accident, a large one near the top of her head from the glass from her car window imbedding into her face. The cuts, the scrapes, the bruising...it caused a lot of scarring, and she just wasn't the same after that. She didn't present herself with the confidence or high self-esteem that she had once had. She sort of became a bit of a recluse and didn't want to hang out with many people. She didn't date anyone, didn't feel pretty enough."

I begin to feel dizzy. This isn't happening.

"And you know how mean girls can be," Mandy continues playing with her napkin and sniffling.

"She missed the beginning of her senior year recovering from surgeries. She wanted to be home schooled the rest of the year because she knew the gossip and the teasing would be so bad, but she never told anyone that she was actually experiencing it. Not even me, and I was one of her best friends and I loved her very much. I would've done anything for her. Had any of us known, we could've stood up for her, helped her; but she carried the burden herself, and one day just couldn't do it anymore. She chopped up an entire bottle of sleeping pills and mixed them in with some alcohol. Or at least that's what her autopsy said. She died in her sleep. That night, Finn found a video on her computer that she had recorded with an apology and a short explanation of why she just didn't want to carry the burden anymore, as if she had anything to be sorry for. God, it ripped Finn apart to watch that video. She was almost there. Halfway done with her senior year, but she just...."

I'm going to be sick.

My head is spinning.

My legs are shaking.

My body is cold, and I'm sitting outside on a hot spring day.

Mandy looks up at me and my expressionless face. "Olivia? Are you okay? Your face is...you look like you've seen a ghost."

I swallow slowly. This girl was me. She could've been me. We were the same age. We had life changing accidents in the same year. We both lived with painful truths that nobody knew about, only I lived - she died. There's no way Finn knows about me and my past, does he?

He wouldn't...

No, there's no way, but this might just explain his overwhelming need to see me the other night to make sure I was okay. He didn't want to be the cause of my hurting myself. He had to have realized that he had hurt me and thought maybe I would react the same way. He's seen some of my scars. Oh God, I obviously remind him of her.

"Yeah, um, I'm just not hungry anymore." I say as I wrap up my sandwich and stand to throw away the rest of my lunch. What I wouldn't give for a huge swig of vodka right now.

"I should get back to work. I still have so much to learn and research before my shoot later this week."

"Yeah okay, cool. I'll walk back with you. I'm sorry, Olivia, I didn't mean to be a downer."

"No, really it's okay. I'm the one who asked, and I appreciate you telling me all of that. I had no idea."

"Finn's a really great guy and has transitioned into a fantastic CEO since his father passed away. He's had a rough couple of years. He really does care about the people he works with, though. You'll love him once you get to know him."

I'm pretty sure Mandy is absolutely right about that. My heart is already aching for Finn, and I have no idea how I'm going to handle the information I now have in my brain while spending the evening with Finn at my celebratory dinner. I'm going to have to sit on this new insight into Finn's family life until the moment presents itself, even if that moment is weeks away.

Chapter 8

Six weeks later, and the moment still hasn't presented itself. It's the first week of July, and I am finally settled into my job and my routine and loving it. I'm cultivating some strong friendships with my colleagues at work. Mandy is quickly becoming a second BFF to me. She's no Abby, of course, but she makes my work day enjoyable. Abby refers to her as my work wife, which I find amusing every time, so it's sort of become a thing. Due to my friendship with Mandy, her mother Karen, who is also my boss, and I have a strong working relationship as well. She has her bitchy moments, especially when we are nearing a deadline, but what managing executive doesn't?

Austin Rivers and Luke Prescott are nice guys, too, and certainly add that essence of college male that seems to level the office vibe on a daily basis. For all the girly talk between Mandy and me, Austin and Luke do an excellent job of telling us how often they are getting laid and by whom, just as much as they let us know when they are going to take a dump…pinch a loaf…drop the kids off at the pool…(their words, not mine). All in all, I really love coming to work every day.

My client pool is growing as well. I made contact with the Boston Harbor Cruise line and am setting up a portfolio for them to view my photos so that we can move on to develop their new marketing materials. I'm excited to share my experience with them. I've also scheduled my trip to Napa Valley to begin my digital portfolio of the winery I'm working with. One week from now, I will be relaxing at the Seal Lake Winery; working of course, but enjoying myself, nonetheless.

Finn does an excellent job of keeping our relationship under wraps for the most part. I am amazed at myself with every passing week that I don't let the cat out of the bag to Mandy for as much time as we spend talking about our love lives. Mandy tells me that she's not interested in any of the guys at the office, but that she does keep an eye on one of the girls that assists Austin on his shoots from time to time. Her name is

Solving Us

Kym. She seems to be pretty friendly to many around the office, but I do take notice of the time Kym lingers around Mandy's desk when she's in. I think it's cute. Mandy knows I have a boyfriend and that he treats me like a princess, but somehow, I've gotten away with never having to say his name. The name Finn can't be that popular that she wouldn't figure that out, so I always refer to him as "My hot runner guy". I guess I'll need to tell her soon so I don't hurt her feelings when it comes out. I want to tell her before she hears it through other family members. I feel like that's the friend thing to do.

At any rate, those in the office who need to know about Finn and me, like Mrs. Hoover, Finn's administrative assistant, know; but other than that, work is work, and love life is…well…it's OH MY GOD hot! We try to not let anything happen while at the office, but I would be lying if I said we don't make out just a few times on occasion when I conveniently have to stop by his office. Every now and then when we're alone, he steals a kiss; and once I swear Karen caught sight of Finn leading me into a room with his hand on the small of my back. But she's never said anything, and Mandy hasn't brought it up in conversation, so I let go of my concern. We haven't reached awesome-mind blowing-clear-the-desk-with-your-arm desk sex yet; in fact, we haven't gone down the sex road at all yet. Six weeks is a long time to ask a guy to go without getting some action, so I allow my shirt to come off but only when it is pitch black wherever we are. It's bad enough that Finn's fingers have touched my scars a few times; I'm just not ready for him to see them. As much as I worry about the snail's pace of our physical relationship, I'm appreciative of the fact that Finn never pushes me further than I'm ready to go. He seems to sincerely want to get to know me and not just make me another notch on his bedpost. Regardless, our relationship is heading in a more serious direction, and as anxious as I am about the fact that there is still a huge part of my life that Finn doesn't know, I might be starting to fall for him.

My favorite part of any work day, aside from actually seeing Finn, is reading the emails he sends me. He always knows how to put a smile on my face. This morning, though, I almost killed my computer with coffee in response to Finn's email.

From: Finn Kellan
Subject: The Help
Date: July 3, 2014 9:22
To: Olivia McGuire

Good morning, Beautiful. Thanks for giving me a HAND last night. I enjoyed it immensely and look forward to repaying the favor again soon.

Thankful,
Finn Kellan, CEO The Kellan Agency

I spit my coffee all over my desk reading his casual thank you to me. I am forever grateful that he is the CEO of this Agency when it comes to email content, but I imagine the guys in the Tech Department can read between the lines. I guess if Finn doesn't care, I don't.

From: Olivia McGuire
Subject: Clean up
Date: July 3, 2014 9:26
To: Finn Kellan
Thank you for the distraction so early this morning. I now have to clean up the coffee that I just spit all over my desk. I'm all wet now thanks to you.
Now smelling like coffee,
Olivia McGuire
Commercial Marketing, The Kellan Agency
Ps. You're welcome by the way, for the "help".

From: Finn Kellan
Subject: Satisfied
Date July 3, 2014 9:28
To: Olivia McGuire

Wet huh? Who's distracted now? That's something I would like to see...except

Solving Us

I'VE ALREADY SEEN YOU WET. #WHALEWATCHING
NOW PREOCCUPIED BY YOU,
FINN KELLAN, CEO THE KELLAN AGENCY

FROM: OLIVIA MCGUIRE
SUBJECT: REMINDERS
DATE: JULY 3, 2014 9:30
TO: FINN KELLAN

HA! YES WHAT FOND MEMORIES. AND THANKS FOR THE REMINDER! I NEEDED TO GIVE THE CRUISE LINE A CALL THIS MORNING TO SCHEDULE OUR MEETING. I HOPE THE REST OF YOUR DAY IS FREE FROM DISTRACTION, BUT IF YOU FIND YOURSELF NEEDING TO BE PREOCCUPIED...
OH AND DON'T FORGET I'M GOING OUT WITH ABBY TONIGHT BEFORE SHE HEADS OUT FOR THE WEEKEND, SO I'LL SEE YOU IN THE MORNING?

CAN'T WAIT TO SEE FIREWORKS WITH YOU, BUT MAROON 5 HERE I COME! OLIVIA MCGUIRE
COMMERCIAL MARKETING, THE KELLAN AGENCY

FROM: FINN KELLAN
SUBJECT: FIREWORKS
DATE: JULY 3, 2013 9:34
TO: OLIVIA MCGUIRE

HAHAHA! YOU'RE WELCOME FOR THE REMINDER, AND YES I'LL PICK YOU UP AROUND TEN TOMORROW MORNING. WE'LL NEED ABOUT AN HOUR DRIVE TIME TO GET OUT OF THE CITY AND OUT TO MY MOM'S BEFORE LUNCH. SHE'S LOOKING FORWARD TO MEETING YOU, BEAUTIFUL.

OH....AND OLIVIA? I SEE FIREWORKS EVERY TIME I'M WITH YOU.

YOURS,
FINN KELLAN, CEO THE KELLAN AGENCY
PS. DON'T LEAVE ME FOR ADAM LEVINE OKAY?

From: Olivia McGuire
Subject: Anticipation
Date: July 3, 2014 9:35
To: Finn Kellan

Deal…although if he wants to buy me a drink I'm not sure I can pass that up! Flattery will get you everywhere! Gotta get to work. Will text you later. Excited for tomorrow!

Olivia McGuire
Commercial Marketing, The Kellan Agency

Our daily morning email banter always helps make my day a happy one. I look forward to each ding my computer lets off when new email comes in. It's always Finn, Abby, or one of my clients. Other than that, I receive the occasional sales email that I try to siphon into my spam inbox. I look through the remaining list of emails I haven't yet opened before calling back the Boston Harbor Cruise Line. There is one from Seal Lake Winery including my itinerary for next week, one from Abby reminding me of our Girls Night Out tonight, and then another from an email address that I don't recognize. I recognize the subject line immediately, so I open the email:

To: Olivia Cardman, The Kellan Agency
Subject: Finn Kellan
Date: July 3, 2014 9:57
From:

He'll never truly love you.

I blink a few times staring at the screen and pick my jaw up off my desk.

What the fuck is this?

Anxiety shoots through me rapidly.

He'll never love me?

Solving Us

I never said I wanted him to love me.

Who are you kidding, Olivia? You're falling for him, and you know it.

Who could've possibly sent this email to me?

I look around the office trying to see if one of my colleagues catches my eye but to no avail. Everyone is quietly working at their desks paying no attention to me. I read the email over and over, trying to find some clue as to who sent this email to me, because obviously whoever sent it knows about my relationship with Finn. To my knowledge, nobody in the office knows except for Mrs. Hoover, and maybe Karen; but I doubt it because if she knew, Mandy would know, and she would certainly say something to me about it.

Note to self, tell Mandy soon.

Hmm, I don't know anyone in the Tech Department yet, so I don't feel comfortable asking them for help looking into it. Maybe Finn could figure it out for me, but the more I think about it, the less I want to involve him. I'm a big girl and can take care of myself. I don't need him fighting stupid little personal fires for me, especially if they're not burning out of control; and, God, let's hope this fire remains contained. I can't let one silly email bother me for the whole day.

"So what are your plans for the long weekend, Mandy? Doing anything fun?" I ask as we're packing up for the day. I grab my purse and shoulder bag with my work files in it as quickly as possible and just make small talk until I can quickly get out of the building. I know I don't want to spend the rest of my day thinking about this email, but I can't not think about it. I feel like everywhere I go today, someone is watching me. That's never a good feeling. I hope I'm just off today, and the long weekend will put everything back to normal for me.

"Having lunch with my mom and some family, but then," Mandy leans in closer to me and whispers. "I'm meeting up with Kym! We made plans to hang out at the harbor and see the fireworks!" She looks like a kid in a candy store as she tells me about her plans with Kym. I'm happy for Mandy. It's cute to see a couple potentially come together. I smile at her when she speaks, trying not to giggle at her excitement.

"How about you? Plans with…what do you call him again? 'Hot Runner Guy'?" she asks me, smirking. In the past six weeks, I have given her just a little information about how I met my hot runner guy boyfriend and how he followed me to Starbucks just to ask me out. I was sure to never divulge Finn's name. Not until I feel one hundred percent comfortable in my friendship with Mandy, which I do now. I suppose after this weekend, if all goes well meeting Finn's mother, I'll make it official in the office. Then this semi-sneaking around can be done.

"Yeah we're spending the day together, and I'm meeting some of his family. I guess if that goes okay, we'll sort of be official, huh?" I wrinkle my nose at the cheesiness of our relationship status.

"Ooh yeah! You totally will be. I'm sure it will be fine. What's not to like about you, Liv? Good luck anyway, though. I'm sure you'll be anxious."

"Yeah thanks. I'm sure it will be fine. He talks pretty highly of his mom, and I know he loves her dearly, which makes me like him even more. I'm a sucker for a family guy," I admit. "Have a great weekend, Mandy. I'll be thinking about you." I suggestively raise my eyebrows at her so she knows what I mean when I tell her I'll be thinking about her. I let out a light laugh as I walk out to the lobby to catch the elevator.

Riding the elevator down to the lobby I think back to the surprise email I received earlier. I had forgotten about it for a very short time, but now that I'm alone, my insecurities creep back into my brain. I'm not really sure what to think about it. It's not like the email said anything ridiculously mean or outlandish, but somehow the possibility of someone being able to anonymously reach out to me in that manner feels a little violating. The ding announcing my arrival to the ground floor shakes me from my thoughts. The elevator doors open, and as I walk out to the lobby, I'm surprised when I catch two of my favorite people chatting just outside the front doors.

Abby is here, obviously waiting on me, but she's talking to Finn, who looks to be consoling her, though she doesn't appear to be that upset. I'm not sure how I'm supposed to approach their conversation since most people don't know about Finn and me yet.

Solving Us

Finn sees me come through the revolving door and immediately smiles at me. He turns in my direction as if he's about to welcome me with a hug or kiss, but I quickly shake my head, silently pleading for him to not shower me with affection outside of our office building. His expression feels like a sucker punch to my stomach, but then he nods in understanding.

"Olivia." He welcomes me to the conversation. "How was your day?"

"Mr. Kellan." I nod professionally in case anyone exiting the building hears our conversation. Abby smirks at my clear avoidance of affection towards Finn. "My day was great. Very productive, Sir, thank you for asking."

Except for this one email...

"Glad to hear it." Finn grins. "I was just walking a client out and ran into Ms. Sheridan here. Seems she's had quite a day and is looking forward to a night on the town with her best friend. I really am sorry to hear, Abby," he says quietly.

I'm confused and a little caught off guard. "What's wrong, Abby? Bad day?"

"Meh. It was a day. Long story short, I met Trent for lunch, and we broke up. He's just working too many weird hours at the hospital for his internship to have the time for a relationship. I can't blame him, but the sex was good, so there's that."

Finn and I both laugh, even though inside her statement makes me feel awkward. Finn and I haven't crossed that bridge yet, and I worry that eventually he won't be so patient.

"Oh. I'm sorry to hear that, Abs. I know you liked him."

Abby purses her lips and shakes her head nonchalantly. "Really if all I can say about the guy after all this time was that he was good in the sack, I guess it's not really meant to be. There are other fish in the sea. Anyway, I'm just ready to throw a couple back with my bestie and dance the night away with a nice steady buzz."

"I'm all for that, Girl! Let's get this weekend started." Abby and I lock arms and prepare to stroll together down the street.

"You ladies be safe tonight. Have fun." He's staring at me with need in his eyes that makes me feel guilty for leaving him alone on the street.

"See you later, Mr. Kellan." I say to him in my best sexy voice before smiling and walking away with Abby. I'm ready for a little R and R after all my work these past few weeks. It's time to cut loose on the dance floor with my BFF and drown my worries in a few glasses of wine…or a Raspberry Long Island Iced Tea, my drink of choice.

Chapter 9

We quickly run home to drop our bags and change our clothes. Abby and I plan to spend the evening at the House of Blues since we got wind that our favorite sexy celebrity, Adam Levine, is doing a not-so surprise performance with Maroon 5. He must be friends with the owner of the club or something; Maroon 5 doesn't usually perform in such small venues, but Abby was lucky enough to score tickets through someone at work. Together Abby and I know every single song Adam does and are familiar with just about every picture you can conjure up on the internet of him. I'm surprised we don't have posters of him plastered all over our bedrooms like teenage girls; but seriously, he's hot. Hotter than hot even. I can't wait to cut loose on the dance floor and dance the night away with my best friend. We haven't had a proper girl's night out since I started working.

Knowing I'm not going to be with Finn tonight, I pick out a flirty black halter dress that makes me feel like I'm wearing nothing. It's comfortable and will keep me cool in the heat of the dance floor. The dress isn't something I would wear around Finn, mostly because my leg scars aren't hidden very well in this dress since it's shorter than what I would usually wear; but tonight I don't give a damn. The venue will be dark, and since I'm already sort of committed to someone, I don't have to worry about impressing a guy. Tonight is about me and Abby relaxing together at a well-deserved Girls Night. I pull my hair up into a ponytail and choose some fun hoop earrings. I don't need any other accessories knowing how much I'm sure to sweat tonight.

Finn: Have fun tonight. Stay SAFE.

I smile reading a quick text from Finn. He's always thinking about me. I swipe my phone and shoot him a quick reply.

Me: We will. Promise. Plans tonight?

Finn: Visiting with Toby for a bit and then having a quick drink with some of my college buddies in town.

Me: Ah. Don't drink and drive. And don't hit on any hot girls.

Finn: Nobody holds a candle to you, Beautiful.

"Ready to go, Liv?" Abby asks me coming down the hallway into the living room. She is dressed in red capris pants and a black strapless halter top with black pumps. Her skin is covered in her favorite strawberry lotion that I recognize not because of the obvious smell but because of the glittery sparkles emanating from her neck and shoulders. She looks ridiculously sexy with her long chocolate brown hair also pulled up in a ponytail with silver dangle earrings. She's wearing a leather snap bracelet with diamond-like studs all over it. She looks hot, and she knows it. I smile at her knowingly.

"You look like a smokin' hot, newly single sexy lady, Abby Bryn Sheridan." I wink at her.

"Damn right I do, Olivia. Let's see if I can't find myself a few good men to flirt with tonight."

I shake my head, laughing at the overzealousness that is my roommate and gesture for her to lead the way.

I don't take my keys since I don't have pockets to put them in, but Abby slides her apartment key off of her keychain and into her pocket along with both of our IDs and credit cards. Within twenty-five minutes, we are showing our tickets to the bouncer of the House of Blues and treating ourselves to our first drinks of the evening. We both go for Long Island Iced Teas, a regular for Abby, raspberry for me. We watch the opening act for Maroon 5 while sitting at a table as close to the stage as we can get. Whoever the band is, they're great! They provide an excited energy to the crowd which is growing larger and larger by the minute. I wonder for a second what the maximum capacity of this place is. People on the dance floor are packing in pretty tight. We finish our appetizer along with our second round of drinks when the opening band finishes their set. With a fifteen-minute intermission between bands, we head out to the dance floor to warm up to the tunes that are being played through the speakers. At least we will be assured a great spot when our favorite leading man comes out.

Because of the long span between lunch and the appetizer I just consumed, I'm feeling blissfully buzzed. Not so much that I don't know what's going on around me, but enough to not care at all what anyone thinks. I'm in a happy place, getting my groove on with Abby. I can't remember the last time we enjoyed ourselves this much. We are all smiles and laughs and giggles while out on the dance floor.

Suddenly the crowd reaches a roaring volume, signaling the entrance of our favorite sexy man, Adam Levine. Oh my God, he looks deliciously hot! He's wearing a pair of jeans ripped in all the right places and a grey t-shirt. Watching him walk on stage in that outfit makes me immediately remember what Finn had worn on our first date. In his ripped jeans and a black t-shirt, I remember thinking he looked yummy as well. Adam's arms filled with tattoos, though, give off the bad boy image that I imagine makes every girl like me swoon.

Finn doesn't need tattoos to make me swoon.

Stop thinking about Finn! You're here to let go and enjoy yourself.

Abby bumps into me as she starts jumping up and down to the opening chords of "Payphone". I immediately smile and lean my head back while I jump around and dance as well. It feels so good to let go and dance my day away.

"Payphone" transitions right into "Lucky Strike", which again has us dancing like wild animals as we enjoy moving with the group of people around us. We continue through Abby's favorite song "Harder to Breathe", and by the time the song is done, Abby and I both are tired and very hot so we make a beeline for the bar to refill our drinks and take a short break so we can continue our fun. After two Long Islands, I know I need to not order a third without a glass of water first. I down my water with Abby, and we both decide on shots for the rest of the night so we won't have to carry our glasses around the club. We click our Washington Apple shots together and smile.

"To sisters before misters...or however that goes!" Abby shouts over the music.

"Hahaha! Chicks before dicks!" I shout back at her.

"Amen! Holes before poles, Liv!"

We toast and shoot back our drinks, almost spitting them out we are laughing so hard. I love hanging out with this girl. "Hey I love this song; let's go. I want to see how close we can get," I say to Abby. "Somebody To Love" is one of my favorite songs, and I have to dance some more, especially as good as this buzz is making me feel. I close my eyes as I become hypnotized to the beat of the music and focus on the lyrics. This song makes me think of Finn every time I hear it, which is at least during every morning run since it's on my workout playlist.

My body sways to the beat of the music as I move my hands up my neck and into my hair until my hands are high above my head, and I'm in a happy place or tipsy bliss, all by myself, entranced by the words Adam is singing about falling in love and never being the same.

Ain't that the truth!

The second verse starts as I feel one of the guys nearby slide his hand around my waist and pull me towards him. A giggle escapes me as our bodies move to the pulse of the music. He can dance and move my body with such strength and fluidity. Abby and I have been dancing with a group of people off and on all evening, so I have no idea which one of them is dancing with me now, but I close my eyes and allow myself to dream that I'm tied up in Finn's body dancing to my favorite song.

I should've asked him to come.

I contemplate the thought of Finn seeing me dancing with another guy when the hand that was holding my waist is joined by another. Both hands slide smoothly down my stomach to my thighs and back up lifting the skirt of my dress just a tad on the ascent. At the same time, I feel warm

Solving Us

soft lips touch the left side of my neck, my favorite spot. Before I realize what I'm doing, I lean my head back against the man behind me.

Am I too drunk?

Olivia, you're drunk; this needs to stop.

Open your eyes, Olivia!

Someone is touching you, and it's not Finn.

He's not here, remember?

I open my eyes immediately in alarm and catch Abby's knowing smirk looking back at me as she dances beside me. She knows exactly what I'm thinking. She raises an eyebrow at me and chuckles. I frown in confusion.

Why isn't Abby telling me to stop?

She's drunker than I am for sure.

I whip my body around to see who I'm dancing with and nearly fall over dizzy from the quick movement matched with a little too much alcohol. I'm caught by the same strong arms that were just holding me a moment ago. I look up and come face to face with Finn, who literally takes my breath away. "What are you doi...." I start to ask but Finn captures my mouth with his own in the hottest kiss I've ever had…in a room full of people…smashing their bodies into one another.

Finn…

We kiss like two crazy animals while Adam sings of wanting to touch somebody and wanting to dance the night away. I'm so turned on and buzzed that I couldn't care less what anyone thinks of us at the moment. We haven't moved. Well, okay, we are moving…to the beat of the song, making out on the dance floor. Finn's tongue immediately wants access to the inside of my mouth, and I grant it willingly, wanting to taste him. I can taste the whiskey he's obviously been drinking. His kiss is warm and inviting and then hard, almost forceful, as he kisses me like it's the last kiss we will ever share. I kiss him back with just as much fervor.

Whoa!

Finn breaks our kiss and rests his forehead on mine, breathing hard. I look up at him, into his beautiful eyes, and for one second worry about what a sweaty smelly mess I must be.

Damnit! My scars in this dress...

I gasp lightly, as lightly as I can when I'm damn near drunk, and begin to tug my skirt down. The concerned look on my face and a frantic hand moving through my hair must speak volumes.

"Stop it, Olivia. Stop worrying; you're stunning." He reads my mind. Finn takes a deep breath as he holds me next to him. "And fuck, you smell so good...like sweat, and perfume, and sweetness, and you."

I'm not sure I even can blush given the amount of alcohol already in my system, but he makes me smile, nonetheless. Finn sweeps my sweat-ridden hair from my face that had fallen out of my ponytail and trails his fingers down my cheek.

"I think of you every time I hear this song, so I couldn't let you dance to it by yourself." Finn cups my face in his hands for a moment and slowly presses his lips to my forehead before moving one hand to the small of my back. His hands are big enough that it feels like any moment now he's going to cup my ass, but he doesn't. His other hand is on the back of my head, tangling into my hair so that my forehead remains attached to his. He pulls me as close to his body as he can and closes his eyes.

"Dance with me," he whispers. The volume of our surroundings is deafening, but as I stand in front of Finn watching him, I can hear every word.

Here we are, on the middle of a dance floor in the Boston House of Blues having our very own little romantic moment. You know what I find very attractive in a guy? One who sings and has no problem singing to me, which is exactly what Finn is doing as he holds me on the dance floor. He finishes the entire song, singing the lyrics in my ear, as we move together. I smell him. I feel him. I listen to him as he sings softly to me, never breaking eye contact. Maybe he's thinking I can't hear him above the sound of the band singing, but unequivocally, I hear every word he sings to me. He isn't just singing a song. He's speaking to me, speaking to my heart, right here in the middle of a crowded pub.

And I am hearing every word.

Every. Damn. Word.

He loves me.

He's falling for me.

I'm falling for you, too, Finn.

And what I wish Finn could see is the irony of this situation. I know in this moment, with me in his arms, he's speaking to my heart; but what he doesn't know is that I could just as easily be singing these exact same words to him.

Finn opens his eyes and meets my gaze. Our bodies are still so close to each other that I can feel every breath he takes. His lips part, and he slowly licks his bottom lip. I can feel that Finn wants to kiss me again, so I close my eyes and wait for our lips to connect, for that sure to be sweet taste of him - it never happens. I frown slightly and open my eyes to see Finn still staring at me with such intensity. I almost mistake his expression for a pained one. His lips are parted and basically touching mine without actually kissing me. I can feel his heavy breath against mine.

"Olivia, do you have any idea what you do to me?"

No, Finn. It's what you do to me.

"I could say the same to you," I breathe. "I'm so happy to see you here, but...why *are* you here, Mr. Stalker?" I tease Finn when the song ends. "Did you follow me here?"

Finn chuckles and wraps his arms around me tightly as he kisses the top of my head.

"No, I promise I didn't follow you here. Some of the guys wanted to catch the concert tonight and grab a drink. I've known about it for a while but didn't want to say anything because, as hard as I tried, I couldn't score another ticket to bring you with me. I know your infatuation with Mr. Levine," he teased me back.

Touche.

"Anyway, once you told me that Abby got tickets, I didn't want to tell you I was coming and make you feel like you had to change your plans. So I told the guys I needed to hang out near the back so you and Abby could have your space and have fun without feeling like I was smothering you or that I didn't trust you."

"Oh. That's very sweet, but you didn't have to do that; I'm sure Abby would've understood."

"It's okay, really. I got my show, and it was better than any concert I could've attended," Finn says, smirking at me.

"You were spying on me?"

"No. Not at all, but seeing you relax and have fun with your best friend, the smiles on your face, your laugh. You didn't even know I was here, and I loved it. I can't *not* watch you when you're near me, and I can't *not* dance with you when one of my favorite songs is playing either. That's what you do to me, Olivia."

I smile at Finn lovingly and kiss him quickly just as Abby approaches the both of us.

"Hey Finneus! I believe we girls made a deal tonight…hoes before bros!" Abby shouts, clearly a little more wasted than I expected. She obviously had an extra shot or two while Finn and I were dancing. We both laugh at her.

Finn's eyebrows shoot up in surprise at Abby's exclamation. "Yeah I know, I know," Finn relents. "I'm on my way out, actually. I just didn't want to leave without saying hello and goodbye to this beautiful girl right here. She's a catch, ya know." Finn's eyes lower and slowly trail up my body. I don't worry too much about him seeing the scars on my thigh. It's plenty dark in here.

"Damn straight! You better not forget it either, Finnegan."

"Okay, I guess this means maybe we're done, too," I say giggling again at Abby for calling Finn anything but his actual name. At least Abby is a funny drunk.

"Finn, would you mind getting a glass of water for my beautiful, sexy, and now very drunk friend? I would rather she didn't throw up all over our cab on the way home."

"Yeah, sure. And you won't have to worry about a cab. My car is outside with the valet. I'm happy to take you home. It's safer for both of you."

"Uh, no offense or anything, but if you've been drinking too it's safer for all of us to take a cab."

"I appreciate the concern, Liv, but it's okay. I only had one drink, and it was over an hour ago. I drank two glasses of water while watching you just to calm my body down. I'm good; I promise. I would never, ever drive drunk."

I put my palm on Finn's cheek and look into his eyes with sincere appreciation. He is always so quick to take care of my needs, or in this case, the needs of my best friend.

"Thank you, Finneus." I smirk at him, and we both laugh. Abby drinks her glass of water while Finn goes out to retrieve his car from the valet. We walk out into the fresh air that doesn't feel that fresh given it's a warm summer evening. Humidity is definitely settling in for the night. I get Abby into the backseat of Finn's car where she leans against the driver side door and closes her eyes. Finn helps me into the front seat, and we take off for our apartment building.

He walks us all the way to our door to make sure we both make it safely. In reality, two girls walking alone at night…one clearly drunk…the other tipsy, at the very least, is probably not a good idea. I'm grateful for Finn's presence this evening in more ways than one. I would love for him to stay, but I need to make sure Abby doesn't wake up worshiping the porcelain throne in the morning. And I know I'll be spending the entire day with Finn tomorrow. I get Abby in the door and into the bathroom so she can brush her teeth and sit for a minute to settle her stomach while I walk Finn out to say goodnight.

"Thank you so much for your help tonight, Finn. I seriously don't know what I would've done had you not been there."

Finn chuckles quietly. "You're welcome. It was my pleasure to be there with you, even for a short time. We should go dancing more often. You're pretty good."

"Mmm, you're not so bad yourself. I had fun. And thank you...for letting Abby and me have our time together. I appreciate it as much as she does. She needed tonight."

"I wouldn't dream of taking you away from her. I know better than to piss off the best friend," he jokes. "In fact, I should go so you can get back to her. She did need tonight, and now she may need your help in there."

"Yeah." I can't stop smiling at him.

I don't want to go in and help Abby. I want to keep smiling at Finn.

"Yeah, I guess I should." I'm still smiling at him. I must be more buzzed than I thought.

Finn tries his best to hide a smile but fails miserably. He shakes his head as he chuckles and reaches out to grab my arm.

"Come here, Beautiful." I walk willingly into Finn's arms and connect my lips with his. Alcohol doesn't make me sad or angry or a loud talker, but it does make me lose my inhibitions. What starts as an innocent goodbye kiss quickly grows into a panty melting grope session right here in the hallway of my apartment building. Finn's kiss deepens as he walks me backwards until my back is against the wall next to my apartment door. As he holds on to me, swirling his tongue around mine, I reach up and grab his biceps. Finn pushes his weight into me against the wall a little more. Not having to hold on to me anymore, his hands start to roam, one up the right side of my body and the other around to softly cup my behind. The butterflies in my stomach are fluttering ferociously. I'm nervous to have Finn touch me, but the alcohol in me has me so eager to just lose control. Tonight, the alcohol is making me brave.

It has been too...long...since I've had a physical attraction this strong to anyone. My hands roam slowly down Finn's body towards his waist line, searching for what I know will be the obvious proof of Finn's arousal, but before I know it, our kiss is over, and Finn has stepped back away from me. Our breathing unsteady, Finn and I gaze at each other.

"You should go. Abby needs you, and if you stay out here one more minute, I can't promise I won't take advantage of you, and I'm not that guy."

Damn Finn and his personal control!

How does he do it?

I'm buzzed.

Finn is HOT.

I want him.

Not here…not in this hallway.

Abby needs me…

"Yeah. I should go." I'm still breathing hard and staring at Finn.

"Yeah." Finn leans over and kisses my cheek

"I'll see you tomorrow, Beautiful."

"Yeah," I breathe. "Goodnight."

Finn waits to make sure I'm inside the door safely before he turns and leaves but not before I see him run his hands through his hair. I smile and walk back to the bathroom to tend to Abby, who is sitting on the side of the bathtub with her eyes closed. I help clean the sweat and make-up off of her face. I put two ibuprofen tablets in her hand and give her another glass of water. Hopefully, she won't wake up too hung over in the morning.

"You're the best, Olivia," Abby says with a tired smile.

"Anything for you, Abs. Thanks for a fun night. I really had a great time."

"Yeah, you did." She's smirking at me and giggling every couple seconds. "Seriously, he's a catch, Olivia, and he's seriously into you. Way more than Trent ever was towards me. Don't you ever walk away from him. He's good for you."

I look her in the eye when she speaks to me, but her gaze is clouded by alcohol and exhaustion.

"Yeah, he is pretty special, Abs."

She asks me the one question I've been waiting for but don't know if I'm ready to answer, "Do you love him yet?"

I stop wringing out the washcloth I had grabbed for her. I'm stumped. I've thought about saying the L-word, but it freaks me out a little bit of a lot. Loving Finn means seriously committing, and seriously committing means moving forward, and moving forward means the possibility of an end, and an end is not something I want to consider just yet. In fact, I fear it. I felt the end coming when I was dating Archer in high school, but I fear I won't feel an end coming with Finn; it will hit me out of nowhere, and I will be hurt worse than anticipated. It's morbid of me to have these thoughts I know, but sometimes, I just can't help it.

"I don't know, Abs. I don't *not* love him. I more than just like him but I don't...I don't know if I would say love just yet. I can't say it, yet. He still doesn't know about...about me."

"Hmm, pity. It's obvious after watching him with you that he loves *you*, Olivia...but you must not want to see it, yet." Abby lifts herself off the side of the tub and heads for her bedroom. She stops when she gets to me and gives me a quick kiss on the cheek. "Good night, Liv. Thanks for taking my mind off my shitty afternoon."

"Good night, Abby," I say softly. I consider her words. Finn hasn't yet said those three big words to me, and I've never asked for that; but the more I think of him, of seeing him tonight on the dance floor, hearing him say he didn't want me to think he didn't trust me, his understanding face when he told me to stop worrying about how I look, I guess I really do have to consider what she said about the way he feels about me.

He strengthens me.

When I'm with Finn, he makes me feel like nobody else matters to him but me.

I'm definitely falling for him.

I look at myself in the mirror before heading to bed.

"I'm falling for you, even if I fall because of you," I whisper to my reflection.

Chapter 10

Finn picks me up just before ten o'clock the next morning to make the drive out to see his mother. Apparently, it's tradition in the Kellan family to be together for the Fourth of July. Finn says they keep it relatively quiet with just some close friends and family, but in the past, they used to throw one hell of a party. I'm honored to be asked, even if I am a bit nervous.

"So, where does your Mom live again?"

"Wellesley. It's a suburb of Boston, only about a half hour away, but with all this Fourth of July traffic, I figured it might take us longer to get out there than usual. Mom's planning a lunch for us and a few of her friends since we have evening plans to see fireworks."

"And, Wellesley is where you grew up, I take it?"

"Yes. Born and raised in the house we're going to. It's my home away from home." Finn looks over at me smiling through his aviator sunglasses.

He looks gorgeous today. He's wearing a pair of khaki shorts and a steel blue short-sleeved shirt that rolls slightly at the sleeves. It has three buttons on the front that are all open to show the top of Finn's well defined chest. Seeing him dressed down like this makes me feel like I'm just dating any normal guy and not one of the hottest young bachelor CEOs of Boston, or the eastern seaboard, or whatever.

"Great," I say and smile shyly.

I turn my head and peer out my window to gather my wits. I'm nervous and afraid to admit it. I don't want to be, but I am. It's been a long time since I've had to be introduced to the parent of someone I'm dating; in fact, it's been so long, I really feel like this is all happening for the very first time.

What if Mrs. Kellan doesn't like me?

What if I speak too fast or say the wrong thing or go on some lengthy rant that makes absolutely no sense and then everyone is staring at me like, "hey who's that crazy girl, and is she still talking?" Then they all just stare at me like I'm some sort of alien freak, and I can't just run away because I'll be in a new place and won't know where the hell I can run to?

I take a very deep breath in my nose and blow it out slowly, still peering out my window.

"Hey." Finn puts his hand on my left thigh and squeezes to get my attention. I turn my head and look at him as he grabs my left hand and kisses it before putting it down with his on his lap.

"Stop worrying, Liv. She's going to love you; I promise."

"How do you know that? You don't really know that, Finn. She could hate me."

"Well she could, I suppose, but for one, Mrs. Hoover has already raved about you to her over the phone, and if Grace Hoover approves, my mother will approve. Trust me."

"She what?!" This is news to me.

Finn laughs and rubs my hand that he's holding with his thumb. "I overheard her talking to Mom on the phone this past week. I'm pretty sure you have nothing to worry about if Grace has anything to say about it."

If this goes well, I'm going to buy Mrs. Hoover anything she damn well wants! Or maybe just some flowers or *maybe a bottle of wine.*

"But, Olivia, I also know that she's going to like you because I've never brought a girl home before to meet the family officially."

Yeah right.

He must say that to everyone.

"That's ridiculous, Finn; certainly there have been at least one or two over the years."

"No. Never." He shakes his head adamantly.

"Why not?" I ask shocked and a little confused.

Finn shrugs and looks over at me. "I guess I just never found the right person, so I never saw a reason."

"But you see a reason now?"

He looks over at me with an almost saddened expression. I worry for a second that maybe I upset him, but his hand sliding over to caress my knee says otherwise.

"Isn't it obvious?" He asks quietly?

Is what obvious?

We pull into the Kellan estate around eleven o'clock. We park in the large circle driveway behind a few other cars, and Finn walks over to open my door and help me out.

"You look absolutely breathtaking today, by the way."

"Thank you."

I chose a long navy chevron maxi dress that has a solid navy halter neck top. I'm wearing my wedge sandals that I love and left my hair down because, after blowing it dry, I could see it was going to be a good hair day, and also because I love when Finn plays with my hair. He can't really touch it much when it's up off of my face. After seeing what Finn is wearing, though, I feel a tad overdressed. I guess since I'm meeting his mother and seeing the estate where we just pulled up, airing on the side of too dressy is a good thing. I take a deep breath and smile at Finn as he kisses my temple and places my right hand in his left to lead me into the house.

We walk into the foyer, and I immediately start looking around. From the entranceway, I can see a grand oak staircase leading to the second floor, a sitting room off to the left that has walls lined with filled bookshelves, *I could spend all damn day in there*, and what seems to be a formal dining area off to my right. These rooms look immaculate and also untouched by anyone. I guess most of the family living happens in the back of the house. The place is palatial, and I can't understand why or even how just one person lives here now. We can hear laughter and talking coming from the back part of the house ahead of us, which is where Finn leads me.

We walk back towards the kitchen and round the corner to the casual dining space when Finn stops suddenly dead in his tracks causing me to walk right into him. I stumble and trip over my sandal and start to fall, but Finn catches me and steadies me so that I don't look too much like a huge klutz. I look up at Finn and then around the dining room to see what caused him to stop so suddenly, but it turns out I don't really need to look, the excited screaming is evidence enough.

"OH MY GOD, OLIVIA!!!! You didn't tell me you were dating FINN!! Why the HELL didn't you tell me you were dating FINN?"

My eyes rapidly dart across the room like a deer in the headlights to Mandy, whose jaw is on the floor. Well, okay maybe it isn't on the floor, but it's definitely only inches from the table.

Umm, awkward.

What the hell do I say now?

What do I do?

No seriously, what do I do?

I glance at Finn and try to swallow. He leans over and kisses my cheek and whispers, "I'm so sorry. I didn't know they were coming," into my ear.

Finn smiles at the group seated around the table and puts his hand now around my waist. He turns to face Mandy and Karen.

"I'm sorry Mandy I...uh," he says frowning and shaking his head slightly. "I didn't know you guys were coming today." He hitches his thumb in the direction of the driveway. "And I didn't see either of your cars in the driveway."

"Mandy got a new car just this past week," Karen spoke up smiling. "We decided to take it for a spin today."

Finn's eyebrows shoot up in surprise. He looks back at me; I'm flushed with anxiety, and I try to calm my nerves without making it obvious that I'm overwhelmed. It's not that I didn't want Mandy and Karen to know, I just wanted to be the one to tell them. Now I feel like I've purposely been keeping this from them, which I have, so they have every reason to think I'm untrustworthy, which I'm not...but still.

"Well I guess the cat's out of the bag now, huh? Um, everyone, this is my girlfriend, Olivia. Olivia...this is everyone." Finn gestures around the room to those seated at the table

Solving Us

Mrs. Kellan gets up from her seat and immediately walks over to me with her arms open. She is a beautiful woman with shorter light brown hair with gray streaks that make her look like the elegant and sophisticated woman I'm sure she is. Her deep blue eyes are warm and welcoming as she smiles at Finn and me. Seriously, I could be looking at an older Mary Poppins right now.

"Olivia, it is so lovely to finally meet you dear. Finn has told me so much about you, and I'm so excited you could join us today." She hugs me tightly. I relax a little and hug her back.

"It's a pleasure to finally meet you as well, Mrs. Kellan. Thank you so much for having me today."

"You're always welcome in this house, Olivia. Any friend of Finn's is a friend of mine."

"Thank you." I smile.

Finn kisses my temple again and gestures around the room introducing me. I meet two of Mrs. Kellan's good friends, Tracy and Eliza, and then say hello again to Mandy and her mother Karen. Lucky for me, they're both smiling approvingly.

Phew!

There are two seats beside Mandy and Karen, so Finn and I sit next to both of them for lunch.

"So," Mandy whispers not so quietly to me. "Why didn't you just tell me it was Finn? We've been talking about 'Hot Runner Guy' for weeks now." She laughs.

"Hot runner guy?" Finn asks grinning proudly. Thank God he's holding my hand under the table. He squeezes my hand, and I feel myself blush.

I look at both Finn and Mandy and also at Karen who, by virtue of her placement at the table, is listening to our conversation.

"I um…" I can feel my expression sadden slightly. I'm feeling unbelievably guilty for keeping this secret but know there's no way I can talk around the now bright pink elephant in the room.

"I just didn't want to give everyone the wrong first impression. I didn't want to be that girl. I'm *not* that girl," I say emphatically.

"That girl?" Mandy asks. "What girl?"

"You know; I didn't want everyone to think I just got the job because I was dating Finn."

"Didn't you, though?" Mandy asks smirking. She winks at me when I give her an oh-my-gosh-I-can't-believe-you-just-said-that expression.

"Mandy!" Karen chides.

"In Olivia's defense," Finn chimes in. "I was the one who found her. She didn't know who I was when we met. It was sort of a serendipitous encounter." He squeezes the hand he's holding under the table again, leaning over to place a quick kiss on my cheek. If I wasn't blushing then, I am now.

"There's no reason to be embarrassed, Olivia." Karen assures me. "When preparation and passion meets opportunity, you take the leap. I think it was a great decision for you given the great work you've done so far."

"Thank you."

"And I know it was a great decision for Finn." She eyes Finn at the table and smiles when her eyes meet Mrs. Kellan's. "He's never been happier."

Mandy nudges me with her elbow and giggles. "So, I guess we have you to thank for Finn's good mood lately, eh? Keep it up, girl!"

Finn saves me from embarrassment. "Okay, okay enough of embarrassing Olivia. Let's eat; I'm starving."

Chapter 11

The rest of our meal time is delightful. We lunch on chicken salad sandwiches, pasta salad, hummus and vegetables, and for dessert, strawberry shortcake a la mode. My stomach is happy, and my nerves are settled. I can feel my body relaxing next to Finn's. I find myself laughing and blushing at times, as Mrs. Kellan, Eliza and Tracy and even Karen tell old stories of Finn growing up. Even Mandy pipes in laughing at a few key moments. It's clear that everyone around the table loves Finn. Not surprisingly to me Sydney's name is referenced a few times throughout conversation. The last time I hear her name, though, I steal a glance at Finn who looks a bit nervous and uncomfortable but smiles shyly, nonetheless.

He leans over and whispers in my ear, "Would you like a tour of the rest of the house?"

"I'd like that very much." I accept, grateful for some alone time with Finn.

Mandy catches my attention quickly raising her eyebrows and then winking at me.

Finn clears his throat and begins to push his chair out from under the table.

"If you'll excuse us, I'd like to give Olivia the grand tour."

"Not at all, sweetheart, go right ahead," Mrs. Kellan replies, smiling adoringly at her son.

Finn takes my hand and leads me from the informal dining room, which is attached to the kitchen, and around the corner to what I guess is the main living room. There's an armoire that houses a flat screen TV, a white sofa and loveseat with yellow chevron accent throw pillows, and a grey throw blanket. The walls are a light grey color with white crown molding. The room reminds me very much of Finn's office.

"Well I see where you get your decorating taste," I joke.

He squeezes my hand and laughs. "Yeah I guess it's a little obvious that my mommy helped me design my office. Maybe someday you can help me make some new changes."

"To your office? No way. I love your office just as it is...well, for the most part anyway."

"For the most part? What part don't you like?"

"There aren't any parts I don't like. There are just some parts that we um...well, we haven't gotten to try out yet."

I tilt my head and shrug my shoulder suggestively. "I mean, who knows how comfortable some parts really are."

Finn's look of confusion slowly morphs into one of amusement as he catches on to what I can't believe I just said.

Filter, Olivia! Filter!

I squeeze his hand and then lean over to peck his cheek.

"I'm sorry; I don't have a frame of reference for you. I'm not used to decorating my office with women; though for you, I would definitely be willing to make some changes. My desk might be pretty comfortable, my chair for sure."

"Hmm, we'll see." I wink at him. He kisses the top of my head and laughs with me. Playful banter comes so naturally with Finn.

"Hey," he says, pulling me to him and wrapping his arms around me. I lift my eyes to his, unsure of his worried expression. "Are you okay? I mean, I feel like I should apologize to you for leading you into the lioness's den earlier. I should've known that Karen and Mandy would be here; they come every year. But when I talked to Mom earlier this week, I guess I just wasn't thinking, and none of them seemed to mention it at work. I never meant to put you in a potentially uncomfortable situation."

"It's fine, Finn. No apology necessary. Your mom is stunning and so sweet, and as far as Mandy and Karen are concerned…well…" I think for a second. "I guess now I can stop calling you 'Hot Runner Guy' at work."

Finn laughs as he holds me, and I can feel his body move against me as I embrace him.

"What if Karen had been pissed or didn't approve? Or what if Mandy were green with envy? Jealous of my hot runner-guyness?" he teases.

I chuckle. "Well first of all, no offense, but I know who Mandy has an eye for, and let's just say it's not you. Secondly, if Karen didn't approve, I would like to think that you or your mother would've felt that tension. Thirdly, your mother would have never allowed that type of reaction, I'm certain. She's a compassionate person, and I'm sure protective of you. And fourth, you make me feel, I don't know…safe, I guess."

I squeeze Finn a little tighter and rub my hands down his back as I hug him. "I knew you would protect me, would protect my feelings."

Finn leans his head down towards mine, moves his hand from my hair to my cheek, and kisses me. Not an 'I want you, need you, have to have you' kiss, but a slow, loving 'I adore you' type of kiss. There is never any denying that Finn is kisstacular.

"Olivia, if I have my way, you'll never have to worry about needing protected again. I want to be that man for you like I've never wanted anything before. I'll always take care of you." Finn ponders for a moment and then turns and pulls my hand to follow him.

"Come on; I have something to show you."

Finn leads me back towards the foyer and up the large staircase. As we walk up the steps, there are beautifully framed photographs to look at. Finn takes the time to point out certain family vacations or special trips he took with his father, like the picture of both of them in front of the Eiffel Tower, or of the two of them on camels in Jerusalem. I'm amazed at how well traveled Finn is and so happy for him that he got the opportunity to spend such precious time traveling with his father before he got sick.

"You're a lucky man, Finn."

"What makes you say that?" he asks me softly.

I gesture to all of the amazing pictures hung on the wall. "This, Finn. All of this. All of the amazing trips and experiences you got to have with your Dad before he died. What a blessing and a ton of memories you now have to remember him by. So many people aren't so lucky, ya know?"

"Yeah. Yeah, I guess so," Finn says almost too sadly for my liking.

"I mean, I don't mean to belittle the sadness of his passing." I put my hand on Finn's arm. "I just mean that it looks like, in these pictures anyway, that the two of you were really living. Adventures, time spent together, and love - those are the important things in life."

We reach the top of the staircase, and I stop suddenly with Finn right by my side. Hanging on the wall at the top of the steps is a beautifully framed family portrait of Finn, his parents, and of course, Sydney. They all look so happy in the picture, like they were an extremely close family. Sydney looks so much like Finn. She has the same blue eyes and the same brown hair, only hers is long enough to be pulled back and in a beautiful knot at the back of her head. She's gorgeous, and she looks young; in fact, Finn does as well. This was obviously taken before her accident.

"Sydney," I whisper under my breath.

Finn's head whips in my direction, his head tilting as he eyes me curiously. "You know about Sydney?"

Damnit...is it ok for me to know about her?

"Um, yeah. I do. Well, I mean I don't really know about her, I just...well, Mandy told me over lunch one day. Please don't be upset with her for telling me before you, Finn," I plead. "It just sort of came up in conversation when I was asking how you guys all knew each other. She told me she was Sydney's best friend, and I, I just didn't know about her, I mean. I'm sorry."

"Don't be. It's okay. She's right; Mandy was Syd's best friend. Of course she would talk about her. I'm sorry I didn't tell you sooner. I should have."

"No, Finn, I'm sorry. I'm sorry I didn't tell you that I knew. I just...didn't quite know how to bring it up."

Finn takes a deep breath and gazes at the portrait with me.

"She was beautiful, wasn't she? She was my best friend, too. An annoying little sister sometimes," he chuckles lightly and shakes his head. "But as we grew up we really enjoyed each other's company. I tried so hard to be there for her, to support her...to remind her how proud of her I was when Dad was a little too busy to be around. I guess it just wasn't enough."

More than you know.

"Her boyfriend broke up with her for another girl. I could see her demeanor changing a little bit, so I started coming home more often on the weekends and some week nights to hang out with her. I told her all the time how beautiful she was. I mean, she still had Mandy so she wasn't alone, but I felt compelled to check up on her, make sure she was okay, that nothing was happening to her. She was being bullied and made fun of at school for the scars on her face, and I never knew. I never knew a damn thing. Syd never told me; Mandy never told me."

"Do you think Mandy knew?" Why wouldn't she say anything to protect her friend? I'm a little confused all of a sudden.

Finn nods his head slowly.

"Mandy told me one...day. She told me that she knew Syd was bothered by a few select girls at school but that Sydney didn't want to make a big deal about it. She just wanted to get through her senior year and graduate and be away from everyone. You remember being that age; girls don't want to admit defeat."

That age? How about now?

That stupid email I got yesterday pops into my mind, as does my decision to not bother Finn with it.

"I can understand her logic."

"Yeah, well, she ended up with too many wrong pieces in her inner puzzle and just couldn't figure out how to get them all to fit, so she threw the puzzle away. She couldn't solve herself."

I watch as Finn looks back at the family portrait on the wall.

"November sixteenth," he whispers. "I'll never forget that day. She took a bunch of sleep-aid medicine along with a couple shots of bourbon from my Dad's cabinet, went to sleep, and never woke up. Mom tried to wake her up for school the next morning and well...you know."

"Oh, God!" I gasp silently. "Your poor mother."

"Yeah," Finn agrees. I looked down at our hands when I feel my ring moving on my pinky finger. Finn is twisting it around and around on my finger while he's talking to me. I'm not even sure he knows he's doing it. I can't help but stare at his fingers, though, as he turns my ring over and over. Such a small act is keeping him calm and bringing him peace, and that's exactly what I do when I'm nervous or anxious.

"It was devastating for her, for all of us really. It was a very rough couple of years, especially finding out about my Dad's condition, and then his passing away as well. If it weren't for Mom's friends, and Karen and Mandy, I'm not sure she would still be here, either. People die of broken hearts all the time, right?"

"I guess that's highly possible." I take a deep steadying breath and rub Finn's arm. "But what about you? Who takes care of you Finn?"

Finn grins easily. "Toby. I was lucky enough to meet Toby after Syd died, and he's been my most supportive friend ever since. Well, that is until you came along."

I smile sincerely at Finn. "Well I'm grateful for Toby then and so glad you have him in your life. Everyone needs someone they can lean on. And I would love to be that person for you, someone you can lean on. I'm sure that wasn't easy, Finn, what you just did. Opening up to me and letting me get to know your family. I want you to know that means a lot to me."

Finn tilts his head and holds my gaze for what feels like minutes.

"I know we haven't been together for very long, Olivia. It's only been a couple months, but something about you overwhelms me. You make me feel peace and happiness again in a way I never really thought about before. You make me want more out of my life. It's like I'm hypnotized by your veela-like powers, and I don't ever want to be woken up. I don't ever want to walk away from you."

I giggle at Finn's Harry Potter reference, knowing he's thinking about Sydney's love of the iconic series. Good thing I'm also a fan and can follow his references.

Solving Us

"Well…" I nudge Finn with my shoulder. "I'll take that as a compliment, and lucky for you, I don't *want* you to ever want to walk away from me."

Finn smiles and lowers his head. He's still playing with the ring on my finger. I think for a minute about his veela reference, narrow my eyes and warn, "But just so you know…" Finn looks up at my face as I speak.

"If you ever make me mad, or decide to walk away, you better watch out. Veelas turn into harpies when they get upset…and I've been practicing throwing those fireballs from my hands."

Finn laughs a hearty loud laugh. "Good to know!" We both crack up in a fit of laughter, but as I I'm laughing Finn quiets enough to look at me and shake his head. "God, I love you, Olivia."

I laugh again.

Wait…what?

I stop laughing.

Did he just say…?

"What?"

I'm pretty sure my heart just somersaulted.

"I said I love you, Liv." Finn smiles adoringly at me.

I am speechless.

"What?" I don't know why I'm finding this moment so unbelievable.

I swallow the huge lump in my throat.

"You love me?"

Finn nods. "I think I've loved you since the day I met you and followed you into Starbucks, watching you take a picture of your blueberry muffin." He takes a deep breath and continues his thoughts. "But today? Today, you being here, the fact that I *want* you here…" Finn lets out the breath he had taken in. "I don't usually bring girls here, Liv." He shakes his head. "I've never really introduced girls to my family because I've never felt for anyone the way I feel for you. I'm just a guy who loves his family and a guy who protects what's his, so bringing you here is a big step for me. Except…"

Finn grabs my hands and holds both of them. The heat rising to my face is overwhelming, my breathing unsteady, and I'm sure my eyes must look like saucers.

"Except it isn't a big step for me, Liv. I mean, it doesn't feel like a big step at all to me. It feels right. Having you here feels right and normal and wonderful and..." He grabs my face and kisses me hard. It feels good to feel him relax with me. As we kiss, Finn leans over and slides his right hand under my legs and moves his left hand to my back. He swiftly picks me up and carries me up the last step.

I gasp and grab tightly onto his upper arms so that he doesn't drop me. "Whoa! What are you doing?"

"One more thing to show you." He smirks in between kisses.

Finn carries me down the hallway and into the last doorway on the right.

Chapter 12

"My room," Finn states, as he carries me into the room and sets me down on his bed.

I look around the blue and white bedroom that looks almost as if a college student is still living in it. There are bookshelves lined with old college textbooks, a desk along one wall, and a flat screen TV hung on the wall opposite the bed. There are two doors that I suspect lead to most likely the bathroom and the close;, but, honestly, I don't care to get up and walk through Finn's room. My stomach is a hot mess.

The butterflies in my stomach are fluttering so fast, I think they might rip right through me. The myriad of emotions flowing through me are confusing the hell out of me. I'm overjoyed that Finn told me he loves me. I feel guilty that I didn't say it back immediately; but then again, he didn't really give me the chance to, which I'm sort of okay with. I'm scared out of my mind to tell him I love him because love means committing, and Finn doesn't know me the way he thinks he does. What if after he really sees me he can't commit to me? What if he sees me, the real me, and decides he doesn't want me anymore? If I tell him I love him and grant him full access to my heart, it'll devastate me when he walks away.

But, I want him to love me

I want to tell him I love him, too.

I just can't.

"Hey," Finn says softly. We're both sitting on the edge of his bed. He's looking at me and turns my face with his hands so that he can look into my eyes.

"Where did you go just now?" he asks quietly.

"I...umm..."

Oh my God, what do I say?

"Olivia, listen. I'm sorry that I dumped all that on you...about Sydney, and I'm sorry if I caught you off guard. I just...I couldn't bring you here and introduce you to my family without telling you how I feel. I told you before that I never had a reason to bring a girl home; but now, you're my reason. You're all the reasons. That's not exactly how I planned it to go, but..."

"Finn?"

"Yeah?"

"Stop talking." I smile at him. "It was perfect. *You* are perfect."

"Olivia, I'm far fr..."

"Shh," I say placing a finger on his lips to stop his words.

"Finn...you're perfect for *me*. Everything about today has been...perfect. I loved meeting your mother, I loved hearing all about Sydney and seeing the pictures of you and your dad. I love talking and laughing with you. I love being with you. I love that you love me."

"But..." His eyebrows raise in quiet question.

God, he's killing me here.

I don't want to break his heart.

"My 'but' isn't really a 'but'. It's more like...."

How do I put this?

"Liv?"

"Yeah?"

"It's okay. When I told you I loved you, I didn't mean to make you feel like you needed to say it back right away. I know I have a lot of baggage, and..."

"Oh God, Finn, no, no, no, you have it all wrong," I interrupt. I grab Finn's face with both of my hands. I let out a heavy breath and close my eyes to gather my wits.

"I'm scared, Finn. I told you before, you're not the only one with baggage. I'm not judging you for yours, but, I...I wouldn't blame you if you didn't want to deal with mine. There are things you don't know, and every day that we're together, I get closer and closer to wanting to tell you because I do have feelings for you, Finn, very strong feelings...and that...scares me."

"What scares you?"

Solving Us

"Love. Love scares me, Finn. Everybody I love I lose and," I let go of his face. "My past is…"

"Lonely? Dark? Confusing? Like your puzzle pieces don't fit?" he asks me.

"My puzzle pieces…" I ponder his thought for a moment. "Finn...my past feels like a fucked up Rubik's Cube."

"Mmm… Rubik's Cube, huh?"

"Yeah"

"Sounds perfect," he mutters.

"Perfect?"

Did he hear me correctly?

"I just told you my life is like a fucked up Rubik's Cube, and that's perfect?"

"Yeah." He smiles at me. "I know how to solve a Rubik's Cube."

Finn takes my hand in his and folds our fingers together, our hands now looking like a completed puzzle. The gesture isn't lost on me.

"Olivia, I understand exactly what you're saying; in fact, I could've used the same metaphor. You feel like your life is a cluster fuck of colored cubes that just don't seem to match up."

I look at Finn stunned. He sees me. He gets me.

"Yeah. That's exactly how I feel. So, I work hard to get one side to completely line up, and I love it; but as soon as I try to line up another side, I lose everything I had before."

"Yeah but, Liv, sometimes in order to solve a Rubik's cube, you have to go backwards before you can move forward. And no matter what, I'll go backwards with you so that we can move forward together. You don't have to feel alone anymore. I *want* to be here with you. You have me. You have my heart. I'm giving it to you. Use it."

I shake my head slowly. "That could take a long time Finn."

"I'm not going anywhere, Liv. I just told you that I love you. I'm hardly going to just give up on you."

Finn pushes me gently back on the bed. He lays down next to me but supports himself on his elbow so that he's looking down at me. He lightly brushes the hair from my face and kisses my forehead.

"I know something happened to you to cause your scars, Olivia, inside and out. I don't know when, and I don't know how, but I do know that they've caused you to feel inadequate just as Sydney did, and I can't let you feel that way. I can't bear to see the pain on your face some days, just like Sydney did when she looked in the mirror. Olivia, you're beautiful. I will always tell you how beautiful you are, even when you're tired of hearing it. I'll never ask you to do anything you're not comfortable with okay? That's not me, and you know that."

"I do."

"Take all the time you need, then. I'll do whatever I can for you; I'll protect you, give you everything you need, I just don't want to lose you, Liv."

The almost desperate look in Finn's eyes reminds me of the look he had that first night he stopped by my apartment and saw that I had been crying.

That night...

The texts...

Sydney...

"That night," I look at Finn questioningly. "Our first date, that night you came to my apartment after I left you in the bar."

"Yeah you never returned my texts, and I...."

"You thought of Sydney. You thought I might...do something rash?"

Finn shakes his head, his breathing heavy. "Liv, I couldn't have ever lived with myself if something would've happened to you. I saw the scars that first day we met, but I could also feel that you didn't want me to ask about them, so I didn't. That doesn't mean I forgot about them. I knew you were obviously bothered by them or else you would've talked about it with ease. I couldn't have something happen to another girl because of me. I couldn't leave you alone until I knew you were safe...I just couldn't."

"No...no, Finn, I get it. I scared you that night. I'm so sorry! Had I known then what I know now, I wouldn't have been so insensitive."

"It's okay. Really. It's okay; I just need you to forgive me in advance if I seem overprotective of you. I don't want to smother you or get in the way of achieving your dreams. I just want to keep you safe, and happy, for as long as you'll let me. I don't want to lose what we have, what we're building."

"I don't want to lose you either, Finn."

"Then it's settled. You're mine, and we're together, you and me. I know you still feel like you come from some sort of darkened past, and, Liv, sometimes I feel the same way. Sometimes I have days where the puzzle that is my life feels like it's falling to pieces; but then I met you, Olivia, and after getting to know you a little bit and falling in love with you, I wonder...if maybe my life is actually starting to fall into place."

Be still my fluttering heart.

"Those are feelings I haven't experienced in...well...a very, very long time. I want to spend every day with you. Sometimes, I feel like I can't breathe without you...I just...I feel like I can be free with you."

"I love it, too, Finn," I whisper.

We both smile, and Finn looks around his room for a few moments like he's considering something before settling his eyes back on me. He rests his hand on my waist pulling me into him so that our bodies touch before he clears his throat.

"Right now...we're together, in my *bedroom*, on my *bed*, and I haven't brought anyone in here since high school, so you'll have to excuse me if I take advantage of this situation for just a moment. I really need to kiss the beautiful girl lying next to me."

"She really needs to be kissed," I whisper.

"You're beautiful, Olivia...God, I'm a lucky man," Finn whispers back to me.

*****

We rejoin the group downstairs as Mandy and Karen are preparing to leave. I remember that Mandy has plans tonight with one of our photography assistants, Kym, and I'm grateful I haven't missed the chance to wish her good luck.

She approaches me happily as we reach the bottom of the stairs leading into the foyer and hugs me quickly.

"I'm so happy for you, Olivia. Finn's a great guy. He'll treat you like a princess," she whispers in my ear.

As I let go of her shoulders, I can't hide the elation from my face. I just spent the most wonderful half hour or more with my perfect guy, who just expressed his love for me. He made me feel like a princess. He made me feel like my past didn't matter, that we were made for each other.

I smile and nod my head in Finn's direction but keep my voice down so only Mandy can hear me. "He does treat me like a princess. I'm really not sure where I got lucky with this one. I feel like my clock is going to strike midnight at any moment."

Mandy chuckles as she looks back and forth between Finn and me. "I'll pinch you all you want, but you're not dreaming, Liv. I've seriously never seen him so…relaxed, content, happy. He's a catch, and believe me, if you don't take him, there will be a long line of others who will try!"

My breath catches, and my heart stops. The pang of jealousy and possessiveness rears its ugly head, and I feel heat rise up to my face. No way is some other woman going to waltz in and steal one of the best things to ever happen to me! I take a deep calming breath and raise my eyebrows at Mandy's comment.

"Well, I guess I better work on keeping him interested then," I say with a smirk.

"Interested in what?" Finn asks.

Mandy and I burst into a fit of giggles. What Finn didn't hear won't kill him.

I wish Mandy lots of luck with Kym and say goodbye to Karen before they both leave to head back to the city. The remainder of the afternoon is spent walking through the grounds of the Kellan estate and relaxing on the patio outside with drinks with Mrs. Kellan and her friends. We planned on staying here in town long enough to see the fireworks tonight. They're small, nothing like they do in downtown Boston I hear, but it doesn't matter to me at all where I am as long as I'm with Finn.

"So Finn tells me you're from New York, Olivia?" Mrs. Kellan asks.

"Yes, I am, but it's actually only minutes away from the Pennsylvania border. I'm from a very small town called Narrowsburg. Have you heard of it?"

Narrowing her eyes, Mrs. Kellan kindly replies, "No, I'm sorry I haven't."

"Oh it's okay; not many people know about it. That's what makes it a gem of a place. It's up in the mountains right on the Delaware River. Always so quiet and peaceful...well, except when a storm rolls through. You can hear the thunder roll down the river valley for miles. It's spectacular. Its sounds like our own fireworks show." I smile to myself as I reminisce about my hometown.

"Growing up in a technology age was a bit of a challenge because the cell phone and satellite reception aren't great up there, too many hills and valleys, I guess. But it's great for growing up outdoors...especially as an artist. Narrowsburg is one of those towns you want to tell everyone about so they all can witness its beauty but also don't want anyone to know about so that it always remains the local cultural gem that it is."

"Does your town have a Fourth of July celebration? Ours is small, but it's what we've grown to love."

"Oh, yes, our town throws a celebration for sure. There's the annual parade, which is about ten minutes long, and in the past used to end with just some guy riding his little lawn mower down the street." I giggle. I frown, just then realizing I hadn't seen him at last year's parade.

"Usually the fire department handles the fireworks display, and we all stand along the bridge leading into town to watch them explode over the river. It's beautiful every year."

"Sounds magnificent." Mrs. Kellan smiles taking in every word. "And your family? Do you have siblings?"

"No, it was just me and my parents as I grew up. My dad is a musician at heart, but he and my mom own a small local art gallery downtown. They feature all the local artists from the area: painters, photographers, sculptors."

"Oh, that sounds wonderful! So, you obviously got your passion for photography from them?"

My mind goes blank.

Memories begin to flood my brain.

"She'll never be the model she thought she could be now."

"Nobody would pay to see those scars."

"I heard they're all down her body."

"They can't hide that with any amount of makeup."

"Olivia?"

I felt a hand on my leg, and I jumped in my seat as I'm brought back from the trance I had just fallen into.

"What? Oh…I'm sorry, no. Um, well I guess. I mean, I used to dream about modeling but found that I've enjoyed being behind the camera instead," I explain dismissively.

I feel a slight squeeze on my thigh and look over at Finn's face. His look of concern catches me off guard but only because I didn't realize I had spaced out. I place my hand over his and squeeze to reassure him that I'm fine. Out of the corner of my eye, I see Finn shrug his shoulders to his mom but I pretend not to notice.

"Well it sounds to me like you're a perfect fit at The Kellan Agency, and I can see how great you are with Finn. I hope we get to see a lot more of you around here, Olivia, dear. You are always welcome here."

I smile at her gratefully. "Thank you so much Mrs. Kellan, I appreciate the welcome very much. You have a beautiful home. I love it here." I lean my head back on my chair and squeeze Finn's hand as I smile at him. This has been an unforgettable afternoon.

*****

Solving Us

The sun is bright and warm but will be setting soon. Everywhere around us I can see pink, purple, and red tulips and yellow and white daffodils blooming in flower pots outside homes on the lane. Dandelions are sprouting up in the fields across the road. Lawns are green with fresh grass, and the smell of spring is in the air. It has been a gorgeous day, and I'm feeling happy and content with my life. School is going really well. The end of my junior year is approaching, and I plan on hanging out with my girlfriends over the weekend to plan our dresses for the junior prom. Archer, my high school boyfriend of two years, just asked me to go with him, but I haven't really started looking into dresses yet, though I have some idea of what I'm looking for. I want something strapless to show off my neck, or if Mom doesn't approve, maybe a one shoulder strap sort of deal.

Max and I leave for our nightly walk down the road and back through the wooded path by my house. It's our favorite route because many times Max will get a treat from the old man who lives a few houses down, as he often frequents his front porch in the evenings and will watch us walk by. Most evening runners also keep treats in their pockets in the event that they pass a dog along the way. It's always good to make friends with the animals. Max is such a great companion to walk with at night. It's our chance to bond every day and my time to clear my head from any stress, but this night - this night stress was the least of my worries.

I open my phone to check my last text message from Archer that reads: *I LOVE YOU* <3 when I feel the tug of Max's leash. The force of his pull makes me drop my phone, and I trip and fall onto my left knee scraping it on the pavement. "Fuck! Max!? What the…" I scream trying to look up to see what happened.

Did he get spooked by a squirrel or something?

Instantly my hands get tangled trying to hold on to Max's leash that is already wound around my wrist. I can feel the nylon cutting into me like a huge serrated knife and feel the tug so strong on the other end that I swear my hand detaches from my forearm. There is nothing else I can say or do before my face hits the pavement.

I can't let go of the leash. I'm being dragged in circles and then down the road for what seems like miles. When the dragging stops, I am instantly pummeled by animal feet jumping up and down on top of me. WHAT THE HELL? I'm being trampled! OH GOD! WHAT'S HAPPENING? I can feel my skin peeling right off along my right side and burning in pain with every move my body makes against the pavement. It's like someone is slashing me with tiny razor blades all over the right side of my body and then pushing pebbles inside my already bleeding wounds. I can hear growling and barking, and when I open my eyes, which are swollen and scraped up so badly I can barely see, I do see Max still attached to the end of his leash.

Thank God he's okay!

I feel the tug and pull as he continues to move and jump and…fight?

"MAX, NO!" I scream as loud as I can, hoping he'll stop fighting, but I know in my heart he is in protector mode. My eyes quickly focus on the other dog. I don't know what kind of dog he is, but he's big. He is definitely bigger than Max and stronger. This dog doesn't have a leash and obviously isn't a dog from our neighborhood, and something about this dog has set Max off.

As both dogs fight for position of alpha male, I can't stay out of their way because my hands are still tied up and twisted in Max's leash. All I can do is lie there and be trampled by claws or accidentally bitten by Max, maybe the other dog, I don't know. All I know is that it hurts so damn bad. I think I'm dying.

PLEASE LET THIS STOP!

I try to keep my head down, but every time Max moves to reposition himself, I am dragged along the ground with him. Suddenly I feel claws on my neck and then pressure on my right side, as the other dog uses my body as a springboard in order to jump on Max. I hear Max yelp as he is bitten by his opponent.

"MAX!!" I scream. By now I can't see a thing, not just because of my swollen scraped eyes, but because of the huge fat tears that are streaming down my face.

Solving Us

"It's okay, Olivia. I'm here." Tears are being wiped from my cheek. Pain is searing through my body.

"NO! PLEASE!" I scream.

"Olivia, wake up." The voice calls to me through the chaos.

I shoot straight up in bed panting and exhausted. Immediately I twist my body to the side to check that everything is intact. I wipe more tears from my eyes shocked that I actually cried in my sleep.

"Olivia? Are you okay? God, you're sweating and shaking!" Finn says sitting up next to me. He wraps his arms around me, and I sink into his embrace, trying to wake up enough to realize what's going on. I look around the room a bit disoriented before I finally realize that I'm in Finn's room, in his bed, wrapped in his arms.

Taking a deep breath I whisper, "I'm okay."

"Okay? Olivia, you're shaking. What were you dreaming about?"

"I...umm..." I shake my head, not wanting to tell Finn anything about what just happened to me. "I don't remember." It's a bold lie; I know. I can remember every fucking detail.

Finn's hands slide smoothly up and down my back calming me down. "Shhh. It's okay, Olivia; I've got you. You're okay. It was just a nightmare."

I'm so tired, but I'm afraid to close my eyes. I don't want the dream to continue. I know how it'll end, and I don't want to see it again. I close my eyes, leaning against Finn's chest, allowing his steady breaths and the gentle pulse of his heartbeat lull me back to sleep.

"No. It's okay. I'm good. I'm sorry, Finn."

I don't want to talk about it. Ever.

Finn reaches over to his nightstand and hands me the glass of water sitting there.

"Thanks." I empty the glass in just a few gulps, hand it back to him, and slide back under the covers turning my body away from Finn.

"Come here, Liv. I'm here," he says cocooning me in his arms. "You're not alone." He kisses the back of my head.

"I love you, Liv," is the last thing I hear, as I slip back to sleep.

Chapter 13

From: Olivia McGuire
Subject: Thank you
Date: July 7, 2014 9:03
To: Finn Kellan

Thank you, again, for a fantastic weekend. It meant more to me than you could know.

Yours,
Olivia McGuire
Commercial Marketing, The Kellan Agency

From: Finn Kellan
Subject: Always my pleasure
Date: July 7, 2014 9:07
To: Olivia McGuire

Olivia, you never cease to amaze me. I was honored to introduce you to my family. I hope Mandy hasn't given you too much of a hard time....yet! Dinner tonight?

Always,
Finn Kellan, CEO The Kellan Agency

From: Olivia McGuire
Subject: Hard time
Date: July 7, 2014 9:11
To: Finn Kellan

If by a hard time you mean she hasn't stopped talking to me from her desk even as I sit here emailing you, then yes I would say she's giving me a hard time, but I can handle her :) Don't forget I leave for CA on Wednesday morning, so I need

Solving Us

to get stuff together and pack tonight, but I could make time for a quick dinner. If I pack tonight I could have all evening tomorrow...

Yours,
Olivia McGuire
Commercial Marketing, The Kellan Agency

From: Finn Kellan
Subject: Toby
Date: July 7, 2014 9:17
To: Olivia McGuire

I'm supposed to meet up with Toby for a bit tomorrow evening, but why don't you plan on being with me for that? I would love for you to meet him, and I know he'll be happy to meet you. We'll just hang out at my place; I'll grill something, we can relax a little before your trip. (PS. Don't remind me...I'm already missing you).

Now sad and lonely,
Finn Kellan, CEO The Kellan Agency

From: Olivia McGuire
Subject: Toby
Date: July 7, 2014 9:23
To: Finn Kellan

Any friend of yours is a friend of mine! I would love to meet him. It's a date! (PS. And don't worry, I'll only be gone a few days! Absence makes the heart grow fonder...right?...right?)
Feeling guilty but not really because it's my job, and you're paying me to go sip wine.

Olivia McGuire
Commercial Marketing, The Kellan Agency

FROM: FINN KELLAN
SUBJECT: YOU
DATE: JULY 7, 2014 9:30
TO: OLIVIA MCGUIRE

ARE BEAUTIFUL. I LOVE YOU. SEE YA TONIGHT.

XO,
FINN KELLAN, CEO THE KELLAN AGENCY

Finn's emails always make me smile. He knows how to start off my day with a quick dose of happy to keep me going. With the incessant talking and line of questions coming from Mandy this morning, I needed something to boost my energy. I'm thrilled that she's happy about Finn and me, though, so I really don't mind it all that much. It really is nice to be able to speak freely about him at work to someone who understands. I haven't even gotten to ask Mandy how her date with Kym went. I guess that's going to have to wait until lunch. My email pings one more time. Knowing it will be from Finn, I smile and quickly click it open:

FROM:
SUBJECT: THE TRUTH
DATE: JULY 7, 2014 9:38
TO: OLIVIA MCGUIRE, THE KELLAN AGENCY

IF HE TELLS YOU HE LOVES YOU HE'S LYING.
YOU ARE NOT THE ONE HE WANTS.

I sit at my desk, staring at the screen. Another one? My stomach drops out, and I feel nauseous all of a sudden. Why is this happening? From what Finn says, he's never been in a serious relationship and hasn't been on a real date for three years before he met me, so why is this happening to me?

He did tell me he loves me.
Was he not being honest?

Solving Us

With a shaking hand, I quickly click delete, so I won't have to look at the email anymore.

I take a deep breath and look around the work room to make sure I haven't attracted attention to myself. I need to clear my head and think for a minute. I stand up and walk down the hall so that I can get a drink and splash some water on my face. As I stand in front of the bathroom mirror, I can feel the tension building in my body. I swallow back the tears, so I won't have to explain my puffy red eyes to anyone in the office, and I certainly don't want word getting back to Finn that something has upset me. I know his overprotectiveness will set in and he'll be at my desk in minutes. I don't want that kind of attention. I need to figure this out on my own. I just don't know how to do it.

Because there is no return address on the email, I have no idea how to figure out where it came from. I'm assuming it must have come from inside this building somewhere, has to be on our server, but I could be totally wrong. I'm not tech savvy enough to know how to go about sending an anonymous email, and now I'm not sure if I can trust anyone in the tech department to ask them for help. What if it's one of them? Until I find out, I need to keep a file of these emails in my computer. Once I get back to my desk I click back through my trash inbox and move the email into a private folder. I also move the first email I received a few days ago into the same file to keep everything together. At some point, when I'm feeling brave enough, I can try to piece this puzzle together. Maybe Abby can help me.

After lunch, I spend my afternoon finalizing my itinerary for Wednesday's trip to California. I print off my boarding passes for my flights, directions to the Seal Lake Winery from my hotel, and contact numbers I will need while there. I also pack up my camera and product information, so I can plan my shoot while I'm traveling. By the end of the day, I'm feeling a little more relaxed, ready, and excited to take my first big business trip. I wish Abby could travel to California with me. We could get into a lot of fun together out there; I'm sure. I'm sort of glad Finn's schedule is filled with meetings here, so he can't accompany me either. I know if he did, the subject of sex would come up, and I'm just not sure how I want to handle that part of our relationship.

Of course, I want him. More than anything, I want to be in his arms and more than just in the dark. I want to kiss him and touch him and be held by him, and I know he wants those things, too, but I always allow my insecurities to get the best of me. I'm easily falling for Finn, and we both want more for sure; I'm just not ready for him to quietly walk out of my life once he sees the real me. I fear the inevitable heartache. And with heartache, will also come the inevitable loss of my job.

I finish making a few copies of my itinerary in the work room and head back to my desk. Usually seeing Karen in our office isn't an anomaly, but today something feels off kilter. When I step into the room, Karen's head shoots up from Mandy's cubicle. She sighs heavily before I see her look back down at Mandy and hear her say, "Nevermind, we'll do it later."

I look at both Mandy and Karen curiously but only because something about Karen's demeanor feels oddly suspicious. Nevertheless, she looks up from Mandy's cubicle excitedly smiling at me.

"Olivia, how are your trip plans shaping up? Do you need anything, or do you have any questions you want to go over before you leave? I'll be in meetings most of the day tomorrow, so I wanted to be sure to touch base today."

"Uh," I blink my eyes and shake my head, willing myself to focus on her words. "Yeah, I think I have everything I need. I was just printing off my boarding passes and copying my itinerary. I'm excited to do this!"

Karen smiles and looks at me like a proud mom. "Great. I'm sure you'll be just fine. Be sure to keep my phone number or email handy just in case you run into any issues or have last minute questions. I'm happy to help."

"Thank you, very much. I appreciate the vote of confidence."

"Absolutely. Have a nice glass of wine for me, will ya?"

I smirk and chuckle as Karen walks away. "Sure thing!"

I watch Karen walk out of the office and turn back to Mandy's desk. "What was that all about?"

"What was what all about?" she asks.

"She just seemed . . .I don't know, a little put-off that I walked into the office just now. I'm sorry, was I interrupting something?"

"No not at all; well, I suppose to her maybe you were," Mandy scoffs quietly. "I don't know why she thinks it's a big deal, or that nobody should know about it, but she's taking classes to earn her photography degree since her degree is in Graphic Design. I think she wants to do more for the company one day; I assume something more creative like we do. So, anyway yeah, she was asking me for help on one of her class projects. It's basically an ad campaign so she wants me to go over things with her."

"Oh. Well, I think it's great that she's getting another degree. Seize the day as they say, right? Good for her!" I nod smiling.

"Yeah absolutely. I'm proud of her, but I'm not sure she's really interested in announcing it to the entire agency; so… "

"No worries! My lips are sealed." I wink at Mandy and get back to work.

Chapter 14

I wake up Tuesday morning with a smile on my face. I'm getting excited for my first real business trip. I know in my heart I'm made for a job like this, one where I can use my talent, my passion, to help create something awesome. I'm excited to meet my clients in person and spend a few days taking in the Seal Lake Winery so that I can do my best work for them. I've never been to California before, so I'm hoping I might also have time to take a few hours at some point to just be a tourist. I'm not sure how much of that I will really want to do alone, though; and being in wine country, I know I'll be several hours away from Los Angeles or San Francisco. I'll just have to be flexible and be ready to take full advantage of any down time.

I step back into the apartment from my morning run and see Abby washing her breakfast dishes at the kitchen sink.

"Hey, Abs!"

"Hey, girl! You ready for your trip tomorrow? I'm so jealous! I want to go with you!" she whines.

"Yeah I'm as ready as I can be. I'm anxious to get out there and do my thing. Is it normal to be so excited? I feel like a kid about to go to Disney World." Abby has traveled for work before, so she understands my feelings. Several of her clients are in New York City, Chicago, and even Seattle.

Abby laughs. "This is your first big business trip; of course it's normal to be excited. Just keep your head on so you can stay focused on your task, and you'll be great! Oh, and bring me back a nice expensive bottle of wine, or three."

"You got it, girl. I promise to bring you something good, sweet not dry, white not red." I remember how Abby likes her wine because I have the same tastes. Sweet Moscatos or Rieslings are our favorite.

"So I'm meeting one of Finn's best friends tonight, Toby? I've mentioned him to you before."

Solving Us

Abby frowns for a minute trying to recall what I've told her about Finn and Toby. "Oh yeah right, this is the friend he made after his sister died? I'm a little surprised it's taken this long to introduce you to him if they're such good friends."

"Well, I get the impression that he's not from here in town. They don't see each other all the time. I think every couple weeks or so."

"Ah, gotcha. So," she changes the subject. "Is tonight the night? You know...you're going on a trip...you'll miss each other. Are we finally going to give in to our desires this evening, hmm?" It's no secret with Abby that Finn and I haven't slept together yet. I mean, yes we have slept together, meaning we've fallen asleep in the same bed and woken up together the next morning, but sex hasn't happened, yet; and I know that's all because of me and my insecurities. Finn has definitely tried a few times to get me to loosen up. He says all the right things and touches me in all the right ways; but when push comes to shove, the scars on the lower half of my body make me feel too unattractive for him. He never gives me any indication that my scars bother him; I know it's all in my head. I'm my own worst enemy.

I sigh and look up at Abby while I move my cereal around in the bowl. "I don't know, Abs."

Abby sits next to me. She places her hand over mine getting me to stop playing with my food. "What are you waiting for, Liv? You want it, you know he wants it. So, what's stopping you?"

"What's stopping me? Oh, I don't know. Maybe the fact that I know as soon as he sees me naked, he'll bail just like all the rest of them. Why bother putting myself through that again?"

"Liv, after all this time you can't still be feeling insecure. Are you?"

I close my eyes briefly taking a deep breath. "Yeah, that's exactly how I feel. I don't have a reason to not feel insecure. Abby what if...what if when he runs his hand up my thigh, or when he touches my..."

"Stop. Just stop right there." Abby interrupts putting both her hands up in front of her. "Olivia McGuire you listen to me. Finn Kellan loves you. He fucking LOVES YOU. He took you to his house. He introduced you to his mother; he told you all about his sister. Olivia, guys aren't just open books for any girl to read. Sure, some guys are players and, they'll sleep with anything that moves; and some guys, like Archer, are immature high school dicks who don't know what they have when they have it. But, most good guys aren't that way, and at some point you have to take risks when you find a great guy. And Finn Kellan is a great guy! This one has chosen you to be his person, and I know in that big heart of yours, you have chosen him as well. You're just too afraid to say it. Look, I know guys have walked away from you in the past, and that's their loss. Any guy who says 'no' to you simply isn't worth it. But this guy. Liv, this guy is saying yes. It's you this time. You have to say yes back before he thinks you don't want him."

A tear slips down my cheek at Abby's words. She's right, and I know she's right. Finn is my strength and my weakness. I love him but haven't told him yet. Somehow, I know I have to face my fears and tell him how I feel. The outcome will either go one way or the other, and then I'll finally know.

"I do love him, Abs. I'm so scared to tell him, but I do love him," I cry softly.

"I know you do, Babe. So, stop beating around your own damn bush, yes pun intended, and tell him how you feel. Love is happy this time, Olivia. You have the opportunity to be happy! Don't walk away from that without taking the leap and having a little faith first. Otherwise, you'll always wonder what could've been."

"Now, I have to get to work, and you need to shower! So, let's hug it out, and then I expect to hear good things later. In fact, I take that back. I don't expect to hear good things because I don't expect to see you tonight, if you know what I mean, okay?"

I smile at Abby and wrap my arms around her neck. "Okay, Abs. And thank you, for listening and for not putting up with my shit."

"HA! My pleasure girl! Talk to ya later."

The rest of my day goes pretty quickly. I spend my time at work making contacts with my clients in California, planning part of my photo shoot, and working a little more on the Boston Cruise Line account, editing pictures and layouts. I'll be meeting with them when I return from California to finalize their plans. Thanks to my date with Finn, I already have all the pictures I'll need for that layout. It's just a matter of editing and coming up with a clever new campaign to move the company brand forward.

The end of the day comes quicker than I'm ready for, and before I know it, Finn is walking in to my office laughing with Karen about who knows what.

"Hey, Beautiful. You ready to go?" Finn's eyes light up when he sees me, and he acts as if there is nobody else in the room. In three strides, he's at my side, slipping his arm around my waist, and kissing me.

"Ew gross! I can hear that kiss from over here. Get a room, guys!" Mandy laughs. I open my eyes and smile at her. She winks at me in response, so I know she's only kidding.

"Hmm. Not a bad idea…" Finn jokes. "There's a dark room around here, isn't there?" Finn's eyebrows shoot up in excitement. I'm pretty sure if I said yes, he wouldn't hesitate to pull me in that direction. Instead, his suggestive comment shocks me. I playfully smack his arm and push him away.

"No. No dark room and no more kissing me at work. Do you see what I have to put up with when stuff like that happens?" I gesture to Mandy who is giggling and to the guys in the office who are also smirking at Finn and me.

"S'alright, Liv." Austin laughs. "We'll take our entertainment wherever we can get it,"

Finn nods at Austin and grabs my bag for me. "Okay, okay, I'll settle down, but let's get out of here, so I can kiss you somewhere else."

I shake my head at Finn but can only giggle at the cuteness of him. He certainly knows how to make me blush, and right in front of my boss, too. I know she's a friend of the family but still. Luckily for me, she's laughing right along with everyone else.

"Have a safe trip, Olivia." Karen says on my way out. "Call me if you need anything."

"Thank you. See you all on Monday!" I wave to my colleagues, who I'm happy to say are also my friends, and then step into the elevator with Finn.

Finn wraps his arms around me and buries his face in my hair breathing me in. "Mmm you smell good, and have I ever told you how beautiful you are when you blush?"

"Every time you get the chance," I respond, grinning at him.

"Good." He kisses the top of my head and rubs my back. "Let's go home. I'm excited for you to meet Toby. I know he's going to love you."

"Oh really? And what make you so sure?"

Finn shrugs dismissively. "Because I love you."

He melts my heart.

I lean my face up towards Finn's and kiss him. I kiss him with all the love and passion I can muster in this elevator to show him that I love him, even though I haven't said it yet. Maybe tonight will be the night. The elevator dings, and the door opens, signaling an end to our kiss. Finn takes my hand and leads me to his car.

I've been to Finn's penthouse apartment many times before. It's beginning to feel like a second home for me. Not that he needs it right now, but his apartment boasts three bedrooms and three bathrooms, a bar and lounge area, a small gym, and even a wrap-around patio, complete with a hot tub and a small garden. The walls in the apartment are all a warm beige color with black molding and doorways. Wherever possible, there are floor-to-ceiling windows that provide a breathtaking view of the entire city. It's really hard to imagine just one person living in this space.

Finn changes out of his suit into casual shorts and a vintage t-shirt. He looks delicious in his flip flops out on the patio grilling our dinner. There's something about a man cooking that turns me on. It must be the domesticated look. It's sexy…just like a guy who does dishes…or folds laundry. I decided to stay in my yellow shift dress, rather than bring clothes to change into. It's dressy enough to wear to work but comfortable enough for me to wear all evening. I love that my dress has pockets. They come in handy at work, and honestly, I love that Finn likes to sneak his hand inside them when he hugs me.

"So, what are we dining on tonight, oh grand master chef?" I tease.

Finn grins as he turns his head to look at me. "Tonight, Madame nous allons régaler sur une délicieuse galette de boeuf grillé garni de votre choix de mon meilleur ketchup, la moutarde , la mayonnaise ou , laitue, cornichons , oignons, et bien sûr que le fromage cheddar vieilli mieux."

Whoa! He can speak French?

I can't hold back my laugh any longer. Finn's attempt at describing a food, that isn't at all French, in French makes me giggle uncontrollably. "Okay, first of all, I didn't know you knew French, and secondly, I think I heard ketchup, mustard, mayonnaise, and onions, which means we must be having cheeseburgers?"

Finn lets out a laugh of his own and nods his head. "Yeah, we're having cheeseburgers, Beautiful. I hope you're okay with that."

"Well, who can turn down a Finn burger that is topped with only your finest ingredients, Mr. Chef, Sir?"

"Damn straight." Finn smirks. "They're almost done. Want to pour us a beer?"

"Sure."

Dinner on the patio is magnificent, and to my surprise, Finn's burgers are excellent. He can cook!

"Where did you learn to cook so well?"

Finn takes his last bite and wipes his mouth with his napkin. "Well, after Sydney died, my dad sort of buried himself in his work to stay busy, and Mom checked out for a while. She was too depressed to do anything, and that left me. I needed something to do so that I wouldn't go crazy, and I knew Mom needed me to help take care of her because my dad wasn't helping. I guess it was their own ways of coping, ya know? Anyway, I came home from school more often to be with Mom and Dad, so Mandy would come over sometimes, and we would cook together. She taught me a lot because Karen had taught her. She at least taught me the basics: how to cook rice, spaghetti, chicken, steak. That sort of thing."

"Sounds like you really leaned on each other then, huh?"

"Umm, yeah." Finn swallows looking at me and then immediately looking down at his plate. "Yeah we did. It was, umm...a weird time for all of us, Mandy included, but it's in the past now. We're all moving forward the best way we can."

I tilt my head and smile lovingly at Finn, who looks like he had just gone through the hardest conversation of his life.

"Well, you're right. You do make a mean burger. Thanks for dinner."

"My pleasure, Liv."

The doorbell rings just then. I recognize the sound from all the times we've had food delivered to the apartment. Finn and I both stand up from the table, holding our plates in our hands. Finn takes my plate from me and stacks it on top of his own.

"I'll take care of this if you don't mind getting the door? That'll be Toby; I'm sure." Finn's eyes are wide with excitement. I can tell he can't wait for me to meet him, which excites me in return.

"Absolutely."

I step into the apartment from the patio and make my way down the hall to the front door. Anxious to meet Finn's friend, I unlock the deadbolt and swing the door open with a smile on my face. A smile that quickly fades.

My hand is on my mouth as I gasp in surprise and confusion. My stomach tightens and threatens to give me back my dinner. I can feel myself breaking out in a sweat all over my body. I feel sick and dizzy, but I cannot keep my eyes off of the figure standing at Finn's door.

Max?

Darkness consumes me. I can feel my breath slipping away. My body feels weightless. My eyes close, and I hear a lady scream and then the bark and whimper of a dog, as my body hits the floor.

Chapter 15

Screaming. I'm screaming. I hurt so badly all over my body, and as I open my swollen and puffy eyes, all I can see is blood. My blood. I can feel my skin burning from the pebbles and dirt and debris that has embedded into my thigh, leg, and stomach. My clothes are ripped all over the place. I'm barely even still wearing a shirt.

Where am I?

Max? Where's Max?

I can still feel my hands wrapped up in Max's leash. I'm lying on my back, but my arms are bent to the left side of my stomach. The searing pain coming from my right arm tells me that it is, undoubtedly, fractured. I feel the weight of something or someone laying next to me, so I roll my head to the left. It's Max. He's curled up next to me with his head on my stomach. He's whimpering.

"Oh God, Max! Max!" I try to scream, but my voice just isn't there. I've screamed so much that my voice has completely given out on me. This has to be one of those nightmares where you try and try to scream, but you can't. I'll wake up any minute and, this God-awful nightmare will be over.

I'm not waking up.

This isn't a dream

This is really happening to me.

My throat is aching for a drink, anything to take away the razor sharp pain anytime I try to speak or swallow. I move my hands as much as I can and lay them on top of Max's head, petting him slowly. I can see blood coming from him - or is it me? I can't tell, but either way, there is nothing I can do. My body defies me as I try to move it. All I can do is roll over towards Max and cry.

"I'm so sorry, Max," I sniffle. "I'm so damn sorry." Tears are burning my eyes as they mix with the dirt and pebbles around my face, but I just can't keep them from coming.

"Max, I'm sorry, buddy. I never meant for you to get hurt. Please forgive me, Max."

I cry so hard that I have to keep from vomiting. How the hell am I going to get out of this mess? What the hell happened? Was it another dog? The claw marks on Max are much bigger than I expect them to be. There's a huge gash on his back running down to his hip. It looks like it could've easily been from a bear. He's bleeding so much.

Max saved me from a freaking bear?

"Max," I whisper realizing that Max has most likely just saved my life. Well, if I ever get out of here alive he will have saved my life.

"Max, you're my hero. You stay with me here, buddy. I'll be your hero, too. I promise I will. Don't leave me, Max," I sob.

I roll my head and scoot my body so that I can kiss Max. He saved my life, protected me from another animal. The least I can do is love him until I figure out what to do next. I don't know how long I've been gone from the house. Eventually, if I'm gone long enough someone will come looking for us, right?

"Please let us make it. Please let us be okay," I pray.

Max whimpers next to me, and I cry. I cry so hard I cry myself to sleep right there on the pavement lying next to my hero.

"Liv?"

"Oh my God! Olivia?"

I can hear someone saying my name, and I can feel my body being checked quickly before I'm lifted, but I can't get my brain to tell my eyes to open.

Someone found us, thank God.

I can hear voices talking, but it sounds like mumbles to me. A man's voice? A woman's?

"What could've possibly caused this?" the female voice asks.

"I have no idea. She has to be okay. Oh, God, please let her be okay," the male voice says.

Dad?

"Olivia, Beautiful, open your eyes. Please baby, open your eyes."

Solving Us

That voice doesn't belong to my dad, but it is one I recognize. The fog in my brain starts to lift, and I open my eyes slightly, tears rolling down my face. I stare at the face looking back at me and allow myself a minute to let my brain catch up.

Finn?

What happened?

I look around the room. I'm lying on a couch in Finn's living room. Finn's on his knees, in front of me on the floor. The concerned look on his face is terrifying.

"Olivia?" Finn brushes my hair away from my face and kisses my forehead.

"Baby, you fainted; are you okay? What's wrong? What can I do? Tell me, please!"

My left arm and shoulder hurts, and I have a headache. I look around the room, frowning slowly in confusion. I remember having dinner with Finn and then hearing the doorbell ring. Finn asked me to get the door for him. It was Toby. No, it was some woman with a dog.

Toby.

Toby?

Toby is a dog?

Toby looks like Max...

Dog?

Toby is a dog?

Finn's best friend is a dog?

I gasp and sit up on the couch, immediately hugging my legs and resting my head on top. I sit there trying to breathe. I feel the wet nose on my leg before I hear the whimper of the dog sitting next to Finn. I can't hold my stomach back this time. I can feel the bile rising in my throat. I throw my hands over my mouth and dart off the couch for the bathroom where I slam the door just before I violently throw up.

Is this a sick joke?

How the hell does Finn know about Max?

Why would he do this to me?

He said he loved me...

The email...
Is Finn sending me those emails?
I'm sobbing into a towel when I hear Finn knock on the door.

"Olivia please, are you okay? What can I do? Please let me help you."

"Go away, Finn." I whisper unable to talk.

"Liv, I'm coming in. It's okay; you just fainted. I need to make sure you're okay, that you didn't hurt yourself."

I muster up the energy to shout a little louder. "I'm fine, Finn! Go away!"

"I'm not leaving you, Liv. I'll give you your privacy if you want it, but I'm not leaving this spot. I'm worried about you, Beautiful."

I am so sad, hurt, and confused. I don't know which way is up or down, in or out. I clean myself up, rinse my mouth out, and wash my face. I can't keep the tears from streaming down my face, so I give up and let them fall. I can feel a storm brewing in my soul and have no idea how to tame it. Quite frankly, I'm not sure I want to this time. I open the door and immediately come face to face with Finn, whose eyes are as big as the moon. I don't even give him time to speak before I lay into him.

"What is this, Finn? What kind of sick joke is this?"

"Olivia?" Finn asks confused.

"How did you know? Tell me? How did you know about Max? Just how much of my life do you know about that you're not telling me?" I realize I'm beginning to shout, but I'm not in the mindset to try and control my emotions.

Finn's eyes shoot up in shock. "Whoa! Olivia, slow down. What are you talking about?" He reaches out and cups my cheek with one hand, but I immediately slap him away.

"Don't touch me, Finn!" I sniffle. "And don't play games with me. Why did you bring that dog here? Why did you make up some fucked up story about your friend Toby...who is a DOG...a dog JUST like my Max? Why? Why would you want to hurt me like that?"

"Max?" Finn is shaking his head frowning. He looks totally confused, which I don't understand. "I don't... Olivia, who is Max?"

Solving Us

"Stop it. I'm not playing your games, Finn. You said you loved me," I cry. "They all say they love me, and then...damnit!" I let out my breath in a huff. "You're just like them. I can't. I just can't."

I make my way quickly to the foyer, grab my purse and bag from work, and open the front door. I take a deep breath and turn around to look at Finn, tears streaming down my face. "Just when I thought my heart was healing, when I thought I was falling in love again..." I shake my head. "I really thought you were different."

I walk out the door and into the elevator, slamming the button for the bottom floor. The last thing I hear before the elevator door closes is Finn shouting, "Toby, stay! Olivia, wait! I love you. Wait please let me..."

I'm done. I've just endured a full-fledged panic attack brought on by the one person who promised to protect me. I can't handle this. I want to run; I want to scream. I want to cry. How can he hurt me like this? Why not just tell me he doesn't love me anymore? Why throw my past in my face like this? How did I wrong him to make him want to do this to me? I run off the elevator when the door opens and hurriedly get into the first cab the doorman can find for me.

"I need to stop at home for just a second, and then could you drop me at Boston Logan Airport please?" I am going to run. I'm going to fly to California tonight. I'll just change my ticket and take the last flight out. That way, Finn can't follow me and try to explain himself. He won't even know where I am tonight, and that is just fine with me. I won't have to put up with anymore tonight. I just need to calm myself down enough to text Abby and get home to get my stuff before leaving. I need to do it quickly before Finn drives himself to my place and waits for me.

The cab pulls up in front of my apartment building. I shoot out of the car and up to my apartment as fast as I can. My cell phone has already rung three or four times in the cab ride over here, and I can hear it ringing again, the chorus of "What Makes You Beautiful" by One Direction now etched in my brain. Finn set my ringtone a few weeks ago to that song as a reminder to me that he thinks I'm beautiful, regardless of my own personal insecurities.

For right now though, I'm intentionally ignoring it. I don't even want to see Finn's face on the caller ID. I grab my suitcase that I had packed, along with my bag from work that has my files and camera inside. I packed light enough that I shouldn't have to check any of my luggage, which should make traveling easier. Before I leave, I scribble a note quickly to Abby telling her that I had been here and am leaving early for California. I need someone trustworthy to know where I am just in case. My parents don't know what's going on in relationship world because I didn't want to give them all the details just yet, so there is no sense in calling and confusing them. I make my way downstairs and outside, back into the cab that was waiting for me. I'm grateful for my cab driver. He seems like a nice enough man who can see that I'm distressed. I'm sure he knows I'm running. He just doesn't know what I'm running from.

In about an hour, I'm registered, checked in, and boarded on an evening flight to Chicago, which at this time of night is the closest I could get to California, but I don't care. Chicago will put me halfway to my destination for tomorrow's trip. I pay the extra money for a first class ticket, since those are the only seats they have left. I just need to get out of Boston. I sit back in my seat, open my bottle of water and take a long healthy drink. I close my eyes and try my best to relax until the plane lands. Easier said than done.

Chapter 16

My flight to Chicago is under three hours, so I'm on the ground by eleven, Eastern Time. I turn my phone on quickly to see if I've received a text from Abby and also to call a hotel to find a room for the night. As soon as my phone is on, it practically explodes in my hand with text messages and voicemails. Most are from Finn, begging me to tell him I'm okay and that he loves me. I knew he would be beside himself with worry over me, but as far as I'm concerned he deserves it. I also have a text from Mandy asking where I am, which I choose not to return. I'm sure she's only asking on Finn's behalf, and I don't want him to know where I am just yet. He'll know where I am in the morning.

I'm just about to turn my phone off and return it to my purse when it rings in my hand. Seeing Abby's picture come up on my caller ID, I decide to go ahead and answer it.

"Abby, hey."

"JESUS CHRIST, Olivia! Where the fuck are you, and what the hell happened? Are you okay? Did he hurt you? What the fuck, Liv?"

"I'm okay. I'm in Chicago, on a layover to California. I'm staying here tonight. I just had to get out of town, so I decided to leave early."

"What the ever-loving fuck? Oh my God, Liv, I...I'm so sorry. This is absolutely not the way I saw your night going, Babe. What the hell happened?"

"Did Finn call you?" I ask curiously.

"Only about fifty fucking times, yeah! He's worried sick about you. Even more so given I didn't know what he was talking about, or where you were, when he stopped by here looking for you. He's confused and doesn't understand what happened either. He just said you kept talking about Max, but he doesn't know who Max is."

"Bullshit," I mumble. "Abby, you know Finn's so-called friend, Toby? The friend I was supposed to meet tonight?"

"Yeah?"

"Well Toby is Max. No, wait. Toby is a dog! A fucking chocolate lab who looks somehow, ironically just like Max did, except Max is DEAD, Abby! Max saved my life and died for me, and he's never coming back, so what the fuck was Finn trying to do to me?" I yell into the phone. Realizing I'm in an airport terminal, and that people are staring at me, I try to quickly find the nearest private corner.

I hear nothing but silence coming from the other line for what feels like long minutes. "Oh, Olivia, are you...wow...I don't even...Liv, are you okay?" Abby asks, flabbergasted.

"I'm better now, but when I opened the door, I saw Max and I - I fainted. I had a killer flashback and woke up on Finn's couch with this dog whimpering and wiping his wet nose all over me. I panicked, threw up in Finn's bathroom, screamed and cried at him, and left immediately. I mean, what kind of sick twisted game is that? How does he KNOW all of this stuff about me, Abby? And why would he even consider doing this to me?" I can feel my tears racing down my face. I'm sure I'm great entertainment for anyone sitting around me or passing by.

"Wow..." Abby whispers. "I don't know, Liv. I really don't know. I'm speechless. I mean...is it even remotely possible that this is a huge misunderstanding? I mean, please Liv, I'm not trying to make excuses for him. This just all seems so...weird, ya know?"

"I don't know, Abs. Maybe he thought I would get over my fears if he brought me face to face with a dog, but how did he even know about Max or that my fears stem from anything dog related at all? We've never talked about it! Ever!"

"Olivia, honey, I don't have any answers for you this time. All I can do is try to talk to him if, and most likely when, he calls me again to check on you. What do you want me to say to him?"

"Fuck off would be nice," I huff.

Abby chuckles. "I can do that. I can definitely do that, but since you won't be here, can I hear him out on your behalf? I promise you, if I find out he's being a douche on purpose, I'll kick him in the nads for you myself."

This time I chuckle as I sniff my nose and wipe my tears. "Yeah I trust you...and I'm glad I don't have to be there. At least I have something to do a few miles away to keep me busy."

"Okay I'll find out what's going on, and I'll keep in touch with you if I can. Where are you staying tonight?"

"Umm...I don't know yet. I'll just find the closest one."

"Liv, stay at the Hilton. It's connected to the airport, and it's where I stay when I'm there for business. Just find the indoor walkways. That way, you don't have to worry about cabs or being out late in the city by yourself. You just travel safely and try to relax on your trip. Drink some extra wine, and if you do need someone, call me. I'll be on the next flight out there."

"I love you, Abs. Thanks"

"You're welcome. Love you too, Liv," she says sympathetically before she hangs up.

I spend the night in Chicago, in a hotel as close to the airport as possible, so I can be ready to go in the morning. I already have my new boarding pass for the flight I was supposed to take as my layover flight tomorrow, so I don't have to be up too early in the morning. I haven't heard anything from Abby throughout the night and have purposely not checked my phone for texts or emails. I know I'll have more missed texts from Finn that I don't want to see.

By noon Pacific Time I've landed in Sacramento. I spot the man who is my driver from the Seal Lake Winery almost immediately after walking off the plane. He is an older man, grey haired and short in stature, wearing a dark green Seal Lake Winery polo shirt with dark blue khaki pants. He introduces himself to me as Tom Haught and escorts me to a Lincoln Navigator SUV waiting outside.

Once I'm in the car, I open my phone and email Karen quickly to let her know that my plane landed, and I'm on my way to the winery. I'm praying that Finn didn't get so worried that he called kingdom come searching for me. I don't need people thinking I disappeared. I have faith that Abby will have set everyone straight. The drive to the winery takes almost two hours, so I lay my head back and catch a quick nap before starting my day. I've gone over all my plans, so I feel more than prepared to meet my clients. The music Tom has playing in the car is just relaxing enough to lull me to sleep peacefully. I awake as we are pulling into the winery, quickly adjust my clothes, and gather my belongings. I braided my hair earlier in the day, so I knew I would at least look presentable stepping out of the car after a long morning of travel.

Chapter 17

"Good afternoon, and welcome to Seal Lake Winery," a smiling young man greets me from the front desk. He looks like someone I might see if I Googled "California surfer dude". He's tall and obviously lean with shaggy blonde highlighted hair that hangs over his ears. I almost laugh at the cliché of him but bite the inside of my mouth to keep focused on why I'm here.

"Hi." I smile at him. "My name is Olivia McGuire. I'm the marketing photographer from The Kellan Agency in Boston. I have a meeting with Mr. and Mrs. Taylor."

"Oh yeah, right. They're expecting you, sorry." He holds his hand out to shake mine. "My name is Jason. Mr. and Mrs. Taylor are my parents. Welcome. I can take you to the conference room."

"Great. Thank you very much."

We walk through the main lobby and outside onto the lake side of the estate. From where we are walking, I have a perfect view in front of me of Seal Lake, but I can also see fields of gardens all around us. There's a field off to my left of nothing but what I can only guess is lavender; the light purple blooms sway effortlessly in the breeze off the lake. The entire estate seems to be nestled between what looks like dry rolling hills. I wonder to myself if the winery might look sort of like a desert mirage from a helicopter view. I can't wait to get a tour of the place. The grounds around me are breathtaking. I secretly wish I would have reserved a room here instead of a local hotel nearby.

"This is all so beautiful here. How do you not just want to sit outside and breathe this all in everyday?" I ask Jason.

"Many people do want to just sit outside and breathe it all in every day. I imagine that's why we keep a full calendar of visiting guests all year round. There's never a time during the year when it's not beautiful here, and there's rarely a time when we aren't booked to capacity. We get a lot of honeymooners and retired couples looking for new travel adventures, and execs from the city are constantly bringing clients here for business meetings."

"Well, I can see why."

"Don't worry," Jason says, chuckling at my obvious tourist-like behavior. "You'll like where you're staying tonight. It's one of our more popular bungalows."

I frown at Jason in confusion but keep walking. "Oh you must have me confused with someone else. I'm reserved at the Hilton this evening."

"You were, yes. But someone called this morning and asked that we reserve a bungalow for you. Mrs...." He couldn't remember the name, but there was only one obvious choice.

"Hoover? Mrs. Hoover?"

"Yeah that's it. Mrs. Hoover called to make the reservation. She said Mr. Kellan thought you deserved to experience everything we have to offer while you're here."

I narrow my eyes at Jason's mention of Finn. As much as I want to be in charge of my own plans, that's not how it works when you're on a business trip; and I certainly don't want to be rude to anyone by refusing to stay here just to spite Finn. That would make the company look bad as well.

"Oh. Okay, but didn't you say you guys are always booked to capacity?" I ask.

"Yes, but we were able to pull some strings for Mr. Kellan. No worries. You'll love it; I promise."

I nod my head thankfully. "Sounds absolutely wonderful. Thank you."

My stomach knots all of a sudden, and anxiety washes over me.

Please tell me Finn isn't coming here...

"Umm...there isn't anyone else staying here is there? From the Kellan Agency, I mean? It's just me right?"

Jason looks at me almost annoyed with my question, which in hindsight does sound a bit crazy. You would think I would know if someone else from my own agency had traveled cross-country with me.

Solving Us

"You're name is the only one on the reservation. It makes sense really, that you stay here on the property. You'll have anything you want at your fingertips for this ad campaign," he explains. Jason is right, and I'm relieved. I'll be able to take pictures all afternoon and evening and then have some private time to work on a layout. We make it to the conference building where Jason introduces me to his parents and owners of the winery.

"Pleasure to meet you, Mr. and Mrs. Taylor. I'm Olivia." I say shaking both of their hands. "This place you have here is absolutely breathtaking. You both must be so proud."

"Pleasure to meet you as well, Olivia, and yes. Kate and I are very proud of what we've been able to accomplish here at Seal Lake. It was an opportunity we couldn't pass up." Mr. Taylor wears a smile that can light up a room as he puts his arm around his wife.

"Thank you, Olivia, for traveling all this way to meet with us. We know the Kellan Agency is one of the best in the country, and Mr. Kellan sent us your name under his highest recommendation."

I'm sure he did...

"Well, I'm looking forward to this project very much. I'm excited to get to work."

We spend the next hour going over ideas and plans for pictures around the winery. The Taylors are looking to focus on their newest organic approach to farming the ingredients used in their wines, from soil choices to compost production. Every aspect has an extraordinarily natural feel that I find to be exciting and innovative. From there, I help them brainstorm ideas on how to emphasize their organic farming to best suit their wine brand. When we're done talking, it is then up to me to spend the remainder of my day and part of the day tomorrow walking the grounds to take pictures of the natural aspects of the winery so that I have an array of images to work with when I get home.

"There are still several hours of sunlight left, but when the sun sets, it creates a beautiful color palette over the lavender fields! You won't want to miss it," Mrs. Taylor explains excitedly.

"Fantastic. Then I'll be sure not to. Thank you both very much for meeting with me." I shake both of their hands again. "I'll get to work and let you know if I need anything."

"Sounds great. Enjoy your stay, Olivia. We'll have your bags delivered to your bungalow. Just stop back at the welcome house to get your key when you're ready."

"I will. Thank you again." I smile. I take my camera out of my bag and get to work. This should be the best part of my day. I need time to be alone, to work, to think...just my camera and me. I'm too afraid to turn my phone on at this point because I don't want to deal with the hundreds of text messages I'm sure are waiting for me from Finn, or Abby, or Mandy, or even Karen.

I walk down through part of the lavender field, snapping several shots along the way. The smell coming from the field is magnificently sweet. Eventually, I end up on the pier at the lake. Looking out at the water reminds me of my apartment view of the river, except that here, everything is calmly quiet. There is no traffic noise, sirens, car horns, or even helicopters. I did, however, notice on my walk down here that the winery has their own helipad. I shouldn't be surprised. I'm sure some of their executive clientele take advantage of it regularly, especially given the lengthy drive here from any major city.

I walk for a while, taking advantage of the sunlight to snap pictures of some of the other gardens in the area. I see vine gardens, flower gardens, walnut gardens, and vegetable gardens. I photograph the free roaming chickens and a small group of sheep. I even find the compost piles. By sunset, I'm back at the lavender fields, and just as Mrs. Taylor had told me, the colors emanating from the field are stunning. Beautiful shades of purple, gold, green, yellow, and pink reflect off the water as the sun sets behind the lake and shines through the fields. It is a glorious evening.

I eat a late dinner on the winery's restaurant patio so that I can enjoy the ambiance around me. I've even found my favorite new wine here. It's a Muscat canelli wine that has a sweet peachy flavor, something I've never tried before. It's delicious, and I can easily see myself drinking the entire bottle, so much so that I purchase the entire bottle rather than just a glass so that I can take it back to my bungalow with me. I make a mental note to pick up a bottle, or seven, for Abby before I leave. My dinner is five-star, which doesn't surprise me at all. I even take a minute to snap a few pictures of my food before I eat it, thinking I can somehow use the images in my project.

Do you always take pictures of your food?
Finn...

I've been able to distract myself for most of the afternoon, but now I sit at my table feeling more alone than I've felt in a long time. The events of the last twenty-four hours come crashing down on me. I can feel the tightness in my chest, as my anxiety grows stronger. I bring my feet up to my seat and wrap my arms around my legs, resting my chin on my knees. I stare out at the lake for long minutes. Sighing to myself, I replay everything that I remember happening yesterday in my head a few times. Opening the door and seeing Max, no, Toby. Was that even his name? Who was the woman who had the dog with her, and why was she even there? The more I think about it, the more I just don't understand.

How did he know about Max?
Who would have possibly told him?
Why?
What was he trying to prove?
I loved him.
Correction...

"I still love him," I whisper to myself. "That's why this hurts."

I sigh again, wipe the tear from my cheek, grab my camera and my bottle of wine, and start my walk down to the lake where my private bungalow is located. The smart me would've gone to the welcome house to ask for a golf cart ride down there, as I'm positive I've had at least two too many glasses of wine. Being inebriated on the job isn't very respectable, though, so I decide to walk it off so nobody sees me. I've done enough work for the day. It's time to drown my sorrows in the rest of this wine and sleep my heartache away. Maybe I'll turn my phone on and call Abby first to let her know I'm okay and see if she spoke to Finn today. Hopefully, I'll be strong enough to avoid Finn's messages. I fear if he calls, I won't be strong enough to not answer it.

Chapter 18

It's dark as I make my way to my bungalow, but the pathway down to the lake is lit with antique hanging lanterns. It's like a page out of a magazine, which makes me chuckle and shake my head as that's what I'm doing here in the first place. The pleasant weather and the sweet smells coupled with the warm glow emanating from the lanterns create a beautiful, dream-like atmosphere. It's like this is my private little aisle of Heaven, and at the end of my walk, I'll find the love of my life waiting for me.

"If only," I say to myself.

I reach my bungalow from the back and walk around the building, grabbing the key out of the pocket of my dress. I raise my head to see the steps leading up to the porch so that I don't stumble, and I immediately know the beautiful little dream I envisioned during my walk here has either just come true or is about to become another nightmare. Finn is standing at my door. He's facing my door with his hand raised, like he's trying to decide just when to knock. He must not know I'm not in there. Well, obviously, he doesn't know, or he would've come looking for me. Do you know that feeling you get when you're about to be pulled over for speeding? The anxiety, the racing heart, the adrenaline rush, the fear…whatever it is. That's me right now. I'm not sure whether to be afraid or excited. Did my white knight just come to rescue me, or are we about to end whatever it was we had?

"Finn?" I say quietly from behind him, so quietly I'm not even sure I say his name out loud.

I must have said it loud enough, though, or he heard me walk up to the porch. Either way, Finn turns away from the door toward me, his arm still raised in the knocking position, his eyes wide. I surprised him.

"Therapy dog," he says quickly.

I'm standing approximately five feet from Finn, who is now standing on my porch steps. I stare at him blankly. I think I'm just as surprised to see him as he is to see me. Finn takes a deep breath and closes his eyes, steadying himself. His next words are so quick I'm not sure my fuzzy, wine-filled brain is keeping up correctly.

"Olivia, Toby is my therapy dog. I've been spending time with him once a week, or sometimes more, ever since Sydney died. He's my therapy dog, and that's all, and I'm sorry. I'm so fucking sorry that I didn't know about Max. Please, Liv, he's my *therapy* dog. He's the only steady thing in my life besides you, Olivia. He's my *therapy* dog. Please, Liv. Don't run off, and don't walk away. Please talk to me," he desperately pleads. He could easily be on the verge of tears.

I stand frozen. All I can do is stare at Finn. I can feel the emotions coming, but the wine I just consumed has blurred my brain enough that I'm actually having trouble processing what Finn just said.

Therapy dog?

"Olivia. Please, Beautiful...talk to me." Finn starts to walk towards me but stops short when I snap my head up to look him in his eye. His proximity to me causes my adrenaline to spike, which helps my head clear a little.

"You have a therapy dog? You got on a plane and came all this way to tell me that you have a therapy dog?" I need to try to put these puzzle pieces together.

"Yes, Olivia, and his name is Toby. The woman with him yesterday was a friend of my mom's and Toby's owner. He's a trained therapy dog, and once a week she brings him to my place to hang out with me. He calms me and brings me back to reality sometimes when I feel overwhelmed or stressed...or scared, especially when I'm missing Syd or my dad. My therapist recommended him, said I was experiencing PTSD sometimes, but I didn't want medicine," he quietly explains. He's still trying to approach me slowly as he speaks. "He's been in my life for years now, and I'm so damn sorry I didn't tell you all about him before. I just..."

Finn takes another deep breath and sighs heavily. He looks tremendously sad and bewildered. I begin to feel bad for him. "I can't imagine many girls are attracted to a powerful young CEO who carries lots of excess personal baggage and has a therapy dog to help get through the stresses of life. I was scared you would leave and never look back." He puts his hands out in defeat and shrugs his shoulders. "This is me, Liv. I love my job, and I'm good at what I do, but it's not enough for me. Emotionally, I feel like I'm this little kid whose family has been leaving him one person at a time, and when they're all gone, Liv, when my Mom is gone, it'll just be me all by myself in this world, and I don't want that, Liv. I want you. I love you, and I never, ever meant to hurt you yesterday. I just didn't know. You never told me about Max, so I'm sorry. I just didn't know."

My breathing is getting faster as I listen to him speak. Tears are falling off my cheek that I hadn't even noticed I was crying, and my fingers are absentmindedly turning the ring on my finger that I wear in memory of Max. I shake my head to refocus on what is happening and stalk forward past Finn up onto the porch to unlock the door.

"What are the chances, Finn?" I ask turning to look at him painfully, as I step into my bungalow. I'm so distracted by my emotions I don't even take a minute to look around and take in the beauty of the room around me. I do hear a radio playing, though. I'm guessing the maid who was here earlier to prepare the room must've left it on, or maybe it's what they do for all guest rooms. I try not to roll my eyes at the irony of the song I hear coming from the speaker, Pink's "Don't Let Me Get Me".

"What are the chances that your therapy dog looks exactly like my Max? A damn chocolate lab, Finn...really?"

"Probably about a million to one, Liv, but I swear to you I didn't know about Max. I spoke to Abby last night, and she told me your reaction was because of an old dog you used to have named Max, but she didn't tell me the whole story. She said it was your story to tell and that you would tell it if, and when, you're ready; and I totally understand that, probably more so than most people. I understand not wanting to talk about your past, Liv. I get it. I do. And I'm not ever going to push you; but I need you to believe that I would never, ever, ever hurt you, and I just - I didn't know. I'm sorry. It killed me watching you go through what happened yesterday. I would do anything to take that pain away from you. Had I known, I would've given you a heads up or not invited him at all until you were ready."

Tears are pouring down my face now as I stand there listening to Finn apologize over and over again. I want to collapse and let him catch me. I want to run into his arms and let him hold me. I want to take him to bed and let him touch me. He flew across the entire damn country to talk to me. There's no way he's making this up, and I'm actually grateful that he is here talking to me now, making me listen; but what he doesn't understand is that I am also broken. It's not just him.

"That pain, Finn? That pain never goes away for me. It will *never* go away for me," I sob. "Every fucking day I'm reminded of what happened to me. Can you understand that? Do you want to know what happened to me, Finn? Do you want to know why I look like this?" I pull my right sleeve down past my shoulder to expose the scars on my neck and collarbone. I tilt my head to the left to be sure Finn can see what I'm showing him, not that he hasn't seen them before. I've just never shown him my body with the lights on.

"Do you want to know Finn why every time I see a dog, let alone one that looks like Max, I freak out? Why I have continuous nightmares and flashbacks? Why I have so much anxiety around dogs?"

Finn shakes his head. "Olivia you don't owe me any explanations. That's not why I'm here."

"I took my dog for a walk one day," I continue, not listening to him. "And ended up with a body torn to shreds, bleeding from head to toe, a broken arm, broken fingers and a dying dog who laid with his head on my stomach for almost twelve hours before someone found us."

"Olivia…"

"HE DIED, FINN!" I yell. "Max DIED saving my life! He saved me from a bear. Max tried to fight him off, but my hands got tangled in his leash, and I couldn't let go, so I had to endure the GROWLING and the BARKING and the SCRATCHES and being DRAGGED along the ground as they fought and ran through the woods and down the road. I laid there and took the blow when Max would jump and accidentally land on me. I couldn't let go, Finn. And now every day when I shower, or when I look

Solving Us

in the mirror, I'm reminded of that day. Every day I look at my hideous scars and wish that it were ME that died that day and not Max because nobody wants this." I gesture to my body sobbing.

"Olivia, please don't say that. It's not true," Finn says softly shaking his head again.

"ISN'T IT?" I shout. "You can't honestly tell me that after looking at my ripped up scarred body that you would prefer me over some other perfect girl out there. Someone whose body isn't flawed like mine."

Finn's eyes grow large. He snaps back at me. "You must not think very highly of me, then, if you honestly believe I would choose some other girl over you because of a few scars."

"What I think is what I know, Finn, and what I know is that every other guy who has ever told me he loved me or has held me in his arms has left me once they've seen the real me. I'm not beautiful, Finn. There's no making love to me. Being with me is like fucking some old lady with wrinkled flabby skin."

"STOP IT, OLIVIA!" Finn shouts back at me. "I don't ever want to hear you talk about yourself that way again. That's enough! You're wrong! You're wrong about the way you look, and you're wrong about my love for you. Why can't you see that?"

"I'M NOT WRONG, FINN! I'm right, and I'll prove it, and then you can laugh or be disgusted or turned off or whatever the hell you want. Then you can get the hell out and leave me alone," I cry.

I quickly lift the hem of my dress over my head and throw my dress on the floor. I'm standing in the middle of the living room in my bungalow wearing only my pink lacy bra and panties. My breaths came fast and hard, and I can't stop my sobs.

"This," I say trying to keep my pride in check. "This is what you get with me, Finn. Go ahead, look all you want." I throw my head into my hands and cry. I'm pissed and ashamed and embarrassed. This is how it happens. The guy I start to give my heart to sees the monster that I really am. He realizes that I'm a puzzle that can't be solved, and he leaves me to pick up my own pieces. I know I'm right when I hear the door close that I had left open when we walked in. I'm standing alone and exposed in the middle of the room, left with no more dignity, nothing but an ugly cry.

    Finn is gone.
    I've lost.
    He isn't my Prince Charming.
    I'm devastated.

Chapter 19

Son of a bitch.

I can't believe what a nightmare this night has become. How could I have let myself fall in love so easily when I knew what the outcome would be? What am I going to do when I get back to Boston? Do I even still have a job there? Do I even still want a job there?

Hell, no.

I need to get out of here.

I need Abby.

She'll know how to help me.

I wipe the tears off my cheeks and open my eyes so I can find my dress, but instead, to my disbelief, I find Finn, standing in the middle of the room watching me. I'm so startled, I gasp loudly.

He didn't leave.

He's not looking at my body, though; he's looking into my eyes. Not with pity but with love, and dare I say it, adoration. Keeping his eyes on mine, he approaches me slowly and sinks to his knees in front of me. He doesn't say a word. My eyes are puffy from crying, my head is pounding, and I now have goose bumps all over my body; but I bow my head towards Finn so I can see what he's doing. He is now face to face with the ugliest part of me, the part of me I hate the most.

Like it's perfectly timed choreography, Finn's hand wraps around my right thigh as Labrinth's voice begins to sing, "Beneath Your Beautiful" on the radio. Finn softly runs his right hand over my scars. I gasp, and my lips part at his touch. I'm scared and a little confused but also instantly aroused. I'm not sure what to do, or how to react, so I stand there allowing him to touch the ugly parts of me while I listen to the lyrics of the song filling the room around us. He takes his time and deliberately traces every scar on my thigh and my hip as if he is healing me with his touch. When he reaches the scars on my stomach, he places both of his hands on me, one on my stomach and one on my lower back to hold me still, as he leans in and kisses my belly. He continues up the roadmap of scars on my abdomen and all the way to my rib cage, placing kisses over each one. I release the shaky breath I didn't know I was holding, and with it comes another flood of tears. Standing here in this well-lit living room, my body on display, I'm facing my biggest fear, and I'm not alone.

My walls are crumbling for the man in front of me, the man I'm allowing to see beneath my beautiful as the song is saying to me. It's all so overwhelming, and I can't stop my emotions. Finn stands up and wipes the tears cascading down my face, watching me as I cry, allowing me to let go of my emotions the only way I know how.

"Listen to me," he whispers. "I'm in love with you, Olivia; I'm in love with all of you. I'm in love with the way your hair feels when I run my fingers through it. I'm in love with the way your nose scrunches up when you laugh. I'm in love with your voice when I get to hear it on the other end of the phone or when I catch you humming in the car. I'm in love with your hands and how they feel when they're inside mine...like abstract puzzle pieces that fit together perfectly. And when you cry?" he says softly, wiping another tear from my face with his thumb. "I fall in love all over again with the warmth of your tears and the sincerity in your eyes."

"Finn…"

Finn quickly places a finger on my mouth to silence me. He isn't letting me speak.

He isn't letting me speak because he wants to be heard.

He trails his hand down the right side of my body over my neck and down my rib cage just under my breast. "Your scars are so beautiful. They don't show your weakness, Olivia; they show your strength." He tilts his head as his hands roam up and down my torso. His feather light touch sends sparks of excitement through me. "Sometimes, Liv," he whispers to me. "Sometimes the ugliest parts of ourselves are the parts others love the most. And these parts here, they're my favorite part of you because they remind me of who you are. You're strong, Liv, so much stronger than my sister." Finn's eyes start to water. "And I love you for that, so much. For reminding me every day that strength and love and happiness can come from pain."

All the air in my body escapes me. If I wasn't in love with Finn Kellan before this moment, there is no going back now.

I look up at him astounded that he would even say such sweet words to me. I don't even have a response. All I can do is sniffle and wipe more tears from my face. Finn cups my head with both hands and sweetly kisses my lips, and before I know it, we are swaying together in an emotionally charged slow dance. He bends over and picks me up cradling my body in his arms as we continue to sway together. I wrap my hands around his neck and weave my fingers through his hair. Spying the large king-sized canopy bed on the other side of the room, Finn carries me in that direction.

He lays me down on the bed and hovers over me, wiping away my remaining tears with his thumb and kissing each of my cheeks. He sits up for one moment and slowly pulls his shirt up over his head. There is no mistaking where he wants this to go, and this time, I'm right there with him. I'm ready.

I want him to love me. I need him to love me in this moment, right here, right now, like I need my next breath.

I reach up as Finn lowers his body on top of mine and weave my fingers into his hair, pulling his lips down to mine. We stay in this position for a moment, not kissing, just breathing each other in, together. Feeling his tongue brush across my lips when we kiss sends fireworks throughout my body, and I'm instantly on fire for him. I can feel the strength in his hand as he grasps my right thigh and pulls it towards him. I immediately tense when I feel his hands running across my scars, but he doesn't allow me to feel fear.

"It's okay, Liv. I love you. Please, let me love you." He runs his hand down the back of my thigh and gently squeezes my behind, and I immediately relax. He brings out the calm in me. The moan that escapes my mouth makes Finn smile against my skin as he trails kisses across my jaw and down my neck. I giggle slightly when his lips touch the spot just under my earlobe, and he chuckles next to me. He knows this is one of my more sensitive spots, and where I love his lips to linger, so he stays there, in the crook of my neck tasting my skin.

I secretly hope he leaves a mark.

I lightly run my fingernails down Finn's back as he's folded over me, and he releases his breath into my neck as his hips push toward me, enough that I feel how aroused he is. I arch my back to press my body as close to his as I can get, and as I do, Finn slides his hands underneath me. He unhooks my bra and quickly helps tear it off of me, tossing it on the floor. We're skin against skin now, well, mostly. I place my palm on Finn's chest reveling in the firmness of him before dragging my fingers down his sternum to his belt buckle. I slip my fingers into the waistline of his shorts, and I feel the tip of his erection waiting to be released. Finn hisses as he sucks in a breath. I hastily unbuckle Finn's shorts and help pull them off. Before he throws them on the floor, he reaches into his pocket and pulls out a foil packet I immediately recognize and places it on the nightstand next to us.

"Was I a foregone conclusion?" I ask teasingly

Finn smiles but looks at me with caution. "Never. A guy can dream, Liv, and I've been dreaming of you for so long now. You're the answer to my prayers, Liv; you're the air I need to breathe. You're the one I want to share my dreams with, every single night."

We have been semi-intimate many times before, but never like this. It's never gone all the way. Never with so much love and passion and affection for one another. And never with the lights on. Tonight, though, I feel like Finn is freeing me of the bonds that have been holding me back from not only my ability to love but to be loved. I feel like a genie freed from its bottle. I want to give this man everything that he desires because in this moment, I realize that that's all he's ever wanted to do for me.

Finn loves me.

And I love him.

He kisses me again, tasting the inside of my mouth with his tongue and granting me access to do the same. As he leans down to hover over me once more, his mouth covers my breast. One flick of his tongue over my nipple and I am gasping for breath, my mouth open and my hands grasping at the sheets around me. I feel Finn's other hand slide down my stomach, his fingers tucking inside my panties. He leisurely extends his hand forward until his fingers are sliding into me. I gasp for breath again and cry out.

"Oh my God, Finn!" I'm panting. Hard.

His tongue.

His fingers.

My body.

I raise my body to meet Finn's, kissing his cheek, his ear, his shoulder, his arm, any part of him that I can reach all while he relentlessly continues to suck on my body. I can feel the heat rising in me, and I know I can only last another few seconds.

"Finn," I whisper. I'm starting to hold my breath. When I feel his fingers flick inside me, I explode inside. I bite down on his shoulder to muffle my scream.

I'm floating. Like a balloon cut free from its string, I am floating in the air and never want to come back down.

A satisfied grin spreads across my face, and I stretch out my body as I feel myself deflate from my floating cloud of pure bliss. Finn sits up quickly and climbs off the side of the bed leaving me bereft of his warmth. I watch him as he sheds his black boxer briefs finally freeing his erection.

Holy hell.

The size of him.

He climbs back on the bed, having grabbed the condom from the nightstand, and sits up in the middle of the bed, and that's when I see it. He has a birthmark just below his pelvic bone on the left hand side. I try not to stare, but the shape of it makes me want to giggle. It sort of resembles the shape of a horseshoe. It's not huge, but it's definitely there, and it's ridiculously cute and sexy as hell all at the same time. He reaches his hands out for me. I sit up with Finn, nearly straddling his lap, as he rips open his foil packet. Before he can roll on his condom, I take his erection firmly in both of my hands. He is rock hard but so velvety soft. At my touch, he inhales sharply. I hold onto him with one hand and trail my other hand down his chest and over his abdomen until my finger reaches his birthmark.

"Lucky." I whisper to myself.

"Hmm?"

"Your birthmark," I say to him as I trace the shape on his pelvis. "It sort of looks like a horseshoe. Aren't those supposed to symbolize luck?"

Finn is speechless for a second, and I look up fearing that perhaps I just ruined the mood with my comment.

"Nobody has ever noticed before, I guess. I don't even think about it."

"It's sexy as hell, Finn. I love it...maybe it's your good luck charm, but I think I'm the one who is lucky."

I look slowly down to the gloriousness that is Finn and try unsuccessfully to hide my lust for him. I kiss his lips before leaning down to trail kisses down his chest. He doesn't let me get very far before he pulls me up kissing me again.

"Olivia," he breathes. "Keep that up, and this will be over way too soon."

I smile at him as he places his hands over mine, moving our hands in tandem up and down his length. Finn closes his eyes and breathes in a deep breath.

"Mmm yes..." he growls softly. I can tell he's trying to remain in control. I look down at our combined hands and back up to his eyes.

"I want you inside me, Finn, please; let me feel you."

Finn grabs my face and kisses me hard, filling me with the taste of him. He lets go of my face long enough to roll his condom on before he wraps his arms around me and lifts me, connecting our upper bodies. His skin touching mine fills me with a carnal desire to meld our bodies together as one.

"Olivia," Finn whispers. I look at him, assuming he's unsure of my decision to proceed. "My love for you is all the anchor you will ever need; once it's down, it stays. I want nothing more than to sink into you right now, Liv, but I need you to know that I will never force you into something you're not ready for."

The longing and absolute love I see on his face overwhelms my heart. I'm so ready. I've been ready. I want this with him. I place my hands on his chest as I lower myself down onto him slowly reveling in the sensation of every inch of him filling every inch of me.

"Fuck," Finn gasps. "You're so tight like this. Are you okay?"

"Finn, yes. I'm good. I'm so good," I groan. He feels so damn good inside me, filling me completely. In this moment, I don't think we could possibly get any closer.

"Olivia, you feel incredible."

I flex inside, my muscles gripping him tightly, making him gasp. "Oh, fuck, Olivia; I need you."

I wrap my arms around Finn's neck and begin to move my hips slowly. I can feel my arousal build in me hearing him grunt in my ear as he flexes his hips. He wraps an arm around the small of my back and holds one hand around the back of my neck. We are connected in mind, body, and soul, and it is beautiful. Our rhythm begins to quicken. I can feel the sweat on our bodies as we rub against each other. I weave my fingers into his hair and kiss him forcefully, licking the inside of his mouth. I can't stop kissing him as our bodies move together in rhythm.

"Ah, Jesus Christ, Liv," Finn moans loudly, squeezing me tighter. "Hold on to me, Beautiful."

"Always, Finn. Always." He's thrusting harder into me, driving me wild, as he hits me at my core. I'm about to go over the edge again; I'm so close.

This is the perfect time to tell him.

I lean my head down to Finn's ear and nibble on his earlobe.

"Olivia..." He grunts.

I whisper in Finn's ear the only words that can be spoken, and I feel them sincerely to the center of my soul. "I love you, Finn."

"Olivia...Ahh...!" he says as he lets go and erupts into me. He buries his head in my neck and holds me as he allows his body to release. We're in the middle of this bed, connected from head to toe in an embrace neither one of us wants to let go of.

"Say it again," Finn whispers, his breathing shaky as his body starts to relax.

I smile, even though he can't see my face. "I love you, Finn Kellan. I love you so much."

Chapter 20

We sit there in the middle of the bed, embracing for a few moments, while we each try to catch our breath. Still holding on to me, I feel Finn lean back so that he can look into my eyes. He kisses me sweetly, reverently, almost like he's thanking me for sharing in the passion that we just created. He lifts me off of him and quickly discards his condom into the wastebasket by the bed. We both lay down together, facing each other, and cover ourselves with one of the sheets on the bed. I'm exhausted, emotionally and physically. I can't remember a time when that much emotion poured out of me at one time, and by the look on his face, I'm guessing Finn must be feeling the same way.

"Are you okay?" he asks me softly.

"Yeah, I'm okay." I'm lying here staring at him, unsure exactly of what to say. What happened here tonight was nothing short of intensely emotional.

"I'm sorry," I whisper.

"You have nothing to be sorry for."

"I feel like I do."

"Why?"

"Finn, the things I said…"

"Never mind about the things you said, Liv," he interrupts. "The things you said were things I needed to hear, and I needed to hear them exactly how you said them because now I feel like I know you. That was the real you standing over there a little while ago, Liv, bearing your heart and your soul, and your body to me. You had nothing left to give, nothing left to hide, so you finally let me in."

"You didn't leave. They always leave." The words come hoarsely out of my mouth as I try to choke back tears.

"I'm not them, Olivia. I'm not those other guys. I'm sorry they treated you so poorly, but you know what? I'm not sorry they left you."

I look up at him a little surprised at his remark, but he's smirking at me. "They're loss is my gain, Beautiful, and I'll take all that I can get with you. I'm glad you're not with someone else. I'm grateful you weren't with someone else when I met you."

I can feel myself blushing.

"I'm so in love with you, Olivia. I would do anything for you; you know that, right? All you ever have to do is ask. I want to help you, to protect you, and not because I perceive you as weak because I don't think you're weak at all. I just want to be a man you can depend on to be there all the time."

"I love you too, Finn; and I want you to be that man for me, too."

We both lay in the bed for a few minutes, soaking in the emotions we just shared together. I'm not quite sure if I should keep myself awake, or just close my eyes and drift to sleep; but either way, I know I need to freshen up first. Finn's voice answers my thoughts before I can say them.

"Come take a bath with me? It's a Jacuzzi bathtub…plenty of room for two."

"Yeah. Okay." I slowly sit up and reach for one of the blankets to cover my body, but after watching me for a moment, Finn's hands catch mine. He shakes his head at me and smiles. "Olivia, there's no need to cover yourself now. You're beautiful, and I like looking at you. Please. You have absolutely nothing to be ashamed of. I'm not going to leave you. I promise."

I gulp loudly and look at Finn in apprehension. I don't know why I'm feeling so shy now, but I try hard to push it back and follow Finn's confidence. As he slips out of the bed, he keeps a hold of my hand and helps me, showing me that he's not shying away from me. It's true that Finn strengthens me. When Finn is touching me, I feel like nobody can hurt me. I secretly pray that he holds on to me forever.

We both sink into the tub, relaxing our bodies in the warmth of the water. Finn grabs me and positions me in front of him between his legs. He rubs my shoulders, washing me with a warm soapy sponge. I revel in his soft touch and relax into him, laying my head back against his chest. I could easily fall asleep in his arms right here in this warm bath.

"Can I ask you a question?" he asks me cautiously. "I know it's getting pretty late, so you don't have to answer if you don't want to talk about it."

"Of course you can ask me, Finn."

He's quiet for a minute squeezing the soapy water out of the sponge over my body. "Will you tell me about Max?"

I sit very still in the water waiting for the anxiety to creep through my body, for the fear and raw emotion to overtake my words; but as I release my breath, I realize that feeling isn't here, and it's not coming. I'm able to take another deep breath and release it without pain or fear or anger. My break down with Finn earlier is beginning to feel more like a successful cathartic exercise in airing out my dirty laundry. I feel better talking about Max than I ever have. Maybe I had just cried it all out and have no more emotion to give; I don't know. Either way, I'm just fine not having another PTSD moment in front of Finn.

"What would you like to know? He saved my life, Finn."

"I know he did, and I'm grateful for it; I am. But I don't want to hear about your accident, I want to hear a good memory, like, when did you get him? And where?"

I smile remembering what Max looked like as a puppy. His paws were so big, like a clown wearing big red shoes, and his eyes were a piercing blue, much like Finn's. "We rescued Max, actually. There's a retriever rescue kennel in my hometown; the owners are friends of my parents, family friends now. Anyway, I was probably in fifth grade or so and really wanted a puppy after our previous family dog had passed away. I bugged my mom and dad about it for almost the entire school year before they finally caved. I think they weren't ready, but I really needed the presence of a dog in the house; it just seemed empty without one, ya know?"

Finn stops rubbing my shoulders, causing me to turn my head and look back at him. He shakes his head and purses his lips. "No, actually, I don't know. I never had a dog growing up. We traveled too much."

"Ah. Right. I can understand that. Anyway, my mom's friend, Eileen, is a huge dog lover and runs her own rescue shelter. Someone had brought in a pregnant chocolate lab. She ended up having four pups while at the shelter, so Eileen gave us one knowing how badly I wanted a dog. He was the cutest little puppy with huge paws and piercing blue eyes...like yours, actually." I say, looking at Finn.

Finn's eyes sparkle. "Are you saying I have puppy dog eyes?"

I giggle back at him nodding my head. "Yes, sometimes Finn, you do!"

"Mmm, I'll take that as a compliment."

"As you should. Max was an adorable puppy, and I loved him very much."

Finn wraps his arms around me from behind and kisses my neck. "So you didn't get another dog? You know - after?"

"No." I shake my head immediately. "I couldn't. I just...I don't know. My accident really changed my life, put me in a dark place for a while, more than a while I guess; and honestly, I just didn't want to do that to Max...start loving another dog, I mean. I couldn't betray him like that. So no, we didn't get another dog. I haven't even been to see Eileen at the dog shelter since my accident."

"I can understand your logic. I just wonder if putting yourself 'back on the horse', as they say, would've been good for you, ya know. You loved Max; you still do love him. I can tell, and I don't mean to belittle that at all. I just wonder..."

"You wonder what I could be like with a dog like Toby." I already knew what Finn was getting at. "A therapy dog, I mean."

"Well, I'm not suggesting a therapy-trained dog is going to replace Max in any way or bring back your confidence overnight, although, I'll be the first to admit it's done wonders for me. I just mean that you obviously have a love for dogs, or you did at one time. I just wonder if another dog in your life somewhere down the line could bring you comfort again that's all."

"I don't know." I quietly move my hands slowly through the water. "If my reaction to Toby is any indication of how I would be around other dogs, I'm not sure I'll ever be okay with them again."

"Olivia, your reaction to Toby was entirely my fault. Had I known about your past, I would never have put you in the situation you found yourself in. At the very least, we could've talked about it first. Liv, it sickens me to think about yesterday, you fainting at the door, being literally sick all because of my actions. I'll never be able to take that back, but I'll spend my lifetime trying to make it up to you if you'll let me. I just want to see you happy and not afraid to be you. I promised you I would never push you into something you aren't ready for, and I meant that, okay? I'm here for you, Liv, whatever you need, whenever you need it."

"What kind of therapy does Toby provide for you? You don't own him, so it's obviously not an around-the-clock type of thing?"

"Toby can sense if or when I'm about to have a panic attack or a flashback or a nightmare in general. He's actually trained to lick my face or nudge me with his nose when it happens so I'll wake up. He stays with me for a few days when I'm feeling particularly stressed or overwhelmed. That's when I seem to experience the most nightmares. A dog can be a wonderfully calming influence; I just don't have the ability right now to own a dog full time in my home. I mean, before I met you, I was working all hours at the office and traveling whenever I could just to get out. That's no life for a dog."

"So he's trained for PTSD?" I ask.

"Yes. He nudged you last night with his nose because he knew you were having a nightmare or flashback of some sort. That's what woke you up once I had you on my couch."

"I see."

"His owner is a foster owner and volunteer with the pet therapy program. That's how we met. I would love to own Toby, but with my traveling, I know I can't provide him with a stable home life. So I'm sort of like a step-parent. I see him every other weekend or so. Sometimes more if life is stressful."

I turn around and straddle Finn's legs. My fingers are pruny, but the water is still warm, and I'm very much enjoying my closeness with Finn.

"I love you, Finn. I'm so sorry if I've made life more stressful for you, but thank you...for proving to me what my heart already knew but was too scared to admit."

"Olivia."

Finn's arms encircle my body and hold me against him in a comfortable embrace. Laying my head against his chest, it feels like our bodies were made to connect. We fit together like two matching puzzle pieces. Life feels perfect when we're together. Finn is everything I ever wanted and everything I never knew I needed.

"We should get some sleep, Beautiful," Finn whispers in my ear before kissing my neck one last time. "We have a big day tomorrow."

I frown at him in confusion. "We do? There isn't anything on my itinerary. I was just going to be a tourist for a while and work a little on my layout for the winery. Are we meeting with another client?"

"Nope. It's a surprise, but I'll tell you this," Finn says smirking knowingly. "Tomorrow Olivia, you're mine. For the whole day, just you and me and California."

"Hmm...sounds like fun, if you think you can handle me for the day."

Finn's eyes narrow, and he grabs on to my waist. "Liv, I would love to handle you right now, and if we didn't have an early flight, I would certainly take full advantage. That and I don't have another condom easily accessible at the moment."

My heart rate speeds up as I feel Finn's arousal underneath me. I dip my hand in the water and close my hand around him, smiling as his breath hitches. I push myself up just enough to adjust him underneath me, so that I can sink down onto him.

"Olivia," Finn gasps. "Baby, we can't..."

"Shhh." I kiss him, taking his words away from him. "I'm on the pill Finn. I've been on the pill for years."

"But, I thought..." Finn's eyes grow large, and he shakes his head, frowning slightly. "Why didn't you tell me before?"

"Because I wanted to know that the guy I was going to share my body with was responsible enough to take care of himself and me. Well, that and you never really gave me the chance to tell you. We were sort of in the moment."

A chuckle escapes Finn's lips, which only heightens the electricity flow between us, making me gasp. "Olivia, you amaze me. I love you."

"I love you, too. Now shut up and kiss me."

"You'll never have to tell me twice," Finn whispers, grinning against my lips.

Chapter 21

The smell of coffee penetrates my nose before I even open my eyes. And what else am I smelling? Maple? Bacon? I slowly stretch my body in the sheets, expecting to reach out and touch Finn, but to no avail. I turn my head to see that Finn isn't in bed with me. I don't remember him getting up out of bed. I obviously slept harder than I expected.

Must've been the wine.

And umm...last night's exercise.

I climb out of bed and reach for the white fluffy robe waiting for me on the chaise lounge sitting next to the bed. Finn thinks of everything. I make a quick pit stop in the bathroom to freshen up and then follow the mouthwatering smell wafting from the kitchenette on the other side of the bungalow. There he is as I peek around the corner, the man I am lucky enough to call mine, looking sexy as ever in his lounge pants and no shirt.

Holy Hell how does he look so hot so early in the morning?

"Barefoot and in the kitchen," I joke. "Just the way I like 'em!"

My unexpected appearance and humor catches Finn off guard enough that he misses the bowl as he cracks an egg that now bleeds all over the countertop. I try to cover my mouth to hide my laughter, but it's too late. He hears my giggles and is laughing at himself, or me, as well. His smile lights up my soul.

"Isn't that supposed to be my line?" he asks as he grabs for a towel to clean up the mess he made.

"Hmm. We'll see. Maybe one day, but I never said I could cook, so be careful what you wish for."

"I'll remember that. I guess you should feel pretty lucky to have me then, huh? A guy who can cook…"

"Finn, I would still want you even if you couldn't put jelly on peanut butter, but this," I say motioning to the breakfast he's preparing. "This is all bonus, but what are you doing cooking breakfast so early? It's only six o'clock in the morning."

"Yeah, I know." He says serving me a plate of delicious-looking French toast and bacon. "Room service doesn't open until seven, so I ordered a few groceries to be delivered to the room so I could cook for you. Eat up; our flight leaves in thirty minutes, and we need to be ready to go."

"Wait, what? What flight? Where are we going?"

"I told you, it's a surprise, but we only have a small window to get there before what I want you to see is gone for the day. So, eat your breakfast, Liv, and throw on some clothes...or go in your robe, whatever you like, but don't forget your camera."

"HA! Okay, okay I get it. Food in mouth, clothes on body, grab camera. I'm on it." I pick up my fork and take a bite of my breakfast as Finn brings me a cup of coffee and a glass of orange juice. We both eat our beautifully prepared breakfast quickly. Finn really is an exceptional cook. We dress for a casual day out and leave our bungalow in the early morning light. I thought we were walking back to the welcome house to catch a cab to the airport, but instead, Finn has a golf cart pick us up outside and drop us off at the helipad where a black helicopter emblazoned with the Seal Lake Winery logo is waiting for us.

"Oh my God, Finn! Is this for real? We're really flying in that?"

Finn chuckles at my shock. "Yes, we are. Trust me; you'll love what we're going to see, and you'll be glad you have your camera with you."

"Wait, before we go, speaking of cameras..." I pull my camera out of my shoulder bag and stand as close to Finn as I can get so that I can snap a picture of the both of us. "I should've done this last night, but in all honesty, I don't need a photograph to remember any part of those moments."

"I don't either, Olivia. Pictures can say a thousand words, but there's not a picture you can take that can say the three words I got to hear from your lips last night."

I hug Finn as he holds my camera out at arm's length to snap a quick picture of the two of us again before we begin our adventure for the day. We climb into the helicopter with the help of the pilot, strap ourselves in, and place our headphones over our ears. Before I can even turn to look out my window, we are off the ground and flying across the winery. The view during this spectacular sunrise is breathtaking. The water of Seal Lake glistens like shiny diamonds in the early morning sunshine, and from a birds-eye view, the lake provides a mirror image reflection of the trees and gardens surrounding it. I swear, if the helicopter would land right now, I would be happy and content with the stunning treat I just experienced. I grab Finn's hand and look over my shoulder to find him watching me. I tilt my head and smile at his awed grin.

"You've done this before haven't you?" I yell into the microphone that hangs down from my headphones. I can tell by his lack of enthusiasm for wanting to look out the window that helicopter rides are, obviously, not a new thing for him.

"Yes I've done this before, but, Olivia McGuire, there is nothing I love more than watching you experience something new for the first time. It's my pleasure to be able to do this with you and for you."

"Thank you for this, Finn. I'm really looking forward to sharing the day with you; and if I forgot to say so, thank you for a most delicious breakfast."

"You're welcome, and it's far from over, Beautiful," he says, kissing the back of my hand and laying it down in his lap.

I spend the next half hour or so peering out the window and watching the landscapes change around me. The scenery below me of the countryside puts me in a trance that I don't want to get out of. I feel like a kid in a candy store. I just can't stop watching everything going on around me and below me. I lean my head against the window and close my eyes for a moment feeling more relaxed than I have felt in weeks. I start humming one of my favorite songs from my workout playlist.

Finn squeezes my hand bringing my out of my relaxed trance.

"What?"

His smile is endearing. "Nothing. You're just cute when you're humming."

"Oh, sorry, I forgot you could hear me."

"Are you kidding? I love listening to you sing, *especially* when you don't know I can hear you." Finn wraps his arm around my shoulder as he winks at me.

"Do you know that song? 'Fly' by Rihanna and Nicki Minaj?" I ask.

"Nope, I don't think so."

"It's one of my favorites that I listen to on my morning runs. I guess flying in this helicopter made me think about it. What do you usually listen to on your runs? Do you have a favorite work-out song?"

"I don't have favorites necessarily. 'Thunderstruck' usually gets my blood pumping, I have some Green Day, some Metallica, Pitbull...I'm not usually too picky."

I smirk at Finn, thinking about what I would find on his playlist if I looked right now. "So, you have to have a guilty pleasure song that nobody knows about right? You know, that song that you don't want to admit that you like...what is it?"

"I don't know what you're talking about," he says, deadpanned.

"Liar!" I poke Finn in his side making him jump and laugh. "Every guy has one; out with it!"

After a minute of trying to hold back his smile, he looks at me guiltily and says, "'Chasing Cars', Snow Patrol."

"I love Snow Patrol! There's no reason to be ashamed of that song; I love it."

"Can I tell you why I love it?"

"Yeah, of course."

"Ironically, it's what was playing in my headphones when I first spotted you."

"Shut up."

"I'm not kidding. It was also one of Sydney's favorite songs when she was in high school."

"Yeah, it was popular when I was in high school. In fact, it made it on the ballot for our prom song," I say raising one eyebrow. "Not the best prom theme song, obviously, but didn't matter anyway, I guess."

"Why didn't it matter?" He asks curiously.

I shrug. "Because I didn't go to my junior prom."

"Why not? You had to have had a boyfriend."

"Yeah, but I had my accident right before my junior prom, so I never got to go."

"Right. Sorry, I didn't realize it was that long ago. Wait - you had your accident during your junior year?"

"Yeah, 2007," I tell him, knowing that he's now putting the pieces together. Sydney and I both had accidents in the same year of high school.

We're the same age, or would be if she were still alive.

"Oh."

"I'm sorry I didn't tell you before, Finn."

"No." He shakes his head. "There's no need. I just...I'm sorry I guess I never really put two and two together until just now."

"You couldn't have. I didn't tell you about my accident until last night."

"Yeah, I guess. It's just all so - I don't know, weird?"

I nodded my head in acknowledgement. "I can agree with that."

Finn lets out a quick breath and half smiles to himself. "Is it weird, too, that sometimes I love the similarities between you both? You and Sydney, I mean? Not like I'm in love with my sister weird, but like, I feel her around me more and more when you're around. Is that too weird for you?"

"No. Not at all. I understand."

He wants to protect me because he couldn't protect her.

Finn squeezed my hand again. "Anyway, Sydney would listen to Snow Patrol over and over again. I used to get sick of it. Now that she's gone..."

"You listen to it all the time. I totally get it."

"Mm-hmm. It just doesn't get old anymore. Anyway..."

"Tell me a happy memory of her. Something fun you guys did together."

He looks out his window quickly before looking back to answer me. "The X-Men," he smirks. "God love her, Sydney was never a super princess girly girl. Movies were something we could do together. She loved Harry Potter, and she loved when I took her to see the first X-Men movie. She was ten when we saw the first one together. We would rent them when we could and sit at home pigging out on graham crackers and Hershey bars."

I throw Finn a questioning glance. "You mean s'mores?"

"Haha. No. Syd didn't like marshmallows, but she always thought the idea of s'mores would be fun, so she would make Hershey bar sandwiches with graham crackers. Messy as hell because of all the crumbs, but I have to admit, they were damn good! "

"That sounds like a lot of fun."

"Yeah." We both sit quietly holding each other's gaze before Finn looks over my shoulder out my window. "We're here, Beautiful. Look out your window, and get your camera ready," he says, sitting up and pointing out my side of the helicopter.

I kiss Finn's cheek quickly and then scoot over to get a better look out my window. We are flying over my surprise of the day, and

It.

Is.

Breathtaking.

The white fleece blanket of fog rolling through the air is like something I have never seen before. Flying high enough from it that our pilot will be able to safely maneuver the helicopter, we are able to look down and watch the fog envelop the entire first half of the Golden Gate Bridge. As the fog continues to cover the bridge, it looks as though all of California, at least all that we can see, has slipped smoothly into the ocean, covered by waves of white. I quickly ready my camera and snap as many shots as I can. Within minutes, the fog is completely covering the bridge, but I can still clearly see the tops of the two bridge towers.

"This view - Finn, this view is incredible!" My face is plastered as close to the window as I can get. I swear, if the helicopter door were open right now, Finn would have to hold my feet just to keep me inside.

"Isn't it? It's one of my favorite things to see when I'm out here on the West Coast."

"How many times have you done this? Come to see the fog I mean?"

"This is my third trip. The other times were with my Dad. Once from the air, and once from land. It's incredible either way."

"I don't doubt it. Holy Shit! Finn, this is amazing! Thank you for showing this to me!" I turn my body back in Finn's direction, grab his face, and plant the biggest most endearing kiss on his lips before leaning back to share my smile with him. "This is something I'll never forget. This has to be on that list of one hundred things to see before you die, don't you think?" I say excitedly.

"Haha. Well if it's not, I guess we better send a letter to the publisher of that list, but let's not plan on dying anytime soon. We have many more experiences to have together, and more things to see today. You ready?"

"I'm ready for anything, Finn." I can't keep the smile from my face. I feel so blessed to be able to share in these kind of experiences with the man I love and with the man who loves me in return.

Chapter 22

Finn: "She Is" - Lady Antebellum
This song makes me think of you. You're a little of everything, and I want everything you are. Love you.

He always makes me blush.

"Earth to Olivia," Abby says from across the table. We are enjoying a quick lunch date since I was in California for so long. We really needed to catch up after everything that had happened between Finn and me, since we hadn't gotten to talk much before I left town.

"Sorry." I smile. "Just a text from Finn."

"Yeah, I can tell by your googly eyes, Miss Lovestruck Puppy. I take it the weekend turned out okay since I never heard from you, *and* you were gone longer than anticipated."

"It was a bit of an intense start, but um, yeah everything is great now. I'm really glad he flew out to see me. It makes me nauseous to think of how things could have ended up between us."

"No shit, sister; you should've seen him here that night. Olivia, he was a fucking mess of tears when he couldn't contact you. He had no idea where you were; I had no idea where you were. He was freaking out that you were lying dead in a ditch somewhere. It was all I could do to not have him call the police...or your parents."

"Oh God! My parents! They don't know, do they? Nobody called them?"

"No, not that I know of. You haven't even told them about Finn yet, have you? I certainly didn't want to freak them out."

"They know about Finn but they don't know how serious it is or isn't. I haven't really talked to them about it. I haven't talked to my parents in the last couple weeks, actually. I need to check in with them."

"Sooo, spill it, Girly. What happened in sunny California?"

I take a deep breath and then a bite of my grilled chicken salad before answering. "Well, I spent the day at the winery working. After supper, I walked back to my bungalow, pretty much drowning in my sorrows and an entire bottle of wine, and there he was, waiting for me on my porch, trying to decide if he had the courage to knock I think."

"Yeah." Abby takes a drink of her Diet Coke, nodding. "Once I had talked to you and knew you were safe in Chicago, he wanted to go there immediately; but I had to convince Finn that by the time he would get there you would be on your next flight. So, he waited until morning and borrowed a friend's private jet to make the direct flight to you. Seriously, girl, I've never seen a guy so consumed with his feelings for someone that he would fly across the country, not knowing how things were going to work out. It was like Superman had lost Lois Lane or something."

I nod my head at Abby's last statement. "I know. He really feels like he failed Sydney in her darkest time of need, which is bullshit, but he's not ready to hear that. Anyway, so he shows up and forces me to listen to his explanation of Toby. I'm screaming back at him about how I'm just a hot mess of a person. He gets upset that I must not think highly of him, at which point I try to prove him wrong by tearing off my dress and standing in the middle of the bungalow in just my underwear."

"What?!" Abby almost spits out her drink. "Oh my God Olivia! That's HOT! Keep going…and then what?"

I sigh, taking another bite of my salad. "I stood there crying my eyes out because I thought he had left."

"Wait, so he didn't leave at all?"

I shake my head. "No. When I opened my eyes, he was there, kneeling before me, mapping out my scars like they were a maze or something. After that…" I shrug and take a sip of my drink, like what I just said was no big deal, even though I know better than to shrug at my best friend.

Abby looks at me from across the table after I don't continue with my story. The blush on my face can't hide my secret, though. Abby is too good. "I knew it!" Abby says, dropping her fork. She looks at the smirk on my face, smiles back at me, and leans forward towards me as close as she can get. "You finally fucked him didn't you?"

Solving Us

"We didn't fuck, Abby. That's really not the right word for what we did because it was the most passionate, loving, intimate moment we have shared since we've been together. The way he makes me feel, Abs…"

"I know, Liv. You don't have to explain. I can see it in your face. I can see it on his when he talks about you. You finally let him see beneath your beautiful."

My head snaps up and I gasp, "What?"

"What? Did I say something wrong?"

"No." I smile, shaking my head. "Not at all; it's just ironic that you said that because as he started touching my scars that night, that song came on the radio in our room. 'Beneath Your Beautiful'. Remember that song?"

Abby's eyebrows shoot up, and she gives me the look that says she's impressed. "Well, Olivia, maybe that's your theme song. It fits you. It fits both of you, come to think of it."

"Yeah." I start to thinking about the lyrics of the song and how they pertain to Finn and me. Abby is right. The song is perfect for us.

"Okay, so you had lots of sex. Is that all you did for the past five days? I mean it is Monday, and you left last Tuesday night for Pete's sake. Dang, girl, you have to be sore!"

I tilt my head and look at Abby disapprovingly before laughing. "Of course not. He took me for a helicopter ride to San Francisco so I could photograph the Golden Gate Bridge covered in fog. It was breathtaking! Then we landed in San Fran, took a trolley ride around town, and shopped for the day. Typical touristy things. We spent a day in Los Angeles and a day on the beach before heading back east. It was really a great mini vacation and just the time that we needed."

"I'm so happy for you, Liv. You deserve this, ya know. After all you've been through, I hope you're happy, Babe, because I really am happy for you, and Finn, too, but…you're my bestie so…"

I smile endearingly at Abby and grab her hand. "Thanks, Abs. Really. I always feel guilty that you're the friend who has to put up with my relationship drama all the time; but then the more I think about it, the more relieved I am that it's you. You're my best friend, and I can't imagine sharing my life with anyone else."

"Hoes before bros, Liv. Remember that."

"HA! I will; I promise. Let's get out of here; I have a mountain of work to catch up on."

"Right behind ya. I have a design to finish myself for a client, so don't be surprised if I'm a little late getting home."

I split from Abby on our walk back to our respective office buildings and head inside to settle in for the afternoon. Before getting into the elevator in my building, I pull my phone out of my purse quickly to shoot a text to Finn. I'm pretty sure he won't know the song title I'm texting him, but I also know he'll look it up.

> Me: "Kissin' U" by Miranda Cosgrove because you're the puzzle piece I've been trying to find.

Smiling as I enter the elevator, I ride up to my office floor feeling content and happy with my life for the first time in weeks. I have a great guy in my life who goes out of his way to take care of me, a best friend who helps me through life and all it has to offer me, a fantastic apartment, and the best job I can ask for with a lot of growing potential in my future. Bring it on world; today I'm feeling like an untouchable million bucks!

I step off the elevator and head down the hall towards my office. Karen is standing at the end of the hall, which would seem like a normal thing to do, except that she is peeking around the doorway to my office like she is watching someone or trying to see what's going on without actually walking in. It's almost humorous in that weird, creepy sort of way. She turns her head in my direction, no doubt hearing my shoes tap across the floor startling her, and causing her to drop the file she was holding onto the floor.

She looks like a scene out of some weird movie or something, and I try hard not to laugh at her because I have no idea what's going on.

"Karen? Are you okay?"

"Uh, yes. Fine. Thank you," she says quickly scooping up her papers and stuffing them back in her file folder. Seriously, this is the weirdest behavior I think I have seen from an adult in a long time.

"Were you looking for Mandy? Is she not in there? You're welcome to go in, ya know."

"No, no. I mean, yes I was looking for Mandy. Um, she and I just...um...had a tiff this morning, that's all. I was just checking on her. You know, to make sure she was okay," she says dismissively. "Anyway, how was your trip, Olivia? I heard things at the winery went very well."

Do not blush. Do not blush. Do not blush.

"Yeah everything went great. I had a great time. Mr. and Mrs. Taylor are fantastic, enthusiastic clients. I'm excited to show them my campaign - that is, when I finish it, which I need to get started on, so if you'll excuse me." I pass Karen and step into the doorway of my office. I turn back to Karen, quickly remembering why she was there in the first place.

"Don't worry, Karen. Whatever it is with Mandy, I'm sure she'll be fine. I'll talk to her if you want."

"No, don't!" Karen exclaims.

Geez, woman. Slow your roll!

"I mean, no thank you; it's fine. She's fine, I'm sure. I don't want her to know I was checking up on her. You know, she'll just think I'm a hovering mom anyway."

"Right. Yeah, I get it. Lips are sealed. Gotta get to work." I watch Karen take a deep breath almost calming herself and then turn to walk back down the hall.

"Yeah, me, too. Thanks," I hear her say.

I walk over to my desk and throw my purse in my desk drawer. I open my laptop and file of photos from the winery so I can get started with my campaign design.

"Hey, Mandy, you over there?" I call from my side of the cubicle wall that separates our two work stations.

"Yep!" I hear her say. "What's up?"

"I just saw your mom in the hallway. Is everything okay?"

"Yeah, why?"

"Umm, no reason. She just...didn't seem herself I guess."

"Huh. That's weird. She seemed fine when I saw her an hour ago."

"Oh...so she's talked to you today?"

"Of course. She's my mom and sort of my boss. Why wouldn't she talk to me?"

"I thought you guys had a fight this morning?"

"A what?"

"A fight."

Mandy stands up and peeks over the wall at me sitting at my desk.

"A what?"

"A fight. An argument, a tiff?"

"Not at all. Why would you ask that?"

"Oh...um...Nothing. No reason. Sorry. I must've misunderstood."

What the hell?

She said they had a fight.

Didn't she say that?

"Are you okay, Liv?" Mandy asks chuckling at the expression of confusion wiped all over my face.

"Yeah," I say, shaking my head. "Sorry. I'm just being stupid."

"No problem," she chuckles. "I'm sure you're just jet lagged."

"Yeah...and sex-lagged." I mutter.

I type the login passwords into my computer and then look up to see Mandy still looking over her cubicle at me. Her face is frozen in shock and awe. She gasps loudly.

"WHAT? And you didn't TELL ME?"

"SHH," I say putting my finger to my lips to silence her and then smirk.

"Sorry, I didn't know you heard me say that."

"Yeah, well I did! So when were you going to tell me about all this, you little private bitch? You can't run away to California for five days with Finn and not tell me every detail! Especially after spilling THOSE beans!"

"Well," I start. "First of all, I didn't run off to California with Finn. I went there for work but he followed me. Secondly, I'll tell ya tomorrow at lunch, or you can give me a call tonight, and I'll tell you all about it. Right now, I have to get my work done, or I'll be sleeping here tonight."

"Deal! I can't wait!" She smiles. It's all I can do to not roll my eyes at her excitement over my love life. Honestly, though, I'm just as giddy as she is, but not everybody here needs to see that.

Chapter 23

The rest of my afternoon is taken up with phone calls to clients, email correspondence and editing of my photos from Seal Lake Winery. I sketch out a few campaign ideas to run by my marketing team in the morning and make a note to touch base with the Boston Cruise Lines to confirm and finish up their ad plan. I haven't heard from Finn all day, and although his absence from my day makes me miss him, I'm grateful for a work day without distractions so that I can get caught up on my workload without distraction. I hate taking my work home with me. I like knowing that if I give my all at work, I can unwind and be me in the evenings. I'm very much looking forward to chilling out with Abby tonight, doing laundry, and maybe going for an evening run. My cell phone dings quietly, alerting me to a text message. I swipe the screen and smile at the text from Finn.

Finn: "Moves Like Jagger" - Want me to show ya?

Not going to lie, this text makes me laugh out loud. It is completely unexpected but comes at just the right time as I'm getting ready to be done for the day.

Me: Like Jagger, huh? I have a thing for Jagger, ya know....

Finn: You'll forget his name after you see me. I promise.
Traveling to one last meeting. See you soon, Beautiful.

This is the perfect ending to a perfect work day. I grab my purse out of my desk and reach to close my laptop when my email dings with a message from the representative of the Boston Cruise Lines that I have been working with on my ad campaign. I would've let it go until morning but the email subject caught me off guard.

Solving Us

To: Olivia McGuire
Date: July 14, 2015 4:56PM
Subject: Campaign ad approval and confirmation
From: Promotions Dept. Boston Cruise Lines

Ms. McGuire,
Thank you very much for your timely response to our new advertising requests. Though your finished product is not what we had previously discussed, we trust your ideas and are impressed with your ability to think outside the box. Assuming there are no further additions or corrections, we approve your campaign design and look forward to receiving the final print. Please let me know if there is any other info that you need at this time.
Sally Jones
Boston Cruise Lines
Promotions and Advertising Department Head

Attch: bostoncruisead.pdf

What the hell?

Did I miss something?

"I didn't send them a finished campaign design," I whisper to myself. "Why the heck would they send me an email approving a design that I haven't shown them yet?"

I sit back in my chair flabbergasted. I can't even comprehend what I've just read. I sit for a moment staring at my computer screen, my eyebrows in a permanent scowl. I read and reread the email from Sally no less than seven times, each time feeling more dumbfounded than the time before. Finally, I think to scroll down and open the attachments she sent with her email. The file attached to the email is what looks like a finished brochure including pictures that do not belong to me. The layout is not at all what I had planned, not to say that it's bad because it isn't. It just isn't my work. I don't get it. How am I going to deal with this predicament? Did she send an email to the wrong person? That couldn't be unless they were for some odd reason working with two separate advertising companies. That can only mean that someone here in my office sent them a design having not spoken to me first. Who the hell would do that and why?

I look around the office. Everyone has left for the day except for Austin who is finishing up an edit. "Hey, Riv, do you know anything about my ad campaign for the Cruise Lines? Did someone offer to step in and take care of it without asking me first?"

Austin stops his work and looks up at me, confusion written all over his face. He chuckles at me before giving me an "are-you-mental" look. "Who the hell would do that? Your clients are your clients, Olivia. I mean, I'm not saying we don't all help each other now and then, but uh...I'm pretty sure you would know about it, Doll." Austin shakes his head again in disbelief at what I just asked him. I admit I must sound like I'm from a different planet. I just don't get it.

"Yeah...I know it's just...yeah...never mind. I'll figure it out."

"Figure what out?"

"Nothing," I say immediately. "I think someone just miscommunicated, that's all. I'll figure it out. Thanks."

"Yup."

My stomach immediately knots as I sit at my desk racking my brain over how to handle this situation. Do I call Finn? Could he have done this, thinking he was helping me out given the stress between us? Where did those pictures come from?

Rather than replying to Sally's email, I pick up my phone and dial her number. I have to get to the bottom of this before I leave for the day, or I know I won't sleep tonight.

"Boston Cruise Lines Promotional office, this is Sally speaking; how may I help you?"

"Sally, I'm glad I caught you. This is Olivia McGuire from the Kellan Agency. I just received your email in regards to the new advertising campaign."

"Oh yes. Mr. Porter likes it very much. We're good to go here on our end. Did you need more information?"

I have no idea how I'm going to ask for what I need. "Umm, yes actually, and I know this might sound a bit strange, but who sent you the finished design because we weren't scheduled to meet until next week?"

"Right. I noticed that it wasn't your name on the email. Let me look it up quickly for you." I sit quietly while listening to her fingers hit the keys on her keyboard. "Yes here it is. I received the email from a Karen Elena. I'm assuming you know who that is."

What?

"Yes I do. I'm sorry for the confusion, I was just taken aback by your email because, well, to be honest, that design isn't my work at all. You're right. It's not at all what we had discussed, but I've been away from work for the past few days and haven't had the chance to touch base with Karen yet, so I apologize for disrupting your day."

I mean how do I say in a nice professional way, "That bitch stole my homework"?!

"It's not a problem at all. I do remember now that she mentioned that you weren't well. I hope you're feeling better, dear."

"I'm sorry?"

Did I hear her correctly?

Karen told them I was sick?

How sick?

"Oh...um...yeah. Much better thank you, and thank you again for your time. I'll be in touch if we need any further information."

"You're welcome, Olivia. Have a good evening."

"And you as well, Sally. Goodbye."

I can feel the heat rising in my face. My heart is racing, and somehow without consciously knowing that I even started, my knee is bouncing up and down ferociously, in time with the pen that I'm tapping on my desk.

What.The.Fuck?

Karen?

Why?

I jump out of my seat, causing the chair to roll backwards and crash into the wall behind my desk and walk down the hall towards Karen's office, hoping she is still here. As luck would have it, I peek into her office to see her shutting down her laptop and opening her desk drawer for her purse.

"Karen, excuse me, but do you have a quick second?" I realize I probably sound like a bitch about to explode, so I do everything in my power to calm myself down.

It's not working.

"I'm just about on my way out, but sure. What can I do for you?"

"I just got off the phone with Sally Jones, from Boston Cruise Lines, after receiving an email from her that left me a bit confused. I was hoping you could shed some light."

The red splotches creeping over Karen's cheeks confirm for me that she has a part in this. For just a moment she looks like a deer caught in the headlights.

"Oh. Right," she says, squaring her shoulders and standing up a little straighter. "Did they not like the design?"

I frown at her from the doorway of her office. "Um, no they approved it," I say with disbelief and, dare I say, disdain in my voice. "I'm just confused as to why you sent them a design at all? I mean, I don't mean any disrespect, but they were my clients that I had been working with for weeks. What was sent to them is not at all what had been discussed in our previous meetings."

"Of course it's not. That's because I did it. Henry Porter and I go way back, so I knew he wouldn't mind if I sent him what I was thinking. Don't worry though, I know you've been stressed with things…with Finn, so I was just doing you a favor." Karen continues to carefully place her file folders in her briefcase bag, but I know it's a way to distract her from my confrontation.

What is she hiding?

"I didn't ask you to do me a favor." My eyes narrow as I watch Karen across the room. "And since you didn't tell me earlier about this, you sort of made me look bad when I had to call Sally and ask her what was going on. I just saw you in the hall a few hours ago. I don't understand why you wouldn't tell me something like that."

Shrugging her shoulders carelessly, Karen turns around folding her arms in front of her and responds, "Nobody told you to call Sally, Olivia. You did that on your own, so yes, I can understand why you might feel that you look a bit...ridiculous and scatterbrained. Perhaps if you had spoken to me before making that call you wouldn't feel so...stupid? The fact of the matter is I know a lot of people around here, in this town, in this business. I know Mr. Porter, and I know what he likes, so I took care of this one for you since you were otherwise detained. End of story. Finn will tell you. He knows Mr. Porter and I are old friends."

"Well that would insinuate that I run to Finn with all of my concerns and questions in this office, but, in actuality, I do not. Our relationship is separate from what we do here, and I intend to keep it that way."

"Is it?" she asks, raising an eyebrow as she walks towards me, ready to leave her office for the day. Her voice is instantly cold, and her comments snide. "Is that why he followed you to California? Is that why he extended your stay an extra few days...because your relationship is...separate?"

No.

She.

Didn't.

Karen rolls her eyes and walks out of the office and down the hall to the elevator, leaving me speechless standing in her office doorway. My anxiety level is ready to shoot through the roof. The knot in my stomach just pulled even tighter. I pick my jaw up off the floor and turn back towards my office to get my things before leaving.

I have never seen Karen like this before. She's always been nothing but nice to me, so what the heck happened? I can't think of anything I may have done to upset her. Maybe this whole thing isn't even about me at all. Maybe she just had a shit day, and I was in the wrong place at the wrong time, except that that's not possible given that she knew what she was doing when she did it. And she did it while I was out of town. My "boss", who doesn't even have experience doing what I do in this profession, just took over my project and purposely made me look like an idiot in front of a client. I've completed several small accounts during my short time here but the cruise line and Seal Lake Winery were to be my first big accounts, and now it looks like I don't know what I'm doing.

"Shit."

That's all I can say.

"You okay?" Oops. I forgot I wasn't alone. Austin is just walking down the hallway towards the elevators.

"Yeah, I'm fine. I'll see ya tomorrow, Riv."

"Okay, see ya." I grab my purse and head out of the office. In the elevator, I think through a few scenarios of how to deal with this problem.

Do I tell Finn?

No. I absolutely do not run to Finn after I just told Karen I keep my relationship separate.

But he's the CEO and my boss's boss.

And they're friends, practically family, with a long history. Who knows what she'll say to him, and that's sort of like tattling.

Do I scrap the entire project and start over with Sally?

No. That only makes me look like a bitch. Not just a bitch but an irresponsible, unorganized bitch.

"Damnit!!" I shout shaking my head. I need a drink. No, I need a long hard run…and then a shower, and then a drink. I grab a cab as soon as I step out of the building and take off for home, not wanting to deal with overcrowded sidewalks. It's already a little later than normal for me getting home since I had to deal with Karen before leaving. As soon as I get home, I strip out of my clothes and throw on my running pants, my pink sports bra, and a tank top. I pull my hair up into a ponytail and grab my shoes. I write out a quick note to Abby in case she gets home before I get back. I need to run. I need to run fast and far and hard. I pick up my earbuds and plug them into my phone, shove my apartment key into my shoe, and stretch quickly before taking off. I start up my running playlist and program it to shuffle songs. My phone is smarter than I give it credit for sometimes. It obviously senses my mood. Adam Lambert's angry voice fills my ears as I start to jog. It's the perfect song to fuel my now-pissy attitude and push me forward, so I turn up the volume and begin to run. In this heat, I'll be sweating in no time.

I run for miles. I run and I run until I can barely feel my feet beneath me, and then I run some more. Every step I take is freeing and I fear that if I stop running the hell that was the last thirty minutes of my work day will all come crashing back around me; and I just don't want to deal with it. I notice that my playlist is recycling songs, which means I've been running for almost an hour. My body feels like I am melting. The soles of my feet sting every time they hit the pavement. I'm hot and sweating like a glass of iced tea on a hot summer day. Come to think of it, a drink of anything sounds really good right about now. I can feel the drips of sweat running down my neck and dripping off the sides of my face. My tank top clings to my sticky wet skin. I'm not one of those girls who looks stunning, even when I'm running. You know, like those girls who never seem to sweat and their running attire always matches their shoes. Nope, I'm a hot sweaty, most likely very smelly mess, but I know that means I'm pushing my limits and feeling the burn. No pain, no gain right? I want to kick myself right about now, though, for not downing a glass of ice water before leaving because now, getting a drink is all I can think about. I have about a mile left to get home and decide to push myself forward and continue running until I make it back home. My frustration with Karen fuels my adrenaline enough that I start sprinting back to my apartment. I make it about half a mile down the road before I feel the tightness in my chest and the numbness in my legs.

Damnit, Olivia, why didn't you get a drink before you left?
It's hot as Hell out here.
I'm a hot sweaty mess.
But I'm cold.
Why am I cold...in the summertime?
I need to slow down.
I can't breathe.
Shit. I can't breathe.

I don't remember my body hitting the pavement, but somewhere in my subconscious mind, I can feel someone pouring water over my head and on my knees. My knees hurt. My right knee is burning, stinging my skin over and over again. I'm back in my past, seven years ago, laying on the pavement with a ripped up bloody body. My eyes shoot open, and my body snaps up into a sitting position. I look down, and sure enough, my pants are a shredded mess, and there is blood trickling down my right leg.

I scream, "MAX!!!!"

"Whoa, be careful sitting up. Don't worry; it's not a deep cut. Once I wash it off, a small bandage should be fine. What the hell were you doing to yourself, Olivia? You could've gotten seriously hurt...and who is Max? Here, drink this."

A pair of hands holds out a water bottle to me, and before I tip the bottle to my lips, I lean my head back squinting into the now-setting sun to see Austin Rivers staring back at me.

"Riv? What...what are you?" I feel dizzy and lightheaded and nauseous.

"God, you're white as a ghost. Just drink, Liv. Small sips," he says, watching me inhale the water like it's the elixir of life. The coolness of the water does make me feel better. I pour some onto my hands and wipe my face and neck.

"I live around the corner and was just getting back from a short run myself when I saw you sprinting down the road. Damn girl, you can run, but why the hell were you sprinting in this heat? Do you always work out like that? No steady pace, or do you always like it fast and hard?" he asks, raising an eyebrow and smirking at his own humor.

I roll my eyes at his innuendo. "No, I don't usually work out like that. Just a bad afternoon and I needed to let go of some stress. That's all. I'm fine."

"Shit. You most certainly are not fine, Olivia. You're damn lucky you didn't break a leg running and falling like that...and even luckier that you didn't give yourself a heart attack or something. Have you had anything to drink today? It's well over ninety degrees out here this afternoon, and with this humidity..."

Solving Us

"No, I'm the idiot who forgot to drink her water before running. Sorry. I thought I could make it back. Obviously, I should've walked." I can feel my attitude heading south quickly.

"Obviously." Austin takes a deep breath picking up on my mood and stands watching me as I empty the water bottle. "Let me get you back safely. You shouldn't walk on that leg right now. You'll just make it bleed more."

"I'll be fine. Thanks for your help."

Austin crouches down and picks me up with ease. "Where do you live?"

"Austin Rivers put me DOWN! I can walk just fine!"

He glares at me, and I know there's no way I'm going to win this one. I swallow hard and wince slightly at the pain in my knee.

"Morgan Estates, but really, Riv, it's not far from here, I can walk it. You can put me down."

"Shut up and let me be a gentleman for a few minutes, all right? Seriously, that knee is going to be sore for a few days. Let's let it stop bleeding, so you don't leave a trail all the way home."

Austin is easily as fit as Finn. He is strong enough to handle me with ease, but he just isn't as comfortable as Finn. Austin Rivers is more the biker type than the fancy car or sail boat owning type. If someone asked me to describe him, I would have to say he's a little bit country and a little bit rock and roll. His brown hair is usually buzzed pretty short, but right now, it's hiding under a ball cap, which in all honesty, boosts his sex appeal up a few notches. He sports an earring in each ear as well as a short beard and goatee, which I also find very sexy about him in that bad boy sort of way; but I don't think now is exactly the time to tell him this secret, so I keep it to myself.

"So, ya want to tell me what got your feathers all ruffled at the end of the day?" he asks as we were walking through the park next to my apartment building. Thank God we aren't walking down the sidewalk. I can only imagine the stares and car honks we would be getting right now.

"No…it's nothing. I don't really want to talk about it. I'll be fine. It just sucks when a totally perfect day goes sour right before you walk out the door. I wasn't prepared for it, and it pissed me off."

"Hmm. Been there. Well look, I know we all joke around and have a good time when we can, but don't sweat the small stuff. We're all willing to help out when things get stressful which happens sometimes especially with dickish clients…or bitchy bosses."

Austin winks at me as if he totally understands what my issue is and that I don't want to say it out loud.

"Yeah. Thanks. I'll remember that."

We make it to my apartment quicker than I expect, and Austin carries me into the elevator before putting me down. He helps me as I limp down the hall to my apartment and open the door. We both step inside and are met with two worried stares.

"Olivia!" Finn drops his phone onto the counter and runs over to me, sweeping me off my feet and into his arms.

"Liv, what the hell? What happened to you? You look like death!" Abby says.

"Thanks, Abby; you definitely know how to make a girl feel great." I roll my eyes but smirk at her, letting her know I'm joking. Well, okay I'm half joking, but whatever.

"She's fine," Austin speaks up. Finn and Abby turn their heads noticing him for the first time, as if he wasn't the one who walked into the apartment next to me. "I was out jogging when I saw Olivia sprinting down the road covered in sweat. She looked like she was about to pass out, and I just couldn't get to her fast enough before she fell."

"Oh my God, Olivia, you fainted?" Abby asks shocked.

"Yeah, it's my fault. I'm dehydrated, and I ran too hard. That's all. I'm fine. Really. It's just a skinned knee." I'm beginning to get annoyed with all the attention. I really just wanted to take a shower and relax.

Finn carries me over to the barstools at the breakfast bar and sits me down. Abby is already following with the first aid kit and a wet washcloth. Finn rips off the remaining shreds of the right side of my pants and wipes up the blood that has dried on my leg, before tending to

Solving Us

the open wound on my knee. The feel of the water burns, or maybe it's just the pressure from Finn's hand. Either way, I flinch and try to pull my leg away, but Finn has a firm hold on my shin.

"Guys, I'm not a six-year-old. It's just a scrape. I can handle it. Okay?"

"Hey," Finn says softly looking me in the eye. He can sense my frustration. "Just let me look at it so I can make sure it's okay." I sigh heavily and nod at Finn. I lean back, resting my elbows on the countertop behind me but immediately wince when my right elbow hits the countertop.

"What?" Finn asks alarmed. "Did I hurt you?"

"No." I sit up and turn my right arm over to see what the damage is to my elbow.

"Damnit." There's blood oozing slowly from a scrape right near my funny bone, which clearly isn't funny, but I chuckle anyway.

"What's so funny?" Abby is scowling at me from beside Finn.

"This is. It's ridiculous really. I mean, I don't know what there is to get so upset about. What's one more scar on an already ripped up body?"

"Olivia..." Finn eyes me cautiously.

"What, Finn?" I look at him, and then to Abby, and then back to Finn trying to figure out what they are both thinking as they both stand there staring at me with concerned looks in their eyes.

"Ooooh. I get it. You guys think I'm going to have a flashback, huh? Poor Olivia gets trampled by her dog in a bear fight and lives with ugly fucking scars, and now you're waiting for me to freak out? Is that it?"

"Olivia, that's enough!" shouts Finn in disbelief.

"I AM NOT A CHILD, FINN! I had a shitty afternoon, and I tried to run off my stress, but I overdid it and fainted. That's it! No big deal! I'm over it!"

"Uhh, I'm gonna go." I hear from across the room. Austin is standing in the doorway, wide eyed and speechless. As this was the first time he had ever seen me outside of work, I feel guilty having just screamed at my friends, one of them being his boss, in front of him.

"Riv, I'm..." I sigh heavily. "Thank you for helping me. I really do appreciate it."

"No problem, Olivia. I'll, uh, see you tomorrow," he says, backing out of the door, closing it behind him but not before I see him eye my roommate from head to toe.

Yes, Rivers, we all know she's a knock-out.

I stand up for a moment, looking at the floor trying to decide what to say next, but what I really want is to be alone.

"I'm going to take a shower."

"Olivia," Finn starts.

"SHOWER!" I shout slamming the bathroom door behind me. I immediately turn on the water and then turn to examine my face in the mirror. I can feel my breakdown coming; the tension in my body is almost unbearable. I want to scream and cry big ugly tears at the hot mess that was my afternoon, but I want to do it in private so I don't have to explain it to anyone. Sometimes a girl just needs to cry a pissed off, angry, ugly cry and scream into her towel until she can't scream anymore.

I slowly peel off my sweat-soaked tank top and what's left of my running pants, letting them fall in a heavy heap to the floor. Bending my arm to peel off my sports bra proves to be a challenge, and I can definitely tell that I'll be pretty sore in the morning, or in about fifteen minutes.

I step into the shower and stand under the cool water. I imagine myself standing under a refreshing waterfall, showering myself in the cleansing waters, but even that doesn't keep the tears at bay. As I wash my face, I can feel the warm wetness spilling from my eyes. I don't know how all this shit happened, or what I'm really going to do about it; but at this very moment, standing in my shower, I want to punch Karen in the face. I want to punch her for being such a bitch to me this afternoon! I want to punch her for messing up my perfect work day and for causing me to stand here crying my eyes out! I want to punch her for stealing my client. Her attitude was one I had never seen from her before, and I really don't understand what I could've done to deserve it. And what's worse is that there is no way I'm going to be able to tell Finn about it. Karen is like a second mother to him. I'll either sound like I'm a cry baby, or I'll cause tension in his family, and neither option sounds like fun.

Abby knocks lightly and then enters the bathroom as I'm finishing up my shower. "Olivia? Babe, what is going on?"

Why didn't I lock the door?

"Let me guess...Finn sent you in here because he thinks I won't scream at you?"

"Uh, no. Chillax there, Hot Stuff, he went to get us some dinner. He said we shouldn't worry about cooking tonight and knew you needed a minute, so he went to get Chinese. I reminded him to get an extra egg roll for you."

"Oh. Thanks."

Open mouth, insert foot.

"So, talk to me. You're usually not like this, so I know something had to have happened at work. I also know if you wanted to talk about it around Finn, you would have immediately; so you're welcome for sending him out for a bit. He won't be gone long, though, so start talking."

I turn off the water and grab my towel hanging over the shower curtain rod and wipe off my face and neck. "Karen Elena stole my client."

"She what?"

"She fucking STOLE my client, Abby. I mean literally...the Boston Cruise Line account? Yeah, while I was working in California, she just decided to take it upon herself to come up with a design, sent it off to the cruise line for approval, which she got by the way, and didn't think to tell me about it! So, who do you think looked like a fucking idiot when she had to call and talk to someone there after receiving the approval email today?"

"Whoa..." Abby says in disbelief.

"Abs, she told them I was sick and hadn't been into work! She lied to them!" I continue to recount my story and conversation with Karen to Abby, filling in all the gaps as she asked for details. Talking about it again certainly isn't calming me down.

"Olivia, you have to tell Finn."

"Do I? I mean, as far as I see it, there's no way I can tell him! I told Karen that I don't run to him because I want to keep our relationship separate, which she clearly doesn't believe based on her bitchy reply and the rolling of her eyes; but, whatever, I mean…who does that? What did I do to her? She wasn't like this before I left town!"

"Okay, take a deep breath. You're getting yourself all worked up, and that shower was supposed to calm you down," Abby says from the other side of the curtain. I wrap my towel around me and pull open the shower curtain to find Abby sitting Indian style against the bathroom door. She had a pensive look to her, as though she was trying to solve the world's trickiest mathematical equation.

"Liv, you don't think she could've sent those emails," she looks up at me, her eyes round and bright. "Do you?"

"NO," I say immediately before stopping in my tracks as her words hit me in the face. "Maybe. No. I don't know. After this afternoon, I suppose anything is possible, but what I don't understand is why Abby? What reason would she have to treat me like this?"

"Jealousy?"

"Jealousy? Jealousy over what? Finn? Ew, he's like a son to her!"

"Do you think Mandy knows? Seems like she would know it happened since she was there while you weren't." Abby scowls and then gasps as her eyes brighten like a lightbulb just went off in her head.

"I don't know. I haven't talked to Mandy about it yet. She wasn't there when I found out."

"What about Mandy and Finn? Is there a history there?"

I actually laugh out loud at Abby's accusation. Obviously, I forgot to tell her more about Mandy. "Uh, I don't think so…especially since Mandy is gay, Abs. She's infatuated with this girl from the office who helps her out."

"Well anything is possible; don't count anything out, Liv. If you're not going to tell Finn about it, and you obviously haven't told him about the emails yet, then you have to watch your back. Nobody there can look out for you but you. In my short experience, a job is a job, and people will do whatever they can to keep one these days, even if it means hurting other people. Don't let her bully you, Liv."

"She's my boss, Abs."

"Who the hell cares? Nobody deserves to be disrespected. She can dislike you for whatever convoluted reason she's come up with, but as long as you're doing your job well, she can't touch you...not that I think she can get near you with a ten foot pole while you're with Finn anyway." Abby smiles and sighs happily. "Aww, Finn is the Dumbledore to your Voldemort, Liv!"

I roll my eyes at Abby's comment but chuckle anyway. I know better than to think that Finn can always protect me from having to fight fires at work.

Especially if I don't tell him.

"I'm going to go get dressed. Finn should be back soon."

"Hey, "Abby stands up and puts her hands on my shoulders. "I'm here if you need to vent some more, okay? I won't tell Finn. That's your business."

"Thanks," I say before walking out of the bathroom and down the hall to my room. I throw on a comfy pair of capris sweats and a t-shirt. My body is beginning to feel stiff from running so hard and then falling. I walk out to the kitchen to grab some Ibuprofen when Finn walks through the door with dinner. His gaze catches my eye, and we stand staring at each other for a second before he looks away to begin emptying the contents of his bags onto the dining room table.

"Hey," I say softly.

"Hey."

"Finn listen, I..."

"I know, Liv. It's okay"

"No you don't know." I walk over to him and place my hands on his biceps forcing him to look at me. "I'm sorry, okay? I didn't mean to scream at you. You aren't to blame for my bad mood, and I shouldn't have taken it out on you. I'm sorry."

"I understand. It's okay. I don't mind being that guy once in a while; I just want to know that you're okay. Can you tell me what happened today that upset you so badly?"

"No, I can't."

"Why not?" He looks perturbed.

I sigh and look at Finn, searching for the right words to help me explain my thoughts to him. "Because I can't run crying and screaming to the big boss man every time something doesn't go my way just because I'm dating him. That's not fair to everyone else I work with, and really, it's not fair to me. I put myself in a potentially problematic situation when I took this job and agreed to date you at the same time. Please don't make it any more difficult than it already is."

"Are you saying I'm difficult for you? Or that I make working at the Kellan Agency difficult?"

"No, not at all. Neither of those statements is true. I just don't want everyone I work with to view me as your tattling bitch so nobody can trust me or wants to be around me. Can you understand that? What happened today threw me for a loop and pissed me off; but it's nothing I can't handle. So please allow me the opportunity to handle it myself. You don't have to be my babysitter...and I mean that in the nicest way."

Grinning at my explanation, Finn nods in agreement with my request. "I understand. I don't want to smother you, Olivia. Just promise me you'll come to me if things ever start to get out of hand."

I reach up on my tip toes and kiss Finn on his cheek. "I promise. Now let's eat, I'm starving, and then maybe tonight, you can help me forget the bad day I just had."

Chapter 24

New England in the fall is a spectacular fireworks show of warm-colored crayons bursting all over every tree in town. Yellows, reds, oranges, browns: they're all there on display as the weather changes to a cooler crisper feel, especially along the waterfront. Late September always gets me in the mood for pumpkin spice lattes and baked apples. Sometimes I like to pretend that I know what I'm doing in the kitchen and spend an entire day baking just to experience the smell of cooked apples in my apartment, or in today's case, Finn's apartment. We planned to spend the entire weekend together just relaxing in the fall weather. We ran from his place through the Boston Commons and back this morning and stopped at the marketplace on the way back for everything I needed to make apple crisp and Dutch apple pie, two of my favorites. It's nice to spend the day relaxing in our sweats together, just being a normal couple. Work is definitely starting to stress me out more than I want it to, so hiding away with Finn for a couple days feels like a nice escape.

Things at work are changing, and I still can't understand exactly why. I still love my job and everything I have the opportunity to do; but for whatever reason, I'm no longer one of Karen's favorite people, and I know it. My work with the Seal Lake Winery was great, and although Karen tried to make my life a living hell by getting involved in my decisions and making changes to my design, I successfully won when Mandy disagreed with her mom and put her in her place. Score one for me. Whatever Karen's problems are with me, I still have Mandy on my side.

I confronted Karen about what happened with the Boston Cruise Lines but got nowhere. She knows I won't go to Finn for help because that would admit my weakness and would also prove me to be a liar, which I am not. Soon enough, though, Finn asked me about it. He knew that the ending product was not what I had originally planned at all. I found myself in the position to either be a tattletale or a "team player", so I explained to Finn that since Karen and Mr. Porter knew each other so well, she said she knew what he would like and spoke with him about changes while I was in California. Yep, that's right, I defended my bully. I don't know what else I'm supposed to do. I know Karen is a second mom to Finn, so there's no way I will win that fight. It's easier to just let it go. I figure as long as I'm doing a kick-ass job with everything I do, there's no way Karen can hold anything against me. I just wish I knew what I did to upset her so much.

"That smells unbelievably delicious."

I'm standing at the stove, pouring the remains of a cinnamon apple syrup I made a bit ago to put over vanilla ice cream tonight in a bowl, when Finn walks into the kitchen, wrapping his hands around my waist. He brushes my hair off the right side of my neck, granting himself access to my "O.M.G. spot", the spot right behind my earlobe that somehow shares an electric circuit with all the other important girly parts. I stop what I'm doing so that I don't accidentally lose control and pour all the syrup onto the floor, except that just makes me think of how hot it would be to slide around on the floor in warm cinnamon apple syrup naked with Finn.

Oh my God, that's hot!

"You think so?" I ask, smiling as I lean my head to the right, reveling in the warmth of his lips on my neck.

"Mmm-hmm," he says, trailing kisses across my shoulder and back up my neck. As he does so, he slides his hands across my stomach, trailing his fingertips along the waistline of my pants. He's obviously hungry for something other than dessert, so I decide to play along. He will soon be in for a bigger surprise than he anticipates.

"You want a taste?"

"I'm getting my taste right now, Beautiful."

"No silly, that's not what I meant. Here." I hold the bowl up to him and dip my finger into the syrup. He watches with lustful hungry eyes as I put my finger in my mouth, licking and sucking the delicious sweet syrup. "Mmm," I moan, closing my eyes in appreciation. It really is delectable.

"My turn." Finn dips his finger into the bowl and slowly moves his fingers toward his mouth. I gasp in surprise when I feel the warm syrup being spread behind my ear and down my neck. It feels like warm mud, or better yet, warm chocolate fudge. A whispered moan escapes my mouth at his surprise touch.

"Shhh. Put the bowl down, Beautiful. We wouldn't want to lose any of that when you lose control of yourself and drop it on the floor."

"Who says I'll…lose…con…trol?" I drop the bowl back to the counter clumsily as Finn's hands begin to move in opposite directions from one another. His left hand slides up under my shirt and glides smoothly over my skin until it comes to a halt just underneath my right breast. His right hand slips underneath the waistband of my pants and heads south where his fingers quickly come into contact with my now warm, wet skin. Luckily, the bowl makes it back safely to the counter because when Finn begins to slowly lick the syrup that is spread behind my ear while simultaneously cupping my breast and rubbing his fingers between my legs, I do indeed lose all control.

And I don't care.

I'll let him win.

Over and over again.

Because I love this game.

"You're so sweet, Olivia. I could lick this off of you all day, and you're not wearing a bra…or panties. What the hell are you trying do to me?" Finn's breathing is heavy and quickly speeding up. I can feel his breath as he licks and sucks on my neck.

"We're just spending the day here at home, so I guess I just assumed they would end up on the floor eventually. So why bother?"

I smirk, unsure if he can see my face or if he is even looking at my face at all. It's all I can do to stand up straight and not lose all the feeling in my legs. I push my chest out slightly signaling my enjoyment of Finn's fondling, and he answers my request for more. I watch as his hand slips out of my shirt and back into the bowl of apple syrup. He slides his hand back under my shirt, grabbing me with now warm sticky fingers, and I cry out with arousal as he pulls me tightly into his embrace. Even through his black sweatpants, there is no mistaking his excitement.

"Olivia."

"Finn," I moan with pleasure. "Please…that feels…sooo…good."

"You smell divine, Olivia," he whispers, trailing his tongue up my neck to my ear. "Babe, I promise to give you whatever you want for the rest of the weekend, but if I don't lather your beautiful body with this warm softness and take you over my kitchen table, I'm not sure I can call myself a man."

I back up into Finn a bit more, grabbing his leg behind me. "Well you are certainly all man, so who I would I be to turn you down?" I'm so turned on he could ask me to do the Hokey Pokey, and I would say yes.

Finn turns my body while still in his arms and walks us both the few steps over to the small kitchen dinette to our right. He pulls my shirt over my head and cups both of my breasts from behind, rubbing and squeezing them, slowly spreading the sugary substance all over me. It feels like a light exfoliator and a bottle of warming lube all rolled into one.

It's Heaven on my body.

Finn bends me over the kitchen table and slowly pulls my sweatpants down trailing kisses down my butt and thighs.

"Olivia, you are so beautiful. I need to have you now, right now before I explode just looking at you."

"Yes PLEASE, Finn. Hurry."

I hear Finn's pants hit the floor and know he steps back for a minute. I grab onto the sides of the table, ready for him to mount me like an animal. I'm all for making love, but sometimes messy carnal sex is just what the doctor ordered. This is just straight up messy fun.

Before I can take a deep breath, Finn's hands are grabbing my breasts, lathering them with what has to be the remaining cinnamon apple syrup. Fuck the ice-cream. I don't care. Dear God, I don't care.

"Hold on, Beautiful. I don't want to hurt you." Finn kisses my shoulder and then my neck and then kisses me between my shoulder blades all while continuing to fondle my breasts, spreading the warmth with every movement he makes. I can feel his erection between my legs and feel him spread my feet a tiny bit more with his own. He grabs my nipples and pinches them both as he slams into me, rocking me into the table with a grunt.

"HOLY SHIT, FINN!!" I scream.

"Are you okay? Am I hurting you?"

"No God, please keep going! Don't stop!"

He feels fantastic inside me this way. I feel him as he slowly pulls nearly all of the way out, but rather than bracing for impact of his next thrust, I meet him halfway as he slams into me again. The kitchen dinette scrapes on the floor and repeatedly slams into the wall in front of us with the force of our weight as our bodies move together. We continue with this rhythm accelerating together until we are both so frantic we can't hold back anymore. I hear Finn grunt as he pumps his release into me on his final thrust, which in turn, pushes me over the edge into my own sweet release. There we are, both standing naked in Finn's kitchen, both a sticky, sweaty, sweet smelling mess and happier than we have ever been.

"I love you, Liv." Finn's forehead is resting between my shoulder blades, his heavy breathing matching my own.

"I love you too, Finn.

Finn kisses my back once more before I feel him pull out of me and stand up. I turn around to face him and snuggle into his embrace. The warmth of the apple substance on my chest causes our bodies to stick together.

"Baby, you smell delicious but we should probably shower and then clean up our mess."

"Only if you'll join me."

"Olivia, that is an offer I will never refuse."

Once we are both showered and redressed, Finn orders us a pizza for dinner. I guess he had had his fill of making a mess with food for the day, but I don't blame him. It's nice to just relax on his living room floor together making small talk, and quite frankly, staring at Finn in his black sweat pants and fitted t-shirt is something I could do for the entire rest of the weekend. I relish in the way he makes me feel when I'm with him: so safe, so cared for, so loved. I don't know how you ever really know when a guy is "The One", but looking at Finn today, I could easily see him as my forever person.

"Finn, I want to talk about something for a minute."

Finn chews his bite of pizza and nods his head at me. "Okay." He takes a big breath and wipes his mouth with his napkin. "Actually I wanted to talk to you, too, but you go first. What do you want to talk about?"

"Toby."

Finn cautiously tilts his head. "Toby? What about Toby?"

"I want to meet him...again, I mean."

Finn sits stone still for a moment, looking at me with a vacant expression. He shakes his head slowly. "Olivia, you really don't have to do that for me. I can plan to see him when you're not here. I understand."

"Yeah but..."

"But what?"

I sit there on the floor, folding up my napkin one hundred different ways trying to think about how to explain what I'm thinking to him. I just can't come up with the right words.

"Liv?"

"I....umm," I start as I take a deep breath. I may as well get it all out in one breath before I change my mind. "Okay, well what if there comes a time, and I mean a while from now not like right now, but even some time in the next year or so, where maybe we're together more often than we are now?"

enter cricket sounds here

"I mean, I don't want you to feel like you have to be alone just so you can hang out with Toby, although, maybe you would rather be alone, and you won't want me around more; I don't know. I didn't mean to invite myself I just, I meant, maybe it would be nice to have him here with us you know, when we're together."

More crickets...

Why isn't he saying anything?
Even more crickets...
Oh, God! What did I do?

"Finn? Can you please say something because you're starting to freak me out here?"

Finn blinks finally and tilts his head, watching me curiously.

"You would do that? For me? You would be willing to meet Toby again, for me?"

"I love you, Finn. And up until about eight years ago or so I loved dogs. Sometimes I look at you and think of Toby and think to myself that maybe God put you in my life for a reason. Maybe it's some sort of fate that Toby looks so much like Max, and he's your therapy dog, I mean, isn't it ironic?"

"Yes, Alanis, I think it is."

I chuckle and shake my head at Finn's Alanis Morissette reference. I stare at him for a moment, allowing my thoughts to play catch up. "Maybe you're that missing puzzle piece I lost years ago. Maybe you're the entire red side to my fucked up Rubik's Cube. I don't know, but I know I love you, and I know I love being with you, and I love being a part of your life and an important part of your life is Toby, so I want him to become an important part of my life as well. That is, if it's...if it's what you want."

I shake my head in uncertainty. "I can't promise it will be easy or that it will go perfectly the first time, but the fact that I'm even able to talk about a dog and not break into a panic-induced sweat means something is changing for me."

I can't make out the expression on Finn's face, but when I finish talking he immediately throws down his pizza slice and crawls over to me, and before I know it, my back is on the ground, and he is cradling me in his arms.

"Olivia McGuire, I'm not sure I could be more in love with you than I am right here, right now. I don't know where you came from, or how I was lucky enough to find you but...thank you. Thank you for even wanting to try this for me. For trying to overcome your fears...for me. I'm not even sure what else I can say other than you're amazing, and you're beautiful. Even beneath your beautiful you're beautiful, Olivia, and I love you. Every part of you."

"Right back at ya, Hot Runner Guy." I smile and quickly wipe the happy tear away that is floating down my cheek. "You make me so happy, Finn Kellan."

Finn sits up and stares at me for a moment, contemplating something. I can't tell if he's coming up with a mischievous plan or if he's just thinking back to our conversation, so I let him sit there for a minute.

"So, in the past couple of hours you gave me the unbelievable opportunity to spread apple syrup on your body and take you over my kitchen table - that part I've been fantasizing about for a while now - and now you're telling me you want to meet Toby." Finn shakes his head. "What did I do to deserve all this, and what can I give you in return? I'll do as you wish, Olivia. All you have to do is ask."

As you wish...

As you wish...

"Well, how about you call and see if we can meet with Toby tomorrow while I clean up this pizza and get us a drink, and then we'll have the movie night we originally planned. Then if we're still awake after that, I can challenge you to a game of Twister." I smirk.

Finn's eyes light up like a little kid on Christmas at my suggestion. "I think that sounds like a perfect Saturday night with my girl; but before I call about Toby, I want to tell you about an opportunity that could come our way, your way, if you want it."

"Ooh I'm intrigued!"

What could this possibly be?

"Well, I ran into a friend of mine the other day who is on the board at Mass. General Hospital, and he mentioned that they're working on revamping their pet therapy program. That's where I met Toby, so that program and supporting its success is sort of personal for me. Anyway, I told them I would do whatever I could to help with their advertising. It would be pro-bono of course, my gift to them for all they've done for me and...my family."

"Finn, that's incredible! I'm willing to help in any way I can if you want it. You don't even have to ask." I'm elated to be able to do this with Finn and for Finn. My intrigue of the entire project perks up immediately. I could skip movie night and go right to the planning stage of this project if it weren't for Finn's expression.

Uh oh....there's bad news to this?

Would Karen be on the team too?

I feel the smile slip from my face as I swallow the huge lump in my throat. He looks scared. This can't be good.

"Yeah I do need to ask you actually. That's just the thing, Liv. Asking you to help me with this project would mean possibly subjecting you to being in the company of dogs. I would never, ever want to put you into an environment that would cause you pain or anxiety or stress of any kind, but if it's something you're interested in, I would love to do it with you. Just you and me, together. Consider it your, uh, extra-curricular activity. I would pay you on the side." Finn leans in to place a kiss on my neck. "Maybe with chocolate syrup next time if you know what I mean."

"Ah. Yes I think I understand very well, and I think it sounds like an amazing opportunity. Can we talk about it more tomorrow once I've spent some time with Toby? Maybe I'll have a better idea of how I'll be around dogs in general after that."

"Yeah, of course. I just want you to be comfortable. This is just one of those major opportunities that comes up now and again that will help push the company name in the spotlight and could be a huge springboard for your career. If it's what you want, Liv, I want it for you."

I lean forward from where I'm seated and kiss Finn. As our lips separate, I nuzzle his nose with mine and give him another swift peck. "You're the best, Finn. I love you."

"I love you, too, Beautiful. I'll go see if I can schedule Toby. Can you get our movie started?"

"As you wish," I giggle picking up the pizza box and our plates to take to the kitchen.

"What's so funny?" Finn asks, confused.

"You'll see!" I shout from the kitchen as he makes his way into his office to make his call.

It's an epic fail that I've allowed Finn to go this long in our relationship having never seen "The Princess Bride", so that, of course, is the movie I select for us to watch for the evening. We relax on the couch, snuggled under my favorite ivory throw blanket, and enjoy the rest of our evening together, including our late night game of Twister. I won this time, by the way.

Chapter 25

We are just cleaning up breakfast when the doorbell rings. Trying to remain as nonchalant as possible, I continue to put away the last coffee mug. Placing the mug onto the shelf above my head, my hand shakes slightly, making the mug wobble before I let it go and slide it back further on the shelf. I quickly clear my throat in an effort to hide the wobbling sound of the ceramic mug. Meeting Toby is my idea, and I know in my heart I'm brave enough and willing, if not also a little excited; but my nerves are telling a completely different story. I don't want Finn to think I'm weak and can't handle it. I really don't want to disappoint him.

"Hey." Finn places his hand on my shoulder and lightly kisses my neck. The physical touch of Finn's hands is more calming to me than he could ever know. It makes me smile.

"It's okay to be nervous. I would be worried if you weren't."

Obviously, he heard my wobbling coffee mug. Damn shaky hands.

"I'm sorry. I really do want this," I try to explain away my nerves. I give Finn a slightly panic-stricken look that he would disagree with our visit this morning. I pray that won't be his decision.

"I know. And I know you can do it, but don't rush yourself, okay? I'll get the door this time. Let me get Toby settled, and I'll come get you. We'll do this together."

I squeeze Finn's arm that was wrapped around me. "Thank you, Finn."

"Anything for you, Beautiful."

Moments later, I stand in the kitchen listening as Finn answers the door and greets Toby's owner and then Toby. Listening to the way he treats his favorite dog makes my heart happy. Thoughts run through my head of Finn responding to his son or daughter in the same manner. He will make an excellent father one day.

Whoa! Not too soon, Liv!

I hear Finn talking with Toby's owner about me before she says her goodbyes and retreats out the door. She wishes us both a calm and relatively uneventful day. I chuckle, understanding her reference to my panic attack the last time I met Toby.

It's now or never.

I want this.

It's not Max; it's Toby. It's not Max; it's Toby.

"Liv?" My head snaps up, and my eyes meet Finn's, as he stands in the archway to the kitchen. I must've let my mind wander. I didn't hear him walk in.

"You ready to do this?" he asks calmly, walking towards me, slowly taking my now clammy hands in his. "If you've changed your mind, it's okay. I would understand."

I swallow hard and take a deep breath, smiling at Finn with all the bravery I can muster. I feel the anxiety start to build inside me. I'm feeling hot, and my legs are slightly weak, but I stubbornly push it as far down inside me as it will go. I have to do this. I want to do this. I can do this.

"It's now or never. Let's do it," I say.

He smiles and shakes his head at my resolve. "You're so brave, Liv. It's one of the many things I love about you. Come on."

Remaining hand in hand, Finn is by my side as we walk into the large living room where Toby is sitting waiting for us. As we enter the living room, Toby stands up and wags his tail in an excited welcome. Finn raises his right hand, slightly holding his hand up, and as he does, Toby sits down, and a sense of calmness washes over him. As we start to approach Toby, I pull back on Finn's hand in retreat.

I don't know if I can do this.

He looks so much like Max.

Why does he have to look like Max?

Finn immediately lets go of my hand so that I don't feel trapped, as I take a step back, crossing my arms in front of me.

"Olivia?"

"I...I just..." I wipe the one stupid tear that escapes down my cheek. "I just need a minute. I'm sorry."

Solving Us

"It's ok, Liv. You take all the time you need."

I close my eyes and lower myself to my knees. Finn lowers himself as well to be by my side.

"I can do this." I blow out my breath like I'm pumping myself up to enter the boxing ring.

"You can do this, Liv. I'm right here."

"He's not Max. He's Toby. He's not Max. He's Toby. He's not Max. He's Toby." I open my eyes, ready to face my fear.

"Hey, Bud," Finn says to Toby, running his hands down Toby's back and scratching him behind his ears. "I have someone special for you to meet. She means a lot to me, so show her your best tricks, okay?"

Toby licks Finn's face, which makes me chuckle, chasing away some anxiety. Seeing this strong bond between a man and his dog reminds me again just how attracted I am to Finn. He shows compassion, love, patience, loyalty; these are all the qualities I look for in a husband or a father for my future children.

"Toby, this is Olivia. Olivia," Finn looks at me and squeezes my hand. I immediately lower myself to the floor next to him. "This is Toby."

As if he understands my hesitance, Toby immediately lays on the floor, putting his head on my knee. It's a natural gesture to just reach out my hand and pet him like any dog-loving human would. I shakily reach out to touch Toby. When my hand meets his fur, I'm breathing hard and fast like I'm about to cross a finish line. I run my left hand down Toby's head to his side. He's soft and warm and comforting, just like Max used to be. I feel the tears spring to my eyes. Not because I feel immensely sad. Sitting here with the man I love and the dog he loves, who looks like the dog I loved, fills me with a sense of peace.

"Hi, Toby," I whisper, sniffling back the tears and smiling. I feel Finn's eyes on me, worried for me. I turn my head to look at him and reassure him that I'm okay. This is nice. As I look away from Toby, I feel his body shift and turn back to see him flipping to lay completely flat on his back with his paws dangling in the air. I laugh out loud, knowing exactly what it is Toby is looking for.

"Of course I'll rub your belly, Furball. I bet you love that, don't ya?"

It's easy to love on Toby. It's way easier than I had anticipated, and I can tell by Finn's expression that he is just as surprised if not more so than me, at how easy this seems for me.

After a couple hours of getting to know Toby, and giving him a much-needed belly rub, Finn and I decide to spend the day inside with our furry friend, snuggling and watching television. We sit next to each other on the floor, flipping through T.V. channels until we come across something we could both agree upon, "Harry Potter and the Prisoner of Azkaban". It must be a Harry Potter weekend on ABC Family.

"This one might be my favorite of them all."

"Why is that?" Finn asks me.

"I don't know. I think I'm just a Gary Oldman fan, and he does such a great job in this movie. What about you?"

"'Order of the Phoenix', obviously," Finn says quietly. Toby is resting practically on my lap, and Finn hasn't stopped petting him while he lays here between us.

"Why do you say obviously? We've never really talked about Harry Potter before, have we?"

Finn is silent for a few seconds before looking at me. "Well, I guess it's my favorite and least favorite really. It was the last Harry Potter movie Sydney and I saw together. It was also the night of our accident."

I had forgotten all about the fact that he had taken Sydney to the movies that night. I want to smack myself for forgetting because now I just don't know what to say.

I hear Finn quietly chuckle and shake his head as if he is remembering something. "She used to call herself 'The Girl Who Lived'. Did I ever tell you that? She thought she was so clever."

I smile at the familiar words. "No you never told me that."

Mandy did.

"The girl who lived," Finn sighs. "Until she didn't anymore."

More silence falls between us as we continue to stroke Toby's soft fur.

"I don't really hate dogs, Finn. It's just easier to make myself believe I do, so I don't have to force myself to relive the past, ya know?"

Solving Us

"Yeah. I get it. I don't really hate Harry Potter movies. Actually, I loved the first four movies. I wish I would've seen the rest of them."

"Wait, what? You haven't seen the rest of the series? You stopped after number four?"

"Yep. Never had a desire to see the rest after Sydney was gone. Just didn't feel right seeing them without her."

"Finn, I never knew Sydney...but I just have this sneaking suspicion that she would be pissed to know you never went to see the other movies. You did read the books, right?"

Silence...

I gasp looking at Finn's face, which clearly says he has not read any of the Harry Potter books.

"You know this could be a deal breaker, right? I mean, it is one thing for you to have never seen 'The Princess Bride', but to have never read Harry Potter?" I shake my head in playful disgust. "I'm just not sure I can be with you until you sort this all out, Finn."

Finn looks at me fiercely. "No, no no, Miss McGuire. You don't get to get rid of me that easily. I'll have the fifth book checked out of the library tomorrow." Finn leans over Toby, who has now woken up between us, and kisses me hungrily.

"I love you Olivia," he breathes.

"I love you, too, Finn Kellan."

Chapter 26

Six months.

I've been with the Kellan Agency for six months to the day. I love the opportunity for creativity and teamwork. I love that my client list is growing exponentially and love the working/personal relationships I've formed with many of my colleagues. Grace Hoover has become my "work mom" more and more as of late. Her excitement towards Finn and me as a couple is never ceasing. Her pride in Finn is obvious in everything that she does for him, which inspires me to always put him in the spotlight when I can. He deserves the success that he has in this city, and I'm proud to be the woman on his arm and the woman in his heart.

Mandy and I have become inseparable at work most of the time. At times, I think she looks a little frayed around the edges, like maybe her relationship with Kym isn't going anywhere, or that she's not happy with what she does here; but she's never said anything to the contrary. She's a good friend to me but seems to be more of a private person as of late, not wanting to chat about her personal life much, which is perfectly fine with me, even if at times it seems our relationship is one sided. The less drama I have in my life, the better.

Austin Rivers and I have worked together a few more times since the day he carried me home after fainting on my run. He's a walking contradiction: the tattooed motorcycle-riding bad boy who has a passion for art and photography, and shall I say, all things in regards to the female form. On the inside I know he's a big teddy bear who enjoys a nice cup of coffee and has had a hard time finding his forever person. I imagine finding the right person is complicated when your outward appearance portrays one persona, but your inner soul is almost completely different.

Maybe I should put him together with Abby.
She could easily see through his bad-boy exterior.

Solving Us

Hmmm, not a bad idea, Olivia!
Mental note: Austin and Abby?

Finn and I are happier than ever. I love and respect that he allows me to use my job at the Kellan Agency to push myself further and challenge myself professionally. Our huge pride and joy right now is the pet therapy program at Massachusetts General Hospital. Finn and I have been volunteering our time there in order to get a strong idea of what their program is all about so that we can create for them a stellar new ad campaign. We've been volunteering twice each week for a month now. We help recruit newly trained dogs into the program and help sift through applicants to match the dogs to the right patients. We also spend time with many of the dogs at the training complex so that they can feel comfortable with Finn and me as well as the trained staff. I have to admit, after all this time I sort of enjoy having a dog around once in a while. The best part about this experience? Karen Elena is not involved! I finally feel like I can breathe when I work because she doesn't get to have a say in this project. Thank God for that.

So, yeah, I love most aspects of my job; but there is one aspect of my daily grind that is really starting to wear on me, and her name is Karen. It's bittersweet every single day having to wake up for work. I love that it means another day of being near Finn and at the very least, sharing texts and emails throughout the day, if not lunch once in a while. But the other part of me loathes having to walk through the office doors in the morning knowing that I have to deal with Karen's shit again. I'm not sure how much more I can take of dealing with the stress of her while keeping my emotions in check in front of everyone in the building, Finn and Mandy especially. No matter what I do, it's not good enough for Karen. She's backed me against the wall, sometimes literally, on every single project I've done here so far. I realize this is my first "real job" in the big leagues, but I'm also not an idiot. I did graduate in the top of my class. I'm pretty sure I understand what I'm doing. I'm not an intern, and I don't need, or want, Karen Elena as my mentor. I wish I could be brave enough to tell her to back the fuck up and let me do my work.

"If that bitch asks me to do one more thing for her…" Mandy stomps into the office throwing a file on the table in the back of the room.

"Uh, everything okay?"

Mandy sighs and stands with her hands on her hips, looking up at the ceiling, shaking her head. I can tell she's trying to calm herself down.

"Yeah it's just Mom. She's been a stressed out bitch for weeks, and it's really starting to piss me off. She's always asking me to finish her work for her. I'm like that nerdy girl in middle school that everyone wants to have do their homework. GAH! She needs to handle her own shit, so I can handle mine!"

Ah, speak of the Devil.

Yes, I've decided Karen is the Devil.

"I don't understand. What has her so busy? We're not under any strict deadlines right now. Our projects aren't due for another couple weeks, or am I missing something?" My heart races for a moment wondering if perhaps I've forgotten an important deadline.

"It's not work." Mandy sits on my desk and slumps against the wall to my cubicle. "She's been taking classes online to earn her marketing photography degree, so she can do more in the company, but she's behind on her work here, of course. She keeps trying to get me to help her with her class projects so she can focus more here. Really I mean, I commend her for trying to better herself, but ya know what? If she can't handle the work, then maybe…" She releases the rest of her deep breath.

I look up from my computer. "Maybe what?"

"Maybe she should just take some time off. Or maybe she should put her degree on hold. She's in over her head in so many ways."

Isn't that the truth!

I wish she would leave me the hell alone, too.

"What kind of project is she working on?" I'm too curious for my own good

"I don't know. It is something to do with Photoshop, or photo editing; something like that. It's just too time consuming for me to help her with that and get my work done here, know what I mean?"

"Does she not want to be the accounts coordinator anymore? She wants to start her own business or what?"

Please let her be starting her own business.
Get her the hell out of my life!

"I think she wants to do more of the creative work like we do, ya know? It's not the mundane paperwork life. We get to be artists, and I think sometimes she envies that. Truth be told, and you didn't hear this from me, but I think she had an interest in your position before you came on board. She doesn't have the exact training for it, but she figured it was a logical move for her. I mean, this is a great place to work and gain experience because Finn treats us all with so much respect. We've really built a great team here, and Mom just wants to be able to do more, ya know? I think she's bored."

I think she's a bitch.
Does Mandy know that Karen hates me?
Should I tell her?
Nope. I can't give Karen that win.

"So, she wants my job?"

"NO, no. Not *your* job per se. Just something different. Hell, I would give her my job if I knew she wanted it that badly. I mean I love it here; I do, but I don't want to be working with my mother for my entire life. I'll never feel freed, ya know? I want to live. I want to socialize more and not feel like she's judging everything I do."

"I understand," I sympathize. "That's why I left my hometown and came to Boston. It was comfortable being back home, but I wasn't growing. I wasn't experiencing anything new or meeting new people. Everyone knows everyone where I'm from. Anyway, I'm sorry she's stressing you out. If you need help with anything, you know I'm here, right? Even if you just need to drink or vent."

Mandy chuckles. "I know you're really involved with the Mass. Gen project. How's that going by the way? Mom asked about it earlier." She stands up and walks back to the table where she dropped the file she carried in but not before I see her cringe.

I tilt my head watching Mandy curiously as she walks to the back of the room. "It's going wonderfully, actually. Finn and I are just about ready to finalize our campaign to show to the client. It's been a fun experience working with them. I've learned a ton about pet therapy. It's a whole world I would've never seen myself in before. What these dogs can do is amazing. And it's awesome getting to spend so much time with Finn. I mean, I would never ever want to take advantage of his position to further my career, but doing this project with him has helped me get my name out there a little more with clientele. That never hurts, ya know? And I learn so much just watching him do his thing. He's very good, very competent and confident. It's attractive." I can feel my cheeks heating up. I'm obviously blushing.

Mandy walks back to her desk. "That's great. Glad to hear it's almost done, though. I'm sure you'll feel better when it's all over, you know, given your fear of dogs and all. I don't know how you do it."

Freeze!

My body is still. I can feel the heat rising in my cheeks. Like I just walked into a sauna I'm not ready for; my body starts to sweat.

Say something Olivia!
How does she?
Why would she?
I never told her about…

"What? Um, I'm not sure I understand what you're talking about."

Good one, Liv.

Mandy peers over the cubicle wall. "Oh shit! I'm sorry, Olivia. Finn told me a while back about your accident with your dog. I'm sorry I totally forgot to tell you that I knew. Don't be mad at Finn, though. He was just worried about you and needed to vent one night. He told me what happened with Toby."

One night?
Is that what he did when I was in California?
He didn't know the whole story then…

"Oh. Well, thanks but that's all in the past now." I shrug, playing it off.

Solving Us

"Good! Phew!" Mandy playfully wipes her brow as if she is relieved to hear my news. "I mean, that could've been a deal breaker with Finn right there, ya know? That guy loves dogs now that Toby is in his life. He would adopt him in a heartbeat if he could. There's always something sexy about a man and his dog, am I right?" She chuckles and sits back down at her desk.

"Yeah," I whisper to myself since I'm quite certain Mandy doesn't hear me.

What the hell was that conversation all about?
If Mandy knows about my past, Karen knows about my past.
If Karen knows, who else knows, too?
Is this ever going to go away?

My phone rings at my desk. I look down at the caller ID and see Finn's name flash across the screen. I take a deep breath and shake my head to clear my thoughts as quickly as possible before picking up the receiver.

"Yes, sir?"

"Hey, Beautiful. I have something to show you, but I would rather do it in person; can you stop by my office quickly?"

"Sure. Be up in a minute."

"Great. See you soon."

I hang up my phone and close my laptop before exiting the office.

"Going somewhere, Olivia?"

Seriously?
Is she keeping constant tabs on me, or what?

I turn around in front of the elevator door to face Karen once again.

"Finn needs to see me for a moment. Did you need something?"

Karen shrugs and shakes her head. "You've just been spending a lot of time in his office lately. You know, for someone who likes to keep her relationship separate from work. Those were your words, weren't they? I just want to make sure you're getting your other projects done in a timely manner. I would hate for you to miss a deadline."

Bitch!
Enough. I've had enough.

You don't get to treat me like shit.

I take a deep breath and smile at Karen refusing to give her what she wants, to see me riled up and emotional over something she said. "First of all Karen, you know very well that Finn and I have been working on a pro-bono project for a while now. Second, my other projects will most certainly be completed in a timely manner, as all of my projects have since I started here. Clients have been contacted, and my team is working diligently. Third, if you have a problem with the amount of time I'm spending with the *CEO* of this company," I annunciate Finn's title as clearly as humanly possible. "Then why don't you accompany me to his office, so we can have that conversation with him? I'm sure he would be more than happy to hear your concerns. He is an excellent listener."

Take that, Bitch!

The elevator dings and the doors open. I step inside and turn around while holding the doors open for Karen. I tilt my head and hold her stare. It's one thing for her to have a say over whether or not I'm doing satisfactory work for this agency; it's a total cross of the line to attempt to call out any of my personal relationships. Karen's nostrils flare, and her eyes narrow momentarily before she recomposes herself.

"Oh believe me, Olivia, Finn knows how I feel, and yes I agree, he is an excellent listener." She rolls her eyes. "I have work to do."

I scoff, quietly standing in the elevator, as I watch her walk away before the doors close in front of me.

Bitch

Bitch

BITCH!

"What the hell have I done to piss her off so much?" I mutter to myself. I work my ass off around here. I've more than proven myself as a competent and successful member of this team, and yet the sand in her vagina just won't wash away. She makes me want to drink. I need Abby to calm me down. I need my person, a stiff margarita, some loud music, and night of dancing until I can't move anymore.

"Ugh, she's a bitch!"

Solving Us

"Who's a bitch?" Finn asks me wearing his amused expression. The elevator doors had opened simultaneously to me talking to myself I suppose a little too loudly. Oops.

I sigh and roll my eyes. "Nobody."

"Olivia?" Finn's amusement washes away quickly and is replaced with concern. "What is it?"

"No, nothing. Sorry. I'm fine. Just...it's nothing. I can take care of it. Nothing a good run and a strong drink can't fix."

"Yeah, because that fixed whatever was bothering you the last time you ran after a stressful day. Do you have an angry client or something?"

"It's fine, really. I don't want to talk about it right now." I put my hand up in front of me as if to shoo away the questions and concerns.

Finn takes a deep breath and assesses my expression before conceding to my request. "Okay, but promise me if it starts to stress you out that you'll come to me."

"I'm a big girl, Finn. I can handle it, but thank you for your concern." I smile at him as sweetly as I can and take a quick deep breath. "So, what did you want to show me?"

"Right. Yes, come with me to my office."

I walk with Finn down the hallway to his office, saying hello to Grace Hoover along the way. "So, I have us scheduled to meet with the hospital board on Friday to present our campaign. Do you want to do the honors? You don't have to, but you taking the lead would absolutely put your name in the spotlight."

"You really want me to do that? I mean, this has been your idea all along. It's kind of like your baby. I would never piggy-back on your position, Finn." I feel his hand on the small of my back as he escorts me into his office shutting the door behind him. He grabs my right hand and tugs me into him, kissing me soundly before stepping back and cradling my face in his hands.

Whoa!

Whatever that was, I'll take two please!

"And that response is why I'm in love with you, Olivia McGuire. You didn't know who I was when we met. You've given this company one hundred and ten percent, and you've never asked me for a professional favor. Don't think I haven't noticed. I want to do this for you."

"If it's what you want, Mr. Kellan," I tease. "Then I'll be happy to lead the presentation, thank you." I softly kiss his cheek and smile at his amusement.

"There's something else I need to ask you," Finn says excitedly.

"Okay; I'm all ears."

"Well, the hospital is planning a fundraising gala for December eighteenth, and they would like to unveil our ad campaign, assuming they approve it, at the gala. They have extended us an invitation to attend the gala, everyone at the Kellan Agency in fact."

My eyebrows rise in surprise. "Wow! That sounds like a fun evening."

Does Karen have to come, too?

"Yeah, it does. I've been to hospital galas before, and I can promise you this one will be every bit as phenomenal."

Finn leaves me and walks over to his desk where I just happen to see his Rubik's Cube resting on his planner, completely red on one side. Was I supposed to notice that? He picks up a single long stemmed red rose and a box that looks eerily like a shoebox.

"We talked a long time ago about the fact that you never got to go to your senior prom." He smirks. I can't help but chuckle out loud.

Where is this going, and what is in that box?

"Okay, yeah. Keep talking." I laugh at the twinkle in Finn's eyes. I'm pretty sure I can feel what's coming next.

"Well," Finn starts. "I was going to send you a check-yes-or-no letter, but I thought nah, that's too old fashioned. I was going to plan a flash mob performance, but I just don't have the time to rehearse, so screw it. I can do better than a high school prom anyway, so Olivia, would you do me the honor of attending the Gala on my arm? If you say yes, I'll show ya what's in the box, but if you say no...well, I guess I'll just have to return the box." He winks.

Solving Us

He presents me with the rose, and I laugh again at his extreme cuteness. "Well..." I pretend to think about my options for a minute, scrunching up my nose and twisting my mouth. "I would say no but...I have to know what's in that box, so you're in luck Mr. Kellan; I would love to go with you." I wink back at him.

Finn laughs with me as he hands me the box wrapped in shimmering silver paper complete with a silver bow. "Here. A little something I thought you might like to wear on prom night." Finn gives me his shit-eating grin that makes me blush immediately. He wouldn't dare present me with lingerie at work, so I hope these are shoes...or gloves or a shawl or something. I rip open the paper, and my eyes grow huge at the white box I'm holding in my hand. I know by the name printed neatly across the top of the box that this is no cheap gift. I slowly open the lid and lay my eyes on the most stunning pair of shoes I think I have ever seen: champagne metallic leather platform heels.

"Jimmy Choo? Finn, oh my gosh I can't believe...what did you...why did...? These are gorgeous!" My mind is completely blown as I take a shoe out of the box, handing the box to Finn to hold. I turn the sparkling shoe over and around in my hands, inspecting every detail from the curved lines of the straps that almost cross in the front of the shoe to the adorable zippers in the back.

"You'll be my Cinderella wearing the most beautiful almost-glass-slippers at the ball. I can't wait to have you on my arm."

"Finn, this is so incredibly sweet. Thank you so much. This is too much, really. I'm so flattered that you even remembered my not going to my prom. You're such a gentleman, and I would be proud to attend the gala with you."

The remainder of my day is blissfully calm since Karen has left early to work on her classwork. It's nice to laugh with the guys and quietly get my to-do list accomplished. I still make sure to tell Abby all about my run-in with Karen when I get home from work. Sure enough, as soon as I'm done talking, we order Chinese food for dinner and then rip open the tequila, vodka, gin, rum, and triple sec and for me, the raspberry liqueur. We crank up the wireless speaker and dance out to every angry song we can think of. My personal favorite is wholeheartedly dedicated to Karen Elena. I sing the lyrics to "You're a Bitch", by Cars Can be Blue louder than I think I ever have without a care in the world of any of our neighbors. If anyone comes knocking to complain, we'll just invite him or her to join us. Sometimes you just have to dance the bad day away with your best friend.

Chapter 27

Finn and I put in many long hours together working on the new ad campaign for "Paws for Patients", Mass. General Hospital's pet therapy program. The hospital board loved our presentation and unanimously voted to approve the campaign for print. In just one month, we will be with our clients as they roll out the red carpet for their fundraising gala, where they will unveil the new campaign. This event is shaping up to be huge! Excitement abounds around the office as everyone prepares for the formal party. Ladies talk animatedly about dress shopping, while the guys talk about how much free alcohol will be on tap. This is all typical, but what has me excited is not just that I'll be on the arm of the most attractive man in Boston but that my BFF and roommate, Abby, will get to attend with me. I wasn't surprised when Austin called Abby for a date several weeks ago. I could see the interest there the first time they laid eyes on each other. I'm pretty sure I called this pairing not too long ago, and to be honest, I sort of like the idea. Austin is a great guy and seems grounded enough for Abby's live-by-the-seat-of-her-pants ways. They seem good together so far, and I'm happy for them, even if they do move pretty fast.

Abby and I spend Saturday afternoon dress shopping at Saks Fifth Avenue. We go through gown after gown after gown until we both find what we are looking for. Abby, of course, picks out a V-neck gown in black and white. It is stunning, and although a little short in the front for my personal taste, the dress screams her name when she puts it on. It hugs her in all the right places and shows off her gorgeous long legs that every guy seems to drool for. Abby is never afraid of taking risks, and as she puts it, "It's easy access in case he wants to cop a feel." I just shake my head, roll my eyes, and laugh.

That's my Abs.

After what feels like thirty different gowns, I finally find the perfect dress for myself. I want something with sleeves, given the winter season upon us. I want something dark in color that will still look magnificent with my Jimmy Choos, and I want something understated. It's not my intention to stand out among the crowd at this gala. I just want to feel like Cinderella spending an evening with her prince. I find a long-sleeved, midnight blue duchesse satin gown with a V-back and tiered train. It is beautifully understated but exquisite. It also covers all of my scars flawlessly, so I know I won't be distracted with insecure thoughts throughout the evening. Ironically, when I step out of the dressing room, I know it's the dress for me when Abby says, "Well shit, Olivia. If you had glass slippers and a tiara, you could be Cinderella in that gown. I think that's the one."

We both decide to make these dresses and our manis and pedis we scheduled for the day of the gala our Christmas gifts to each other. This is just a little splurge among friends. Finn offered to pay for our shopping spree earlier this week, but I politely turned him down. Damn if he isn't the most thoughtful man I have ever met, but I'm not with Finn for his money. Abby and I are doing just fine on our own, and what better way to celebrate the holidays with my BFF than painting our nails and dressing up like princesses for one night. After we make our purchases, I send a quick text to Finn to let him know of my success.

Me: Found a dress! Can't wait to be your Cinderella!

Finn: Great.

Me: Miss you though. Are you having a good day?

Finn: Yeah.

Me: What are you up to?

Finn: Not much.

Me: Are you working?

Finn: No.

Me: Hey. Why the short answers? Are you okay?

Finn: I'm fine.

I frown at Finn's last text. He's definitely not fine. I'm not sure why he's giving me such short answers; this doesn't seem like him at all. He almost sounds pissed off or sad or...
Wait.
Oh no.
"Abby, what's the date today?" I ask cautiously.

Abby pulls out her cell phone in the cab and checks the date. "It's November fifteenth. Why? Something wrong?"

"Shit," I whisper to myself.

"What? What is it? Did you miss a deadline or something?" she asks.

"No. This is the weekend Sydney died. November sixteenth. I was just texting with Finn, and his answers are short and straight and that's usually not like him. That has to be it. He's upset. It's an anniversary for him, and I forgot about it! How could I have been so stupid?"

"Liv, it's totally okay. Go to him! Spend the night with him, and give him some love to help him through. We had a great day, but he needs you."

"Maybe he doesn't want me there. He could've told me when we talked about this weekend that he wanted me there, but he didn't. But then again, maybe he's upset that I didn't even think about the date. Ugh! I'm the worst girlfriend."

"Trust me, Liv. He may think he doesn't want you there, or that it's okay that you're not there, but I'm positive if you walked into his apartment right now he would hug you and thank you for coming. Men need us as much as we need them. They're just too proud to say it. Go. You need to be there."

"Yeah? You sure you're okay with that? I don't ever want to just split on you, Abs. This was a fantastic girls' day."

"Are you kidding? We're both going to look drop dead gorgeous, and we did get to spend the morning and afternoon together. It would be terrible for you to not be there for him when he needs you. He just doesn't know he needs you. Or maybe he does and doesn't want to spoil your weekend."

"You're the best bestie a girl could have; you know that?"

Abby throws me her cat-ate-the-canary grin as she likes to do as our cab pulls up to our apartment building. "Sure as hell do. Now give me your dress, and get out of here. Go do your thing. And give him a little hug from me."

"Thanks, Abs. And don't think I don't know that you're going right upstairs to call Austin, so you can get some tonight."

"I have no idea what you're talking about, Olivia!" That's all I hear as she waltzes into our building.

I sit back in my seat and give the cab driver Finn's address. "Oh, but can we stop somewhere first? I need to pick up something."

"Yes, Ma'am."

Twenty minutes and a quick trip to Target later, I'm thanking my cab driver and heading into Finn's apartment building. The guard already knows who I am and doesn't question my appearance, so I head up on the elevator. Finn has no idea I'm here, so I'm hoping he's happy to see me. When I knock on his door, I immediately hear Toby barking.

Of course Toby would be here.

Good. This is good.

The door swings open, and I'm greeted by two of my favorite guys.

"Olivia? What are you doing here?" Finn looks a little worried, so I do my best to put him at ease as quickly as possible.

"I'm a terrible girlfriend who didn't even think about what weekend this was, and I'm so sorry for that. It wasn't on purpose; I promise," I breathe. "But, I'm here now."

Finn gives me a weak smile and tilts his head, watching me like I'm a cute puppy dog doing tricks. "You didn't have to break your date with Abby, Liv. I'm okay."

"Really?" I ask quietly. I don't want to offend him or make a bigger deal out of this weekend than I should, but his sweatpants, t-shirt, messy hair, and a beer in his hand tell me something different. "Because I can…"

Solving Us

"NO!" He interrupts. "I mean, you're here now, so I don't want you to leave."

I hold up the bag in my hands to show him. "I have a bag full of X-Men movies, graham crackers, and Hershey bars. Want to share?"

The look on Finn's face says it all. He's astonished that I remembered the stories he's told me about him and Sydney. He reaches out his hand and pulls me into his arms, wrapping them tightly around me. I feel him kiss the top of my head before he inhales deeply.

"Thanks, Liv. I'm really glad you're here."

Toby barks beside us and paws my leg. He's wagging his tail as I bend down to pet him. "Are you glad I'm here, too, big boy? Is this guy not snuggling you enough, or what?"

Finn laughs and picks me up, throwing me over his shoulder as I yelp in surprise. I watch Toby follow along behind us as Finn carries me to the living room couch. "I'll show you snuggling, Woman. I can snuggle with the best of them."

"Hahaha! I know you can, Captain. I know you can!"

Finn throws me onto the couch and lowers himself on top of me. He locks eyes with mine before sharing a very slow, very sweet kiss. "I really am glad you're here, Liv. This is the first time in seven years that I've shared this anniversary with anyone other than my parents."

"I don't want to be anywhere else, Finn. Thank you for letting me share it with you." I kiss him gently. "I love you. You know that, right?"

"Yeah," He nods. "Yeah, I do. I love you, too, Olivia."

I give him another quick peck on his cheek. "Now get a blanket or two, and let's get started on these movies. We have a lot to watch."

"Why don't *you* grab your favorite blanket from the bedroom and go change into your pajamas, so I don't feel so underdressed. I'll get us some drinks to go with our snacks."

"You got it."

Once I'm comfortably snuggled next to my two favorite boys, Finn and I relax and settle in for a weekend of X-Men movies, junk food, puppy cuddling, and all around laziness, loving every minute of it.

*****

"It's right over here," Finn says, pointing to the gravestone with Sydney's name on it.

"It's beautiful." That is all I can say when we reach the spot.

We stop in front of a gorgeous gray marble stone in a row of other headstones. Nearby is a beautiful oak tree and a small reflecting pond. Though a cemetery wouldn't be my first choice as a place to hang out, the feeling here is serene, quiet, and quite welcoming. I hold Finn's hand as he steps forward and places the red and yellow calla lilies on Sydney's grave.

"Hey, Syd," Finn says quietly. "I miss you." He releases a big breath that I watch escape into the cold air around us. "Every day I miss you, Syd, but especially today. I'm sorry, Syd. I'm so sorry."

I squeeze Finn's hand in mine to let him know I'm with him and to help encourage him to be strong. He looks at me standing next to him, tears welling in his eyes. I shouldn't be so surprised that this is still so hard for him. Hell, I still have my bad days, too, and my story hasn't ended. I step into him a little more and wrap my arm around him, placing my hand on his chest to comfort him. We stand silently for a minute or two. I'm not certain of what I should say, if anything, so I remain silent and follow Finn's lead. He clears his throat quietly before continuing his conversation with his little sister. "I know I usually come alone, but, Syd, I brought someone I want you to meet. Her name is Olivia, and, Syd, I know you would love her as much as I do if not more since, well, you know she's a girl and stuff. You guys are the same age, so you would probably like the same stuff. I don't know, but I love her, Sydney. She's my everything, and I just wanted you to see her."

"It's nice to meet you, Sydney," I say. "I've heard so many wonderful things about you. Thank you for sharing your brother with me. I promise to protect him and take care of him."

Solving Us

"Oh and, Syd," Finn grabs the bag off the ground that we brought with us. "I wanted to bring you something but couldn't decide what to bring, so we decided you might want a snack. Here you go."

Finn takes out the graham cracker and Hershey bar sandwich we made for Sydney and lays it on the ground next to the flowers. I smile endearingly as he leaves the gift for the sister he loves so much.

"Enjoy. Love you, Sydster." Finn sniffles as he backs up to where I'm standing. I wrap my arms around him and hug him with everything I have. I don't know how many people fall in love in cemeteries, but I swear I fell deeper in love with him just now.

"Thank you, Olivia." Finn breathes into my ear as he kisses my hair.

"For what?"

"For coming here with me. For being with me this weekend. For knowing what I needed when I didn't know it myself. I love you more than you can possibly know."

"I love you, too, Finn. I'm honored to be here with you. You know I would do anything for you. I never got to meet your sister, but I have to think in my heart that she would be very happy to see where your life has gone since she left you."

Finn takes my hand and leads me around the pond back to where we're parked. We drive slowly out of the cemetery; the musical voices of Coldplay fill the car around us.

This one's for you, Sydney.

Chapter 28

I wake up on the morning of December 18th with a smile on my face. I'm ready to spend the day with Abby preparing for our night of celebrations, but first, a good steady run is in order to kick my energy into gear. I pick up my phone and send a quick text to Finn before heading out on my run. I smile to myself knowing that the slightly cheesy song will make Finn laugh as he starts his morning, too.

Me :"Good Time" - Owl City and Carly Rae Jepsen

My phone dings, alerting me to a text message while I'm running through the park outside of our apartment building.

Finn: Animals - Maroon 5

I almost trip when I read the song title Finn sends me. He knows how much I obsess over Maroon 5. That song is one of those songs that can turn me on like nothing else, and Finn knows it. I roll my eyes at the innuendo I know he is giving me with his text and continue running. It's a chilly run through town, as the forecast calls for cold temperatures and overcast skies for the next few days. A nor'easter is on its way this weekend, so I'm glad this gala is happening now. It'll be nice to be snowed in for a few days with my Prince Charming. I take a quick break to stretch my calves before turning around to run home. My nerves for this evening have been creeping up on me, and I can feel the tension throughout my body. I just want everything to go perfectly. I shoot another quick text to Finn before heading back.

Me: Don't forget the flash drive I gave you yesterday for tonight.

Finn: As if I could forget that. Haha! Nervous much?

Me: Ooh touche. Sorry. Just going through my mental checklist before I get ready. On my morning run. Love you.

Finn: Don't worry. Karen is here helping me gather everything up. We'll be fine. You'll be great! Can't wait to see you!

"WHAT?"

"NO!"

"SHIT!"

I begin pacing with my phone in one hand and my other hand on my hip. My anxiety level climbs another five notches.

What does he mean Karen is helping him?

Why is she even at the office today?

Can I trust her?

How can I trust her?

How can I possibly tell Finn?

I've kept him in the dark for six months.

"SHIT!" I scream looking around quickly in hopes that nobody is within earshot; it appears I'm alone, which is good because I don't want anyone to see me panic. I feel like I don't have a choice anymore. I have to tell Finn everything. He has to know the truth now before everything is ruined; but what if she's already spoken to him, and if she has, what has she said? I know I'm about to make a rash decision, but I don't have time to think any more. I start running in the opposite direction of home, hoping that when I reach my destination I'll know exactly what to say. In about twelve minutes, I'm jogging into the Kellan Agency, surprisingly a sweaty mess given the temperature outside. My face feels windblown and chapped, but my body is on fire with rage, anxiety, and worry about what Karen may or may not be doing to our campaign. She wouldn't dare do this to Finn, would she?

I jump off the elevator as soon as it opens and run into the lobby near Finn's office. Mrs. Hoover isn't here, which I think is a little odd. She's usually here whenever Finn is here but then again, he was only stopping in for a couple hours this morning to finish a report and reply to a few emails before packing up for the night. I suppose I shouldn't be surprised that she's not here; she's probably out getting ready for the gala herself. I continue briskly down the hall towards Finn's office and barge through his door without even thinking to knock first. As soon as I do, I immediately regret it.

"Olivia? What are you...? Are you okay?" Finn drops the brochures that he was holding onto the conference table in front of him and dashes to my side. He runs his hands down my face and arms lifting them as he goes.

What's he looking for?

Injuries?

He thinks I'm hurt and came running here?

"Yeah I'm...fine. I'm fine." I try to brush his hands off of me to show him that I'm okay, but he just looks at me in shock.

"I don't understand, Liv; what are you doing here?"

"Yeah, Liv. I thought you and Abby had manis and pedis this morning?" I look across the room and see Karen and Mandy standing at the conference table. It looks as though they're filling boxes. I had no idea Mandy was here, too. Finn never told me that she was here helping him as well. Now I'm the one confused.

"Umm, yeah I do, but they're not until twelve-thirty and I..."

Think of something to say fast, Olivia!

"Well, I was running in the area this morning and thought I would stop in and help. I uh...I'm sorry I didn't know you guys were both here. I thought I would just surprise you." I look at Finn and try my damnedest to smile, even though smiling is the very last thing I want to do.

"Well I *am* surprised, so thank you for that. And you must be more nervous than I thought," Finn chuckles and kisses me on my cheek. "Because I texted you about twenty minutes ago that Karen was here helping me. You didn't need to worry about it. You're sure you're okay?"

"Right. Yeah. You did tell me that. I'm sorry; I guess I'm just anxious about tonight. I know what a huge deal this is for you, Finn." I turn my head to stare at Karen as I speak. "I just don't want anything to go wrong that would make the company look bad."

Solving Us

"Of course you don't, Olivia. Your feelings are completely normal," Karen tries to assure me. "I was just telling Finn how proud of you both I am. This campaign is magnificent. You've both put in a lot of time and effort for a great cause. I'm certain tonight will be your time to shine, and everyone who loves you will be there to celebrate with you."

"Liv, all the work is done. We were just packing up all the promotional materials. The huge campaign banner was directly delivered to the hospital, and Finn has the flash drive with tonight's presentation. We just went through it together before you walked in. It's fantastic!" Mandy winks as she walks toward me.

"Now, you stink, and you look all windblown from running. Go home and relax, and then get your pretty self ready to shake it off with me and the gang tonight! You're going to need your energy! In fact, maybe you should take Finn with you and work off some that nervous energy with him, if ya know what I'm sayin'." She gives me the double eyebrow raise and winks again which makes me laugh. Seriously, this girl has no filter.

"That sounds like a great plan!" Finn turns to me. "I'm sure these ladies can close up the office. I'll take you home."

"NO!" I say a little too emphatically.

Mandy, Karen, and Finn all turn to look at me curiously; a little taken aback by my outburst.

I cringe. "I mean, no thank you."

"Olivia."

I'm obviously looking like a sporadic nutcase to Finn. The confounded look on his face says it all. He's not sure what to make of my presence.

"Mandy is right," I try to explain. "I'll need my energy for tonight like she said, and besides…Abby would kill me if she knew I was here right now. She's playing the part of my father today, and doesn't think I should see you until gala time."

Finn sighs and places his hands on each side of my face. "Okay. I understand. I won't argue with Abby. She can have you for lunch, but I get you for after-hours dessert." He whispers as he leans in for a kiss; a kiss that is so warm and soft that I forget everything going on in my life for about fifteen long seconds.

"I'll be there at four to pick you up."

"I'll be waiting." I smile with my eyes half closed. I look around the room for a moment, to Finn's desk, to his couch, and sigh softly when my eyes reach the conference table. What I wouldn't give to be able to kick Karen and Mandy out of this room and lay myself out for him on that table right now.

"Soon." He whispers in my ear and chastely kisses the side of my neck, my OMG-spot. "I know what you're thinking, and it will happen soon. I promise you that, and I assure you, Beautiful, that table's never seen that much action."

I start to melt into Finn's kiss when I spy Karen watching us from across the room. Mandy is obliviously closing a box and moving it from the table to the floor. Karen raises one eyebrow in my direction, giving me a very clear indication of what she wishes she could say but never would in Finn's presence. It would be some snide remark about mixing business with pleasure.

I clear my throat and lean back quickly away from Finn as inconspicuously as I can. "Right. Well, umm...I look forward to that meeting, Mr. Kellan. Until then, I should be on my way. I have a hot date tonight."

"Yes. You do, and it's already taking all of my focus to not be at your door right now, wanting to spend this entire weekend with you, so go. Get out of my sight until I can really have you in my arms for the night."

Finn kisses me one more time, rubbing the tip of his nose with mine, before letting me go. I smile and say my goodbyes to Karen and Mandy and walk out of Finn's office. In hindsight, I feel a little guilty for barging in on their work, but I'm also glad I did. At least I feel a little more assured that Finn has seen the final product today, and Mandy is helping to pack it all up. Karen would have to work pretty hard to try and sabotage our work.

Chapter 29

At ten minutes till four, there's a knock on our apartment door. Knowing Finn likes to be a little early, my heart is aflutter as I open the door. I'm excited for him to see me in my dress.

"Well if it isn't the most beautiful princess I've ever seen."

I smile warmly at the handsome gentleman standing at my door. I'm flattered. "Well thank you, Mr. Rivers, and don't you look absolutely dashing yourself. You clean up well, you sexy thing."

"Hey! Who are you calling sexy?" Abby shouts walking down the hall toward the front door looking dazzling in her black and white gown.

"Whoa!" Austin says as his jaw falls toward the floor. He shakes his head in disbelief and awe. "God, I'm a lucky man that this princess here has a smokin' hot roommate. Come to daddy, you beautiful woman."

Abby and I laugh at Austin as he walks through the door to Abby, dipping her in a sexy as hell but very cute kiss. I turn to close the door only to find Finn standing in the doorway looking like he just saw a ghost. My smile dissipates immediately.

"Finn?"

"Olivia...you...you..." His eyes scan my body, my face, my hair, and I wonder for a moment if there's something wrong with my dress.

I frown slightly. "Finn? What's wrong?"

"You're gorgeous. Stun-stunning even," he stutters. "Shit. Those aren't even the right words to describe how you look right now; I'm sorry. You sort of took my breath away for a moment."

I can't hide my smile, obviously. I feel myself blushing at his sweet compliments.

"Well, I don't see anything wrong with that!" I let out a deep breath and laugh at Finn's amazed expression "You scared me, you big hot handsome hunk! Get in here!"

I tug on Finn's arm and pull him inside the door and into my embrace. He is dapperly dressed in a black three-piece tuxedo with a black bowtie. He smells divine, and I immediately remind myself that we actually have to go to an event. We can't stay here in each other's arms; really, I could do this all night and be quite content.

"You smell fantastic, Finn, and I'm not sure you could look more handsome if you tried."

"Thanks, but I'm pretty sure I don't hold a candle to the gorgeous babe I'm holding in my arms right now. I brought you something."

"What is it?" I look around quickly even though I don't remember Finn having anything in his hands when he was in the doorway a moment ago.

"Well, I would've gotten you a corsage or something to wear on prom night, but since this isn't actually a high school prom, I thought maybe you deserved an upgrade."

I watch as Finn digs his hand into his hidden jacket pocket producing a little light blue gift box with black lettering and tied with a white bow. I gasp in shock.

That's a Tiffany's box.

He went to Tiffany's.

It's not....

Is it...?

It's not....

It can't be....

I study the box quickly as he hands it to me. It's not a small enough box to be a ring and not the shape of a necklace box. I untie the bow and open the box. Inside is a light blue pouch, which I pull from the box and open. Inside the box is a pair of stunning olive leaf drop earrings in sterling silver with a pearl dangling on the end. They're beautiful; they're classy and sophisticated.

"Oh Finn! These are gorgeous. They're more than gorgeous, but you spent way too much. I can't."

"Yes you can, and yes you will. I promise I didn't spend a fortune on them, and I promise that they will look exquisite with your dress this evening."

Solving Us

Abby looks over my shoulder to see the earrings in my hand. "And I have just the thing to go with it, Liv! Be right back," she says as she makes her way down the hall to her bedroom. She reappears seconds later with a bracelet in her hand.

"This will go perfectly. Here, put this on." Abby hands me a silver bangle bracelet with three small pearls set in between antique filigree. It's beautiful and compliments my new earrings perfectly. I can't help but smile, feeling like Cinderella getting ready for the ball. All of the people in this room with me right now care about me and want to see me happy. This is our night, Finn's and mine. We've worked hard for this, and I can't wait to share the evening with some of my best friends. I smile to myself as I see another side to my Rubik's Cube of a life lock into place.

Within the hour, we are stepping out of our limo and into the lobby of the historic Fairmont Copley Plaza Hotel. Adorned in pine wreaths wrapped with glimmering red ribbon, silver and gold sparkling chandeliers, and shimmering snowflakes, the hotel looks like a royal palace expertly decorated for the holiday season. It is breathtakingly beautiful and cheerfully warm, causing a small burst of excitement to bubble in my stomach. There are two smells during the holidays that bring me Christmas cheer and take away much of my anxiety. My very favorite is the fresh balsam-scented candles from Bath and Body Works. They remind me so much of the freshly cut Christmas trees I used to pick out with my parents each year. The other of my favorites is also the same smell wafting through the air in the lobby right now. The mixture of oranges, cranberries, and cinnamon fills my senses with euphoria. I pinch myself slightly to make sure I'm not dreaming, but Finn just laughs at me adoringly. My breath hitches as I'm escorted down the hall and catch a glimpse of the grand ballroom I'm about to step into.

"Wow," I whisper looking around the room and taking it all in.

The historic ballroom is trimmed in long red velvet curtains, golden archways with sparkling lights, and what has to be no less than twenty Christmas trees, each uniquely decorated with glass bulbs, shimmering snowflakes, red satin bows, and ribbons with coordinating patterns. Tables are covered in red tablecloths and set with immaculate white china. The centerpieces on each table are huge silver and gold candelabras covered in Christmas pine floral displays. Really this entire room looks like a Christmas dream that I could never imagine in my own mind.

"Beautiful isn't it?" Finn asks squeezing my hand.

"That's the understatement of the year, Finn. Never in a million years would I…."

"Mr. Kellan. Ms. McGuire, welcome! Great to see you."

Mr. Sparks, the Pet Therapy Program Manager, spots us as we enter the room and casually interrupts my thoughts to greet Finn and me. He shakes Finn's hand first before turning his attention to me. "You look absolutely lovely this evening, Ms. McGuire."

"Thank you very much, Mr. Sparks. I was just telling Finn how overwhelmingly beautiful this all is."

"Yes it is, thank you. Our fundraising department knows how to get the job done when it comes to pulling off an event of this magnitude. Do make sure you make your way to the auction table to see all of the donations up for grabs tonight. There are some spectacular surprises over there."

I'm eager to see it all and can't wait to pull Finn in that direction. A girl loves to shop, after all.

"Wonderful. I look forward to it, Mr. Sparks. Thank you again for inviting us all here."

"Oh we wouldn't have it any other way, Ms. McGuire. I'll meet you and Mr. Kellan up front by the main stage at nine o'clock for the unveiling, okay? Enjoy yourselves tonight!"

"Thank you again, Sir. We'll see you then." Finn nods, shaking Mr. Spark's hand again.

"Liv!" I hear Abby say from behind us. She pulls my arm in her direction. "Let's go look at the auction table. I'm dying to see what I can bid on!"

"Uh, okay." I turn around to look at Finn who nods and smiles at me. He and Austin stand together smiling at the pair of us girly girls who are quick to shop till we drop.

Solving Us

"What can we get you ladies to drink? It's a full bar, of course, so whatever you want," Finn suggests.

"Well, if you're offering, I would love a cranberry martini?"

"Oooh, that sounds wonderful. I'll have the same; thank you!" Abby grins.

"Coming right up, ladies. Take your time."

"Come on, Liv." She turns me in the other direction, and arm-in-arm we walk across the ballroom to the auction tables.

The auction tables dressed with black tablecloths hold twenty-five different auction items as part of tonight's fundraiser. Everything from signed sports memorabilia baskets to ticket packages for Broadway shows in New York City are up for bid, but there are a few others that actually peak my interest. A cruise to the Bahamas for a party of ten, a four-day trip to Nova Scotia, and shopping spree in downtown Boston, just to name a few!

Abby stands over my shoulder reading the details on the auction bid sheet. "Holy shit, Liv!" she says. "Do you know how much fun the two of us could have with some of this?"

"Yeah, I do. Too much probably, but it's worth it if the money is going to such a great cause..." I hear my voice slipping away a little bit but that's because my attention stops on the last item up for bid. The oversized framed picture I'm looking at is one I know I've seen before. It looks identical to the one hanging in Finn's office lobby near Mrs. Hoover's desk. Perhaps I shouldn't be so shocked to see this auction item, but when I see Finn's name attached to the sheet as the donor, I have to work hard to choke back my tears.

Auction Item 25

Two week all expense paid vacation to Ireland and Scotland
Highlights: The Cliffs of Moher, Kiss the Blarney Stone,
St. Patrick's Cathedral, Loch Ness, Edinburgh Castle
and shop the Royal Mile

Donated by Mr. Finn Kellan, CEO The Kellan Agency
in memory of his father and sister.

"Ahh, you found it. I wondered how long it would take you." I look up to Finn's gaze as he hands me the drink I ordered.

"Finn, I had no idea you were donating a gift like that."

He turns toward the framed picture and shrugs his shoulders lightly. "This was just something I felt I needed to do, ya know? I guess it's another one of those healing moments. Dad and I made a lot of great memories on that trip. To give someone else that opportunity would mean a lot to him...and Sydney. She would've loved trying to search for the Loch Ness Monster or shop in Edinburgh." He chuckles.

"I love it," I say. "I think it's a magnificent idea, and I hope it makes a ton of money. It's a great cause."

"Me, too." He kisses my forehead and then lightly kisses my lips. "Come on, let's go find our seat. We're table thirteen. Dinner should be starting soon."

I turn around to see that Austin is already with Abby, and they are following us to our table. We reach our seats, and my stomach turns.

Maybe it won't be so bad

Around table thirteen are Austin and Abby, Finn and me, Mandy and Kym from the office and Karen along with Mrs. Kellan, Finn's mother. I'm happily surprised to see Mrs. Kellan here only because I didn't know she would be at our table. I know that she's a huge supporter of the hospital and of the pet therapy program.

Karen wouldn't possibly do anything stupid with Mrs. Kellan around.

Please, Karen, don't do anything stupid.

It's just a seat.

We'll be dancing and working most of the night anyway.

I take a deep breath and smile at everyone at our table. I'm seated in between Finn and Abby, so no matter what, I'm comfortable, happy, and content for the night. Cinderella has made it to the ball.

Chapter 30

Dinner consists of filet mignon, duchess potatoes, and fresh green beans, followed by a dessert of Ghirardelli chocolate mousse. Tables off to the sides of the dining room are teeming with Christmas cookies, tea, coffee, and a hot chocolate bar so guests can help themselves throughout the rest of the evening. The auction will be starting soon, so tables are being cleared of dirty dishes, and people are mingling again and double checking auction items.

Table thirteen has been a lot of fun so far this evening. I'm enjoying myself very much, even without much alcohol in my system. I want to have my head on straight for tonight's presentation, so I'm letting Abby do all my drinking for me for now. One Cosmo earlier was enough. Since Mrs. Kellan is with us tonight, it's been a trip down memory lane as she recounts story after story of Finn's childhood and what he was like as a squirrely little kid. Mandy even had a few great zingers for him. You would think they were brother and sister the way they act around each other. I suppose in a way they are, having grown up in two families that are as close as theirs are. Watching them laugh together makes me wish I would have known them both years ago as young kids. I have a feeling I would've liked Sydney very much if she was anything like Mandy is.

"Good evening, ladies and gentlemen! My name is Thomas Sparks, and I am your emcee for this evening's auction! We are about to begin; if you'll all turn your attention to the stage."

One by one, items are auctioned off to the highest bidder. Mandy, Abby, and I practically drool as a set of four large Coach purses goes for five thousand dollars, a luxury pontoon boat goes for forty-eight thousand, and the trip to Nova Scotia goes for seventeen thousand dollars. We are lucky enough, though, to win a complete spa package for two for fifteen hundred dollars split between us.

"Hoes before bros, Olivia!"

"Amen, Abs! Holes before poles!" I wink at her.

As Mr. Sparks announces the final auction item, I look around the room to see if I can tell who might be interested in the trip to Ireland. "The bidding starts at twenty-thousand. Do I hear twenty-thousand?"

Bids begin to climb higher and higher, and before long, they're past ninety-four thousand dollars. Even Karen placed a bid earlier in the auction for fifty-two thousand but stopped once the bidding hit seventy grand.

All of a sudden from the west side of the ballroom we hear another bid.

"Five hundred thousand dollars." There's an audible gasp in the room. The Red Sea of people parts as most everyone turns to see who is placing such an enormous bid. A soft chuckle comes from Finn, and I see him shake his head slightly and smile. His eyes look as though tears could pour from them at any second.

"Mom," he whispers.

"What?" I say. "Your mom placed that bid? Oh my gosh!"

"Five hundred thousand dollars to the beautifully stunning Mrs. Kellan! Do I hear five hundred and one?"

Mr. Sparks repeats himself before we all watch him say into the microphone, "Going once! Going twice! SOLD to the beautiful lady in the black velvet gown!" After a moment, he comes back to the microphone to thank everyone and let the guests know that the unveiling will happen within the hour.

"Because of your generosity this evening, our new pet therapy program has raised one point three million dollars! We are forever grateful for all of you tonight. Thank you again for reaching deep into your pockets to help out this fantastic organization; and in case I forget later, a very Merry Christmas to you all and a happy New Year!"

The crowd erupts in applause. Finn and I are both over the moon excited about tonight's outcome. I never dreamed the program would raise that much money. This event is so over the top from anything I've ever been used to seeing. I can't imagine my high school prom was anything even close to this, so I'm feeling like a pretty lucky girl.

Solving Us

We reach Mrs. Kellan, and Finn congratulates her with a huge hug. "Dad would've been so proud of you Mom. What are you going to do with your trip?"

"I was going to donate the money anyway, and I'm not going to do anything with the trip, Finn. You are going to take this beautiful girl on the trip of a lifetime and relax a little. See the sights. Make memories."

"Mom, I...." he says.

"It's for a great cause that has been beneficial to this family. I want someone I love to take someone he loves to the place that still holds fond memories and a great deal of joy for him. Merry Christmas, Finn and Olivia dear." She says to us both.

"Mrs. Kellan." I hug her dearly and try hard to hold back my tears. I can feel the love in this family. It wraps around me like a warm, soft bath towel. "Thank you. Thank you for the donation and for the unbelievable gift," I say to her.

Mrs. Kellan winks at me before departing and says softly in my ear, "I've always wanted to see an Irish wedding."

Wait.

What?

What wedding?

My wedding?

To Finn?

In Ireland?

Oh. My. God.

Is it hot in here?

"Good bye, Sweetheart" Mrs. Kellan kisses Finn's cheek. "You take care of this beautiful girl, and I'll see you both next week for Christmas."

"Yes, absolutely," I say, still a bit stunned.

"Hey. Ya hear that?" Finn asks. "Let's dance."

He takes my hand and escorts me to the dance floor. On the way, he grabs two glasses of champagne from a nearby waiter and hands one to me. We both quickly down our drinks and set them on our table before entering the dance floor.

"You don't have it planned somewhere for Adam Levine to show up here and surprise us all like in his video do you? Because that might make this night absolutely perfect." I giggle as we dance together.

"Nope, sorry; but don't worry. I'm pretty damn sure your night is going to be perfect. I'm making sure of that," he says.

"It's already a perfect night, Finn."

"No, Beautiful." Finn pulls me closer and holds the back of my head with his hand so he can whisper in my ear. "It'll be perfect when I peel you out of that dress."

"Mmm, what I wouldn't give to be peeled out of this dress right now," I tease breathlessly.

Finn's body stops moving to the music; his grasp on me is tighter now. I pull my head back so I can look at him wondering why we stopped dancing. His Cheshire cat grin is almost alarming.

"You have no idea what those words just did to me, Olivia." He checks his watch. "We have plenty of time."

Wait...

What?

Finn takes my hand and starts to lead me in the direction of the ballroom doors.

"Wait, Finn, where are we going?"

He turns around and kisses me. "To peel you out of your dress, or maybe just have some fun with you while you're in it. You're stunning, but since the moment you opened your apartment door all I've been able to think about is the beautiful body hiding underneath it. So let's make this dress worth every penny you paid for it."

We walk out of the ballroom and down the hallway away from the crowds. Finn is clearly looking for a quiet place to be alone.

Why doesn't he just buy a room?

"Finn! We can't..."

"Yes we can, Liv. Yes, we can. Trust me. Do you trust me, Liv?"

"Of course I do, but..."

"Kiss me then. Kiss me, Olivia."

Solving Us

I don't hesitate to follow Finn's instructions. I throw my arms around him, sealing my lips to his. He picks me up and carries me backwards until he runs into the door behind him. He pushes down on the handle, and the door opens. We practically fall into the darkened room, but Finn manages to keep us both upright by grabbing something above his head.

"Where are we?" I ask between kisses. I throw my head back, exposing my neck to Finn's warm, soft tongue.

"Coat room. You taste so good, Olivia."

We make our way toward the back of the room, weaving in and out of row upon row of winter coats belonging to tonight's gala guests. Finally Finn grabs my wrists and pulls my arms up over my head.

"Feel that bar, Liv?"

"Yes."

"Hold onto it, and don't let go."

"I...ahhhhh..." I sigh louder than I should when he wraps himself around me from behind and cups my breasts in his hands. "Okay. I won't let go, but, Finn, I'm not sure I can promise you that my legs will let me remain standing."

"It's okay, Liv. I've got you. I just need to feel you like this. Hold on to the bar as long as you can." He sucks on my neck, right on my OMG-spot, hard enough that I fear he may be leaving a mark.

That'll look great during my presentation.

"You, Olivia, are a stunningly beautiful woman. You drive me crazy every time I look at you; but right now, in the dark where I can't see you, I want to focus on all my other senses instead."

"Finn..."

"So I'll enjoy *hearing* your pleasure as I start with touch." His hands squeeze my breasts as I arch my back, welcoming the feel of his hands on my body. I stand there in front of him, close my eyes, and lay my head back on his chest, feeling his hands glide down my torso toward my pelvis. We're both fully clothed, and already I know my black satin panties are going to have to come off. They're too wet to wear for the remainder of the evening. Finn lowers himself to his knees so that his face is right at my waist.

"And smell..." He whispers as he lifts the front of my dress up over his head enough to be covered by the material of my gown. I feel his hands running up the back of my legs, his nose stopping at the apex of my thighs. I hear him inhale and groan underneath my dress, which causes me to have to hold tighter onto the bar above my head.

"Oh God, Finn ,please...."

"And touch again..." He slips his fingers into the bottom of my panties, my now dripping wet panties, before I hear them rip and feel the release of the elastic from around my waist. I almost lose my footing when Finn rips my panties off of my body, but his strong hands steady me.

"And my favorite one, Olivia. Taste." Finn lifts my left leg resting my foot, Jimmy Choos and all, on his bent knee, granting himself better access to me. His tongue moves slowly over me, tasting my arousal, taking everything my body is offering him. The feeling is so intense that it causes my legs to shake. I'm not sure I'll be able to remain standing much longer.

"Finn..." I cry out my voice shaking.

"Almost there, Beautiful. You taste so good. The sweetest dessert of the night."

Finn continues his sensual torture on my body as I hang tightly from the bar above, trying not to fall. I'm groaning when the door to the coatroom opens and the lights come on.

FUCK!

Who is it?

Oh God! Please don't come back here!

Please don't come back here!

Please don't come back!

My body tenses immediately, and I freeze right where I'm standing. Finn continues his assault, not knowing that the lights have been turned on. If someone walks two aisles over, we're screwed.

"Yes, Sir, let me get that for you."

"I'm sorry we have to leave before the presentation. I'm being called to a patient who needs me."

I feel Finn freeze when he hears voices, but after a quick second I feel his finger slide lazily inside me as he starts all over again quickly and purposely quickening his pace.

Oh My God!

Finn!

I can't....

I....

Don't stop...

"Certainly, Sir. It's not a problem at all. Your coats are right here."

His finger moves in and out.

His tongue swirls around me.

I can feel my climax coming.

I bite my tongue hard and hold my breath.

"Thank you. Merry Christmas to you."

"And to you as well, Sir. Have a good night."

The voices trail off as the lights go back out, and the door closes. Finn's finger picks up speed as he rubs the inside of me, hitting me right where he knows will make me lose all control.

"Olivia," he whispers

"Finn! Oh God! Finn!"

I dip my head down into my chest before throwing it back in a huge release of ecstasy. I release the breath I was holding, and hear Finn chuckle from underneath my dress.

"It's not funny, Finn!" I tell him, even though I'm softly chuckling right along with him.

"Oh, Olivia, but it is. I would ask if the risk of getting caught turns you on, but I already know the answer."

Finn emerges from underneath my dress and grabs a hold of my waist to steady me as I let go of the bar above me. He backs me up through several coats until my back is against the wall.

"Are you okay?" he asks, sliding my ripped panties into the inside pocket of his jacket before taking it off and laying it over the rack behind him.

"Yes." I smirk at Finn though I'm practically panting coming off of my high. "I'm perfect, Finn."

"I know you are, Beautiful. And you're so brave. I'll make this quick; I promise." I watch Finn unbuckle his belt and throw my hand out to stop him from going any further.

"No. Let me, Finn. Let me."

He gathers the material and lifts up the front of my gown as I pull down on the zipper to his pants, smoothly slide my hand into his boxer briefs, and release his erection.

"Shit." Finn gasps. "Damnit, your hand feels good right there." Placing his hands under me, Finn lifts me up and holds me against the wall. "Wrap your legs around me, Liv, and hold on."

In one swift thrust, Finn slides into me, my own arousal covering him like a warm, slick oil. "So good," he groans, leaning his forehead on mine. "So fucking good, Olivia." He pulls out as much as he can and takes his time gradually sliding back in. He fills me with his slow thrusts over and over again until I think I can't take anymore.

"Fiiiinn…." I groan. "Please, Finn. Faster."

He kisses me hungrily, and with one hard thrust after another, says in my ear "As. You. Wish. My. Beautiful. Girl. Olivia!"

"Yes!"

Together we reach our high, breathing against each other, as we float back to reality. My body feels heavy, even more so in this dress, as I slump over Finn's shoulder breathing heavily. He lowers us to the floor, both slightly sweaty, but oh so happy.

"You, Olivia McGuire, are the best Christmas gift I could ever receive. I could enjoy unwrapping you like that every damn day."

"I love you, Finn Kellan."

"I love you, too." He kisses me softly once more and tells me to stay seated for just a moment. I watch him, amused and confused, as he quickly puts himself back together and then searches through coat pockets of nearby winter coats clearly belonging to women.

"A-ha! Yes!" I hear him proclaim before he reemerges from the coat rack. "You ladies are all so predictable". Chuckling, Finn lowers himself beside me and holds out the package of tissues he found in someone's coat pocket. He pulls a couple out and tenderly cleans me off, disposing of everything in the trashcan by the door. He pulls me up from the floor and helps me adjust my dress before we head back to the ballroom.

"I didn't peel you out of your dress, but I guess I really didn't need to." Finn smirks, kissing my neck softly.

I wink at him. "The night isn't over, Hot Runner Guy."

Chapter 31

"Would someone *puh-lease* tell my overbearing mother ta'put her fucking camera away? God, I'm so'over posing for her!"

Finn and I watch from our seats as Mandy throws herself into her chair taking a huge gulp of her cosmopolitan. I'm pretty sure she's had more to drink than she should at this point, as she's already slurring her speech; but hey, when it comes to her mother I won't ever judge her. Karen makes me want to drink, too.

"Posing? What are you posing for?" I ask her.

"Who fucking knows? She's finishing up a project for some Photoshop class and won't leave me the hell alone. 'Mandy, stand against this wall and look this way. Mandy, hold your arm out this way like you're dancing with someone. No, Mandy, the other hand. Mandy, let's go over here. Mandy, are you listening?' Good God, shoot me now." She rolls her eyes and finishes her drink, while raising a hand to signal a waiter to bring her a glass of champagne.

"So wha'have you two lovey birds been up to this evening, huh?" Mandy slurs her speech again, and Finn chuckles at her silently.

"You never could handle your liquor, Mandy," he laughs. "Maybe you should slow down a bit."

"Screw you, Kellan. I'm fine. It's my mother's fault." She grins.

"As long as you're not driving out of here tonight, and don't make an ass of yourself in the name of my company, I don't really care what you do. You're a big girl. I'm not your brother, Mandy. Just be careful. You look lovely tonight, by the way. Green suits you."

"Always watching out for people, Finn. That's why we all love you," she says, fixing the deep V-neck on her green silk dress. She looks up at Finn when she finishes and winks at him, which causes me to chuckle this time.

Solving Us

"Yeah, yeah, keep talking." Finn laughs again. "If you ladies will excuse me, I need to check in with Mr. Sparks about the presentation." He kisses my hand and winks at me. "I'll be right back."

"Can't wait." I watch Finn walk away and can't help but smile at the super sexy man that I get to call mine. In the nine months we've known each other, I've fallen for him more than I ever imagined. He's changed my life by leaps and bounds in what feels like a very short time. I have more confidence in myself and more courage to take risks and try new things. I owe him so much.

"Yep," I hear Mandy say. "You're a lucky girl, Olivia. Finn is a sexy catch, and you've caught him hook, line, and sinker."

Amused with Mandy's demeanor, I flash her my biggest cat-ate-the-canary grin. "You think so?"

"Hell yeah I do, Liv. I mean, look at him." She nods her head in his direction, and we both watch as he talks with Mr. Sparks. I notice Karen walking up to the two of them and shaking Mr. Sparks's hand.

Ugh. Get away from them, Bitch!

"What's not to love? He's the sweetest teddy bear of a man I've ever met, Liv, and I've known him a long time. And his body?" Mandy whistles, causing me to stare at her with eyes of surprise. I've never heard her talk about Finn that way, especially because as far as I know her interest lies with the female variety. You would think she's a high school kid with a little crush. Nevertheless, she has a damn good point. His body is sexy as hell, especially in that sleek tuxedo he's wearing. I can't help but imagine walking up to him and unbuttoning his shirt, one slow button at a time.

Or just ripping the damn shirt wide open!

Catching my bottom lip with my teeth, I watch Finn with a level of lust building up through my body. "You make a great point, Mandy. His body is definitely...mmmmm... it's nice." I remind myself where I am and who I'm with. Finn doesn't need me divulging our sex life to the entire room, and Mandy is too tipsy to be trusted.

"Nice?" She giggles. "Oh, come on. The man has his own lucky charm! He's magically delicious."

Wait.

What?

I try to smile at her, but I can't. My stomach just did a somersault, and my heart feels like it's trying to escape out of my chest.

"What did you just say?" I ask her, hoping to God I heard her wrong or that what she said doesn't mean what I think it means.

"I said he's magically delicious." She giggles and leans across the table closer to me like she's about to tell me a secret. "I mean you've seen it right? His birthmark? It looks like a damn horseshoe, don't you think? Sexy as hell too."

I can't move.

I can't even plaster a smile on my face.

That birthmark is not located in an obvious spot.

Please God, no.

I shake my head slowly in disbelief at what she just said. I feel the furrow in my brow as I look at her silently, pleading for her to tell me I'm wrong about what I'm thinking right now.

"Mandy, I don't...how do you..." I close my eyes and exhale the breath that I've been holding. "How do you know about that birthmark?"

My mouth goes dry as I look into Mandy's eyes to see the realization hit her of what she has just revealed to me. Her eyes pop out of her head as she covers her mouth with the palm of her hand.

"Fuck," she mumbles. She reaches across herself with her other hand and places it on top of mine, but I withdraw my hand immediately startling her.

"Okay, Liv, don't be mad. It was a long time ago."

"WHAT was a long time ago Mandy?" I don't want to hear what I know in my heart is the truth, but I have to hear it from her anyway. I watch Mandy take a deep breath, deciding what exactly to say to me; how will she explain to me something she obviously wasn't supposed to reveal?

"We..." She spits out her next words all in one breath. "We slept together. Olivia, it was one time, a long time ago, and we were so drunk. I don't have feelings for him like that; you have to believe me."

"No. I don't have to believe a fucking thing you say, Mandy. Why didn't you tell me this before? Why are you telling me this now for the first time?"

"I wasn't supposed to tell you ever, Olivia. Finn didn't want you to know about it because he knew how you would react. We were young and stupid, and neither one of us really wanted it, Liv. He doesn't love me. He loves you. I'm so fucking sorry. It was right after his dad died. The night after his dad's funeral. I saw him in a bar in a sad, drunken stupor, so I stayed with him to make sure he was okay. He was so damn sad, Liv. First Sydney, and then his father. He just needed a release."

"Oh I see. So, you took advantage of a depressed man in mourning? How could you do that to him, Mandy?"

I'm going to be sick.

The room is spinning

My thoughts are all over the place.

Is this inconsequential?

Would Abby tell me I'm overreacting?

Where the hell is Abby anyway?

"Olivia, Finn wasn't the only one mourning the death of someone special. Mr. Kellan was like a father to me! He was there when my father wasn't! I grew up with the Kellan family, so no, I didn't take advantage of anyone. We were two people who needed to lean on each other."

"Stop. Just stop. I can't." I put my hands up in front of me and shake my head. I can't hear anymore. One of my best friends slept with my boyfriend and never thought to tell me about it? I get that it was years ago, but why the hell didn't either of them even mention it to me? How could they just keep it from me like it's no big deal?

"Olivia."

"STOP MANDY! You've said enough! I can't do this. Not tonight." The tears begin to release and crawl down my face. I swipe them away just in time to watch Finn walk back to the table. I don't know how to handle this. I don't know what to say, but I can feel my insides breaking apart.

If he kept this secret for so long, what else is he hiding?

Finn's hands caress my shoulders lightly as he bends over to place a sweet kiss on my cheek. He doesn't say anything, but I can tell he feels the tension in my body.

"Everything okay?" he asks in my ear.

I nod affirmatively without speaking. I lean over to pick up my clutch purse from under my chair so that I can excuse myself to the restroom.

"Good. Mr. Sparks is ready for the unveiling. Everything is set for you. Karen is setting up the file for you now. All you have to do is open the program, and it'll all be there. You ready?"

Karen is doing WHAT?
Why is she...?
What did he...?
Oh, God, can this night get any worse?
I have to tell him.
Right here.
Right now.

I jump out of my seat. "No I'm not ready! What do you mean Karen is setting up the program? What the hell did you do?"

Finn smiles and has the audacity to laugh lightly. He rubs both of my arms as if to settle me down.

"Relax, Beautiful. You're just nervous. I get it. Karen's got you covered. She offered to start the program while I was talking with Mr. Sparks. Don't worry. It's fine. I gave her your zip drive."

"Finn," I say breathlessly. I'm starting to panic. "I don't trust her. She's been fucking with me for months now. This is going to go all wrong; I can feel it." I look all around the room as if everyone has stopped to look at me, but all I see are people dancing, drinking, and having a great time. Music is still playing, and I hear laughter all around me.

"Whoa, Olivia, relax. It's just your nerves. Karen is fine. She's done this before. She knows what she's doing."

"No, Finn, you don't understand you can't trust..."

"Ms. McGuire are you ready to begin?" Mr. Sparks interrupts what I'm trying to say to Finn.

Solving Us

Shit!
I can't do this now!
"Um, yes. Yes I'm ready."
Hell no, I'm not ready!
I can't breathe!

"Olivia." Finn holds my shoulders firmly and waits for me to look him in the eye. "You're going to be great. Relax and have fun up there. I'm proud of you." He places an endearing kiss on my forehead before releasing my arms.

I swallow the lump in my throat and nod to Finn. I make one more sweep across the room looking for Abby, but when I spot her dancing with Austin, I know I can't interrupt. I'm already walking across the room with Mr. Sparks. She's the life preserver that I just can't reach.

Suck it up, Buttercup. You're on.

As the music fades in the room. Mr. Sparks stands next to me on the stage while one of the fundraising committee members introduces me to the podium. I clear my throat and look out into the crowd with a beaming smile that perfectly hides every inch of hurt and fear that has crept up inside of me in the past twenty minutes.

Just get this done. and get out of here.

"Good evening. ladies and gentleman! It is my pleasure to stand before you all this evening and celebrate with you the success of a wonderful development for the Massachusetts General Hospital. The expansion of the "Paws for Patients" therapy program is one that I am very proud to have been a part of. It means a great deal to me to see the program continue to thrive because I've seen firsthand how this program benefits many, many people, including several in my life that I love very much. On behalf of Dr. Sparks and the Board of Directors. I thank you all for joining us tonight to celebrate this spectacular occasion. If you'll direct your attention to the screens to either side of me, I'll take you on a virtual tour of the new Paws for Patients program."

For the next ten minutes, I show slide after slide of the new therapy department and explain the hows and whys of the new developments. I breathe a sigh of relief as I go through each slide, knowing that Finn was right. Karen knew what she was doing and wouldn't dare make him look bad at an event like this. I'm able to relax and enjoy the oohs and ahhs from the crowd as I continue to show more slides.

"Although you are all used to the program being called Paws for Patients, the hospital wanted to create a new and improved logo and marketing design in order to rebrand the program and help push its success into the future for years to come. I'm honored to have been given the opportunity to unveil the new design to you tonight. All promotional materials have been printed and mailed, and we are very excited to watch this program thrive as a result of the hospital's efforts. It is without further ado that I introduce to you the new look for the future of the Paws for Patients Program!"

I click my remote with a beaming, genuine smile that my presentation went smoothly. I close my eyes quickly and exhale a huge sigh of relief.

Why aren't they clapping?
Did the slide not change?
Did I hit the wrong button?
Why are there gasps from the crowd?

I open my eyes and look at the screens. I'm staring in horror at my very worst nightmare coming to fruition. In bold red letters above an image of three chocolate lab puppies laying in a pool of blood are the words, "PAWS FOR PATIENTS - MASS. GENERAL HOSPITAL."

Max?
This isn't happening.
I can't speak.
My mouth is open, but I can't speak.

"What the hell is this about, Ms. McGuire? Is this your idea of a sick joke?" Mr. Sparks whispers in my ear, not so silently.

"No sir. I...I..." I can't even finish my sentence because I don't know what to say. I try hitting my remote to go to another slide, but the picture is stuck there. I try to hit a button on the laptop in front of me, but nothing changes.

What is going on?

Solving Us

Why is this happening to me?
She did this.
I know she did this!
I told him this would happen.
He wasn't listening to me.

I feel the tears sliding down my neck, and I feel as though everything I ingested this evening is about to escape my body. I quickly run my eyes across the crowd for Finn or Abby, but when I look up my eyes are filled with water, and I can't see anything in front of me. I thought I was sweating, but when I feel the tears drip silently from my eyes, I realize the water on my neck is from my own tears. I must be panicking to be crying uncontrollably like this.

Run away, Olivia.
Just run.
Don't look back.

I look at Dr. Sparks, who is seething with anger, but shake my head in defeated confusion.

"I'm sorry, Sir. I'm so sorry; I....excuse me." I push past him and make my way off the stage as fast as my feet will carry me. I can't breathe. I need to catch my breath.

"Olivia, what the hell is going on? What have you done?" I turn around and see Karen coming after me.

"I haven't!! How dare you, you sick evil bitch!? YOU did this! How could you do this to me? To FINN?"

Karen gasps in disgust at my accusation as Finn approaches me. He glares at Karen and says, "Fix it! NOW!" and watches for a moment as she makes her way to the stage.

"Finn, I'm so sorry! I don't..."

"Stop, Olivia. I..." He exhales. "I don't understand what the fuck just happened. You need to explain this to me, but I can't even begin to listen right now because I have to do damage control before the company loses a future multi-million dollar contract!"

"What? Finn, you don't ..."

"I said not right now! Walk out of this room, and compose yourself. I'll catch up to you when I'm done here."

Is he serious right now?
He thinks I did this?
How could he even begin to think that of me?
I don't...
I don't understand.
I can't breathe.

"I'm not the only one who has some explaining to do."

"What's that supposed to mean?" Finn asks befuddled.

I'm pissed that there are tears streaming down my face. I don't want to be crying. I want to scream at Finn for even remotely considering that I had anything to do with this. If that's what he thinks, then I'm better off without him. I can't even look at him anymore.

I wipe my tears and turn to walk out the door and down the hall back to the hotel lobby. My Rubik's Cube has been twisted, turned, and fucked up all over again. I'm Cinderella running from her ball...only this time, the prince isn't following.

Chapter 32

I'm alone for the first time today, taking a brief moment to breathe in and breathe out without feeling everyone's eyes on me, watching me like I'm some sort of alien creature. I hear the door creak open and the click-clack of heels on the tile floor. The uneven rhythm of the footsteps nearing the sinks and mirrors tells me that several girls have just entered the bathroom. My sound of silence is gone. I hold my breath and sit as still as I can, praying they will leave soon.

"Did you see her neck?"

"Hell yeah, I did. What the hell happened to her? She looks like she got in a cat-fight and lost."

"I heard it was her dog or something. Who knows? I mean, it's too bad really. I used to think she was sort of pretty and obviously Archer drools all over her all the time."

One of the girls clears her throat. "That's not what he was doing last night."

Huh?

What's that supposed to mean?

Wait a minute; I know that voice!

"Oooh do tell, Roselyn! What was Archer Michaels doing last night?"

Roselyn chuckles quietly. "It's not a question of *what* he was doing last night, Christina, but *who* he was doing last night, and the answer to that question is me."

I can feel my eyes practically bulge out of my head in shock. Bile rises up from my throat. My gag reflex is about to kick in, so I swiftly cover my mouth and hold in my breath. I vow to myself that I will remain as still as I possibly can, even though my body is now trembling in shock and anger.

My best friend and my boyfriend?

"Shut the fuck up! You and Archer? Damn girl, you have balls. Olivia would die if she knew! How does she not know?" I hear Christina exclaim. Someone just unzipped a purse. I can hear the knocking around of cosmetics as they are placed on the counter by one of the sinks.

"I was there for Archer when Liv was in the hospital. We just got closer spending so much time together, and now that Olivia looks like…that, you know, I guess the attraction for Archer is just not as strong, ya know? I mean, it's one thing to be a couple, and I do love Olivia like crazy, but seriously girls, can you blame Archer for being afraid to touch those nasty looking scars? He doesn't have the heart to tell her yet, but it's okay. We'll see how things play out. I mean, school is ending soon anyway. I'm sure he'll break up with her after graduation."

I can't hold back anymore. My body needs to purge the secrets I just heard. I twist my body around just in time to be sick. I pull my hair to the side and hold it out of the way and lean up against the stall door in time to hear the girls retreat.

"Ew, gross. Someone just threw up in there; let's get out of here."

"So disgusting. She's probably bulimic, whoever she is."

I slump to the floor of the girls' high school bathroom. I can feel whatever energy I had this morning drain from my body as I close my eyes and cry.

"Olivia?"

"Olivia! Wake up!"

I'm shivering when I open my eyes just enough to see what time of day it is. It's dark around me, which means it's late at night, or very early in the morning. I'm so cold…and sticky. My clothes are clinging to parts of my body. The cold air nips at the skin on my arms, legs, and stomach.

Am I missing a shoe?

Am I wearing pants?

I honestly can't tell. I'm so damn cold, though, and my body is shaking. I can't control the shivering no matter how hard I focus on it.

"Olivia, honey, you're okay. I need you to look into my eyes. Can you look into my eyes?"

I drag my eyes over to the beaming ray of a flashlight on my face, causing me to squint at the brightness of it. "That's it, Olivia. Good job."

"Vision is responsive," I hear the woman standing above me say.

"You're name is Olivia, right? Olivia McGuire? Honey, do you know what day it is?"

I try to open my mouth to answer her, but words won't come out. I feel like I'm in one of those bad dreams where you try to tell yourself to wake the hell up, but words just fail you. I try to scream, but no noise is coming from my mouth. None at all.

What's wrong with me?

This is a bad dream, right?

Why am I not waking up?

"Patient is uncommunicative but alert," the woman says.

"Olivia, it's okay. You've been in an accident, and I'm here to help you. My name is Elizabeth, and I'm a friend of your parents. You're in good hands, Olivia. It's okay if you can't talk; we're going to get you onto a stretcher and get you out of here. We've been looking for you, Sweetheart, and thank God we found you. Don't try to move, okay? It's better if you don't move."

My breathing picks up as I think back to what happened to me. I really have no idea what day it is or where I am exactly, but the blanket that Elizabeth is putting over me is warm and helps calm my body down. I can feel a slight tug at my wrist and hear the cutting sound of sharp scissors.

"Okay, I've detached her wrists from the leash. Let's get her on the stretcher."

Leash?

Max?

The bear....

Max!!!

"Max!!! Max, come on, boy! Where are you? Max, are you okay?" Finally sounds are coming from my mouth in a hasty panic. Somewhere deep inside I find the energy to make sure my best furry friend is okay, even though screaming like this is like swallowing a hundred razor blades. I have obviously been without a drink for a long time.

"Max!! Where's Max?" I cry. "Someone please get my dog! He's hurt! He needs help!"

My body is being turned and placed on the back board and lifted onto the stretcher. I can feel the wind hit my face as I'm being rolled over to the nearest ambulance. I try my hardest to grab the wrist of the woman who is next to me helping to roll my stretcher.

"Please, Ma'am...my dog. His name is Max. He's a chocolate lab, and he was laying with me when I fell asleep. Help him! He's injured, and I couldn't help him. I'm so sorry, but please. Please get him, too! I'm sure my dad will take care of any expenses! Please!"

I'm lifted into the ambulance. Elizabeth, the woman who is helping me, leans over my stretcher brushing some of my hair off my newly tear-stricken face. "Olivia," she says with a saddened empathetic voice. "I'm so sorry, Honey. He was here. He stayed with you. Max stayed with you the entire time. We found the two of you laying together, but Olivia...he just didn't make it, Sweetheart."

My body convulses, and I break into uncontrollable sobs. My best friend is gone, gave his life for mine. We've been ripped apart, and now I'm alone.

*****

"Oh shit! Austin, she's in here! Get a cab!"

I feel her before I see her. Abby is on the floor of the hotel bathroom with a wet paper towel, wiping my face of the sweat and tears and most certainly smeared mascara. My head is throbbing, and my heart feels like it's been ripped out of my body and crushed into pieces.

"Abby?"

"Shh. Olivia, it looks like you passed out, Sweetheart. I need to get you out of here."

"Okay. Where's Max?"

Solving Us

Abby stops wiping my face and stares at me. She tilts her head and studies my face for a moment before replying, "Olivia, Max isn't here. He died many years ago. You passed out and...oh, you must've had a flashback dream or something." She shakes her head. "Max isn't here, Olivia. Did you hit your head? Are you okay?" She moves her hands around the back of my head to check for blood but doesn't seem to find any sign of injury.

"My head is throbbing, but I think I'm okay." I don't recognize my own voice as I speak. My nose is so stuffy from crying I feel like I have a cold. I sound like it, too.

"Let's get you out of here, Liv. You need to get home."

"He thinks I did it, Abs. He thinks this is all my fault."

"Who? Finn? No, he doesn't, Liv. He's just playing damage control. This will all work itself out. Don't worry."

"But he yelled at me, Abby..." I start to whine until I remember the other revelation I learned tonight. "And did you know Finn and Mandy slept together?"

Abby stops in her tracks and looks at me in shock. "Wait, what? When? Just recently?"

"No, no. It was years ago when his father died. But, they never told me. Why wouldn't they just tell me?"

"Oh good Lord, this night is just like the high school prom you never experienced. Filled with drama and ending in tears. Come on, let's get you home, and then we can talk."

Abby helps me out into the lobby of the hotel where Austin is waiting with a cab to take us home. He helps us both into our coats.

"The snow is really starting to come down out there. Let's get you ladies home before the roads get bad," Austin tells us.

"Thanks, Riv."

"We all know this was Karen's work, Olivia. We've all seen it, the way she is with you. I don't know where it comes from, or what's going on, but don't let her defeat you. Finn will get it all figured out."

"She just humiliated me in front of hundreds of people and embarrassed the Kellan Agency tonight. I feel defeated already. Finn thinks I had something to do with it, Riv. How can he even begin to think that?" I feel the tears reemerge and slide down my cheeks.

"Olivia, Finn is a very smart man. Just trust him. I'm sure he'll have it all figured out before the clock strikes midnight. You won't be turning into a pumpkin any time soon. We won't let that happen."

"Mandy," I whisper.

"Don't know, Liv. We're not sure which way she swings, so let's get out of here before someone overhears us talking. If we don't know who is at fault for sure, then don't trust anyone. Not even Mandy."

I look to Abby quickly, and she nods in confirmation. We all exit the hotel together where a cab is waiting to take us home. It's definitely not the beautiful limo that we arrived in. I nervously turn my ring around and around on my finger while staring out the window watching the snow flutter around in front of the city street lights. My mind replays tonight's events over and over. My stomach turns as I hear Finn yelling at me again to leave the room and calm myself down. I hear Karen ask me what I've done, as if she doesn't already know every detail of tonight's happenings. I think back to those bitches I called friends back in high school talking about my scars and Archer as if I was dead to all of them. I was alone then, and I feel alone now. I would love nothing more than for Finn to show up and apologize for believing I had anything to do with tonight's presentation, but I don't see that happening. Not tonight. At this point, I just want to get home so this night can end. I want out of these shoes, out of this dress, and I want this makeup off my face. I want to curl into a ball under my covers and cry myself to sleep. It's what's bound to happen anyway.

Since I've been home, I don't hear a word from Finn. Not a text, not a phone call. I take that as a sign not to bother him, so I don't reach out to him either. I'm hurt that he hasn't checked on me at all, and I'm pissed off that he and Mandy slept together and hid that from me. Why wouldn't they just tell me?

It's almost midnight. I lay in my bed with my earphones in, listening to all the "I'm-hurting-sad-depressed-angry-confused" songs on my iPhone playlist. I punish myself with songs of self-loathing because that's just how I roll. When girls are hurting, they either eat a lot or they listen to sad songs; and since my stomach doesn't feel like it can handle a bowl of Hershey kisses right now, sad songs it is. I'm weeping alone in my room listening to Coldplay, Gwen Stefani, Rascal Flatts, and Little Big Town. Damn it, why is it that country music always seems to say exactly how I feel? Why do girls do this to themselves? Is Finn at home wallowing in misery to non-stop sad songs?

No, he's cleaning up my mess.

Somewhere in the last few minutes, I must've fallen asleep but the ding of my cell phone awakens me. Finally, I see a text from Finn:

> Riv told me you got home okay. Hope you got some sleep.
> Take a few days off, so I can work everything out here.
> I'll be in touch soon.

Take a few days off? Why does he make it sound like he's putting me on administrative leave? Is that what this is? A time out? Am I honestly in trouble? He has to know I had nothing to do with this.

He has to know.

Please know, Finn.

I don't even bother texting him back. I don't even know what to say. I put my earbuds back in and turn my music up so that I can't hear anything else but the shattering of my heart and cry myself to sleep.

Chapter 33

I wake up with a headache from hell. Not an alcohol hangover but definitely an "I-spent-the-whole-night-crying-my-eyes-out" hangover. My eyes feel like tiny puffs of air are forcing them to stay closed. I can't breathe through my nose. It's like I cried myself to sleep and then continued to cry the entire time I slept. Maybe I did for all I know. I'm facing away from my bedroom door when I hear a light knock at the door.

"Liv? You awake?"

"Yeah," I whisper.

"Are you okay?" Abby asks, stepping into the room.

"That's yet to be determined, Abs. Did you need something?"

"No, not really. I just wanted to check on you. Riv and I are going to go get us some coffee and bagels for breakfast, okay? You should try and eat something. Maybe take a shower. You'll feel better."

"Yeah. Yeah, I will."

"Did he text you last night?"

"Once. He told me to take a few days off while he worked things out…whatever that means."

"Oh, Liv." The sound of pity in Abby's voice hits me like fingernails on a chalkboard. "I'm so sorry. This whole thing is just bullshit, but I'm sure Finn knows it. Everything will work out. Try not to worry about it. In the meantime, we'll hang out here and eat crappy food and watch chick flicks all day okay? Maybe some Princess Bride? The snowstorm is supposed to roll in later today, so there won't be much to do anyway. How about if Riv and I stop by the Star Market, too, and get some Hershey Kisses and more milk. God knows we'll need it."

"Yeah sure, Abs." I'll say anything to appease her at this point. There's no sense in arguing with her. I'm stuck here anyway.

Solving Us

"Liv, I know it's been a shitty twelve hours or so, but have faith in Finn. He'll figure it all out and will call you soon. You know he will. He loves you, Liv."

"If he loves me then why did he treat me like shit last night? Why hasn't he called me since? Why did he tell me to take a few days off from work? Is that how you act when you love someone?" I lean across the bed to grab another Kleenex as fresh tears cascade down my cheeks.

Abby sighs and looks at me sadly. "I don't know, Liv. I don't want to defend him, but something just seems weird about this whole thing. He has to know Karen is doing this to you; and if he doesn't know it's her, he has to know it's not you. He would be stupid to not see it."

"Abby, I told you before, she's like another mother to him. He could be blind when it comes to her for all I know; and even if he does know, will he really do anything about it? I mean, honestly, do you think he's going to fire someone who is like a family member to him?"

"I can't answer that, Liv. We'll have to wait and see."

I nod and blow my nose.

"In the meantime, Riv and I will be back shortly with breakfast, okay?"

"Okay. See you soon. Be careful."

I climb out of bed and head for the shower. Abby is right. The warm water is refreshing and helps clear away some of the stuffiness in my head and the puffiness of my eyes. I vow to myself that I won't spend the day listening to more sad music. As much as I could stay in bed all day, there is no reason to wallow until I hear more from Finn. I slip on my comfy sweats after my shower and make my way to the kitchen for some hot chocolate.

I'm heading to the living room to watch some mindless television when there's a light knock on the door. An anxious excitement shoots through me. I smile for the first time in over twelve hours.

It has to be Finn.

Please be Finn.

I open the door quickly, excited to finally be able to wrap myself up in Finn's warmth and snuggle the day away with him, but instead I'm face-to-face with a man I don't know. He is dressed nicely in black dress pants and black dress shoes with a black wool coat. He looks to be roughly my age, maybe a little older, and is smiling politely. He's not a delivery man I ever remember seeing, and since he's not holding flowers, I'm guessing that's not why he's here. He is, however, holding a large envelope.

"May I help you?"

"Are you Olivia McGuire?" he says, cheerily raising his eyebrows.

"Umm, why are you asking?" I don't know this guy at all. The last thing I want to do is tell him who I am when he's not wearing any identification.

"Oh, I'm sorry," he says sincerely. "My name is Adam, and I'm a courier for the Fairmont Copley Plaza." He unbuttons his coat to show me the name tag he's wearing on his sweater.

"Oh. Yes, I am Olivia." I frown, confused. "I'm sorry; I didn't expect anyone from the plaza to stop by today. Was there something I can do for you?"

"No ma'am. Actually there's something I can do for you. This envelope was dropped at our desk late last night. We were going to deliver it to your room but then saw that you were at the Plaza for the Gala, not as a hotel resident. I'm sorry to bother you on a Sunday, Ma'am, but this envelope was addressed to you, and it looked too important to not get to you. Your address was on the Gala invitation list. I hope you don't mind that our manager looked you up so we could get this to you right away."

What the…?

Must be my botched presentation paperwork.

I forgot I left it there in my hasty retreat.

I roll my eyes at the absurdity of last night and the fact that someone is actually delivering my now-bullshit presentation to me in person.

"Thank you very much, Adam. Please come in for a moment. I wasn't expecting a delivery today; I need to get you a tip."

"Oh, it's no bother, Ms. McGuire. Actually a tip was included when the package was dropped off. So, please don't worry about it. I have to get back. Have a wonderful day."

I nod to him, befuddled. "Oh. Okay, thanks again very much. That was very kind of you."

Adam smiles at me and waves good-bye before buttoning his coat and heading back down the hall.

I kick the door shut behind me as I turn to walk back into my apartment. I sit at the breakfast bar and put my mug of hot chocolate down on the counter before opening the envelope in my hand. Inside the envelope is a handwritten note, a small envelope, and a plastic baggie holding...black panties.

My black panties!

Finn?

I don't recognize the handwriting right away, but as I read the note quickly, my insides start to boil.

>Olivia, congratulations on a fantastic presentation last night.
>The whole town will be talking about it for some time!
>Thought you should see these.
>They make a much better looking couple don't you think?
>Don't bother coming back to work. You'll be hearing from HR by the end of the day.
>It was a pleasure knowing you.
>Oh, and I thought you would want your panties back.
>At least, I'm assuming they are yours.
>>xoxo,
>>Karen Elena

My breath escapes me quickly, and for a second, I find it difficult to breathe.

Now I'm being fired?
What has she done?
Is this why I haven't heard from Finn?

I open the second smaller envelope and pull out half a dozen photos and am punched in the gut with the first picture I see. It's Finn dancing with a woman at the gala. I know the woman he's dancing with isn't me because it's not my dress or my hair, though the beautiful green dress looks eerily familiar. I'm confused as to why this picture should affect me. I don't remember him dancing with anyone other than his mother and me, but we were apart from one another for a while during the evening. Finn is allowed to dance with whomever he wants; I certainly don't tie him to my hip or anything. I look closer to this particular picture, though, and discover Finn's eyes are closed, and he's resting his head against hers, but damn, I can't see her face. It feels like a more intimate picture than I want it to.

My stomach flips when I see the next picture in the stack. Finn is holding hands with the same woman as he leads her across the room. I can't even figure out where this would have taken place. A third picture shows Finn looking over one of the balconies in the hotel. His arm is tenderly around the same woman from the other pictures. The next one in the stack is of Finn...and Mandy? They're sitting at what looks like a kitchen table together holding hands, their foreheads touching. Are they smiling?

Mandy...

I squint my eyes and look at the previous pictures again.

The girl in the pictures is Mandy!

I recognize the green dress in the picture now.

I thought she was gay.

She told me she was with Kym.

Was that all for show?

"NO!" If this is supposed to be pissing me off, it's working.

I throw the stack of pictures from my hands and watch them flutter like dead leaves from a tree to the floor. One last picture that I hadn't yet seen lands at my feet. I don't want to pick it up, but damn, curiosity killed the cat, so I have to look.

This isn't happening.

"Why?"

"Oh God! Why?" I cry out.

The last picture I touch is of Finn clearly kissing Mandy as they stand near a table.

Table thirteen.

Our table.

"NO!" I scream and turn around to slap the countertop with my hands, knocking over my mug of hot chocolate. Wrong place, wrong time, mug. I pick up the tipped over mug and throw it against the wall, watching it shatter into pieces.

Just like my heart.

Just like my soul.

There's no holding back the ugly cry this time. I'm sobbing in the dining room of our apartment alone. Nobody is here to explain this away. Nobody is here to console me or tell me I'm overreacting, so I let go and allow my body to convulse. I let the tears rush down my face like a flash flooding stream. I sob loudly enough that, if someone were here, they would think someone just died.

Because a piece of me did just die.

I sob until there is nothing left inside of me. No energy. No thoughts. No fight. Just a ghost of a girl who once existed in a world of happiness. I'm the Broadway diva singing her lonely soliloquy before the intermission and second act, except there's no second act for me. I'm losing my happy ending, and there's not a damn thing I can do about it. Instead I'm Christina Perri, standing in a room all by myself, hearing the chillingly sad lyrics to "The Lonely" twist and turn and spin around me.

This isn't the life I wanted for myself. I'm reliving high school feelings all over again. My boyfriend and one of my best friends? I don't know what's real and what isn't anymore. I'm letting Karen win because there just isn't any fight left in me. If Finn loved me enough to fight for me, he would've done so by now. I wasn't ready for this world. I should've known better than to open my heart again.

I lay on the dining room floor for what feels like hours.

I'm breathing.

Just breathing.

In and out.
Repeat.
In and out.
Repeat.

My cell phone dings, alerting me to a text message. Slowly, I raise myself off the floor and stand up to find my phone on the counter. I push the small round button under the screen and see that the message is from Finn.

Good morning. How are you feeling today?

My eyes close, and I stand there continuing to focus on breathing in and out, in and out.

"I can't." I shake my head slowly and with a lifeless expression on my face.

I can't even write back.

Without any emotional response, I feel myself put the phone down on the counter in front of me and turn towards the kitchen. I skip the glass and head straight for the refrigerator, pulling the bottle of vodka from the freezer. I open the cap and swallow as many times as I can before my stomach fights back. I just want to numb the pain, make it go away. As I lean on the kitchen counter to steady myself, my arm knocks over an opened bottle of pills, spilling them onto the floor. Like a damn sloth, I make my way to the floor and try to shovel the hand full of pills into my hand. Nothing has ever looked more tempting in my life.

I can't live like this anymore.
I don't want this life.
Make it go away.
Dull the pain.
Just like Sydney did.

I take a few more gulps of vodka before funneling my handful of pills down into the bottle. Grabbing a pen from the drawer in front of me and a piece of paper, I slowly write the name of two songs that are running through my head before walking down the hall to my room like I'm on Death Row. No more tears, no sniffles, no angry words. Just peace and calm. Taking one last look around the apartment I hear myself whisper, "I love you, Abby."

Chapter 34

FINN

It's three o'clock in the morning when I walk through my apartment door after what feels like the longest fucking night of my life. Toby meets me at the door, wagging his tail excited to see me. I planned to have him here while Olivia was with me this weekend, but obviously, now those plans have changed. As if he knows she's supposed to be here, Toby sits by the door tilting his head to the side. It's a look that makes me smile every time.

But not this time.

"Yeah, Buddy, I know. She's not here. Tonight was just a clusterfuck of what the hell happened and I'm sure she's fast asleep by now."

Toby whines as if he's completely understanding every word I say. Maybe he is.

I bend over and scratch lightly behind his ears. "It's okay, Bud. I checked on her earlier. She's okay…for now. I just need to figure out what the hell happened and what I'm going to do about it."

Watching her up there tonight on the stage made me so happy and so damn proud. She was in her element. She was lighting up the crowd. Everyone was hanging on her every word. And then, the floor fell from underneath her, and I watched her crash. God, I wanted to save her. I could see it in her eyes: the fear, the confusion, the horror, the sadness. Everything we had worked on in the past month was washed away with one fucking slide. I can't wrap my head around this night. I just want to crash. I want to sleep this night away and wake up refreshed, so I can fix this mess and make everything right with Olivia. She worked way too hard on this project to go down with a ship that she didn't sail.

I hope she knows I don't hold her the least bit responsible for what happened.

*****

Solving Us

I haven't heard from my sister in a while, so I decide to go home for the weekend after class to surprise her. I know my parents are busy, and since she doesn't go out much anymore other than with Mandy, I figure a little sibling bonding will do her some good. I'm sure there's a good movie playing somewhere; maybe I can find a concert I can take her to.

I'm up earlier than normal for a typical college student, but I need to get my homework done so I can hit the road in time to be home when Sydney gets home from school. I'm just finishing my shower down the hall when my roommate, Lucas, barges into the bathroom.

"Dude, Finn, your Mom's on the phone! She sounds frantic, and I can't get her to calm down. I think there's an emergency or something, but I can't tell what she's saying."

"Shit," I whisper. "Okay, be right there. Thanks. Sorry she woke you, man."

"S'alright, bro. I need to finish my paper anyway."

I run down the hall wrapped in my towel, dripping wet from my shower. Without even saying hello, my ear is flooded with screams and sobs from my mother on the other end of the line.

What the fuck is happening?
Dad?
Oh God, it's Dad.
"Mom?"

"SHE'S GONE! SHE'S GONE! OH MY GOD, SHE'S GONE!" Mom is screaming into the phone, her panicked voice causes my adrenaline to spike. My heart starts racing, and I haven't even figured out what's going on yet.

"Mom calm down. What's going on?"

"MY BABY GIRL, FINN!" she sobs. "WHAT HAS SHE DONE?"

More sobbing.
Gasping for air.
Why is she panicking like this?
Sydney is gone?
She's probably with Mandy.

"Mom, calm down please! I don't understand. Syd is gone? It's a school day, Mom; she's probably with Mandy. Did you try calli..."

"She's DEAD, FINN! SYDNEY is DEAD! OH GOD, PLEASE WHY IS THIS HAPPENING? GOD, WHY DID YOU TAKE MY BABY FROM ME?" The ugly cry I hear on the line is like nothing I have ever heard from my mother before. Ever.

The world around me stops.

Breathe in, breathe out. Repeat.

Breathe in, breathe out. Repeat.

Dead?

Sydney is...dead?

My Sydster...

"No, she's not. No, she's not, Mom. No, she's not." I'm frantically shaking my head back and forth, losing all control of the words coming out of my mouth. There's no way on earth she's dead.

There's no way.

I hear myself say, "I'm on my way, Mom. Mom? I love you. I'm on my way." I leave the phone hanging off the hook and turn in circles around my room looking for whatever clothes are laying around to slip on. I pull on last night's jeans and get a t-shirt from my drawer. Without even putting them on I grab my tennis shoes and car keys and run out the door, not speaking to anyone I run into on the way out of the building. I don't even tell Lucas where I'm heading when he asks, "What the fuck, bro? Is everything okay?"

*****

There's no feeling left in me. No emotion. No fight. No energy. I'm a shell of a man sitting in my sister's room. The coroners were already here and gone before I was able to get here.

I didn't even get to see her.

Mandy and I have been in this room for hours looking for a clue. Any clue as to why my sister would take her own life. I sit at her computer and click through page after page of her internet history, but I come up empty handed each time. I click through school paper after

Solving Us

school paper until I see a file with a title that catches my eye. I open it and see that it's a video of Sydney, dated three days ago.

"Mandy, what's this? Did you know about this?"

Mandy is at my side before I can even turn my chair to look for her. She peers over my shoulder at the screen and shakes her head.

"No, I've never seen her make a video before. I didn't even know she knew how, Finn."

I take a deep breath and close my eyes for a second, not knowing if I want to watch this video or not, but since curiosity killed the damn cat, I have to.

"Close the door, will you? I don't want Mom or Dad walking in."

"Yeah. Sure."

I click the video and turn the volume down so that my parents can't hear her voice. The picture on the computer monitor is just Sydney alone here in the very room we're in right now. Mandy and I watch intently. I'm scared of what she might say. What if I don't want to hear what she has to say? I swallow the knot in my throat and blink a lot to keep my emotions in check. I need to know the damn truth, if that's what this video even is.

"Hey," Sydney says with a quiet calm tone to her voice. "If you're seeing this, then I must've done what I've been thinking about doing for some time now. Either that or Finn, you need to get the fuck off my computer and stay out of my stuff!"

Mandy and I both chuckle at the attitude that is, was, my kid sister. My beautiful sister.

"Anyway, if you're seeing this I'm guessing I'm dead. I'm happier now, so please don't worry about me. I just..." I can see tears starting to drip down Sydney's cheeks, which in turn, causes my eyes to explode with water. I feel Mandy's hand on my shoulder, but it's shaky. She's sniffling, too, so I grab her hand over my shoulder.

"I just can't do it, guys. I tried so hard. So damn hard. I hope you all know that. You tell me everyday how beautiful I am, and I know how much I'm loved; believe me I do but...I can't live like this, and I don't know what else to do. I can't fix me. You can't fix me. Nobody can fix what happened. It is what it is, and I blame nobody."

Sniffle

"Mom, I'm so sorry. I know...well, I think I know what my being gone is going to do to you, and I'm so damn sorry, but I can't do this anymore. How can kids do this to other people, their peers? They were my friends, and now all they do is sneer. I hear the whispers. I hear them say, 'If it were me I would want to kill myself.' Don't they get it? People like me who are hurting, we feel like we're dead inside anyway. We just want to be in a better world. Mom, please, please forgive me and forgive yourself because I know you'll blame yourself for the choice I made."

"Dad, I'll always be your little Syd. I'm sorry that I let you down. I'm sorry I wasn't strong enough to fight back against the bullies at school. I'm sorry I didn't believe you enough when you told me how beautiful I was. I love you so much."

"Mandy, you're my best friend forever and ever, even now. I'm watching over you. I'm with you wherever you go and whatever you do. WWSD right? And Finn..."

Oh God.

"I'll always be your little Sydster."

I'm weeping. Tears are flowing down my face as it falls into my hands. She's not gone. She's right there on the monitor. Like we're skyping. She can't be gone.

"Finn, look at me. Really look at me."

How does she know?

I raise my head slowly and watch Sydney on the screen through the waterfall of tears flowing down my cheek. It feels like Sydney is looking right at me.

Right into my soul.

"This," she says pointing to her face. Her scars.

"This is not your fault. Do you hear me? NONE of this is because of you. If you love me, you'll stop punishing yourself for a sunken ship that you were not responsible for sailing in the first place. I know you've been trying to protect me. I know it's why you've been coming home more, for

Solving Us

me, but you have a life that you need to live. I'm just holding you back from that. Forgive me, okay? And just promise me that you'll spend your life protecting the ones you love as hard as you can because I know after this, you will anyway. You were the best big brother a girl could ever have. I know you're going to make the love of your life a very happy girl one day. Please find her. You deserve a happy ending. I'm giving you mine.

Sydney looks around her room before looking back to the screen in front of her. "Okay, so, that's it. I've said what I needed to say. I've been listening to this song for a while now, and I feel like it's the only song that just...is me right now." She sighs. "I love you all. I'll see you all again on the other side. Good night."

Sydney walks away from her computer screen and can no longer be seen but a song is playing in the background.

"And So It Goes" by Billy Joel

*****

I'm walking into my apartment after a long day at work. I pull off my tie and unbutton my shirt as I walk down the hall to my bedroom. I'm ready to fall asleep next to Olivia, the love of my life. I walk into my room and something feels off. It's brighter than usual. Olivia usually turns off the bathroom light but tonight it's on, and she's not in the bed sleeping.

"Olivia?" I call out to her.

No response.

"Olivia are you here?"

I know she's here. Her car is parked outside.

Something's wrong.

I run to the bathroom and slip in a large puddle of water.

Why is there water all over the floor?

I look to my right where the bathtub is, and there she is leaning back in the water. Her eyes are closed, and her body isn't moving.

I'm soaked. My face is suddenly wet, and I can't get it dry. I don't understand.

"OLIVIA, WAKE UP!" I scream sliding over to the bathtub to get to her. I jostle her body but her head just rolls to the side. "NO! OLIVIA, PLEASE DON'T LEAVE ME!"

I shake her several times…

Why isn't she waking up?

I feel myself shaking her so damn hard, but she's not waking up.

Chapter 35

FINN

I startle awake when I hear a dog barking. Toby is at my side, leaning up on my bed, licking my face all over.

Dream. I was dreaming.

My body is a sweaty mess, and it takes me a minute to figure out that not everything that just happened in my head is real. I take a deep, slow, shaky breath and try to think.

Olivia isn't with me because she's at home.

I know she made it home safely because Rivers told me he took her home with Abby.

I'm okay. Everyone is okay.

I take another huge breath and focus on the here and now for just a moment before reaching over the side of the bed to give my attention to Toby.

"Good job, Buddy. I'm okay. Thank you for waking me. Good job." I pull open the drawer to my nightstand and grab a few treats for Toby, a reward for a job well done. I'm glad I'm no longer living in that nightmare.

The clock on my nightstand reads ten o'clock in the morning, which is late for me; but given that I went to bed so late, I guess I'm not surprised I slept in. I pick up my phone and send a quick text to Olivia to make sure she's okay.

Good morning. How are you feeling?

While I wait for her response, I get up to wash the sweat and dog slobber off my face. It's the only disadvantage to having a therapy dog. On those rare nights that I do have a nightmare, I wake up with a face full of dog slobber, but given the dream I was having when he woke me, I'm not complaining in the least. I love that dog.

In need of a huge cup of caffeine, I step into the kitchen to start up the Keurig. Snow is coming down outside. It's a pretty dusting over the city from my vantage point, but I know it's supposed to get much worse in the next couple of hours. I need to shower and get to Olivia so that one way or another we're snowed in together. She can help me figure out last night's mess. She's good at helping me focus on my work when I need to, and she always has the best ideas. I don't care where the work gets done as long as she's next to me.

Thirty minutes later, I still haven't heard from Olivia. I shouldn't worry about not hearing from her, even though it's unusual for her to not text me within a few minutes. I'm sure she slept in just as I did but still, she usually checks her phone when she wakes up.

Maybe she's in the shower.
She can't text from the shower.
Or, maybe she's mad at me.

I didn't exactly smooth everything over with her last night before she left.

I'll be with her soon. Apologies are always best done in person.
Maybe I should text her again.
If she's mad at me, she's not going to answer my text anyway.

I shower quickly and get dressed so that I can take Toby out for a quick walk, deciding that if I still haven't heard from Olivia by then, I'll head over there immediately.

The walk with Toby is quick and cold. My face is wind-whipped from the snow blowing around outside. I cover my nose with my gloved hand for a second as we walk swiftly to the front of my building. When I return to my apartment building, Mandy is waiting for me in the lobby holding my black suit jacket from last night. I forgot that I even gave it to her at the end of the evening when she was cold. She's pacing back and forth biting at her nails like she's thinking something through, like something is wrong. I'm startled at the sight of her.

"Mandy? What are you doing here? Are you okay?"

"Yeah I'm okay but, Finn," she says almost in disbelief. "Oh God...I think my Mom is behind last night."

"What?" I shake my head and chuckle at the absurdity of what Mandy just said, except the expression on her face tells me she's not joking at all. The small smile slips from my face.

"Wait," I cock my head. "What?"

Mandy explains hastily, "She was going on and on this morning on the phone with someone, and I overheard her, obviously, so I put all the pieces together while I was showering and drove over here as soon as I figured it out. I told Mom I was going out with Kym. Can we talk upstairs? Please, Finn?"

Karen?

"Yeah. I've got to get to Olivia's, but Yeah, of course. Come on up."

We step onto the elevator with Toby and head up to my apartment. Mandy takes a minute to give some love to Toby while I take off my coat and hang his leash.

"Do you want some coffee?"

"Uh, yeah, sure. That would be great," she says nervously. She sits at my breakfast bar and watches me as I pull an extra coffee mug down from the cabinet. I pour coffee for both of us and stand opposite of her in my kitchen, watching her sip her drink.

Scratching my head, I say to Mandy, "You've stumped me, Mands. I don't understand how or why Karen would be involved in anything that went wrong last night, so why don't you just start from the beginning and tell me everything you know."

"I don't know lots of details, but I heard her on the phone this morning. I have no idea who she was talking to but she was laughing about last night and what a basket case Olivia was when it all happened. I mean, from the sounds of things, Finn, she was happy that Olivia had such a terrible night. I don't get it, but before I was about to step into the shower, I heard her say 'She won't be coming back'."

"What do you mean she won't be coming back? Who won't be coming back?" The anger in the pit of my stomach flashes through me to my core; and even though I don't want it to, for a moment, I actually believe what Mandy is saying to me.

"I think she means Olivia isn't coming back, Finn! I don't know what that means, but I didn't want to ask her without coming to you first. I didn't want to raise any red flags in front of her. I didn't know what she would say or do, so I showered quickly and came here."

The clock on my microwave shines eleven forty-five. Time has gotten away from me, and I still haven't heard from Olivia. That feeling in the pit of my stomach, that at first was anger, is quickly changing to worry. The last few times Liv gave me the silent treatment, she was upset and hurting, and it was all because of me.

"Shit."

"What?" Mandy asks wide-eyed.

I shake my head disappointed in myself. "It should've been me. I should've been the one with her last night. I should've been by her side the minute everything happened. Fuck! How could I have been so ignorant? Damnit! I was so stupid."

"Finn, you can't blame yourself. Anyone can understand that the Kellan Agency was the first thing on your mind."

"But I wasn't with her, Mandy! I saw the look on Dr. Sparks' face, and I went into business mode without thinking about Olivia's feelings. In fact, I practically yelled at her to walk away and calm herself down, but then she never came back. Next thing I know, Riv is telling me that she's not feeling well, and he's helping her get home with Abby."

Rubbing my forehead with my thumb and middle finger, I whisper, "I didn't even say goodbye to her. I just let her go so I could do damage control. I was so exhausted by the time I got home, I sent her a text and fell asleep."

"So call her," Mandy says. "Get your ass over there and talk to her, Finn. I'm sure you can iron all of this out. I just don't know how to find out more details about my Mom. What do I do?"

"I'll take care of it. I know a few people I can call to help out where you can't. But, Mandy, I really do appreciate you coming here this morning. If what you're saying is even a little bit true, it takes guts to do what you did. Thanks."

Solving Us

Before Mandy has the chance to answer, my phone is ringing in my hand. I look down at the screen and see Abby's name on my caller ID.

Olivia?

"Abby?" I answer quickly.

"What the FUCK have you done now, Finn Kellan?!" She screams into the phone loud enough that I pull my phone away from my ear.

"I swear to fucking Christ, Finn, whatever the hell you've done, you will fucking PAY! I should drive over there and fucking KILL you with my own bare hands. You don't DESERVE her! You fucking don't deserve her, you son of a bitch!"

"Whoa! Whoa! Whoa! Abby, what do you mean?" I try to speak calmly even though my nerves are on fire hearing Abby's words. "What happened?"

"What the fuck do you MEAN what happened? She's GONE, Finn! Olivia is GONE, and …"

I hear words coming from the other end of the phone, but I also hear nothing at all.

Olivia!

Sydney…no, she's not. No, she's not Mom. No, she's not!

Oh God!

I did this!

Again.

What have I done?

"I'm on my way," is all I can say before I throw my phone into my back pocket, grab my keys and coat, and run out the door. Mandy is right behind me, having overheard my phone call.

"I'm coming with you," she says.

I'm in no mood to argue, so I don't even blink when Mandy gets into the passenger seat of my car. As I pull out onto the street, sliding in the snow already accumulating on the road, Mandy lays her hand on my forearm and looks at my stoic expression.

"We'll figure this out, Finn."

The rest of the ride is eerily quiet, so much so that it's almost uncomfortable. Olivia hates a quiet car. She always has music on, but

Mandy knows me well enough to know that I'm in no mood to talk right now.

Within ten minutes, I'm knocking on Abby and Olivia's apartment door. When the door swings open, I'm staring at a fuming mad woman who looks like she's been crying.

"Where is she, Abby?" I ask immediately.

"What the fuck did you bring her here for?" Abby asks as she looks Mandy over from head to toe.

"What? Abby, she was with me when you called. She's…"

"So, you just assumed it was fucking okay to bring her here? Of all places? Olivia's apartment? Are you fucking nuts, or are you just that much of an asshole?"

What the hell?

Her words cut through me, and I'm taken aback.

"Who the hell cares if she's here or not, Abby? I'm not here for Mandy; I'm here for Olivia. Where is she? Do you know? Tell me everything you know."

"Are you fucking her, Finn? Are you fucking this girl behind my best friend's back?"

"What? NO! Abby, why the hell would you…"

"Oh God…." I hear Mandy mumble behind me. I turn around, and she's covering her mouth with her hand wearing the I-just-broke-my-mom's-favorite-crystal-vase expression. "Finn."

"What, Mandy?" This is getting annoying. "Would one of you please tell me what the fuck is going on?"

"Finn, Olivia knows. She knows about us."

"You're damn right she knows about you! How could you DO this to her, you piece of shit prick?" Abby is screaming at me with tears streaming down her face.

"Whoa! Enough, Abby!" I shout at her to calm her down. "Somebody here has some explaining to do because Mandy and I are not an 'us'. Never have been, and never will be for Christ sake. She's like my little sister, so TELL me what's going on, please!"

Abby backs up into the apartment, and I take it upon myself to follow her in and shut the door. At least now the entire building won't be privy to whatever the fuck it is that's about to happen in here. Riv is now standing in the dining room, glaring quietly at Mandy and me as we walk in.

"This, Finn!" Abby throws a stack of cards my way. Papers? They're papers?

No, they're pictures.

"There's no explanation needed, Mr. Kellan," she spits out. "You're fucking my best friend's friend! It's happened to her all over again; and in one way or another, she fucking caught you, and now she's gone! I need an explanation, and I need one right fucking now before I seriously come over there and punch you in that perfect face of yours."

I slowly go through the pictures one by one, startled and speechless at what I see. Mandy peers around my shoulders and gasps at the pictures I'm looking at.

"I don't get it," she says. "That's me, and that's you, but we were never together last night like that. I spent almost the entire evening with Kym." Mandy looks at Abby, shaking her head in confusion. "Abby, I don't understand. I was never even around Finn, except for at our table last night when I was complaining…"

An audible gasp comes from Mandy. "My mother…no…" she draws out. "It can't be. She wouldn't…"

"What?" Abby and I both ask.

"Finn, remember last night I told you my Mom wanted me to pose for her so she could use me as a model for one her class final projects?"

She doesn't need to explain any further. I get exactly what she's saying. I stare at one of the photos a little closer.

"She photoshopped these pictures," I whisper.

"Yeah. That's exactly what I'm thinking she did," Mandy agrees.

I smirk, looking at one of the pictures in front of me. "She did a sloppy ass job of it, too. Abby look at this."

I hold the picture out for Abby to see. She and Riv both lean over to see what I'm pointing at. It's Olivia's ring. Her favorite silver ring with the paw print on it.

"That's Olivia's ring," Abby states. "She wears it all the time. Never takes it off."

I nod in agreement "Exactly. Karen Photo-shopped Mandy's body into these pictures but didn't bother with appendages, I guess. Maybe she was in a hurry or knew that Olivia wouldn't look too hard at them, which surprises me given the photographer that she is."

Abby is immediately calmer now. "Yeah, well, you stop paying attention when your heart is breaking."

"Abby, I know this is my fault, and I need to fix it. I can fix it. When did she leave, and do you know where she would've gone?"

"No. Riv and I went out to get breakfast and do a little grocery shopping before the storm, and when we got back she was gone. All she left for me were these pictures and a note. I have no idea how to find her, Finn, and she's not answering her phone; and Finn..." Abby walks into the kitchen and reemerges with a small container in her hand. She starts to cry when she looks at me again.

"The vodka bottle is gone, and these pills were on the floor." She opens her hand to show a small handful of Ibuprofen.

No.

She wouldn't.

"You said she left a...uh...a note?" I swallow the knot in my throat.

"Not really a note, actually. Just two song titles. I don't get it."

"Song titles." I clear my throat quietly. "That's how she communicates."

Are they meant for me?

"What were the song titles?" I ask.

Maybe they're a clue?

"Umm, I don't know. The paper is right here on the counter." Abby reaches over and grabs the small sheet of paper where Olivia has written two song titles. She hands it to me so Mandy and I can read them.

As soon as my eyes read the titles, I feel my head slowly turn to look into Mandy's eyes. I suddenly feel like I've been punched in the gut.

My world just came to a screaming halt.

"No," I sigh. I can feel the tears burn my eyes. "She wouldn't. She can't." I'm beginning to panic.

"She wouldn't, Finn. She won't. She won't. She won't." Mandy is shaking her head vigorously, but all I see is myself standing in my doorway hearing the news from my mother that Sydney is gone. I feel the release of my hot tears stream down my face as I touch the words on the paper in my hands.

"Human" - Christina Perri

"And So It Goes" - Billy Joel

Chapter 36

OLIVIA

It's dinner time when I finally pull into the familiar driveway of my childhood. The regularly five-hour trip took me a little over six and a half hours because of the extra snow on the ground. I decided to go north into Albany and down through Poughkeepsie to home, instead of through Connecticut like I usually do. I was able to dodge the heavier snow that way, but still, I'm glad to finally be home as the snow is coming down pretty heavily now. I'm relieved to be away from Boston and from the chaos that is currently my life. Spending a few days with my mom and dad where nobody can get to me puts a calm in my heart that hasn't been there in a while.

"Livvy!" I hear my Mom exclaim from the front door. I've always felt the warmth in my heart at her nickname for me. She and Dad are the only ones in my family that call my Livvy. She comes running outside to embrace me and help with my bags.

"Mom, you're going to catch a cold without a coat on!"

"Oh don't worry about me, Sweetheart. I wasn't expecting you so soon. Are you okay? Where's Finn? I thought we would get to see him. Is he coming later?"

"Yeah umm, no. Finn didn't come with me this time, and he won't be coming later." I say quietly; my head hangs in shame.

"Oh, Olivia…" She can see the defeat on my face and the growing bubble of tears in my eyes. She wraps her arms around me in a warm, motherly embrace.

"Let's get you and your things in the house. You must be starving after that drive."

"I am a little hungry, actually. I was too afraid to stop in this weather, so I white-knuckled it for the last hour of the drive."

"Well come on then, Sweetie. Dad's inside finishing up dinner. We can talk later."

I stop just outside the front door and turn back to look at my mom following me in. "Thanks, Mom. I just needed a time out, ya know?"

She nods and smiles. I can see Grandpa's face smiling back at me through her eyes. "Everyone deserves a little time out now and then, Olivia. I'm sure everything will work out in time."

I'm not so sure this time.

After dinner, I make my way upstairs to my bedroom to unpack a few of my things. A nice hot bath is calling my name, so I grab my headphones and slip into the bathroom to relax in the tub. I've gone all day without contacting anyone about where I am or if I'm safe. When I turn my phone on, I see that I have at least eleven text messages. The only one I can see when I look at my screen is one from Finn that reads

> Please call me.
> At least tell me you're okay.
> Olivia, not hearing from you is killing me. Please!

I don't even want to read the previous ones, so I send them all to my inbox, push my earbuds into my ears, and try to enjoy a relaxing bath.

Nothing about it is actually relaxing since all of my thoughts are of Finn, and then Finn with Mandy, and then Karen, and then the pictures I saw this morning, and then last night. I wish I could just close my eyes and wake up with it all having been a terrible dream, but it's not. It wasn't. This is my life.

"Do you love him?" My mom asks me quietly. We're both sitting on my bed, enjoying a warm cup of hot chocolate before I go to sleep.

"I did love him." We sit in silence for a long minute before I sigh.

"I *do* love him."

"Tell me what you love about him. Every time we've talked, you haven't been able to stop gushing about Finn and how well he treats you. I'm not trying to defend him at all, Sweetheart, but there are two sides to every story. So, start with why you love him."

That's easy. I don't even have to think about my answer. "I love him because he's not perfect."

"Tell me more," Mom encourages.

"He's a man not too much older than me who has a strong head on his shoulders. He's a hard worker. He knows what he wants, but on the inside, he's a damaged young man who is still grieving a great loss. He's a normal person, Mom. He has demons just like I have demons. I love him because he's not perfect. I love him because…he's like me."

That answer came out of my head way too fast, but all I can think of now are the pictures I saw earlier today. "But, Mom, what about those pictures? How could he betray me like that? And so publically, too? Our night was going so well, and then it wasn't, and then it was over, and we haven't spoken since. I feel like the carpet has just been pulled from under me. I don't know how to get up and keep walking." I take a deep breath and look at Mom's face. "I'm not sure if I want to keep walking."

"Oh, that's easy. Of course you want to keep walking, Livvy. If you love him, then you owe it to him to hear his side before you make your judgments."

"Why, Mom?"

"Because," she smirks shaking her head. "Because men are like dogs, Livvy. They're usually excited to see you but have no idea what you're mad about. If you really love Finn, don't you think you owe it to him to at least talk to him?"

I chuckle softly and roll my eyes. "You sound an awful lot like Abby."

"Well, if that's true, then it sounds like you have a wonderful friend on your side. A friend who is probably worried sick about you because you have yet to let anyone know where you are and that you're safe. I hope she hasn't called the police about you by now with this snowstorm going on. She probably thinks you're alone in a ditch somewhere."

My head snaps up, and I stare at Mom. I never really thought about the fact that I hadn't talked to her all day.

"I just wanted to get away without someone trying to talk me out of it, ya know? I just…"

"You needed a time-out. I get it, Livvy. I do. But, don't forget that you're not alone. There are people in your life who love you and care about you and want to know that you're okay."

"Yeah. I hear you. I'll send her a text and let her know I'm okay."

"Good idea." Mom leans over and kisses my forehead before getting up from my bed

"Mom?" I ask before she leaves my room.

"Yes, Sweetheart?"

"How did you know Dad was, you know, The One?"

Mom smiles. "I knew your Dad was the one when I still wanted to be with him no matter how bad any argument was. He never had much money. Hell, we were both starving artists, but we had passion and dreams and a healthy drive for what we wanted out of life. He supported my dreams. That's all I needed. All I ever wanted. Just remember, Honey, that strong relationships, the ones that survive, are built by those who can forgive and by those who don't keep track of the past."

I nod my head, quietly breathing in all of Mom's advice. I hear what she's saying. I know in the end I'll have to talk to Finn, but tonight, tonight I just want to be away from it all. I send a short text to Abby, letting her know that I'm taking a small city break to clear my head and that I'll talk more when I'm ready. Hopefully she can forgive me for running out on her.

I need this for me.

Chapter 37

FINN

"I have to get to her."

"I have to get to her before she does anything stupid."

"Fuck! This is on me! I did this!"

I'm pacing back and forth, talking to nobody, anybody, and myself all at the same time. The knot in my throat is tight, and I'm starting to panic. Mandy, Abby, and Riv are just standing there, watching me like I'm a goddamn freak show.

"What do you mean, before she does something stupid?" Abby asks. "What is it you think she's going to do?"

I don't even slow down my pace to explain. I hear her questions, but I'm lost in my own puzzle, trying to figure out which pieces I need to put together to make everything right again. I grab my phone from my pocket and send a few more texts to Olivia.

Liv, I'm sorry! Talk to me please!

Where are you?

Are you safe?

As I'm texting Olivia, I hear Mandy explaining my worries to Abby.

"Before Finn's sister committed suicide, she played that Billy Joel song in a video blog," she says softly.

There's a gasp, and Abby is quickly at my side. "Finn, did Olivia know that? Did you ever tell her that?"

"No. Never. We've never...." I take a deep breath to steady my panicking nerves. "We don't talk about Sydney much. She knows I don't like to talk about it. Look, Abby, I'm sorry, but please." I stop pacing and take Abby by the shoulders, looking into her eyes with every bit of desperation I have. "Help me help her!"

Solving Us

"I really don't know where she is, Finn," she says, shaking her head sadly. I watch a tear fall down her cheek.

"Can you think of anywhere she would go?" I look around the room. "Mandy? Riv? You guys have any ideas because damn if my brain isn't giving me anything but a clusterfuck of panic and fear right now. I really need your help."

"She wouldn't go to the office, would she?" Mandy asks.

"Where is she from?" Riv asks looking at everyone.

"Umm, a small town in New York." Abby shakes her head and narrows her eyes. "Narrowsburg? It's pretty far away, though, like five hours or so and with this storm, I can't imagine she would go there."

"How can I find out? Do you have a number?" I don't have time to guess or assume. I need to find out for sure.

"Yeah, I have her parents' number written down somewhere, but Finn, we can't just call them!"

"Why the hell not?"

Of course I can call them. Is she nuts?

"Because even if she did decide to go there, she wouldn't be there yet, and if her parents don't know she's coming, we'll cause a major panic when we call there looking for their daughter, who they believe is here in Boston!"

I didn't think of that.

"FUCK!" I shout.

"What am I supposed to do? I can't just sit here while she's out there!" Why do I have to feel so goddamn helpless?

Riv puts his hand on my shoulder and squeezes in support. "Finn, man, the snow is coming down way too hard for you to go anywhere. You're probably better off just staying here. Wait it out until we hear something, don't you think? I mean maybe she just went to a hotel for a night. Maybe she just needed to be alone for a while."

"It's the alone part that scares me." I look to Abby who is watching me with a concerned look in her eye.

For me?

For Olivia?

"You know what happens when she's stressed and alone," I say quietly to her. "I can't just do nothing."

She tilts her head to the side, studying me for a moment. I hear her breath hitch and look at her knowing that she's about to say something.

"You really do love her don't you? I mean, you *really* love her." She says it like she can't believe she's saying it. I don't get that, but hell if I don't love Olivia with all that I am. I would die for her.

"I want her to live with me," I say quietly enough that maybe I'm just talking to myself. "I want to grow old with her. I want to adopt dogs and train them with her. I want to share all that I have with her. Yes, I love her, Abby. I'm so in love with her, and I have to make sure she knows that. I have to tell her. What if she doesn't know it enough? If she does something…" I choke up and feel warm tears slip down my face. "I would never forgive myself."

Abby approaches me slowly, keeping her narrowed eyes on me the entire time like I'm some sort of alien or something. I don't get it, but when she reaches me, she lifts up on her toes and wraps her arms around my neck in a comforting embrace. At first I don't move because this is unexpected. I look over Abby's shoulder to Riv and see him nod before I wrap my arms around Abby and hug her back.

I haven't felt this vulnerable in years.

Since Sydney left me.

"She's not Sydney, Finn." Her words slice through me, causing me to release the breath I didn't know I was holding. I squeeze Abby tighter and allow myself for just one moment to be comforted. "She's much, much stronger than your sister was, and I say that with the utmost respect. She loves you, too, Finn. I know she does, but she's hurting right now. There's a lot that you obviously don't know."

I let go of our embrace and back up enough that I can see Abby's face. "About what? Abby please, please tell me what's going on."

I see her eyes shift to Mandy and back to me before she answers me. "Are you sure you want to talk about this with her here? Her mother hasn't exactly been a stellar employee where Liv is concerned."

What?

"My mother is a bitch, and I'm finding that out more and more as these days progress, so please, don't hesitate to hold anything back in my regard. Olivia is my friend, and Finn is the brother that I never had and…"

Abby gives Mandy a questioning lift of an eyebrow.

"Yes, I know," Mandy says rolling her eyes. "We slept together. It was one time, and it was years ago after his father died, okay? I tried to tell Olivia that it was nothing more than a night of too much drinking and a lot of grieving. We've all done stupid things in our lives that we regret, and I'm pretty sure I can speak for Finn when I say that was one of them, but we can't take it back. It didn't mean what Olivia thinks it meant. I'm in love with a woman for Pete's sake, so please, please help him get the girl because we all care about Olivia, and we want to see her happy, too."

Abby slowly nods her head, and I silently praise her for being an understanding human being who can follow the truth in a stressful situation. She could've kicked us both out a long time ago, but we're still here, thank God. The only other place I would rather be is with Olivia.

Lying next to her.

Holding her in my arms.

"Okay, we should sit down. There's a good bit I can tell you since I'm almost certain Olivia hasn't already."

*****

Stupid Boy - Keith Urban

I still haven't heard from Olivia, but after talking to Abby for the last hour, it's the first song that comes to my mind, so I text it to her. She communicates best through song lyrics, so I'm praying that my texts are getting through to her and that she'll find it in her heart to forgive my ignorance. If she had just told me what was going on at work, I could've helped her. I would've helped her.

I can help her now.

Susan Renee

The snow is coming down pretty heavily, but I decide to brave the weather and take Mandy home so that I can see and speak to the one person who, for some reason, is single-handedly trying to ruin my life.

Chapter 38

FINN

I enter Mandy's childhood home, reminiscing as I do about some of the happy times our families spent together. There are pictures on the walls in the foyer of our two families together, of Karen and my mother, and of Mandy, Sydney, and me as we were growing up. I don't fully understand Karen's motives for doing what she's done to Olivia, or to me for that matter, but it infuriates me most likely because it saddens me to my core. Olivia is a gentle soul. I know she wouldn't hurt a fly, so to think that someone out there has been bullying her right under my nose disgusts me. What's more is that once I'm done here, I'm going to have to break the news to my mother. I'll be breaking her heart. As if she needs that to happen again in her lifetime, but in this case, I have to do what has to be done.

We walk towards the kitchen where I hear Karen talking on the phone. She's laughing. "It's almost too easy. She had it coming…yeah I know…will do. Thanks for your help. I'll keep you posted. Goodbye."

Going along with Mandy's plan, I stand back in the foyer for a moment and watch as she enters the kitchen, clearing her throat as Karen ends her phone call.

"Oh! Sorry, Sweetie. You scared me. I didn't know you were there."

"Hi, Mom," I hear Mandy say. The sound in her voice makes me sincerely believe that she's about as pissed off and hurt as I am. She's a better actress than her mother. "Who were you talking to?"

"Oh, that was just Greg from the IT department. He just had a server question for me."

"Oh I didn't realize you talked to him often. Didn't you tell me he's the one I needed to steer clear of because he's a…how did you put it…a perverted slime ball?" Mandy chuckles.

"Yes, the very same, but he's had a ridiculous crush on me for years, so I use that to my advantage when I can."

Ew.

"How's Kym? Did you guys have a good time this morning?" Karen asks disinterested.

Does she not like Kym either?

"Yeah. Yeah we did. We went to Starbucks this morning to grab a cappuccino. It was busier than we expected with all this snow. Oh, and oh my God, I almost forgot to tell you! We ran into Olivia while we were there. Poor girl was a hot mess. It was obvious she had been crying. Last night really fucked with her, I think. She didn't seem to want to talk to me since Kym was with me. She just got her stuff and left."

There's the info to light Karen's fuse. "Tears, huh?" I hear Karen chuckle lightly. "Mandy, last night didn't fuck up Olivia; Olivia fucked up last night. Plain and simple. I'm sure Finn is ready to have her head, as he should, as far as I'm concerned. After her mess of a presentation last night, Finn has no choice but to let her go. After all, the company's reputation is at stake. We can't have someone who fucks up that big stay with us when she'll most likely just do it again. She's a liability. He'll finally see that I'm the one who should've had that job all along. I have way more experience, and I know how to get the job done."

The nonchalance in Karen's voice infuriates me, but I stand still and continue to listen.

"Wait, what? A liability? How so? You don't think she purposely sabotaged the presentation do you?" Mandy asks surprised.

"Isn't it obvious, Sweetheart? I mean, seriously," Karen scoffs.

I can't stand here and listen to her accuse Olivia of this shit anymore! I slowly walk forward into the kitchen, my hands in fists beside me because it's all I can do to not want to punch Karen's face as hard as I can.

"An obvious liability?" I ask quietly, trying to keep my emotions at bay. She sees me enter the kitchen and pales immediately.

She wasn't expecting me.

I stand stiffly in front of her.

"Please, tell me why on God's green earth you would think Olivia McGuire is a liability to my company?" I'm seething but trying my damnedest not to explode in Karen's face. My father taught me how to be strong, and if ever I needed strength, it is now.

"Finn," she stutters. "I...I didn't..." She puts her right hand across the front of her throat, a clear sign of fear.

Good. I'm scaring her now.

She should be scared.

"Save it, Karen," I sneer. "I couldn't stand there in the hallway and listen to one more lie come out of your filthy damn mouth. Just answer me one question. Why?"

Karen frowns in disbelief as she looks between Mandy and me.

That's right, bitch. Your own daughter isn't even on your side.

"I don't understand what you..."

"Oh for Pete fuckin' sake, Karen, will you grow up and listen to your goddam self? You're pathetic! You've spent the last nine months sabotaging one of my employees, my company! Don't try to deny it. The evidence is already stacked against you."

I spot her work laptop on the kitchen counter. She eyes me looking at it, widening her eyes as she figures out my thoughts.

"Finn, please," she pleads.

I walk to the kitchen counter, picking up the laptop that belongs to the Kellan Agency. "I'm going to guess that everything I need to know is inside this computer, so you won't mind if I take it with me."

I close my eyes for a brief second and inhale. "Just tell me *why* Karen."

Karen looks quickly around the room I'm sure looking for some sort of Hail Mary, but she has none.

"Mom, please." I look at Mandy's pained expression and know that she's hurting because it's obvious that Karen is somehow involved in this mess. "For once, Mom, tell us the truth. What the hell have you done? And where is Olivia?"

Karen lets out an exasperated breath and rolls her eyes. "Finn, you were just too blind to see it." She shakes her head sympathetically. "Olivia isn't the right fit for this company, and she's not right for you. She makes too many mistakes. I understand that you wanted to give her a chance. I mean, obviously, she's a beautiful girl, and you have a little crush on her; but this is exactly why you should never mix business and pleasure. You can't see what I see on a daily basis. You aren't there to help cover up her mistakes, so I have to help out where I can. You should be thanking me, really. It should've been me, Finn. It should've been me in that position from the get-go, and you wouldn't be in this mess." She watches me for a moment to see how I'm going to react to her words. I refuse to give her the reaction she wants, so I stand there in the middle of her kitchen staring at her deadpanned.

"Thanking you?" I ask interested in what she could possibly say next.

"Yes. Thanking me. Listen to me, Finn. I know she didn't come in with tons of experience in the field, but come on. Even the Boston Cruise Line account was shoddy work. And then she skips town without even telling anyone what's going on. Remember when she ran out on you? She's lucky really that I was available to help out with the project. I covered for her, so she wouldn't be so embarrassed when she returned from California. I did it for you and for the company."

"Oh my God! What the fuck, Mom?" Mandy interrupts. The anger in her expression is palpable. "First of all, it was ME who practically did that entire project for you, and that was because YOU told me it was a class assignment you needed help with and wasn't a real deal! So you stole that account right from under Olivia on fucking purpose! Secondly, you know damn well she didn't run out on Finn. She was scheduled to go to California…"

I raise my hand to stop Mandy from talking.

"Not that it's any business of yours, Karen, but Olivia took a flight to California a night early because of me. You see, I'm perfectly capable of making mistakes in my personal relationships all by myself. I don't need your fucking help, so what's your next excuse?"

Karen's expression changes to one of empathy. In her best motherly tone she says, "Finn, Honey, you don't understand. Here, let me show you." She steps forward to grab her laptop that is now safely under my arm, but I instinctively step back from her.

"Don't even fucking think about it, Karen. You may think I'm naïve, but I'm no idiot. My father taught me better than that."

"Yes he did. And he taught you that family comes first in all things...that we protect the ones we love. Isn't that right, Finn?"

"Yeah. That's exactly what he taught me, and that's exactly what I'm doing."

"Of course you are." She rolls her eyes. "That's why I took care of Olivia for you this morning. Because the Mr. Loverboy standing in front of me could never look her in the face and fire her. Seriously, your father would be disappointed that you ever put a girl before his company."

I feel the expression on my face shifting, like the Hulk, to one of overwhelming anger.

"You know NOTHING about what my father wants for me and this company, you crazy, sick bitch!" I shout.

Find a nice girl, Son.

Look inside her. See beneath the beautiful.

"I love her! Do you not understand that?" I ask seething.

When you find your missing piece, don't wait too long to finish the puzzle, Son.

Give her anything and everything, Finn. But most of all, tell her you love her every day.

"Damnit! I love Olivia McGuire! She's my family now! She's my best friend, my other half, whatever the hell you want to call it; but I'm in love with her, and I will protect her until I can't physically do it anymore. So yeah, I am protecting the one I love, Karen. I'm doing exactly what my father told me to do before he died."

Like a lion ready to attack, Karen explodes right back at me, "You CAN'T love her Finn! You aren't supposed to be with Olivia McGuire, Son, because you are SUPPOSED to be with MANDY! She has loved you for YEARS and has stuck by your side when you had NO ONE! She DESERVES to have part of this company after what she's done for you! YOU know it, and I know it, so FUCK your little school boy crush, Finn! Grow some balls, and get the hell over her! SHE won't want you now, anyway."

Whoa!

Is she serious right now?

I look over at Mandy and see that tears are pouring down her face. I'm not exactly sure why she's crying. She's either heartbroken that her Mom just spilled a secret I never knew she was keeping or…

"You don't get it do you, Mom?" Mandy cries quietly. "You've never gotten it. I stand in front of you every single day, and you don't see me for who I am!"

"Mandy." Karen shakes her head in sympathy. "I…"

"I'M GAY, MOM! I'm FUCKING GAY!" Mandy screams. "It was NEVER Finn I had a fucking crush on, Mom! It was SYDNEY! Damnit to HELL, Mom; it was SYDNEY! I LOVED HER! She was my BEST FRIEND, and I couldn't EVER tell her how I felt but I LOVED HER! Finn is like the older brother I NEVER HAD, and you know what Mom? It was FINN who helped ME when I had no one. It's FINN and OLIVIA and KYM who help me NOW, when I have no one, because I sure as FUCKING HELL don't have you!"

Karen's eyes narrow as she stands quietly in her kitchen. I don't even want to give her the chance to speak. She's wasting what little time I have of finding Olivia by tonight. I shake my head slightly at the absurdity of the woman standing in front of me.

"You're fired, Karen."

"What?" she asks in disbelief.

I hold out my hand in front of me and stare her down. "Put your keys in my hand right now, and do not step foot inside the Kellan Agency ever again, unless I am personally escorting you inside. I'll have Mandy empty your desk and bring any personal items left in your office."

"You can't be serious! After all I've done?"

My stoic expression doesn't change. "Don't even get me started on all you've done. I think you've done enough, and I feel sorry for you. You had a great thing going, but now you're just a disgrace to the female population, and you're a bigger disgrace to my family. It wouldn't surprise me now if your own daughter had trouble loving you."

My eyes slide over to where Mandy is standing. I watch more tears run down her face, but she keeps her chin up as she confidently confronts her mother alongside me.

Oops. Hold your tongue, Finn. Mandy is your friend after all.

This is just as hard on her.

Karen's eyes go wide for a moment as she processes what I've said to her before she turns and walks slowly to her purse grabbing her office keys. In her last act of defiance, she hands her keys over to Mandy. As if they're burning a hole in her hand, Mandy tosses the keys to me and quickly folds her arms in front of her, looking away from her mother.

"Mandy, please…"

"I can't, Mom. No. I just…I can't. Not right now. Olivia was my friend, too, Mom. She IS my friend. She was the closest friend I've had since Sydney left me."

My insides are burning hearing my sister's name.

She's not Sydney, Finn. She's stronger.

I clear my throat. "I need to go. I have to find her," I say to Mandy.

"I'm coming with you. I can't stay here right now. Is that okay?"

"Sure. If I can get to my Mom's, you can stay there. She needs to know what's going on, and she needs to hear it from me."

"Kym's is on the way. I'm sure I can stay there."

I nod in agreement. Talking to my mother is probably something I should do alone anyway.

"I'll be in the car." I rest my eyes on Karen one last time, knowing that my mother will be heartbroken to hear that her close friend had a hand in sabotaging the family company. I feel a twinge of guilt on my way out that I've just taken another person from my mother's life. The last thing I hear before the door shuts behind me is Mandy's voice saying, "Goodbye, Mom."

Chapter 39

FINN

Every man feels like a little boy again when he's with his Mom. Somehow the connection between a mom and her little boy is one that can never be broken, and when I'm with my mother, I feel like I can do no wrong. She makes me stronger. She makes me want to be the best man I can be. She makes me want to find a partner who is as beautiful and strong as she is, and I did…and then, like an idiot, I let her walk away.

"I'm sorry, Mom. I'm so sorry," I cry at the dining room table, a mug of Mom's homemade hot chocolate in my hands. "I really messed everything up."

"The way I see it, darling, you have nothing to apologize for. At least, not to me. You did exactly what you needed to do for the company."

"But I failed, Mom. I failed to protect the ones that I love. Olivia is gone, and once again, it's all because of me. I've lost her, Mom. I lost Sydney, and I lost Dad, and now I've lost Olivia, and I'm losing myself. I don't know what to do."

Mom rubs her thumb over my hand as she holds it across the table. I'm a bit confused when I look up at her and see her smiling her 'you know damn well what to do' smile. She sips her hot chocolate and places her mug back down on the table. Scrunching her nose slightly, she tilts her head and whispers, "I'm pretty sure you know exactly what you need to do."

I wipe away the tear that escaped down my cheek. "It's not that easy, Mom. She left. She doesn't want to talk to me. She won't return my calls or my texts. I'm not even completely sure of where she is. And with this snowstorm, how am I supposed to get to her once I find out? I'm pretty sure she wants nothing to do with me." I dip my finger in my mug, stirring the hot chocolate inside.

"If I know anything about women, Finn, and I would like to think I know a great deal, I would say what she wants is a man who is strong enough to save her from herself."

"What do you mean? Olivia is one of the strongest girls I've ever met."

"But, does she believe that about herself?"

"I don't know. Sometimes maybe."

"Why do you love her?"

That's a question I can answer without giving it any thought whatsoever.

"I love her because she's not perfect. I love her because she's beautiful and doesn't know it. She doesn't care about money, or the fact that I come from lots of it, or have lots of it. She's never asked for a dime. I love her because she's never judged me for my imperfections. I love her because she loves Toby. I love her because every day she reminds me of the spirited girl Sydney used to be, and I love her because every day she reminds me of how much stronger she is than Sydney ever was. She has baggage, Mom. She has a past that has scarred her and scares her into thinking she doesn't deserve a future with anyone; but then I watch her in her element when she doesn't know I'm watching, and I'm amazed by her. She's perfect to me, Mom. Everything that's imperfect about her makes her so damn perfect for me. Does that sound ridiculous?"

"Imperfections define perfection."

"Huh?"

"It's a quote from my favorite author, Colleen Hoover. I read it in one of her books, but I'm pretty sure those words pretty much sum up you and Olivia. 'Imperfections define perfection.' Wouldn't you agree?"

"Yeah. Yeah, I guess so."

"So, tell me what it is you want with Olivia. Obviously you love her. Do you see a future with her? A for real happily ever after?"

"I've never felt this way about any girl I've ever known, Mom. It's only been about eight months, but I'm in love with her."

"I know you are, Sweetheart. I can see it in your face."

"Before Dad died, he told me to find my missing piece to complete my puzzle. She's my missing piece, Mom. She's it. This might sound...I don't know...fucking crazy, but I feel like Olivia is my gift from Sydney. When I'm with Olivia, I think about Syd. Olivia makes me happy to live my life. She makes me want a future, a wife, children, a house in the suburbs: the whole grand picture."

"Oh, Finn!" Mom gets up from the table and rounds the corner to hug me tightly. "I've been praying that I would be lucky enough to watch you fall in love and settle down. Your father would be so proud of you right now."

I chuckle at Mom's blatant lie. "Who are you kidding, Mom? You know Dad would be saying, 'Don't worry about those girls Finn. There will be plenty of women draining your bank account soon enough. You just work your way to the top before that happens,'" I say in my best stern father voice.

Mom laughs.

"Okay, you may be right about that, but you know deep down he believed in love. He may have lost sight of it as the company grew bigger, but your father was the biggest romantic when he was your age. It's why I married him. When your sister left us, I think he realized he had missed out on a lot of little parts of life. That's why he didn't want you to be in his shadow. He would want you to make different choices. Be happy. Be you. It's what I want for you, too, Sweetheart."

"Thanks, Mom."

"You're welcome for the hot chocolate," she says taking my mug to the sink and rinsing it out. I watch her lay the mugs down in the dish dryer with a June Cleaver flair. "Everything else you figured out on your own."

She winks at me and smiles turning off the sink.

"Yeah but sometimes a boy just needs to talk to his mom." I kiss her cheek. "I'm going to head upstairs for a bit and see if I can figure out a plan for the next few days. I can't get anywhere with the amount of snow out there, but I need to figure out where she is and what I'm going to do next."

"Okay. Let me know if I can help out at all."

"Thanks. I will."

"Oh, and Finn?" She turns around from the sink, as I turn in the doorway.

"Yeah?"

"If you choose the path that I'm pretty sure you want to choose, her father is the safest place to start." She smirks, and I know exactly what she's referring to.

I smile back at her and shake my head. "Got it. Thanks Mom, but I've got to get her back, first."

Sitting at my desk in my old bedroom, I do a little online searching. I need to see how long it will take me to travel to Olivia's hometown, assuming that is, indeed, where she is. At five and a half hours through the mountains, there's no way in hell I'll get there in the next few days. Roads are already closed on the outskirts of town. If the city is this bad, I can only imagine how my car will get me through the mountains.

Do helicopters fly from Boston to this Narrowsburg?

She's worth whatever that would cost.

My phone beeps, alerting me to an incoming text message.

Thank God! Olivia!

I'm disappointed but not surprised when I look at my phone and see Abby's name. Still, I'm hoping for any news at this point.

Abby: She's at home. Narrowsburg, NY. Parker Rd. That's all I know.

At least she's safe there.

I let out the breath I was holding and text her back.

Me: Thanks. Is she okay? She won't text me.

Abby: She didn't say otherwise. We're here if you need anything.

Me: Okay.

I quickly send another text to Olivia. I know she won't respond, but I have to continue to try and communicate with her.

Me: I love you, Olivia   Gone, Gone, Gone by Phillip Phillips.

I throw my phone down on my desk and continue to search a bit online for the perfect Christmas gift for the girl I love. I spend the next few hours searching one website after another before I find exactly what I was hoping for. It's so perfect; I couldn't have designed anything better myself. I jot down the phone number of the store in Manhattan so that I can make a phone call first thing in the morning. I close my laptop and find a pair of pajamas in my dresser drawer. I chuckle, hearing Mom's voice in my head always telling me to leave a few essential things here because "you never know." I hear my phone beep while I'm brushing my teeth, but I don't run for it, assuming it's Abby. Seconds later, the wind is knocked out of me when I look at the incoming text.

Olivia!

Liv: Broken Ones - Jacquie Lee

Oh, God! I haven't lost her!

She's alive!

There's still hope!

I've never heard of the song title she just sent me, so I bring it up on my Spotify list and listen to it before texting her back, so she knows I received her message.

Please don't run.
I love every piece of you even when you feel broken.
Sleep in peace, beautiful girl.
I love you.

Hearing from Olivia tonight has finally helped to calm my nerves. Laying in my bed, I stare at my ceiling and try to clear my mind of the day's events. It's been a fucked up twenty-four hours, and I'm aching to see Olivia, to fix her broken pieces. I put my hand down over the bed to pet Toby, as I'm used to doing when I'm falling asleep, only I realize Toby isn't here. I'm not at my house. I had Mrs. Pritchard pick him up earlier this morning.

Toby…

Solving Us

It's too perfect!
It could be too much...
It's a great idea, though!

With that final thought, I smile to myself, say good-night to Olivia in my head, and fall fast asleep.

Chapter 40

OLIVIA

These last three days at home have been comforting hanging out with Mom and Dad. The house all decorated for the holidays always brings back feelings of nostalgia. The holidays are usually my favorite time of the year. Mom singing with Karen Carpenter while she bakes and wraps, and Dad working in his rehearsal room with "A Christmas Festival" blaring through his Bose speakers. I always enjoy wrapping up in a blanket on the couch, watching whatever ABC Family has on during their 25 Days of Christmas marathon. Having just watched the end of another Harry Potter movie, it dawns on me that I never did follow up to make sure Finn read the next book. I shake my head chuckling to myself that I allowed him to get away with it.

"Something funny, Livvy?" Dad says with his eyebrows raised in question.

"Nah. I was just thinking about...well...something Finn and I..." I trail off, not really knowing what to say and least of all to my dad.

He sits down on the coffee table in the living room, facing me. "Have you two talked?"

"No. I mean, we've texted once or twice but that's it. I think..." I sigh. "I don't know; maybe I just needed a break. I'm just not sure what to say to him at this point, Dad. I'm not sure I'm the one he wants." I look down at my hands watching my fingers turn the ring that I never take off around and around. Dad sees it, too.

"Look, Livvy, I don't always seem to know the right things to say when it comes to my daughter and relationships. I'm supposed to be the dad that scares the guys off and keeps them away, until you're at least thirty."

We both chuckle as I look at my dad adoringly. He's such a protector.

Like Finn.

"But then I look at you, Livvy, and you're missing something. Something I'm not sure you realize you're missing because you've spent a great deal of your adult life not looking for it and not wanting it...or maybe not feeling like you deserve it."

My eyes start to water. I'm a Daddy's girl through and through, so the very second he starts to say something emotional, I have a hard time holding myself together.

"But, Livvy, Babe, you do deserve it. You deserve to be happy like your mom and me. You deserve a life. You deserve a future. And I know we can't always be the master of our own fates, and we don't always know what's behind the door that opens for us, but you know what I do know?"

I grab a tissue and wipe the tears that are now running down my face. "What, Dad?"

"I know he's looking for you. I know he knows you're here, and I know he wants to get to you very badly. I have to imagine if he has to drive a snow plow up here from Boston, he's probably planning his route right now."

I shoot my dad a shocked glance not quite understanding what he's saying. "What do you mean he knows I'm here? I never told him that."

"Abby sent your mother an email. That's how we know he's looking for you. You won't return his calls, and I suppose you have your reasons for that, so I'm certainly not going to pressure you, but at least now you know he's trying to walk through snow and ice to get to you. Don't forget that."

He is?

What could he possibly have to say?

"I won't. Thanks, Dad."

"Anytime, Sweetheart. It's not often that a dad gives his daughter a thumbs up on going after the guy, ya know."

Again, I laugh through my tears and blow my nose. "I know, Dad. I hear you. I just have to figure a few things out."

"And you will, Livvy. You will. Why don't you get out for a few hours? Riverfront Books is open now that the roads are clearing up a little. And you love K.B.'s cappuccino. Maybe you'll think of a good Christmas gift for Finn while you're out." He kisses me on my forehead and winks at me before heading out of the room. "You can sit here all you want and mope over not getting him a gift, but I know you, Livvy; and I'm one hundred percent certain you have had a plan for a long time in that beautiful head of yours….so go do it. Go get it. Whatever it is you want to do. You'll feel better, whether you see him soon to give it to him or not."

When he leaves, it only takes a moment before my eyes grow big and a sincere smile inches up my face. My dad's right. I know I could stay here and live the lonely life in a small artsy town, but I've been there, done that. That's why I left in the first place. I run up to my room and grab my camera that has been stuffed in my bag. If I'm going to spend time by the river, I may as well take advantage of the gorgeous scenery. I say goodbye to Dad and let him know I'll check in at the gallery where Mom is working for the afternoon.

Narrowsburg being the tiny town that it is, it only takes me four minutes to drive up town and park along the street near Riverside Books. The roads are surprisingly clear for the winter storm that just walloped the area, and I quietly wonder to myself how the roads are in Boston. I check my cell phone out of habit. Or maybe out of anxious hope? Finn has texted a few times, but other than that, he hasn't said much in the last day or two.

Maybe he's letting me go.
I don't want to be let go.

The sleigh bells ring against the door when I enter Riverside Books, the only bookstore in town. It's not much, but when they don't carry what I'm looking for, they've always been good about ordering things for me. I know I could order off of the big box stores online, but I like to keep my business local whenever I can. I've watched Mom and Dad lose business to the big bad internet; and although I know my parents just need schooled on social media and online sales, something I hope to be able to provide them, it feels good to support the local families trying to make a living in this small town.

Solving Us

"Olivia! It's so good to see you! I didn't know you were back in town!" It's Mrs. Michaels, Archer's mother and owner of the book store, standing at the counter as I walk in. I should've remembered she worked here, but it totally slipped my mind. Ugh, she's the last person I want to see, let alone talk to right now. She smiles and comes around the counter to give me a hug. "Are you here for the holidays?"

I hug her back with no enthusiasm. Her son was a cheating douchebag.

Maybe his mom never knew?

Wouldn't I love to let that cat out of the bag?

"Um, yeah. I guess so, yeah. Just for a few days anyway." I do not want to stand here and have a conversation about why I'm really back in town. But since I really don't have a plan, I guess I'm not lying when I tell her I'm here for the holidays. I can go with that story. Mrs. Michaels is one of the town gossips. She knows everyone's business, so I'm praying that Mom hasn't already talked to her, or that maybe this time Mom has enough sympathy for me to not bring up my love life or lack thereof.

"That's great, Olivia. I'm so glad you stopped in. If Archer were in town, I am positive he would love to see you, but he's stuck in Manhattan until at least Christmas Eve."

Good.

He's the last person I want to see.

"Oh, that's too bad. Actually I stopped in hoping you might have the Harry Potter series?" I quickly change the subject.

"Of course we do! After all this time, it's still one of our biggest sellers!" she exclaims with pride as she swiftly walks down the appropriate aisle.

"Great. I need the entire series, please, if you have them all."

Mrs. Michaels looks at me in surprise. "You mean, you've never read the Harry Potter series? I didn't think there was anyone in this town who hadn't read them except for the younger children."

"Oh no, these aren't for me. I've read the whole series more times than I can count. They're a Christmas gift for...a friend."

Damnit, Olivia, you paused!

"Ooh...a boyfriend?" she asks, almost too interested.

"Um, just a friend. My best friend, Abby, actually," I lie. I really don't need to give Mrs. Michaels fuel for her fire. "When I found out she hadn't read them yet, I told her it might be a deal breaker on our friendship!" I wink at her so she knows I'm kidding.

"Well I think this is a great idea then, Dear. I'll get you all checked out."

"Thank you."

I grab my bag of books, smirking to myself knowing that I just totally lied to Mrs. Michaels and don't feel the least bit guilty about it, and knowing that if and when I see Finn again, he'll get a kick out of this gift. I'm temporarily brought back to my solemn self when I realize my being back here and not in Boston impedes my ability to follow through with the other part of Finn's gift I had planned. I suppose, for now, maybe it's for the best since it was going to be a joint gift of sorts anyway. I've caused Finn enough stress. I certainly don't want what I considered a thoughtful gift to cause any more stress for him. This will have to do for now. Back out on the street, I place the bag of books in the trunk of my car and walk down the sidewalk towards the gallery to say hello to Mom.

When I walk in, I see her assistant, Krista, wrapping up a few paintings to ship out. That used to be my job as I was growing up in high school. I smile remembering every step and watching Krista to make sure she does it right. Mom was always a stickler for details.

"Hey, Krista! How are you?"

"Olivia! Your mom said you were in town for a few days. I'm great! It's good to see you."

"Thanks. Yeah, I'm just in for Christmas," I think I lie again. "Just stopped in to see Mom. Is she in her office?"

"Oh, no actually, she's not here. She was here, but she's um...running a few errands she said. I think the post office, and the bank, stuff like that." She shrugs.

"Okay." I nod. "Well, I'm just going to take a walk to the bridge to get a few pictures. Will you tell her I stopped by, and I'll see her tonight?"

Solving Us

"Sure will, Olivia! Have fun out there. It's a beautiful day for picture taking!" She winks at me.

I chuckle as I wave to Krista on my way out. I wrap my scarf around my neck and continue my walk down to the green Narrowsburg Bridge connecting the town to Pennsylvania. This area is one of the best for catching some great photo opportunities. With an eagle's nest close by, I've always considered myself lucky to catch one flying in or out. I spend about an hour walking through town and down along the river before the wind picks up and starts stinging my face. I'm ready for some heat, so I make the trek back up the hill to K.B.'s Pit Stop for a hot drink and a sweet treat before heading home.

Sleigh bells once again hit the door as I step inside. Even when decorated for the holidays, I love the ambiance of K.B.'s Pit Stop. The decor around the shop is all antique race cars, old posters of racing events, and every table is adorned with a checkered flag. I smile at the Christmas tree in the corner decorated with car ornaments. It was one of my favorite places to hang out growing up and is still one of my favorite places now. I walk to the counter and order a hot chocolate and an orange-cranberry muffin from the young barista, whom I do not recognize. I guess it's nice to be home for a bit and not run into everyone that I know. Since it's the middle of the day, there aren't many people hanging around. Other than two other people in line behind me, there is just an older couple in the corner playing checkers while they sip their coffees.

I choose a table near the back of the store where I can snuggle into a cozy booth. I sip my hot chocolate and close my eyes for just a moment, allowing my body to warm up and relax. The smells of orange spice and nutmeg are plentiful throughout the store. Kristy, the owner of the shop, does a lot of extra baking during the holidays for local parties and events. Sitting here feels almost like sitting at home in the kitchen with Mom. The music piping through the shop speaker seems to be a mix of holiday and secular music. I know when I walked in I was hearing "I'll Be Home for Christmas" playing, but now I'm hearing "Falling in Love at a Coffee Shop" by Landon Pigg. I shake my head at the oddity of what is most likely Kristy's iPod on shuffle; nevertheless, this song sobers me and saddens me. Ironic that the song is about falling in love at a coffee shop, yet here I sit, alone and isolated from the world I was thriving in only four days ago.

Trying to ease the sting of this stupid song, I grab my camera out of my bag and click through the many photographs I took outside. Sleigh bells sound a few more times as the hustle and bustle picks up slightly around me while I enjoy some quiet time. Before I unwrap my muffin to dig in, I bring my camera to my face turning my lens to focus in on the beautiful snowflake-like sprinkles decorating the food in front of me.

"So it really is true. You *do* always take pictures of your food."

I know that voice.

I don't even have to move the camera from my face.

There's no way.

"Olivia," he breathes.

I'm frozen. A million thoughts are infiltrating my brain at this very second, and I'm not sure which one to latch on to. I can't move the camera from my face. I feel hot tears wanting to emerge from my eyes, but I force them back with a gigantic gulp.

Why do I feel so anxious right now?

"Olivia, please, Beautiful." He kneels down right by my side placing a hand on my camera helping me lower it to the table. I feel one lone tear escape rebelliously down my face and try to swipe it away.

"No. Don't," Finn says. "Olivia, I need to see this. I need to look at you, please. Just…you don't have to move or say anything. I know what I've done to you. I know you're hurting, and I know you may not ever be ready to forgive me, but please just let me look at you and, and know that you're alive, and you're okay."

I sit quietly for a second, mulling around his words, while he stares at me. The memory of just a few days ago, standing in my apartment by myself, having my heart ripped out of my chest with just a few photographs and a note from Karen, makes my stomach queasy. I no longer want my muffin, and I can't stop the tears that I thought I was strong enough to keep at bay at least until I got out of this place.

"You love her." I choke on my words.

"What? Love who, Olivia?"

I slowly raise my head, quiet tears streaming down my face. I'm silently thanking myself for at least choosing a booth in the back and out of the way.

"Mandy. You love her, Finn. I'm sorry for the mess I caused you, but you could've at least told…."

"Whoa, whoa, whoa, Olivia, stop. Wait. You have it all wrong." He smiles pleadingly. "Olivia, yes of course I love Mandy. She's my sister's best friend and is basically a sister to me, too. I will always have a place in my heart for her, but that's it. Olivia I love *you*. It's always *been* you, Beautiful. It will *always* be *you*."

I watch as he reaches into his inside jacket pocket and lays an envelope in front of me. I recognize it right away. It's the envelope that Karen's note and pictures are in. I turn my head away from the pictures and from Finn instantly. I have no interest in subjecting myself to that pain again. I can't.

"Fuck. Damnit," Finn whispers to himself. "No, no. Liv you have to look. I *have* to show you. They've been photoshopped. Karen photoshopped these pictures, Olivia. She knew after that night that you would be too upset to look closely, and oh my God, how I wish you would have because I wouldn't be kneeling here right now having to watch you go through all this pain; so you have to look. It's the only way you'll believe me. I'm sorry, Beautiful, but please. *Please* for me, look at them one more time. Look closely."

I turn my head slowly and see the pain and the desperation in Finn's eyes.

He wouldn't travel all this way if he wasn't serious.
Listen to him, Olivia.
Hear his side first.

Finn hurriedly pulls out a few of the pictures and points to the girl he is standing with. "Look Olivia do you see? This picture isn't real. It's been altered. Yes, that's Mandy, but look at her arm and her hand. Do you see?"

The bracelet I was wearing that night is on Mandy's wrist, and on her finger sits the small silver band I have known for the last eight years.

"My ring."

"Thank God!" Finn breathes. "Yes! Yes it's your ring, Beautiful, and it's in every single one of these pictures! All of these poses, all of these pictures were originally of you and me! Do you remember this one? We were dancing to "Sugar", remember?"

He pulls out another picture of him and Mandy during the auction, except she was standing by Abby and me during the auction. In fact, come to think of it, I don't remember seeing her at all during the evening, except for when she sat down drunk at our table. I look at Finn my eyes huge in realization.

"Yes, Finn. I do remember."

Finn releases a huge breath. "Oh thank fuck." He closes his eyes and takes another slow breath. When he opens them, there's a tear in his eye that wasn't there a moment ago.

"Finn…"

His hand runs down the length of my face and cups my cheek. I instinctively lean my head into his touch. I've missed this feeling so much.

"I thought I had lost you Liv. I thought…I thought…the vodka…the pills."

"I'm not her, Finn. I'm not Sydney. I spilled the Ibuprofen accidentally and tried to clean them all up."

I watch a tear drop from his face. "I know. I know, Liv. I do. I just, I miss her. If anything would've happened to you…"

"I know you miss her, Finn, and I'm so sorry."

"No," he says confidently. "Olivia McGuire, you have nothing to be sorry for." He kisses my cheek lightly and sits back. "Listen to me, Liv. I'm the one who is sorry. I saw something in you so many months ago that reminded me of Sydney, and I was drawn to you immediately. Like you were an angel sent to me by my little sister. And then you mentioned that you felt like your life was a puzzle and that you hadn't found all the right pieces yet, and I fell in love with you, Liv. I knew. I knew then that

Solving Us

you were indeed placed in my life as a gift from Sydney, and I wasn't ever going to let you walk away if I could help it. She told me in a video that I saw after she died that she wanted me to move on and find my missing piece, and...and I'm not good at this sometimes, Liv. I didn't know about Karen, and I'm so damn sorry! I wish you would've told me what was going on, but I'm so, *so* fucking sorry for everything she put you through. I never meant for any of this to happen."

Well, what do I say to that?

"How did she do it, Finn? How did she sabotage our presentation? Did the hospital drop our service? You were so mad at me. I didn't know what..."

"No. Liv, it's okay. It's a long story that I'll tell you later, but no, the hospital didn't drop the contract. I was able to clear it all up by exposing Karen and letting them know that she's no longer with the company. That's what took me a few days to get here. I had to clean it up, Liv. I had to. I couldn't allow Karen to have any more access anywhere in the agency. Everything is fine now. I came to get you because I need you, Olivia. I need you with me. I need you beside me. I need you in my arms, and I need you in my bed, and I need you in my life. Please, forgive me."

I watch him for a second. I watch his face, slightly tear-stricken and more defeated than I think I've ever seen him. We both have baggage. We both have events that happened in our past that, although are very different in circumstance, they are very similar in how they have affected us as individuals and as a couple. Finn Kellan gets me. He's the only one who has seen past my scars, and not just the physical ones on my body, to see who I am and who I want to be. I would be stupid to walk away from him.

"Well, how can I argue with a plea like that? You would make a shitty lawyer, though, ya know that?" I smirk.

Finn stands up and takes my hand, helping to pull me from my seat. He wraps his arms tightly around me in an embrace I have missed so much. I find comfort in the warmth of his chest as I hear him breathe in the scent of my hair.

"I've got you," he whispers in my ear, kissing the side of my head. "I've got you, Liv. Please don't ever run from me again. Please don't scare me like that again. I love you so much."

"I love you, too, Finn. I'm so sorry I scared you and Abby. I promise I won't run again."

"Move in with me."

Whoa.

What?

I lean my head back to see Finn's face. He's as serious as I've ever seen him. "Move in with me, Liv. I love you, and I need you, and I want to share a life with you. Move in with me. We'll figure shit out together, you and me."

"Finn…" I tilt my hand and look at him sadly. "After all this, Finn, I…"

"No, Liv! Listen to me. I know what you're thinking. You're scared. I get it. I do, but, Olivia McGuire, I love you, and I promise I'll protect you any way I can. I can give you anything you need."

"Finn, I don't need you to do that."

"I know, Liv. And that's why I love you so damn much. You never ask for anything. You never expect anything. You're your own brave strong creative and kind person, and I admire everything about you. We're together all the time, anyway, and you can still see Abby whenever you want, I promise but please, move in with me. I need you."

I watch him for a minute, not quite sure what to say. Moving in with Finn would be such a comfort, but I also love being with Abby.

But Abby and Riv are getting closer.

"You're sure?" I ask. I've never had a guy ask me to move in before. This is new territory for me.

"Do I look like I'm having doubts, Olivia?"

I chuckle at his passionate stare. "Okay, Finn. Okay, let's do it!"

"Yeah?" He asks, shocked, I think, that I said yes.

"Yeah," I laugh through my tears.

Solving Us

Finn wraps his arms around me and picks me up. Instinctively, I wrap my legs around his waist and kiss him as passionately as I can, remembering that we are in a public place in a very small chatty town.

Fuck it. Let them talk!

Finn holds onto me while he grabs my coat and camera bag. I'm not sure how he doesn't drop me. I'm no feather, but I giggle when he wraps my coat around me as best he can, throws cash on the table, and walks out of K.B.'s all while continuing to kiss me.

"Excuse me," I hear him say as we stop on the sidewalk. I turn my head and see Mrs. Michaels from the bookstore, startled that we almost ran into her. I laugh out loud at her expression and squeeze Finn a little tighter."

Yep. That will give her something to talk about!

"Where are we going, Finn?"

"How about a quick walk. Show me the river?" Finn asks letting me slide down so that my feet are touching the ground once again.

"Uh, yeah. Okay. Good idea." I slip my arms into my coat sleeves and zip up to keep warm. Finn takes my hand as I walk him up the street to the viewing area where we can look out over the river. Just as we get there, an eagle is flying down the river and back up to its nest.

"Whoa!" Finn says. "I've never seen one before. I mean, flying in the wild anyway. They're magnificent!"

"Yeah. They're beautiful all the time."

"Like you." Finn leans down and kisses me sweetly. His breath is warm and comforting. I've missed him. I smile shyly, not knowing what to say. This has been a morning I wasn't exactly planning.

"So umm…I'll understand if you think I shouldn't come back to…"

"Stop right there. Do not say another word, Olivia McGuire." Finn holds my face in his hands and looks directly into my eyes as lovingly, yet sternly, as possible, I think. "You did absolutely nothing wrong. Don't think for one second that I don't want you there. That I don't need you there. Because you would be dead wrong."

"But, Finn, there's so much you don't know."

Finn nods his head. "You mean like the emails she's been sending you since you started? Or the Boston Cruise Line account that she stole right from under you? Or the everyday bitch that she was to you? Should I go on?"

I raise both eyebrows, staring at Finn like a deer in the headlights.

"Olivia, how do you think I figured out where you were? Your best friend and roommate wasn't about to play Super Sleuth by herself. Once she was done ripping me a new asshole, we were finally able to sit and talk and solve the problem."

"Oh no!" I nervously giggle knowing exactly how my best friend can be when someone has hurt the people she loves. "Finn I'm sor…"

"Nope. Don't you dare apologize again, Liv. This is on me. I did this. I wasn't vigilant enough. I was too trusting of Karen. She's tried to pull shit like this before. Well, maybe not to this extent, but she's always thought she deserved a different place in the business, but she doesn't have the qualifications. That and she comes across like a bitch sometimes…people skills…she doesn't always have them."

Obviously.

"So, how did you solve umm…the problem?"

"Well…Mandy actually started it. She came to me the other morning and told me she had overheard her mom on the phone and was more than cooperative in exposing her. They have some unfinished personal issues to deal with, I guess. Anyway, once I was filled in on what she had been doing to you, I confronted her, and then I fired her ass."

"Wow."

"Yeah. It was a no brainer. My father taught me to protect the people I love. And I love you, Olivia. I wish I would've known about this as it was happening. I wish you would've told me. I could've protected you."

I shake my head. "No Finn. I couldn't tell you. I couldn't be the office snitch or the whiney girlfriend of the CEO. The ramifications of that would have been terrible for me and most likely for you as well. I just, it's nothing I haven't been through before. I tried to handle it. I had Abby to lean on."

"Liv, I get it. I do, but I need you to put yourself in my shoes for just a minute. Your life parallels my sister's in so many ways that I can't help but think of her in times like this. The bullying she went through, the hateful comments made to her, the way she must've felt every damn day. I can't, Liv…I can't let you live like that. It's my job to protect you. I *want* to protect you."

"But it's not your job, Finn, and you can't do that every day. You can't glue yourself to me and watch everything I do. That's not healthy for any relationship, and I do appreciate my independence. I'm so sorry I kept this all from you. I never thought about how it might affect you because I was only thinking about getting myself out of a hard situation."

Finn looks out over the water. Large pieces of ice are drifting down the river. "Fair point. I get it. But can you promise me that if something even remotely close to this comes up again, you'll tell me about it?"

I smile at him. "You'll be the first to know, every morning and every night."

"HA!" He smiles holding me tightly against him. "Damn right! I can't wait to wake up next to you every morning, Olivia. I love you so damn much." Finn kisses me hard before rubbing his nose against mine. He quickly scoops me up in his arms and begins to carry me back down the sidewalk. "Come on; I need to show you something."

"Wait, Finn." I can't stop giggling. I love when he carries me. "Where are we going?"

"You'll see."

"Wait! I drove here! My car is just up the street."

"It's okay. I don't think anyone will steal it. I'll bring you back to get it, but I need to show you something right now.

"What do you need to show me?"

"Your Christmas present."

"But it's not Christmas yet, Finn!"

"I know, but this can't wait. You have to see it before you move in with me."

I throw him my cute pouty face as he enters the driver's side of the car. "Okay, then. Show me. I hope you know where you're going!"

"I think I can handle it. Won't take long."

In less than five minutes, we're pulling into my parent's driveway.

"Uh, how did you know how to get here?" I don't quite understand. I know it's a small town, but damn, how does he know exactly how to get to my house without his GPS?

"I was here earlier. Looking for you, but you weren't here, so I talked with your parents for a bit."

"My parents? But my mom has been at work."

He smiles and looks over at me through his mirrored sunglasses. "Wrong again, Beautiful. She met me here with your father an hour or so ago."

"What? Why?" I'm laughing, but I'm also so damn confused.

"You'll see very soon. Come on. Let's go in."

We get out of the car and walk the short path to the house. Nearing the front door, I hear a barking puppy.

What the hell?

Toby?

"Did you bring Toby with you?" I ask excitedly.

Again, Finn smiles at me. He takes my hand and kisses it. "Nope. Come on." He opens the front door, and we both walk inside hand in hand.

Immediately the barking starts again, leading me into the kitchen. When Finn and I round the corner, I feel him squeeze my hand, and I look back at him. He's smiling, but I can tell he's also a bit nervous.

Of my reaction?

I turn back to the kitchen where my mom and dad are sitting on the floor. Beside them, held by my dad, is a ridiculously cute yellow lab puppy with a royal purple collar. She's beautiful, and I'm stunned.

"What's going on, guys?" I turn back to Finn, who is smiling and trying to gauge my reaction. "Did you do this for them, Finn? You bought them a puppy?"

"No, Olivia. I bought you a puppy. Well, actually I guess I got us a puppy."

"What the…" I start laughing and immediately drop to my knees holding my hands out for the puppy, who wastes no time running to my lap and licking my face. Wet puppy kisses are the best.

Finn kneels down beside me to watch the puppy with me. "She's not old enough yet, obviously, but if you want, I thought we could train her like the others at the hospital."

"Oh, Finn! What a great idea! Yes! Of course I would love to do that! Oh my gosh, thank you so much!" I squeeze the puppy in a light hug and then pick her up to hold her to my eye level so I can see her cute face. Hanging from her purple collar are two dog tags. One has Finn's address on it, and the other is blank so that we can have her name put on it, I guess, as soon as I think of one. But what distracts me beyond the dog tags is the small shiny band dangling next to the tags. It's a diamond ring in the shape of a heart. It's not huge, but has to be at least two carats. It's stunning, and it's shiny, and I don't know how I didn't see it from across the room. I look up to where my parents are sitting. My mom has tears in her eyes. I can tell she's trying very hard not to cry. I look at Finn, who calmly reaches over and takes the puppy, she who must soon be named, and swiftly detaches the ring from her collar.

"Good girl," he whispers to the dog. He lets her go, but she doesn't run around the room. She sits in front of us calmly and cocks her head to the side wagging her tail. I would usually giggle at something as cute as that, but right now in this moment I'm so stunned by what is going on around me, I can't react. I'm motionless on the kitchen floor, and everyone seems to be staring at me.

"Olivia." Finn turns my body so that our knees are touching on the floor where we sit, and he holds both of my hands in his. Quickly realizing what this moment is about to become, I try so damn hard to pay attention and listen to the words Finn is saying to me.

"Fifteen minutes ago, I asked you to move in with me, and you said yes. What you didn't know was that I had an even greater reason for asking. I'm in love with you, Olivia. I love you so much it physically hurts when I'm not with you. I love you more than fancy cars or trips to the

Cliffs of Moher. I love you more than a risky closet rendezvous and cinnamon apple syrup."

Oh God, he said that in front of my parents!

I chuckle and close my eyes, not wanting to see my parents' reaction, but Finn squeezes my hand and keeps talking. "Olivia, I love you more than Harry Potter, or the X-Men, and I love you more than Hershey bar and graham cracker sandwiches. You're it for me, Liv. I knew the very day that I met you that you were going to be the one for me. The zig to my zag, the light where I feel dark; you're the comfort to my nightmares. You're my missing piece, Olivia. You're the whole damn Rubik's Cube. Every fucking colorful side, and I need you. I need your strength and your determination. I need your passion, and I need your ability to see the world not as a chaotic Hell, but as a world of possibility and promise, of adventure; and, Olivia, I want to experience it all with you. Every last moment until my dying breath; so Olivia McGuire, will you please walk beside me as my wife, my best friend, my lover, and my soulmate? Olivia, will you marry me?"

"Oh, Finn! Yes! Yes, I will marry you!" I don't even wait for the ring to be pushed onto my finger before I leap into Finn's arms, kissing him over and over again. I hug him tightly before he lets go to actually slide the ring onto my finger. I wipe away the tears and look over at my parents who are both crying right along with me. I stand up and run to them both, embracing them in a family hug.

"I told you he was looking for you, Livvy." My dad says, sniffling through his tears.

"Wait, you mean, you knew about this? You knew about everything this morning?"

Dad laughs and nods his approval to Finn, who is smiling with our newest four-legged friend in his arms. "Yes, Livvy. We've known about this for a day or two now. Finn just needed time working out the details."

"Ha! I can't believe you pulled it off!"

"We can't either, Dear. You have been walking around here like a sad little zombie for days, but we didn't want to ruin Finn's surprise."

Solving Us

Mom says, kissing my cheek. "Your ring is beautiful. Well done, Finn, and welcome to the family!"

"Thanks, Mrs. McGuire," Finn says returning the hug. "Oh, but I have more to show you, even though it's a bit premature." He puts the puppy down and puts his hand in his jeans pocket pulling out a small box. The ring box I suppose. When he opens it there is another ring inside made up of four diamonds individually set in a small semi-circle. Finn takes the ring out of the box and slides it onto my finger sitting right next to my engagement ring.

"The ring comes as a set. This will be your wedding band."

I gasp in surprise as I see what becomes of the ring when both bands are connected. My engagement ring that I thought was a simple heart shape is now surrounded by four diamonds to make up one diamond-shaped paw print. It's exquisite and not like anything I have ever seen before.

"Oh Finn…I…this…it's…"

"I know," he says. "It's beautiful, like you. I'm sorry it took me a couple extra days to travel here but it took me a few days to find it. I had to make sure it was perfect."

"It is perfect. You're perfect, Finn. Thank you so much for this, for coming here…for everything. I can't wait to be your wife."

"You have no idea how happy I am to hear you say that. Say it again." He smiles.

With a smile on my face so big it hurts I yell, "I'm going to be your wife!"

"Hell yeah, you are!" He sweeps me off of my feet and spins me around the kitchen as everyone laughs together.

*****

After a wonderful home-cooked meal with my parents, Finn and I spend the rest of the evening playing with our new puppy in the living room. Snuggled under a blanket in front of the fireplace, we watch as the pup chases her tail a few times before she catches it and falls down. She swiftly gets back up and walks right into my lap folding herself up and falling asleep in the warmth surrounding her.

"Luna."

"What?" Finn asks quietly.

"Luna. I want to name her Luna."

"Okay." Finn agrees. "Why that name? What made you think of that?"

"Luna Lovegood. If this puppy was a boy, I would've picked Neville because both Neville and Luna were two Harry Potter characters who were constantly picked on or made fun of. But, in the end just like Neville, Luna is strong, compassionate, loyal, and brave." Reaching down and sliding my hand softly down Luna's back, I say to Finn, "She'll teach us both a lot, I'm sure."

"Luna…" Finn practices rolling the name off of his tongue. "I like it. Luna it is."

I lay my head back on Finn's chest and exhale, closing my eyes and silently appreciating this moment of relief from the last few days.

"Oh, I have one more thing for you."

"There's nothing more you could give me that would make me as happy as I am right now, Finn."

"It's okay. You're getting it anyway. It's just a little thing I saw the other day that made me think of you, of us." Finn hands me a small, oddly-shaped wrapped gift that he pulled out of his pants pocket. "Sorry about the wrapping. I didn't have a box."

He places in my hand a small square shaped gift that obviously has some sort of chain or cord. I rip open the package and shake my head in astonishment at the small key chain in my hand.

"It's perfect." I smile, turning the Rubik's Cube around in my hand. Every side of the cube has been solved except for the top row of each side.

"Not yet," Finn whispers, looking at the cube in my hand and then at me expectantly. "You said yes, Liv. So, I thought you should get to make the last move."

Solving Us

I look back down at the cube in front of me and realize that all I have to do to solve the puzzle in my hand is turn the top row until the colors all match up. I do so with happy tears in my eyes. He thinks of everything.

"Now, it's perfect, Liv. And now you can look at it every day and be reminded of how far you've come, how strong you are."

"How strong we both are," I correct him. "How far we've both come. I love you, Finn Kellan."

"I love you too, Olivia. Merry Christmas."

"Merry Christmas, Finn."

We sit for a few quiet moments watching Luna sleep and listening to my Dad play Christmas tunes on his guitar down the hall. Running his fingers up and down the length of my arms, Finn leans over, kisses my neck, and whispers in my ear, "So, uh...what are you doing for New Years?"

I chuckle at his question and whisper back, "You, I hope."

Acknowledgements

Almost exactly one year ago I sat on my bed reading a blog post of Colleen Hoover's. I sat there with tears in my eyes reading about her humbling successes in life, from where she was in a slightly dilapidated house working from her mother's broken laptop, to a life filled with adventure, best-selling novels, a million new friends and fans, and most importantly better life for her family. What I read from that post that day was that Colleen is first and foremost a mom, doing all she can to give her children the life they deserve while pursuing something she hadn't planned on developing into a future. I'm amazed by her every damn day. I'm amazed by how much she loves, and how much she encourages, and how much she gives back. That night I said to myself "she's just a normal woman like me, and if she can do it, so can I, right?

So yeah, I owe a huge THANK YOU to you, Colleen Hoover, for just being the inspiring, generous, humble human being that you are. You've given me the courage to believe in myself again, to 'decide what to be and go be it', and that all of my imperfections are indeed perfect for me. I hope one day that I will be in a place where I can give back to others as much as you do. All writing aside, thank you for giving me something to strive for, for sending me a signed book last Christmas when my husband wrote asking for help with a "big romantic gesture", and for taking time out of your busy day with your son last summer to meet me, a run of the mill girl from Ohio, at The Bookworm Box. (I should probably also thank Vannoy for that since I'm sure she must've texted you...and it JUST dawned on me that she probably came up with the idea of having me clean up around the store just to keep me in the building until you got there! Now I'm laughing and I super love her too!)

This book, in a small way, is an homage to some of my favorite authors, all of which have impacted my life with the stories they've written. Some of my characters, buildings, businesses throughout Solving Us are named after these authors. So THANK YOU to Colleen, Hoover, Kristy Bromberg, Jamie McGuire, S.C.Stephens, J.Kenner, and E.L. James.

Solving Us

THANK YOU to Kristy Bromberg, Gail McHugh and Kandi Steiner for taking time out of your busy lives to answer my numerous facebook messages about the writing and publishing world. Your help was invaluable and I am indebted to you all.

My beta readers during this process, Dawn Cox, Amanda Douglas, Nichelle Edwards, and Kelli Karns, THANK YOU for your encouraging words and excitement for this project! I needed it to keep going. You all made me believe in myself and my abilities to finish a story that people just might want to read.

Speaking of beta readers, there's one that I was scared to death to have read this book. I lived with her for eighteen years and always teased her about the "smut" she would read all day every day. I knew I would never do that because I thought "those" books were stupid…but damn if the apple doesn't fall far from the tree. The ultimate compliment to me was the day my mother told me she had tears in her eyes and couldn't read anymore that night, that she loved what I was writing and was so proud of what I was doing. Thank you, mom, for sharing in this excitement with me. You'll always be my person and I'm so glad I get to share this with you.

Murphy Rae, of Indie Solutions by Murphy Rae, for my outstanding cover design and for putting up with my uncontrollable over-excitement at getting this process rolling. Your magic is amazing and I can't wait for many future projects together! You are badass!

Devon Anderson, my grammar/punctuation bitch, my book-talk partner, my cheerleader…I owe you a ton. THANK YOU so much not only for your initial enthusiasm of having a writing partner, which kept me going more than you know, but for the numerous Facebook chats, emails, and long phone calls when I was doubting my abilities or needed to talk out my thoughts. You listen, you support, and you encourage at all hours of the day. You've never said no and you've never told me to go away, and for that I am grateful!

Lauren Brocchi, let me say this, Solving Us would not exist without my knowing you. After my twentieth read-through of Fifty Shades you gave me a pool of authors to choose from to continue my new obsession.

Susan Renee

You introduced me to Colleen Hoover's work and many after that and the rest was history. If it weren't for you I wouldn't have a best friend to talk and laugh with about book boyfriends, about whatever latest novel is coming out, or our favorite authors, blog posts and everything in between. No subject is taboo between us and I love it! THANK YOU for being my content editor, for reading and rereading my book more times than I can probably count, and for always giving me the honest truth whether I wanted to hear it or not. Sharing in this project with you has bonded us for life. You've been my bestie since I can remember and I pray that our relationship always thrives and we spend many more years together causing trouble, bitching about nothing and celebrating successes in this new world we've ventured into. Now finish your damn book so we can literally go down this road together!

Although it will be some time before they ever lay eyes on this, I still have to say THANK YOU to my children, Anna and JP. There's so much you don't know about the last five to six years but I hope as you grow up you'll one day understand that every day I pray that what I'm doing will result in a better future for you both. I've learned that sometimes life doesn't go the way you dreamed it would go and the plans you had for yourself aren't what God intended. Did He intend for me to write Romance novels? Who knows. But He did give me the opportunity to be the best mom I can be for you and THAT is what I prayed for years ago, and what I pray for every day. I love you both so much.

Who needs a book boyfriend when you're married to your best friend? There simply aren't enough words in my vocabulary to tell you how much I love and adore you, Doug. You're my person. You encouraged me to go through with this project full force with no regrets. You see beneath the ugliest parts of me and you see beneath whatever beautiful parts there are. You're my whole damn Rubik's Cube, every fucking colorful side and I love you so much. THANK YOU for understanding my obsessions, or at least humoring me as I cannonball into these new waters.

And last but never least, MY READERS. If you've read this entire book and are still reading my sappy acknowledgements I feel like I owe you the hugest of hugs, or some candy or something! THANK YOU, THANK YOU, THANK YOU for reading something that has been the therapeutic ride I didn't know I needed until it was complete. The last five years of my life have left me adrift in waters I was getting tired of swimming in, but YOU, you all have saved me. You've pulled me onto dry land and given my life new meaning. THANK YOU for saving me and for lifting me up and for all of the encouraging words. I hope one day I get to meet you all and hug you and tell you "thank you" in person.

Can I ask one more favor? Every author appreciates reviews in order for more people to hear about their story. I would be forever grateful if you would do that for me. Leave a review on Amazon or Goodreads or Barnes & Noble or wherever you purchased my book so that others might see it, read it, and purchase it so my kids can go to college one day!

About the Author

Susan Renee lives in Ohio with her husband, two kids, and two dogs. After teaching music in the public schools for nine years, Susan is now the proud wearer of many different hats! Her favorites are Mommy, wife, and debut indie writer! On a whim she decided to try her hand writing the type of novels that she enjoys reading and the rest is history. She is currently working on a new standalone novel, expected to be published in the spring of 2016. Susan loves to hear from her friends and fans so be sure to look for her on social media platforms!

Website: www.authorsusanrenee.com
Facebook: http://www.facebook.com/authorsusanrenee
Goodreads: https://www.goodreads.com/SusanRenee
Instagram: authorsusanrenee
Twitter: @indiesusanrenee
Spotify: susan_renee

Contact Susan at authorsusanrenee@gmail.com

What is Susan working on next?

Here's a sneak peek at my next book, SEVEN, a new standalone novel! Releasing in the spring 2016!

"You are my sunshine…"
Breathe Peyton.
"My only sunshine…"
Fight for mommy.
"You make me happy…"
Breathe baby girl.
"When skies are gray…"
You can do it Peyton.
"You'll never know dear…"
Please. Please Peyton breathe on your own.
"How much I love you."
Don't you die on me baby girl.
"Please don't take my sunshine away."
Beep. Swoosh…..Beep. Swoosh.….Beep. Swoosh.

I sit here next to her hospital bed holding her little two year old lifeless fingers, so delicate, so small. I think about her first birthday and how adorable she was with cake all over her face, her tummy and in her hair. Peyton is the happiest little girl and so full of life.

Correction.

She *was* so full of life.

Now she lays in a bed that's too big for her, in a hospital gown that's two sizes two big covered in blankets that don't belong to her because her blankie was lost in the accident. EMTs are trained to do all they can to save their patient but they're not trained to search for blankies or favorite stuffed kittens. I'm all she has. My husband, Peyton's daddy, has been in surgery for the last four hours, so I'm all she has. I can't leave her. I have to believe she'll wake up.

She'll wake up.

She has to.

Made in the USA
San Bernardino, CA
09 July 2016